A WILDERNESS CHRISTMAS

Four captivating Christmas love stories by today's leading historical romance authors at their heartwarming, passionate best!

MADELINE BAKER
"Loving Devlin"

"Madeline Baker is synonymous with tender Western romances!"

—*Romantic Times*

ELIZABETH CHADWICK
"The Fourth Gift"

"Elizabeth Chadwick writes a powerful love story...splendid!"

—*Romantic Times*

NORAH HESS
"Christmas Surprise"

Norah Hess's historical romances are "treasures for those who savor frontier love stories!"

—*Romantic Times*

CONNIE MASON
"Christmas Star"

Connie Mason writes "the stuff that fantasies are made of!"

—*Romantic Times*

D0828099

Other Holiday Specials from *Leisure Books:*
A FRONTIER CHRISTMAS
AN OLD-FASHIONED VALENTINE
A VALENTINE SAMPLER

A Wilderness Christmas

MADELINE BAKER
ELIZABETH CHADWICK
NORAH HESS
CONNIE MASON

LEISURE BOOKS **NEW YORK CITY**

A LEISURE BOOK®

November 1993

Published by

Dorchester Publishing Co., Inc.
276 Fifth Avenue
New York, NY 10001

Printed in the United States of America.

A Wilderness Christmas

LOVING DEVLIN
THE FOURTH GIFT
CHRISTMAS SURPRISE
CHRISTMAS STAR

MADELINE BAKER
LOVING DEVLIN

Merry Christmas to all my readers, especially
Patti Brogden, Yancee Nanning,
and
Mozelle Strickland.
You're the best!

Chapter One

New Mexico, 1873

Devlin Dennehy rested his arms along the top
rail of the corral, his gaze roaming over the
wild horses penned inside the four-rail fence.
He'd made a good catch this year, he mused.
When he sold this bunch of broomtails to the
Army, Sarah would be able to buy that new stove
she'd been pestering him for.

He felt a sense of pride as he gazed around the
ranch. They'd done well in the last four years.
They'd added on to the house, built new corrals,
put up a new barn to replace the one that his
people had burned down.

A slight grin tugged at his features as he recalled
the first time he had seen Sarah. He'd been living
with the Apache then, raiding with his father's

9

people. To his regret, it had been his half-brother who had killed Sarah's first husband and kidnapped her six-year-old son. He'd been sent to the house to kill Sarah, but one look at her face, so much like his mother's, had stayed his hand.

Instead of killing her, he'd become her protector, keeping watch over her, always from a distance, of course. He had provided her with food and firewood. He'd saved her life, and she had saved his, and in the process, they had fallen deeply, hopelessly, in love. And because he'd loved her so much, he'd fought his own brother in order to return Danny to Sarah.

Their marriage had caused a scandal in town, but, in time, people had gotten used to the idea. He was accepted by most of the townsfolk now. He'd traded his clout and leggings for sturdy denim and cotton, exchanged his moccasins for boots. Only the color of his skin and the length of his hair proclaimed his Apache heritage. He couldn't change the first, and refused to cut the second.

Four years, he mused. Where had the time gone? Four years since he'd seen his father's people or his brother, Noche. Four years, and Sarah was with child, again.

His gaze lifted to the graveyard on the crest of the hill where he used to sit to keep watch over Sarah. Two small whitewashed crosses stood out in stark relief against the late summer sky, marking the graves of two infants who hadn't survived. A third cross marked the final resting place of Sarah's first husband, Vern.

Devlin's heartbeat quickened when he saw Sarah step out onto the porch. She was a remarkably pretty woman, with hair as yellow as freshly churned butter and eyes as blue as cornflowers. It still amazed him that she had agreed to marry him, that she had willingly endured the scorn and derision of her friends to be his wife.

He smiled as their gazes met, and then she was walking toward him, her calico skirt swaying provocatively. And he wanted her. Just like that. Always like that. He had thought that, in time, his ardor would cool, but he had only to look at her to want her.

And she knew it.

He saw it in the seductive smile that curved her sweet red lips, in the sudden light that danced in her eyes.

"Dinner is ready," Sarah said, coming to stand beside him. "Are you hungry?"

His dark eyes moved over her face like a caress. "Very hungry."

Sarah felt her heart skip a beat. It was incredible that the fire between them still burned so strong, so bright. When he looked at her like that, it made her heart sing and her soul ache for his touch.

Devlin's arm curled around her shoulders. "Where's Danny?"

"Fishing with the Loomis boys. He won't be back for hours."

His smile was so bright it put the desert sun to shame. Effortlessly he swung her into his arms and carried her into the house.

In their bedroom, he stood her on her feet and

began to undress her, his hands caressing the clothing from her body, his eyes burning with desire as he openly admired the womanly curves now swollen with his child. His heart soared with happiness as he placed his hands on her rounded belly, felt his child's lusty kick.

Sarah stared down at Devlin's hands, so big and brown where they rested on her belly. "I'm getting as fat as old Bessie," she muttered.

"You're not fat." Bending, he kissed her shoulder, her breasts. "You're pregnant with our child, and you've never been more beautiful."

When he looked at her like that, his eyes filled with adoration, how could she doubt him?

Head tilted slightly to one side, Sarah removed the pins from her hair so that it fell in a riotous mass of waves over her shoulders and down her back.

Her heart raced as Devlin buried his hands in her hair, his lips trailing fire as he kissed her cheek, the curve of her neck, the hollow of her throat.

Little tremors of pleasure stirred within her as she undressed him, her hands gliding over his hard-muscled flesh. They were so different, she thought. Her hair was light where his was dark, he was tall and broad-shouldered where she was short and slight. And yet they fit together so perfectly.

Heart filled with tenderness, Sarah traced the awful scar that marred an otherwise beautiful body. Souvenir of an old knife wound, the scar cut across Devlin's left cheek, angled down his neck, then continued across his chest and belly to the point of his right thigh.

She looked at her hand, resting on his thigh. Her skin, despite long hours in the sun, remained the color of ivory; his was the color of burnished copper, smooth and beautiful. She never tired of touching him, of looking at him.

Devlin closed his eyes, Sarah's touch making him weak. She was the only woman he'd ever known who had every right to hate him, the only one who hadn't been repelled by his scars, who hadn't cared that he was a half-breed.

Miraculously, she had never held him responsible for the raid against her home or for the death of her husband.

Opening his eyes, he watched her fingertips trace the scar across his chest. She had touched his scars the first time they had made love, too. It was a memory he'd never forgotten.

"Don't." He had caught her hand in his before she could touch him.

"I want to."

"Why?"

"To prove to you that it doesn't matter."

"Doesn't it?" he had asked, knowing she could hear the bitterness in his voice, his fear of being rejected.

"I love you, Devlin," she had said quietly. "The scars don't matter."

"I'm not Devlin. I'm Toklanni. I'm not a white man, I'm a half-breed. Can you accept that?"

Can you accept that? He'd been afraid to believe they could have a life together, but Sarah had refused to let his fears come between them. She loved him wholly, completely, asking for nothing but his love in return.

Whispering her name, he carried her to the bed and made love to her there, reveling in her softness, her sweetness, in hearing his Indian name on her lips.

"Toklanni." She murmured his name again and again as they soared toward the heights of ecstasy, and as his life spilled into her, he prayed that this time *Usen* would bless them with a strong, healthy child.

Chapter Two

Sarah hummed softly as she prepared the evening meal. Looking out the kitchen window, she could see Danny and Devlin washing up at the pump.

Danny, now almost eleven, was tall and lanky. His hair, the same shade of blond as hers, needed cutting badly. He laughed at something Devlin said, his teeth flashing white in the late afternoon sun, and she felt her heart swell with tenderness. He was a fine boy, honest and straightforward, well-mannered, eager to please.

But it was Devlin who drew her gaze time and again. Shirtless, he was a sight to behold. Drops of water clung to his skin. His muscles rippled as he shook the water from his waist-length hair, then toweled his body dry. He was magnificent, tall and lean, his skin a smooth dark bronze, his hair as sleek and black as a crow's wing. In the four years that they'd been married, he'd never raised his voice in anger. He treated Danny like his own son; he treated her with unfailing kindness and respect, and expected Danny to do the same. She could not have asked for a kinder, more patient man to be a father to her son, could not have asked for a gentler, more loving husband.

He waved when he saw her at the window, and she waved back, marveling that the newness of their love hadn't worn off, that his touch still made her tremble with longing.

Devlin threw his arm over Danny's shoulders and together they walked up to the house.

Sarah smiled at her two men. This was her favorite time of the day, when they sat at the table together, discussing the day's events, making plans for the future.

She felt a flush of pleasure warm her cheeks as Devlin sought her gaze again and again, his dark eyes filled with love and reassurance. He knew how desperately she wanted another child, how grievously she had mourned the deaths of the two little boys they had lost. One had been stillborn; the other, born three months early, had lived only a few moments. Devlin had not wanted her to get pregnant again, but she had begged him to let her try one more time. And because it was hard for him to refuse her anything, he had agreed to try one more time.

Sarah placed a protective hand over her belly, praying that this child would live.

*   *   *

Devlin rose early the following morning, careful not to disturb Sarah as he dressed and left their room. Danny was waiting for him in the kitchen, dressed and ready to go.

After a quick cup of hot coffee, Devlin took up his bow and they left the house. Minutes later, they were riding toward the hills across the river. If *Usen* was with them, they would return with fresh game. A deer, if they were lucky, perhaps a couple of rabbits and sage hens, as well.

Danny glanced at the man riding beside him, his heart filled with respect and admiration. He had only vague memories of his real father, but he knew in his heart that his real father couldn't have loved him any more than did Devlin Dennehy. He vividly remembered the first time he had seen Devlin in the Apache camp. At first, he had been afraid of the tall, scar-faced man who had fought his own brother to rescue a frightened white boy from the Indians. But that fear had quickly vanished, put to rest by the kindness in Devlin's dark eyes, in the quiet patience of his voice.

In the years since then, Danny had learned a lot about the Apache way of life. Devlin had told him that the Apache looked upon all other people as their enemies. A warrior who could kill without being killed, one who could steal from the enemy without being caught, was a man to be honored. From birth, every boy wanted to be a warrior. Pity was an emotion almost unknown among the People. Truth was a virtue held in high regard. An Apache did not steal from his own people; he shared what he had with those in need. Parents loved their children, they treated their old ones with reverence.

Besides telling him of the history of the People, Devlin had taught him to hunt and to fight, to track game both large and small, to conceal his whereabouts, to use a bow and arrow as well as a rifle. Devlin's skill with a bow was nothing short of remarkable. He could shoot an arrow five hundred feet with fatal accuracy.

He was hunting with the bow today. It was a powerful weapon, strengthened with layers of sinew. His arrows were more than three feet long, made of light yet well-seasoned wood.

They rode for over an hour. Sometimes Devlin asked Danny what he saw—did he notice the wolf tracks beside the stream, had he seen the scattered remains of a deer half-buried in the brush?

As they neared the foothills, conversation ceased and Danny felt his heart begin to beat fast as he looked forward to the hunt. But first, there were prayers to be offered to the Great Spirit, asking for His guidance and for His blessing on their efforts.

Sarah pressed a hand to her back as she straightened from the washtub. Devlin had warned her not to overdo, and today she was taking him at his word. The clothes could wait awhile.

Returning to the house, she put a pot of water on for tea, then sat down at the kitchen table, her feet propped up on an overturned crate. Ah, but it felt good to sit down.

Gazing out the kitchen window, she wondered if Devlin had found a deer, if Danny's good trousers would last another year, if the baby she carried beneath her heart was a boy or a girl. Secretly, she hoped for a little girl with Devlin's black hair and dark eyes. But it didn't matter, boy or girl, both would be equally welcome, equally cherished. Her arms ached to hold a child. Devlin's child. How she loved him! In those first terrible weeks after Vern's death, Devlin had brought her food and firewood, had stayed nearby, making sure she was safe. In his arms, she had found tenderness, a sense of peace and belonging, that she had found nowhere else.

She was brewing a cup of tea when she heard a disturbance near the horses. Thinking Devlin had come back early, she hurried out the back door.

The smile of welcome died on her lips as she came face-to-face with an image straight out of one of her old nightmares. Turning on her heel, she fled for the safety of the house, a scream of terror rising in her throat as the Indian grabbed a handful of hair and jerked her to a halt.

"No!" She shrieked the word, sickened by the war paint that covered his face, by the feral gleam in his cold black eyes. "No!"

It couldn't be happening again.

The warrior spoke to her, his words harsh, guttural, and totally without meaning. She watched, mesmerized with fear, as he laid his hand over her stomach.

19

"No apu," he remarked, and then smiled, his teeth very white against the hideous black paint that covered most of his face.

In a distant part of Sarah's mind, she realized the Indian was pleased that she was pregnant.

She also realized that he wasn't Apache. Her first reaction was relief. Apaches had killed Vern. Her relief quickly turned to despair. With an Apache, she might have had a chance. They were, after all, Devlin's people.

She screamed as the warrior dragged her toward his horse; screamed again as he lashed her hands together, then stuffed a dirty rag into her mouth. That done, he lifted her onto the back of a calico gelding and quickly vaulted up behind her.

Only then did she realize that other Indians were raiding the house. She felt an overwhelming sadness as she saw one of the warriors wearing the fancy blue bonnet Vern had bought for her years ago. She'd never had an occasion to wear the hat; now she never would. Another Indian was waving her apron over his head with one hand and carrying her mother's cherrywood music box in the other.

Sick at heart, she saw her few priceless belongings carried off.

A churning cloud of dust filled the air as the Indians turned the horses loose. She thought of all the hours Devlin had spent chasing down the herd, breaking the horses to ride. All that time and effort, wasted. There was a loud squawking as some of the warriors chased down the chickens. At any other time, she might have admired their riding skill, but all she felt now was a mind-numbing despair.

She wept as she saw the first bright tongues of flame lick at the walls of the house. Her house. She'd been so happy there these past four years. She thought of the cradle Devlin had made for their baby, of the shirt she had been making for Danny, of the china she had brought with her from back east. Gone now, all gone.

She sent a last look at her home as the Indians rode away, grateful that Danny and Devlin would be spared the horrible fate that awaited her.

Chapter Three

Devlin smelled the smoke long before he saw the flames. Fear gripped his heart as he urged the big bay mare into a lope.

Sarah! Please, God, let her be all right.

He repeated the silent prayer over and over again as he raced toward home, felt his heart turn cold as he crossed the river. The barn was on fire; the house was almost gone.

He pulled back on the reins, his feet hitting the ground at a run before the animal had come to a halt.

"Sarah! Sarah!" He hollered her name as he circled the house, unable to get too close for the heat of the flames.

"Mom!"

He heard Danny's voice, and then the boy was there beside him. "Is she . . . ?"

"I don't know." Devlin drew a deep breath, held it a long moment before releasing it in a heavy sigh. "Stay here while I look around."

Moving cautiously now, Devlin circled the house, looking for tracks. He knew a moment of gut-wrenching relief when he saw Sarah's tracks, her hard-soled shoes easy to identify amidst the sea of moccasin prints.

The story was there, etched in the ground as clear as words on a page. She'd left the house by the back door, been grabbed by a warrior, Comanche, by the cut of his moccasins. Struggling, she'd been dragged across the yard and lifted onto the back of a horse. Her captor had vaulted up behind her and they'd ridden away from the house, following the mustangs Devlin had been working with for the last three months. But the horses didn't matter. Nothing mattered but Sarah.

Devlin glanced at the house and the barn, now smoldering piles of charred embers, and felt the rage grow within him. Everything Sarah loved, everything they had worked for, had been destroyed.

"Is she . . . can you tell if she's . . ." Danny's voice broke on a sob.

"She's still alive," Devlin said. Choking back his anger, he put his arm around the boy's shoulder.

Danny turned his head away, not wanting Devlin to see the tears in his eyes. Tears were a sign of weakness. Surely his adopted father never cried. He was such a strong man, so self-assured, so confident, a man who knew who and what he was and was comfortable with that knowledge.

"It's all right, *ciye*," Devlin said, squeezing the boy's shoulders. "Never be ashamed of your tears."

"Men don't cry."

"Sure they do."

Danny sniffed noisily. "Have you ever cried?"

"A time or two," Devlin admitted, remembering how his throat had swelled with tears the day he'd returned Danny to his mother's arms. It was a memory he held close to his heart.

Devlin gave Danny's shoulder another squeeze. "We're wasting time."

"Right." Danny fisted the tears from his eyes. "Let's go."

"I'm going alone, *ciye*."

"But . . ."

"I'm sorry, I know you want to help, but I'll be able to travel faster alone." He ruffled the boy's hair affectionately. "Besides, if anything happened to you, your mother would never forgive me."

Danny didn't argue. Wordlessly, he swung into the saddle, his blue eyes filled with silent reproach.

"We'll stop by the Loomis place and see if they'll put you up for a few days," Devlin said, thinking out loud. "You'll be safe there."

The Loomis place was close to town and big enough to make even a Comanche war party think twice about attacking it.

Danny nodded and Devlin felt his heart go out to the boy, but there was no help for it this time. He'd be riding hard and fast, traveling through

Indian territory all the way. It was one thing to risk his own life, but he wasn't willing to risk Danny's, too.

Joe Loomis was plowing his field when they arrived. Loomis was a big bear of a man with shaggy brown hair, brown eyes, and a quick smile. But he wasn't smiling when he crossed the field.

"What is it?" he asked, his hooded glance raking over Devlin's face. "What's happened?"

"Comanches. They burned our place to the ground and took Sarah."

Loomis swore softly. "I'll get my rifle and go with ya."

"No." Devlin laid his hand on the other man's shoulder. "I appreciate the offer, but I think it would be better if I went alone. I'd like to leave Danny here."

"Sure, sure." Loomis nodded agreeably. "You'll be needin' supplies. Danny, go up to the house and tell Mary Kate to put some grub together, enough for two or three days. Now, then, what else can I do for ya?"

"I could use a heavy jacket, maybe some gloves. A bedroll."

"You've got 'em. Anything else?"

"I don't think so."

"Come on up to the house. You can take time for a cup of hot coffee while I collect your gear."

Mary Kate insisted on fixing Devlin a hot meal before he left. She hovered over him while he ate, urging him to have another slice of pie, reminding him that it might be a long time before he had another home-cooked meal. She was a plain woman, with limp brown hair and pale blue eyes. She'd given birth to seven boys in eight years of marriage and the strain was beginning to show. But she was kindness itself as she hovered over Devlin.

"Don't worry about Danny while you're gone," she said, pouring Devlin another cup of coffee. "We'll take good care of him. Poor lamb. First his pa kilt by them no-good savages, and now his ma . . ."

Mary Kate broke off, her cheeks flooding with color as she gazed at Devlin. "I'm sorry . . . I . . ."

She glanced away, but not before he saw the faint flicker of fear in the depths of her eyes.

"Forget it, Mary Kate."

He finished his coffee quickly, thanked her for the meal, and left the kitchen, irritated by her sudden embarrassment, angered by his reaction to it. They'd been neighbors for the last four years. He'd helped Joe raise a new barn, he'd sat at their table, had them to his house, and yet, when she'd looked at him just now, he'd felt like a stranger.

Danny and Joe were outside.

"Everything's ready," Loomis said. "Gear's all packed. I threw in an old coffeepot and a sack of Arbuckles. I stuck an extra Colt in your bedroll, too, just in case."

"Thanks, Joe." Devlin shook the other man's hand, then wrapped his arm around Danny's shoulders. "You behave yourself. Don't be causing Mrs. Loomis any trouble." Heaving a sigh, he gave the boy a hug. "Don't worry, *ciye*. I'll find her."

Danny nodded. "I know you will."

There was nothing more to say. Giving the boy

a last quick hug, he swung into the saddle and rode out of the yard.

Sarah groaned as her captor lowered her to the ground. They had been riding nonstop since that morning, and with each mile, she had fallen deeper and deeper into despair.

She was trembling from head to foot as she made her way behind a clump of brush, too weary to care if anyone followed her or not. A myriad of fears chased themselves across her mind, fear that Devlin and Danny would come after her and be killed, fear that the constant bone-jarring ride would cause her to lose the baby.

Wrapping her arms around her swollen belly, Sarah prayed that the child was safe, that she would be allowed to live until it was born. Devlin had told her that the Indians loved children, all children. She only hoped that her baby would be given a chance to live.

The Indians had gathered into a group, talking and gesturing as they passed a waterskin between them. Another warrior opened a pouch and withdrew several chunks of dried meat. Sarah accepted the one that was offered to her. Sitting on the hard ground, she chewed on the tough strip of jerky, wondering if they'd kill her here or wait until they reached their camp.

The warrior who had captured her came to stand in front of her and she knew a moment of heart-stopping fear, but he only handed her the waterskin and turned away. For a moment, she stared at it in disgust, repulsed to drink from something made from the intestine of an animal, but, in the end, thirst won out and she drank greedily, not caring that the water was warm, trying not to think of the dozen savages who had drunk out of it before her.

Ten minutes later, they were riding again. She tried to keep her mind blank, tried not to think of what awaited her at the journey's end, but all the horror stories she'd ever heard jumped to the forefront of her mind—terrible stories of women who had been raped until they died; tales of women who had been killed, their unborn children cut out of their wombs; whispered accounts of women who had been taken captive, forced to pleasure one man after another in order to survive.

She bit down on her lip as a host of horrible images filled her mind, knowing she would rather die than let any of these savages lay a hand on her.

Closing her eyes, she prayed for help, prayed that Devlin wouldn't come after her, that she would be allowed to die before she could be shamed and humiliated. She wept for her unborn child, for Danny, for Devlin. Wept until exhaustion claimed her and she tumbled into oblivion.

The sudden cessation of movement woke her. Opening her eyes, she saw that it was dark and the Indians were making camp for the night.

She was stiff and sore in every muscle, and a soft cry of protest escaped her lips when her captor lifted her from the back of the horse.

He muttered something to her as he cut her hands free and gestured into the darkness beyond the fire. Hoping he meant what she thought he did, she went behind a bush and relieved herself. For a moment, she closed her eyes. She was so tired. So sore. She hurt in places she'd never been aware of until now.

Rising to her feet, she peered through the underbrush. The Indians seemed to be preoccupied with looking after their horses. At least, none of them seemed to be watching her.

Lifting her skirts, she started walking away from the camp, and then, when she figured she was out of earshot, she began to run. Fear gave wings to her feet and she ran blindly into the night, praying that she wouldn't fall, that she'd be able to find a place to hide.

With only the sound of the wind in her ears, she ran on, a tiny ray of hope beginning to bud within her breast. Please, please, please . . . the silent prayer repeated itself in her mind.

Her side was aching, her lungs were on fire, sweat dripped into her eyes, and still she ran onward. And then, like the harsh echo of doom, she heard the quick tattoo of hoofbeats coming up behind her.

"No!" She'd run so hard, so far, it wasn't fair! "No!"

She screamed in protest as the warrior leaned over the side of his horse and grabbed her around the waist, lifting her onto the horse's back.

His arm was like iron as he held her against him. He was yelling at her, his face distorted beneath the hideous black paint he wore.

When they reached the camp, he lifted her

roughly from the back of the horse, then bound her hands, jerking the rope tight.

"Kahtu!" he said, and pushed her down to the ground, the look in his dark eyes warning her to stay put or suffer the consequences.

As punishment, he refused to give her anything to eat or drink, and at last she fell into a troubled sleep, her dreams haunted by horrible images of rape and torture at the hands of heartless savages.

Morning arrived all too soon.

She was given a hunk of charred rabbit to eat and a drink of water for breakfast, allowed to relieve herself, and then they were riding again, heading south, toward the Staked Plains.

Sarah sent one last glance behind her, a cold shiver stealing down her spine as she bid a silent farewell to everything she had ever known, everyone she had ever loved, certain that not even Devlin would be able to find her now.

Chapter Four

Devlin was bone weary when he reined his horse to a halt that night.

Dismounting, he gathered wood for a fire, huddling deeper into the coat Loomis had given him while he waited for the twigs to catch.

He ate a part of the grub Mary Kate had packed, hardly aware of what he was eating. All he could think of was Sarah, seven and a half months pregnant and in the hands of marauding Comanches.

He chewed on a chunk of brown bread, his frustration rising with each passing minute. He couldn't even hate the Indians, he thought ruefully. He'd been in their place. He knew how they felt, why they'd attacked the house. Why they'd stolen the horses, taken his woman. Not long ago, he'd been doing the same things himself. If he hadn't gone with Noche to raid Sarah's ranch, he would never have met her. And now she was in the hands of another warrior . . .

He felt his emotions surge to life then, but it wasn't anger that roiled through him, it was jealousy; deep, dark jealousy that flooded through every fiber of his being. She was his woman, his wife, and he would kill any man who dared lay a hand on her.

When he'd finished eating, he doused the fire and moved his camp.

He followed the trail easily, seeing where the raiding party had paused to rest the horses, feeling a deep-seated relief when he saw Sarah's footprints. Thank God, she was still alive. That was all that mattered.

He'd been on the trail for almost three hours when he topped a small rise and came face-to-face with three Comanche warriors who were obviously hanging back to make certain the main party wasn't being followed.

They spotted him at the same moment. As one, the three warriors charged toward him. Two were armed with bows, the third carried a rifle. With an oath, Devlin reined his horse around and dug his heels into the bay's flanks, hoping he could outride the Indians.

He heard the sounds of their war cries as they pursued him and he leaned over the mare's neck, asking her for more speed, felt her willing response.

He swore softly as an arrow hissed by his ear. He felt the bay stumble, heard the sharp report of a rifle. Pain exploded in his left leg, and then the horse was going down and the ground was rushing up to meet him.

For a moment, there was only darkness. When the world stopped spinning, he was lying on his back. He could see the bay lying a few feet away, struggling to rise in spite of the arrow quivering in her neck. The sound of hoofbeats drew his attention and he glanced over his shoulder to see the warriors riding toward him. He swore under his breath as he realized his rifle was out of reach.

He was struggling to gain his feet when he heard a welcome sound. On hands and knees, he watched as a dozen Apache warriors thundered across the open prairie, the high, piercing war cry of the People filling the air.

The Comanches immediately turned tail and ran for home. Nine of the Apaches went in pursuit; the other three rode toward Devlin.

"Ho, brothers," he said, the Apache words sounding strange on his tongue.

The young warrior on his left sneered at him. "Brother?" His laugh was filled with scorn.

Devlin nodded. "I am Toklanni, brother to Noche."

The warrior grunted softly, his expression changing from derision to respect.

They gave him a strip of rawhide to bite down on while they dug the bullet out of his thigh; then one of the warriors wrapped the bloody wound with a strip of cloth torn from Devlin's shirttail.

That done, they gathered up his weapons and stripped his gear off the bay. One of the men put the horse out of its misery, and then they set out for home, with Devlin riding behind one of the warriors.

He cursed softly as the sun climbed in the sky. The Apache rancheria lay due west; Sarah's trail went south. But there was no help for it.

It was after dark when they reached the Apache camp. By then, the cloth wrapped around his leg was soaked with blood and he was burning with fever.

He was only vaguely aware of being lifted from the back of the horse, carried into a lodge, covered with furs. He heard the distant sound of voices; a low groan rose in his throat as someone probed the wound in his leg, igniting new fires with every touch.

Sounds and images became fragmented . . . the muted whisper of a rattle, the sweet smell of sage, the taste of strong green tea made from the bark of a tree. He cried out, tension spiraling through his body, as someone laid a heated blade over the wound in his thigh, and then the world went black.

He sat on his heels on the far side of the stream, hidden from view by a tangled mass of scrub brush and cottonwoods as he watched the woman walk toward the stream. She stopped at a flat-topped rock, sat down, and removed her shoes and stockings; then, lifting her skirts to keep them dry, she made her way into the water, squealing a little as the cold water covered her feet and ankles.

He liked looking at her, liked the way she moved, graceful as a willow in the wind. Her hair caught

*the light of the sun, and the water that clung to her
legs glistened like dew drops. Sometimes, when he
looked at her, he saw a woman full grown, ripe and
desirable . . .*

"Sarah." He woke with the sound of her name
echoing in his ears, felt a cool hand on his brow.

"Sleep, Toklanni," murmured a soft voice. "All
is well."

"Sarah?"

"Sleep now," the voice repeated.

He tried to see her face, but all he could make
out in the darkness was the outline of a woman
with long hair. Questions rose in his mind, but
his eyelids felt like lead. He heard the woman
speaking to him again, and the sound of her voice
lulled him to sleep.

When next he opened his eyes, Noche was sitting beside him.

"Chickasay," Devlin murmured.

Noche nodded. "You have been long in the land
of shadows, my brother."

"How long?"

"Two sleeps."

Two days. Devlin swore softly, thinking of the
time he'd lost. The trail would be cold by now.
Each minute that passed saw Sarah that much
deeper into the land of the Comanche.

"You have lost much blood," Noche remarked.
"You should rest."

"I've got to go." Devlin sat up, aware for the
first time that he was naked beneath the furs.
The movement sent a bright hot shaft of pain
down the length of his left leg.

"Where is it you must go in such a hurry?"

"Comanches took Sarah."

"Ah, the white woman you were to have killed."

"She's my wife, Noche. And she's pregnant."

With an effort, he forced himself to his feet, but his left leg refused to support his weight and he dropped back down on the furs, a muffled oath erupting from his lips.

"Toklanni! You must not get up so soon."

Devlin smiled as Noche's wife hurried into the lodge. She had once been a lovely woman, but she'd been badly cut by some buffalo hunters and now her face was badly scarred. It had been to avenge Natanh's abuse at the hands of white hunters that had caused Noche to attack Sarah's ranch four years earlier.

He realized now that it had been her voice he had heard in the darkness.

"How are you, my sister?"

"I am well." She patted her stomach, which was as round as a melon. "We are to have a child."

Devlin nodded. "I see."

He watched her as she prepared them something to eat. He felt uncomfortable in his brother's lodge. They had parted with bad blood between them four years ago. Now the chasm of time and hard feelings lay between them and he didn't know how to cross it.

They ate in silence. From outside came the sound of children laughing as they ran through the village. He heard men's voices raised in excitement and concluded that some of the warriors were gambling nearby.

The scent of roasting mule meat drifted into the lodge, along with the smell of dust and the faint aroma of sage. And over all lay the myriad smells of the mountains, the trees, the earth itself. When he finished eating, he laid the bowl aside and eased himself down on the furs again, seeking escape from old memories in sleep.

He felt a little better the next day. Sitting outside, he watched the people go about their daily tasks. Men he'd known since childhood came by to say hello; others, less well known, regarded him through dark, unfriendly eyes, reminding him that he had been long away, that he was no longer considered to be one of the People. Their censure hurt, but he could not blame them for the way they felt. He had chosen a white woman over his own people and there were some, including his own brother, who would never forgive him for that.

Sitting there, wrapped in a thick fur, Devlin watched several young boys as they set up a target, then took turns testing their skill with the bow.

Memories of his own childhood came flooding back. Surely there was no life better than that of a young Apache boy. He had no responsibilities, but was free to run and play all the day long. He had learned to ride, to hunt the deer and the buffalo, the rabbit and the fox, to read the tracks of man and beast, to distinguish a friend from an enemy by a moccasin print. Each tribe's heel fringes, soles, and toe forms were different. One-piece moccasins were common among the

Northern Plains tribes. The Comanche used buckskin heel fringes; the Cheyenne used two small tails of deerskin or a buffalo tail which trailed behind. Apache moccasins had high tops to protect the wearer's legs from snakebite and keep the sand out. The soles were of stiff rawhide, the toes turned up to protect the feet from cactus thorns.

At first, he had carried a small bow and shot at make-believe enemies, but as he grew older, he began to hunt in earnest, tracking rabbits and small game as his skill with the bow increased, all with an eye toward the day when he would be a warrior.

To be a warrior was not easy, and the training was rigorous. As a novice warrior, he had been required to plunge into icy water, to run long distances over rough country with a heavy load strapped to his back. He must keep his mouth shut and breathe through his nose. He had to be able to make his own weapons and use them with skill. To test his endurance, he was made to go for long periods without sleep, and as his training reached an end, he was sent alone into the wilds, to live by his own skill for two weeks.

By the time he was fifteen, he had been ready to go on the warpath. It had been a time of great excitement. A ceremony had been performed on his behalf, a helmet and shield were made for him. There had been a war dance, and he had been required to take part, to show his agility and endurance. He had been taught the stylized language of the warpath, and when he was ready, he had accompanied the proven warriors on four raids. He had not been allowed to fight yet, but had been assigned menial tasks, like building the fires, preparing and cooking the food, looking after the horses, standing guard at night. Not until the fifth raid had he been allowed to take part in the actual fighting.

It had been frightening, exhilarating. He had learned the true meaning of courage. And he had learned how quickly a life could be taken.

Drawing his gaze from the boys, Devlin stared into the distance, wondering if Sarah were still alive, fretting at his inability to go after her.

It was another two days before he could walk without aid.

When he told Noche and Natanh he would be leaving in the morning, Natanh tried to convince him to wait another day or two.

But Devlin couldn't wait any longer.

"I am all right, my sister," he assured her. "I thank you for the warmth of your lodge, but now I must go."

She didn't argue; instead, she began to pack a parfleche with food for the trail.

"I need a good horse," Devlin told his brother. "And some buckskins."

"Why should I help you?" Noche asked. "You turned your back on us. You have not come to see me or your people in four winters."

"You made it known that I was not welcome in the lodges of the Apache when last I was here."

Noche hesitated. He gazed at Toklanni for a long moment, his expression impassive, and then he sighed. "Perhaps I was wrong."

"Perhaps?"

"Natanh will get you a change of clothes," Noche said. "I will see about a horse." And with that, he left the lodge.

"He is a proud man," Natanh remarked. "You hurt him deeply when you chose the white woman over your own people."

"I didn't make that choice," Devlin said bitterly. "He made it for me."

"He has always been jealous of you," she remarked, her dark eyes filled with understanding. "Many people were angry when he forced you to fight him for the white boy. Many people are still angry because he drove you away." A faint smile played over her lips. "Many people are angry with you because you left us."

"I did what I had to do. I have no regrets."

"None?"

Devlin dragged a hand through his hair. "Your eyes see deep, Natanh. I have missed my people. No matter that I have made my home with the whites, my soul is still Apache."

"I know this. Do not stay away so long this time, Toklanni. It is not good for brothers to be divided."

"I hear you," Devlin said.

Natanh smiled at him, then handed him a pile of clothing she had pulled from a basket in the rear of the lodge.

"Good hunting, *chickasay*," she said, and squeezing his hand, she left the lodge so he could change.

It felt good to be wearing buckskins again. The leggings, fringed along the outer seam, fit like a second skin; the clout fell to his knees. The shirt was fringed along the sleeves and back. The moccasins had hard soles; the upper portion, made of heavy deer hide, reached to midcalf.

Standing there, his nostrils filling with the familiar scents of the rancheria, he felt the thin layer of civilization he'd worn for the last four years fall away. He was no longer Devlin Dennehy, rancher, but Toklanni, the warrior.

It was a good feeling.

Noche was waiting for him outside. Wordlessly, he handed Toklanni his weapons: a Winchester rifle, a Colt revolver, a knife in a buckskin sheath. And then he handed him the reins of a big gray stallion.

Toklanni couldn't conceal his surprise, or his pleasure, as he stroked the stallion's neck. He'd raised the horse from a colt. But when Toklanni had demanded that Noche return Danny to his mother, Noche had insisted they fight to see who would keep the boy. One of the conditions had been that, if Toklanni won the fight, he could take the boy back to his mother, but he would forfeit the stallion.

"Hey, boy," Toklanni murmured as the gray nuzzled his arm. "Remember me?"

"Do you wish a war party to ride with you?"

Toklanni shook his head. He could ride faster alone. A lone rider would not leave much of a trail, or cause much suspicion. And he didn't want to start a fight in which Sarah might be hurt or killed. If he was lucky, he could slip in, grab Sarah, and leave before anyone was the wiser.

"No, *chickasay*, but I thank you for the offer. And for this," Toklanni added, patting the stallion's shoulder.

"May *Usen* direct your path," Noche said, "and guide your steps back to your people when your journey is through."

Toklanni clasped Noche's forearm, held it for a long moment, and then swung onto the stallion's back.

"Good hunting, *chickasay*," Noche said, lifting his arm in farewell.

"My thanks. Be well until we meet again," he said, and then, resolutely, he reined the stallion south, toward the land of the Comanche, his mind empty of everything but the need to find his woman.

Chapter Five

Old habits returned quickly on the trail. Toklanni rode warily, taking advantage of every bit of cover, his gaze constantly moving back and forth across the trackless prairie.

He rode back to where he'd met the Apache and quartered back and forth until he found the Comanches' trail. Though faint, it was still there, heading south, toward the *Llano Estacado*, the Staked Plains, a vast treeless country where the last of the free Comanche roamed wild and free. With winter coming, they would be heading for one of the canyons to take shelter from the harsh weather. There, in the breaks, could be found small streams, grass, and cottonwoods.

In the summer, plums, pecans, walnuts, and persimmons could be found along the larger streams. The rocky hills and the canyon sides were covered with scrub cedar, ash, elm, redbud, oak, and willow. In the summer, the Llano was desertlike, but after the spring or summer rains, there was an abundance of grass.

The eastern part of the *Llano* was made up of rugged hills. To the east rose the Wichita Mountains, to the west lay New Mexico, to the south was a great expanse of wild waste known as the Big Bend country, which was crisscrossed with Indian trails.

The Comanche were formidable fighters. Among their enemies were numbered the Apache, the Utes, the Pawnees, and the Navajos. They were cunning warriors, ferocious fighters, masterful horsemen.

Toklanni had been in their country only a few times, riding with the Apache to steal horses or to avenge a raid.

His mind filled with bits and pieces of Comanche lore as he rode tirelessly day after day. It was said a Comanche warrior would never ride a mare if he could help it, that mares were for women and children. He'd also heard it said that killing a man's favorite horse was akin to murder.

Like the Apache, the Comanche did not eat fish unless food was very scarce, and it was believed that those who ate turkey would become cowardly and run from their enemies just as the turkey flies from its pursuers. The Comanche didn't eat dog, either, because the dog was related to the coyote, and coyotes were taboo.

An old mountain man had once told him that the reason the Comanche didn't eat dog was because once, when the Comanche moved, they left an old woman in camp with a dog, and when they returned, they found that the dog had killed the woman and devoured most of her body.

It was midafternoon about a week later when Toklanni reined the gray to a halt beside a small waterhole. Dismounting, he took a long drink, then splashed some of the cold water over his face and neck before letting the gray drink.

Another day's ride would bring him to the edge of the *Llano.* And somewhere within its maze of canyons and arroyos were the Indians he sought.

Taking a firm grip on his rifle, he clucked to the gray, praying that Sarah was well.

That evening, he huddled in the protection of a rocky overhang, quietly cursing the storm that had forced him to take shelter. Thunder rolled across the black sky, lightning lanced the clouds, while a torrent of rain washed away Sarah's trail.

He stared, unseeing, into the distance, his thoughts turned inward. Remembering how Sarah had taken him into her home and nursed him back to health after he'd been attacked by two white men and left for dead. Remembering how readily she had accepted him, trusted him when she had no reason to trust him. How could he help but love her?

Sarah. He swallowed hard, realizing that she could be dead even now. The thought was like a knife in his heart.

Please. He lifted his face toward heaven, the single word repeating itself over and over again. *Please. Please.* Please let her be all right.

Like the Apache, the Comanche were often cruel to their enemies. Men were killed out of hand, women were taken alive when possible, children too young to run away were adopted into the tribe. Women were not usually abused, but there were cruel men in every society, and he groaned low in his throat as he thought of Sarah being mistreated. And the child . . .

He shook the morbid thoughts from his mind. It would do no good to dwell on the worst that could happen. Until he knew otherwise, he would assume she was alive and well. He had to believe that, or go quietly insane.

Driven by the need to be doing something, he swung into the saddle and headed south, toward the *Llano*.

Chapter Six

Sarah stared at the Indian camp, relief that they had finally reached their destination warring with a deep-seated fear of what awaited her.

The village was located in a canyon alongside a slow-running creek. Horses grazed on the hillsides, dogs sprawled in the shade.

As they rode into the middle of the camp, Sarah stared at the people. For the most part, the men were of medium height, with deep chests and broad faces. The women tended to be a little shorter and slighter, with coarse black hair. The men wore breechclouts, leggings, and moccasins. She saw several young boys wearing nothing at all.

The women wore buckskin dresses with long, luxurious fringe on the sleeves and hem and beautifully beaded moccasins. They wore their hair cropped short and painted the part with vermilion. Some of the women had painted the insides of their ears red and accented their eyes with red or yellow lines above and below the lids. Others had reddish orange circles or triangles painted on their cheeks. Sarah couldn't help staring at them, they looked so bizarre.

Unlike little boys, the little girls didn't go naked. They wore breechclouts, and their hair, uncut, was worn in braids.

The women stared at Sarah with equal curiosity, interested in the color of her hair, her full calico skirt and black leather shoes. They talked excitedly as they gestured at her fair skin and light eyes, then pointed at her distended belly. "*No apu,*" they said, nodding to each other.

The warrior who had kidnapped Sarah slid from the back of his horse. Lifting Sarah, he placed her beside him, his hand resting possessively on her arm.

"*Nu naibi,*" he said, and though Sarah could not understand his words, she knew without doubt that he was telling everyone that she was his woman. The thought made her shudder.

Gradually the people went back to what they'd been doing before the war party rode in. The warrior holding Sarah's arm led her toward a large tipi near the center of the circle and ushered her inside.

Sarah glanced around. The tipi was tilted slightly backward. There was a smoke hole near the top, above the entrance, which was made by folding the skins back. The entrance, which faced east, was an opening covered by a piece of stiff hide.

Devlin had told her that a tipi shed wind and water and was warm in winter. It could be set up in fifteen minutes and taken down in even less time.

She saw what she assumed was a bed in the back of the lodge. Letting her gaze wander, she saw several parfleches. She could see that one held several articles of men's clothing. There was flint and steel beside a fire pit, along with a large black kettle and a few spoons and bowls made from what looked like the horn of an animal.

She looked up when she realized the warrior was speaking to her.

"Esatai," he said, thumping his chest.

"Esa . . . Esatai?" Sarah repeated, frowning.

The warrior nodded. "Esatai," he said again, and then pointed at Sarah.

"Sarah," she said. "My name is Sarah."

"Sa-rah." He grunted softly. Indicating that she should stay where she was, he left the lodge.

Alone, she wandered around, poking into some of the parfleches, seeing that they held food and cooking utensils as well as a variety of ornaments and winter moccasins.

She stood up, feeling guilty, when the lodge flap opened. She stared at the man standing there for several moments before she realized it was Esatai. He had washed the war paint from his face and chest and she noted that he was almost handsome. His skin was a dark reddish copper color, his eyes were dark brown, his lips thin but well-shaped.

She took a step backward as he took a step toward her.

He stopped walking toward her and held out his hand, palm up. "No be afraid Esatai."

"You speak English," Sarah exclaimed.

"*Tue*," he replied. "Little."

"Let me go home."

Esatai shook his head. They had gone raiding to avenge the deaths of three warriors killed by whites. He had not expected to find such a prize when they attacked the white man's house, but now that he had the white woman with hair like the sun, he would not let her go.

"You stay."

"I want to go home," Sarah said. "I have a husband. Please, let me go to him."

"I be hus-band."

"You?" Sarah shook her head. "No."

"*Haa*. Yes." His gaze lingered on her swollen belly. He had lost his wife and child to sickness two winters ago, but now the Great Spirit had sent him another woman to take her place.

Sarah huddled deeper into the buffalo robe around her shoulders, jumping a little as a loud rumble of thunder shook the earth. Three days had passed since they arrived in the village. It had been raining ever since.

Esatai sat on a blanket on the other side of the fire, patiently gluing turkey feathers to the shaft of an arrow. She envied him the task. If only she had something to occupy her hands, something to keep her mind off the rapidly approaching darkness. She glanced uneasily at the single bed in the rear of the lodge, wondering if Esatai expected her to share it with him.

He had said he was going to be her husband.

She had tried several times to tell him she already had a husband, but it didn't seem to matter. He had captured her and he meant to keep her.

Sarah gazed into the flames, her mind filling with thoughts of Devlin and Danny. She knew Devlin would come after her, but how could he hope to find her now? It had taken days to reach the Comanche stronghold; whatever tracks the Indians had left would have been washed out by the rain.

And Danny. Her baby. First his father had been killed by Indians, and now she'd been kidnapped. Thank God for Devlin. At least her son wouldn't be left alone.

After a while, Esatai put the arrow aside. Rising, he left the tipi. He returned a few minutes later with two freshly skinned rabbits, which he handed to Sarah.

"Food," he said. "You fix."

Sarah stared at the rabbits, wondering what he expected her to do with them.

Esatai watched her for a moment and then, sensing her confusion, he pulled two long sticks from one of the parfleches, skewered the rabbits, and laid them over the hot coals.

"You watch," he said.

Sarah nodded that she understood, and Esatai went back to work on his arrow, leaving her to turn the meat so it didn't burn.

When the rabbits were cooked, Esatai cut the meat into chunks and dumped it into a large wooden bowl, which he placed between them. Reaching into one of the parfleches, he pulled out something that looked like a stuffed sausage. Slicing off a piece, he handed it to Sarah.

"What is it?" she asked.

"Pemmican."

"Oh." So, she thought, this was pemmican. Wild berries, cherries, or plums were mixed with pinon nuts, pounded well, and dried in the sun. Tallow or marrow fat was then added. Devlin had told her pemmican was a mainstay of many Indian tribes, and that Indian children ate it the way white children ate candy. It could be stored for long periods of time.

"*Tuhkaru*," he insisted firmly. "Eat."

With some trepidation, she took a bite, surprised to find that it was rather good.

Esatai sat down beside her, helping himself to the roasted rabbit. Once, their hands touched as they reached into the bowl at the same time.

Sarah started to apologize, but the look on Esatai's face stilled her tongue. He gazed at her for a long moment, and then he took her hand in his, turning it this way and that.

Her skin was soft, pale, warm. He let his fingers slide up her arm to her shoulder, and then, after a moment, he caressed her cheek. "*Nu naibi.*"

"I don't understand," Sarah said, although, deep inside, she was afraid she understood all too well.

"My wo-man."

"No."

"*Haa,*" he said with a nod. "Yes."

Sarah stared at him helplessly. She wanted to hate him, to scream at him, but his eyes were kind when he looked at her, his hand was gentle as it caressed her cheek.

He pointed at her, then at himself. "You. Me. Come together . . ." He paused, searching for the right words, and when he couldn't find them, he pretended he was holding a baby. "After."

Sarah nodded, understanding that he would not touch her intimately until after the baby was born.

But that didn't keep him from insisting she share his blankets that night. Silent tears tracked her cheeks as Esatai held her against him. He spoke to her in Comanche, and while the language sounded harsh and guttural to her ears, his voice was soft and unexpectedly soothing.

With something akin to horror, she realized that he reminded her of Devlin. He had the same quiet strength, the same air of self-assurance. She knew, without doubt, that, like Devlin, Esatai would protect her with his life.

Later, after he'd fallen asleep, she stared up at the narrow strip of sky visible through the smoke hole, fervently praying for a miracle.

In the days that followed, Sarah learned more than she'd ever wanted to know about Indian life. She had always thought the Indians were uncivilized, heartless savages, so she was surprised to learn that children were prized and loved, and that they were never physically punished. Most surprising of all was the fact that, when discipline was needed, it was meted out by an older sibling or some other relative.

Once she saw an old woman put a sheet over her head to frighten a little boy who had dumped a handful of dirt into a cook pot. Esatai told her that all children had the fear of *piammpits*, the Big Cannibal Owl, put into them. *Piammpits* lived in a cave on the south side of the Wichita Mountains and ate bad children at night. At least, that was what Sarah thought he said. It was hard to tell, since his English was limited.

On several occasions, she saw little girls and boys playing what appeared to be the Indian version of "house." Each boy chose a wife. They swam together, rode together; then the boys went hunting make-believe squirrels, which they brought into camp for the wives to cook.

The Indian women were busy from dawn till dark, preparing food and clothing, caring for their children, gathering wood, and hauling water. There were no stores in Comancheria. Everything was made by hand. Indian women didn't buy a length of cloth to make a dress. They had to spend hours working over a green hide, soaking the hair side with a mixture of wood ashes and water, which produced lye. After the hide had soaked long enough, the hair was scraped off, along with every particle of blood, fat, and flesh.

Once the hide was dried, it had to be softened. This was done by pounding a disgusting mixture of brains, liver, grease, basswood bark, soapweed, and water into the hide. After the mixture was worked into the rawhide, it was left in the sun for a while, then pulled back and forth across a tree limb, thereby drying and softening the hide. This process went on for several days until the skin was soft and pliable.

Sarah discovered that the Comanche were a social people. Visiting, dancing, storytelling, and games were very popular with old and young alike.

Sarah felt completely out of place when Esatai dragged her into the lodges of his friends. She didn't understand the language, the customs were strange, and she often thought that they were talking about her.

The only social event she enjoyed was the dancing. Sitting on the sidelines, she loved to watch the dancers. Men and women alike moved with a natural grace, a freedom of movement that was beautiful to see. There was something mesmerizing about sitting in the darkness, watching the flames cast flickering shadows on the yellow lodgeskins as she listened to the songs and the rhythmic beating of the drum.

She'd been to several dances before the night Esatai took her by the hand and led her into the dance circle. Sarah tried to pull away, but he refused to let her go, insisting that she dance with him.

She felt the heat climb in her cheeks as she endeavored to follow the steps, but her pregnancy made her feel clumsy, and she felt as if everyone was staring at her, laughing at her.

Fighting tears, she ran out of the circle into the darkness beyond the campfire.

She ran until she was out of breath, and then she sank down on the damp grass and let the tears flow. She wanted to go home. She wanted to see Danny. She needed to see Devlin, to feel his arms around her. Soon, her child would be born. The thought of having a baby here, among enemy people, filled her with soul-wrenching fear. She wanted Devlin to be there when the baby came. She wanted a doctor, a bed, clean sheets.

She let out a startled cry as she felt a hand on her shoulder. Glancing up, she saw Esatai standing behind her, his face unreadable in the darkness.

Wordlessly, he put his hands around her and lifted her to her feet. Wordlessly, he drew her into his arms and held her close, one hand awkwardly stroking her hair.

"Why do you cry?" he asked.

"I want to go home. Please, Esatai, let me go home."

"No." Sadly, he shook his head. In the few short weeks that she had been in his lodge, he had come to love her as he had loved his first wife. He didn't care that the other warriors ridiculed him for taking a white woman to his lodge. He didn't care that the child she carried belonged to another man. She was his woman now, and he would not let her go.

Discouraged and homesick, Sarah rested her head on his shoulder. She wanted to hate him. She could have hated him if he'd been cruel, but he treated her with infinite kindness. She knew the other warriors mocked him because he gathered the wood and the water for their lodge. He ate whatever she cooked, no matter how it turned out, and thanked her for it afterward. He tanned a hide so that she could make herself a warm dress for the coming winter. He made her a pair of fur-lined moccasins, traded his rifle so that she might have a warm robe.

How could she hate him?

He held her while she cried, held her until her tears were gone and her heart was cold and empty.

And then he kissed her, once, gently.

"I . . . be good . . . hus-band," he promised. And taking her by the hand, he led her back to his lodge.

That night, very softly and gently, he caressed her face, his fingertips lightly questing as he traced the curve of her cheek, her lips, the line of her jaw. Desire blazed in his eyes, his breathing grew shallow.

"*Nananisuyake,*" he murmured hoarsely. "Pretty."

Sarah blushed in spite of herself, her whole body tense as she waited for him to attack her, to take forcefully what she could never give. But he only smiled at her, his dark eyes asking her not to be afraid, to trust him. And then, giving her shoulder a gentle squeeze, he left the tipi.

Later, lying beside him in the dark, Sarah listened to the sound of the rain against the lodgeskins, the soft patter of the raindrops echoing the silent tears in her heart.

Chapter Seven

Soaked to the skin and bone weary, Toklanni reined the gray to a halt. Earlier that morning, he'd entered the *Llano* and now he sat there, wondering which way to go.

It had never been safe to be in Comanche country, but it was even worse now. The Indians were on a rampage, riding with a vengeance against the whites, who were slaughtering the buffalo at an alarming rate. Hides were selling for almost four dollars each.

Back in the autumn of '71, several hunting outfits operating out of Dodge City had crossed into the northern panhandle in violation of the Medicine Lodge Treaty of '67. When the buffalo hunters established a trading post at Adobe Walls, the Comanche took to the warpath. Now, almost two years later, the destruction of the herds had escalated.

There were some whites who lamented the decimation of the great herds. Opponents decried the waste of so much meat and argued that continued hunting only served to keep the Indians stirred up and on the warpath, but the buffalo hunters insisted they were rendering a great service in annihilating the animals because everyone knew the Indians depended on the buffalo for survival.

Phil Sheridan agreed, declaring that the buffalo hunters had done more to destroy the Indians in the last two years than the entire Army had done in the last thirty years. He'd gone on to say the legislature should give each hunter a bronze medal with a dead buffalo on one side and a discouraged Indian on the other.

But Toklanni's concern wasn't the buffalo, or white hunters, or the Army. His only thought now was to find Sarah and take her home.

He swore softly as a dozen or so riders came into view. Dismounting, he led the stallion behind a clump of sagebrush and tapped the gray behind its right foreleg, and the stallion immediately lay down. Drawing his rifle, Toklanni squatted behind the horse, hardly daring to breathe as the Indians rode by.

Like the Apache, the Comanche went to war not only for plunder, vengeance, and glory, but for the sheer love of fighting. Any man worthy of the name was a warrior. Success in battle brought admiration and respect, and the highest honor a man could achieve was counting coup on a living enemy because it required more bravery to touch one's enemy with a spear or a coup stick than to kill him from a distance. The taking of a scalp was a matter of small consequence; anyone, even a woman, could scalp a dead man. Stealing tethered horses from within a hostile camp was also considered a high honor. The Comanche allowed two coups to be counted on a fallen enemy. The Cheyenne counted coup on an enemy three times, the Arapaho four times.

Toklanni stayed where he was for several minutes after the war party passed by, offering a silent prayer of thanks to *Usen* for the rain which had washed out his tracks.

Urging the gray to its feet, he swung into the saddle and reined the horse south, toward Palo Duro Canyon.

The next two days passed slowly. Toklanni slept little and only in snatches. Several times he saw small groups of warriors, mostly hunting parties. Once he came upon a village. He watched it for several hours, but there was no sign of a white woman and he rode on, riding deeper and deeper in Comancheria.

The weather grew severe, making travel almost impossible. He was wet all the time, his nerves were raw, every muscle tense.

He reached Palo Duro Canyon late one rainy afternoon. Taking cover on a ridge behind a pile of rocks, he counted thirty lodges where there had once been hundreds, but most of the Comanches were on the reservation now. Only last year, General McKenzie had launched an attack on the

Comanche in Palo Duro Canyon. After the battle, McKenzie had captured and destroyed over a thousand Indian ponies. With their supplies and mounts seriously depleted and winter coming on, the bands had straggled into the reservation one by one, until only a few renegade bands remained in the *Llano*.

With darkness coming on, Toklanni huddled into his blankets, his rifle resting on his knees. There would be no sleep for him this night, he thought ruefully. No sleep, no fire, no hot coffee to turn away the cold. Nothing to sustain him but the hope that he would find Sarah here, alive and well.

Morning dawned clear and cold. Rising to his feet, Toklanni blew on his hands to warm them. After checking on his horse, he squatted on the ridge, absently chewing on a hunk of beef jerky as he scanned the camp.

The women were up now, moving to the stream for water, gathering wood for their cookfires.

Toklanni leaned forward, the cold and his hunger forgotten as he watched one of the women walking toward the stream. She wore a buckskin dress. A heavy robe was draped around her shoulders, her head was covered by a colorful Mexican shawl. But there was something about the way she moved . . .

She turned for a moment, and he saw that she was pregnant. "Sarah." Her name slipped past his lips.

Almost as if she had heard him, she turned

to stare up at the ridge, her gaze searching the rocks and trees. She turned away when a young man came up behind her and took her by the arm, leading her into a tipi near the center of the village.

Toklanni watched the camp the rest of the morning, but Sarah didn't leave the tipi again.

He spent the morning considering and rejecting a half dozen ways to rescue Sarah, but, in the end, there were really only two choices.

He could try to sneak into the camp at night and spirit her away, though he knew that would be next to impossible. Like most Indian villages, the Comanche camp was overrun with dogs, most of them half wild, making it virtually impossible for anyone to enter undetected.

His second option was to ride in and boldly demand her return.

In the end, he decided on the second plan.

With the matter decided, he removed his weapons, then swung onto the gray's back and rode down the ridge, hoping he wasn't making the biggest mistake of his life.

His arrival roused the whole camp. Women grabbed their children and scurried for the shelter of their lodges. Dogs barked. Old women hurled insults at him; old men shook their fists in his direction.

But it was the young men who gathered around him, dragging him from the back of his horse, stripping him of his weapons. He was the enemy. He staggered under the blows that rained down upon him. One man darted into his path, striking him across the chest with his coup stick. Another came up behind him and struck him across the back of the neck with a war club.

Grunting with pain, Toklanni dropped to his knees. He stayed there for a moment, feeling the blood trickle down his neck, knowing that if he stayed down, they'd kill him.

With an effort, he gained his feet and continued forward. He saw Sarah step from one of the lodges, saw her eyes widen and her face grow pale as she recognized him.

The young men continued to torment him, slapping him with their open palms, pummeling him with their fists, hitting him across the back and shoulders with clubs.

He ignored the pain as he walked steadily onward, his gaze focused on Sarah. Gradually, the warriors backed off. Risking a glance to the side, he saw the confusion on their faces, the grudging respect in their eyes.

He came to a halt when he reached Sarah's lodge. There were tears in her eyes now, and when she would have touched him, he shook his head imperceptibly, warning her off.

For a moment, he let his gaze move over her, making sure she was unhurt, and then he concentrated all his attention on the warrior at her side.

"I am Toklanni of the Mescalero Apache," he said, speaking loudly so all could hear. "I have come to get my woman."

The warrior drew himself up to his full height.

"I am Esatai of the Tekapwai Comanche. You not find woman in our lodges. Only death."

"I have found her," Toklanni said. He nodded at Sarah. "This is my woman. She carries my child."

"Woman is mine. Child is mine."

Slowly, deliberately, Toklanni shook his head. "She is my woman. Ask her."

Esatai lifted his chin defiantly. "If I say she is my woman, she is my woman." A faint smile curved his lips. "Dead man has no need of woman."

Toklanni kept his face impassive, knowing that any sign of weakness now would be fatal.

"I have crossed the *Llano*," he said, keeping his voice even. "I have come in peace to claim what is rightfully mine. It has long been known that the Comanche are a brave and fearsome people. Have they now become a people without honor, to rob a man of his wife?"

Esatai's eyes narrowed ominously as he lifted a hand to the knife on his belt.

"You can kill me," Toklanni said, "but you cannot kill the truth."

A low murmuring arose from the crowd that had gathered. Toklanni kept his gaze on Esatai, but he could feel Sarah watching him, feel her heart reaching out to him.

Esatai looked out at the crowd that had gathered around. The Apache had done a brave thing, riding boldly into their camp, alone and unarmed. He could not kill the man outright. To do so would be cowardly, and the Comanche scorned cowardice above all else.

Esatai glanced at the white woman. She belonged to the Apache. It was there in her eyes for all to see, and he knew he would have to give her up. But first he would see just how deeply the Apache warrior's courage ran.

"The gauntlet," Esatai decided. "If you survive the gauntlet, the woman is yours."

A sudden chill snaked its way down Toklanni's spine, but he kept his emotions carefully masked, refusing to let Esatai see his trepidation.

There was a sudden burst of excited conversation from the crowd as they began to speculate on the Apache's chances of survival.

Esatai held up a hand for silence. "What say you, Apache? Will you run for your woman? Or leave as you came?"

For the first time, Toklanni let himself look at Sarah, his smile assuring her that everything would be all right. "I will do as you say."

Sarah shook her head, appalled at what he was about to do. "No, Devlin. Don't. Please don't."

"I'll be all right."

It didn't take long for the Comanches to get ready. The warriors hurried to their lodges, choosing their favorite weapons, then quickly formed two long parallel lines.

Esatai took Sarah by the arm and led her to the far end of the gauntlet.

"Here. Stay," he said, then took his place to her left, at the end of the line.

Toklanni, stripped down to his clout and moccasins, stood at the head of the gauntlet, his hands clenched into fists. Closing his eyes, he took several deep, calming breaths.

Usen, fill my heart with courage. Bless me with the strength of my brother, the horse, with the speed of an arrow in flight, with the surefootedness of a wild mountain goat. Above all, bless my woman with a strong, healthy child . . .

He opened his eyes as he felt a hand on his shoulder. An old Comanche woman stood at his side. She looked at him for a moment, her sunken black eyes brazenly assessing him.

"*Miaru!*" she said, giving him a shove. "Go!"

He stared at Sarah for a long moment and then, taking a deep breath, he began to run.

Hoots and war cries rose on the wind as the Comanche warriors struck out at Toklanni, hitting him across the back and shoulders with war clubs, striking his arms and legs with lances, jabbing at him with sharp sticks.

Toklanni hunched over, shielding his head with his arms as he sprinted between the howling warriors. His body was throbbing with pain by the time he reached the halfway point. He risked a quick glance toward the end of the line, saw Sarah waiting for him, her clasped hands pressed against her chest, her lips moving silently, urging him on.

And beside her stood Esatai, a look of eager anticipation on his face as he raised a war club decorated with scalps.

Toklanni ran forward, dodging left and right in an effort to avoid the blows that descended on him like rain, steadily, mercilessly.

He was near the end of the line when a barrel-chested warrior struck him across the side of the neck with a club. With a grunt, Toklanni dropped to his hands and knees. He heard Sarah's warning scream, heard an exultant cry as Esatai darted forward. Summoning the last of his waning energy, Toklanni rolled to the side so that Esatai's club, aimed for his head, struck him on the shoulder instead.

He felt his skin split from the force of the blow, felt a sudden rush of warmth as blood trickled down his arm. Some deep-seated instinct prompted him to roll back the other way, and as he did so, he felt a rush of air past his head as Esatai swung his war club a second time.

A war cry rose on Toklanni's lips as he scrambled to his feet and sprinted the short distance to the end of the line.

He stood there, glaring defiantly at the Comanche warriors, his breath coming in harsh, labored breaths, his whole body throbbing with pain.

Esatai scowled at him, the hatred radiating from him like heat shimmering on the desert.

With an effort, Toklanni squared his shoulders, and then, in a gesture clearly intended to show possession, he draped his arm around Sarah and drew her up against him.

"My woman," he said, his breath hissing between clenched teeth.

Esatai's hand closed around the knife sheathed on his belt. The urge to draw that knife, to drive it into the Apache's heart, was strong within him, but such an act would forever shame him in the eyes of his people.

Toklanni saw the threat in the warrior's eyes. "My woman," he repeated. "Do you deny it?"

Slowly, Esatai shook his head. "Take woman and go."

Toklanni nodded, his movements heavy and sluggish as the adrenaline that had been keeping him on his feet drained away, leaving him weak and weary.

One of the warriors brought the gray forward. A faint smile curved the Comanche's lips as he handed the reins to Toklanni. "*Hoartch*," he said, a look of admiration in his eyes. "Friend."

Toklanni nodded as he took the reins. "*Hoartch*."

He lifted Sarah into the saddle and then, gritting his teeth against the pain, he swung up behind her, his back straight, his face impassive, as they rode out of the village.

"Devlin, are you all right?"

Sarah's voice, low and filled with concern, wrapped around him.

"Yeah."

Sarah glanced over her shoulder, her gaze sweeping over him. He looked awful. His face was swollen, caked with sweat and dirt. His right shoulder was bleeding, his chest was a mass of bruises.

"Dev—"

"Not now, Sarah."

They rode the rest of the way in silence. As soon as they reached the ledge, Toklanni slid off the back of the stallion and sank to his knees.

Moving slowly and awkwardly, Sarah dismounted, then knelt beside Devlin, wondering where to begin. "Dev? Devlin!"

He blinked up at her. "Saddlebags."

Rising to her feet, she rummaged in his saddlebags, withdrawing a long strip of muslin and a small bottle of whiskey.

Devlin took several swallows of whiskey while she doused the rag with water from his canteen and washed the blood from his shoulder.

When that was done, she rinsed the cloth, soaked it with water, then pressed it against the bruises that discolored his chest and shoulders. There were numerous raised red welts on his arms and legs, more bruises on his back and buttocks, but nothing seemed to be broken.

With an effort, she unsaddled the horse, then spread the blanket on the ground. She bit back the urge to cry as she watched Devlin stretch out on the blanket. Sitting beside him, she cradled his head in her lap.

"Oh, Devlin." She smoothed a lock of hair from his forehead, lightly stroked his cheek.

"Did he hurt you?"

"No." Her fingertips traced his lower lip.

"Are you all right?"

"Fine." She pressed her lips together, fighting the urge to cry. "I was so afraid."

Devlin caught one of her hands in his. "I know."

"Not for myself," she murmured. "Esatai wouldn't hurt me. I was only afraid I'd never see you again."

"Sarah." He gazed up at her, wishing he didn't

69

hurt so bad, wishing he could take her in his arms and hold her close. But this wasn't the time or the place, and as much as he hated to admit it, he didn't have the strength.

"I knew you'd look for me," she said, her fingers entwining with his, "but I didn't think you'd ever find me."

Toklanni smiled at her. "I'll always come for you, Sarah."

"I know. How's Danny?"

"Fine." His eyelids fluttered down as a soul-shattering weariness overcame him. "He's with Joe. . . ."

A fierce tenderness filled Sarah's heart as she stared down at her sleeping husband. He'd crossed miles of wilderness to find her, had suffered a brutal beating at the hands of his enemies. Surely no one in all the world had a man like hers.

Chapter Eight

Toklanni woke with a low groan. Sarah lay close beside him, her head nestled on his shoulder. Sometime during the night she had covered them with a blanket.

He lifted the edge, peering at his chest, which was a colorful mass of greenish yellow bruises and dull red welts.

With a sigh, he sank back and closed his eyes again. He'd been in fights before. He'd been wounded, but never in all his life had he hurt all over the way he did now.

Sarah sighed and shifted a little in her sleep, and her hand, which had been resting on his stomach, slid down to his thigh. In spite of his weariness, in spite of the dull pain that pounded through him, he felt an unmistakable stirring in his groin.

Opening his eyes, he turned to look at her. She looked like a princess in a fairy tale, he thought, waiting for the handsome prince to come along and waken her with love's first kiss.

A wry grin tugged at the corner of Toklanni's mouth. Not by any stretch of the imagination would he ever be considered a handsome prince. Heroes in fairy tales always seemed to be fair-haired with bright blue eyes and near-perfect features. None he'd ever heard of had scarred faces and Indian blood.

He watched Sarah for a long while, saw a ghost of a smile flit across her face. And then her eyelids fluttered open and he found himself gazing into the clear blue depths of her eyes.

"Good morning," she murmured.

"Morning. What were you dreaming about?"

"You, of course." A faint flush colored her cheeks. "Why are you staring at me?"

"I was just thinking how pretty you are." He cleared his throat. "Like a princess in a storybook," he added, feeling foolish as he said the words aloud.

"Funny you should say that," she remarked, laughing softly, "because I was dreaming that I was being rescued from a fire-breathing dragon by a handsome young prince."

"Oh?" Toklanni lifted one black brow. "Who played the prince?" he asked, a trace of bitterness creeping into his voice.

Sitting up, Sarah punched him on the arm. "You, of course. Who do you think?"

Toklanni shrugged, grimacing as the movement

sent a wave of renewed pain coursing through his right shoulder.

Sarah frowned at him for a moment, and then sighed. He was thinking of his scars, she knew without a doubt. It had been a long time since she'd even thought about his scars. She could remember her feeling of revulsion the first time she'd seen him, the bile that had churned in the pit of her stomach when she tried to imagine the pain, wondering how he had survived such a terrible wound. Looking at him now, she saw only the man she loved.

Toklanni held her gaze, his expression impassive. He knew Sarah loved him in spite of his scars and yet, sometimes, without warning or provocation, he couldn't help but wonder if, deep down, she wasn't repelled just a little.

"Devlin—"

He shook his head. "Forget it."

With infinite tenderness, Sarah traced the scar on his cheek and then, leaning forward, she kissed him, her lips trailing over the faint white line that ran from his cheekbone to his jaw, then on down his neck.

"Sarah, don't."

"Why?"

"Just don't."

She stared up at him, taken aback by his gruff tone. "What's wrong?"

"Nothing."

"Devlin Dennehy, you stop this nonsense right now. Those scars don't mean a thing. They never did. I don't even see them anymore." She laid her hand on his arm. "I don't know why you let it bother you."

He was being foolish and he knew it. "I'm sorry. Why don't you put the coffee on?"

"Devlin—"

"I'm fine." He turned away from her, digging into his saddlebags for the jerky and pemmican that would have to pass for breakfast.

His thoughts were grim as he stared into the flames, waiting for the coffee to boil. The house and barn were gone. The stock was gone. All they had were the clothes on their backs, and a baby that was due in less than a month.

Toklanni swore softly. He'd have to take Sarah to town, find a job, a place to live until they could rebuild . . . assuming that Sarah wanted to start over again. After all she'd been through, he wouldn't be surprised if she'd rather live in town, permanently.

The thought left a bad taste in his mouth. He hadn't minded giving up the freedom of his old life to live on the ranch. In spite of having to live within four walls, he'd still been free, able to come and go as he pleased, with no one to answer to but himself. But to live in town, to be forced to work for someone else, keep hours that were set for him . . . he shook his head, knowing he'd hate it. But what choice did he have?

They ate their meager breakfast in silence. Toklanni saddled the gray. He insisted that Sarah put on the heavy coat Joe Loomis had lent him, then helped her into the saddle, wincing as he climbed up behind her.

Sarah placed her hand over the arm around her waist and gave it a squeeze. He was a colorful sight this morning, his whole body discolored and swollen from the beating of the day before. "Where are we going?"

"Pepper Tree Creek, I guess. I'll get you settled into the hotel, then go get Danny."

"Is everything gone? The house, the barn, everything?"

"Yeah."

"Don't blame yourself. It would have happened even if you'd been home. You might have been killed if you'd been there. Danny, too."

"Maybe."

"Devlin, please."

"I don't feel like Devlin right now," he muttered.

He wasn't acting like Devlin, either, but she couldn't quite put her finger on what was different. "What can I do?"

"Nothing. We'll go to town," he said, putting his thoughts into words for the first time. "I'll find a job."

"We can sell the land," Sarah suggested, hoping to ease his mind. "We could use the money to buy a house."

"If that's what you want."

She glanced over her shoulder, wanting to see his face. "What do you want?"

"I don't know."

"Devlin . . . Toklanni, talk to me. Tell me what's wrong?"

Slowly he shook his head.

"We can rebuild if you don't want to live in town," she said.

"It's up to you."

Exasperated, Sarah faced forward again. She tried to figure out what was bothering him as the miles slipped by. He couldn't be questioning her love. Surely he couldn't be upset over his scars, not at this late date. She wondered if he was blaming himself for the attack on the ranch, but that didn't make sense, either. It wasn't his fault the Comanches had burned the house and kidnapped her. It would have happened if he'd been there or not.

It had to be the thought of living in town that made him so depressed. She knew that he'd hate it. Even though most of the townspeople had learned to accept him, there were still some who looked at him with contempt and mistrust. Most of the tribes had been moved to reservations, but there were still occasional outbursts of warfare, raids on outlying homesteads and ranches. Cattle and horses were stolen, fences were cut, telegraph lines were pulled down.

"I don't think I want to live in town," Sarah said, her voice light. "I think we should rebuild."

Toklanni grunted. "With what?"

"We'll get a loan from the bank."

"Yeah. I'm sure old man Simms will be glad to lend us the money."

Sarah uttered a very unladylike oath. Devlin was right. Ralph Simms wouldn't give Devlin the time of day, let alone lend him enough money to rebuild the house and the barn. The banker's wife and children had been killed years ago by a Kiowa raiding party. He'd had no use for Indians ever since.

"Maybe we can build from scratch. I'm sure Joe Loomis would help. And Jim Howell and his brother."

"Maybe."

With a wordless cry of frustration, Sarah grabbed hold of the reins and gave a sharp jerk, bringing the stallion to a halt. Turning around as best she could, she stared at her husband.

"Devlin, I don't know what's bothering you, but you're making me damned angry! I love you. I don't care about your scars. I don't care what anyone else thinks of my choice of husbands. I don't care about the house burning down . . . well, not very much. What matters is that you're safe, that Danny's safe. I don't care if we stay in town, or try to rebuild the ranch, as long as we're together. Do you understand that?"

He grinned at her in spite of himself, amused by the rage that danced in her eyes, by the flush of heated color in her cheeks. He didn't think he'd ever seen her so angry before.

"It's very becoming," he remarked.

Sarah frowned at him, her anger momentarily forgotten. "What is?"

"Your anger."

"My anger." She expelled a deep breath. "Are you trying to make me crazy?"

He shook his head and then, ever so slowly, bent toward her, blocking everything from her sight but the love shining in his dark eyes. His mouth was warm when it covered hers, filled with tenderness.

"I'm sorry, Sarah," he murmured, tucking a wisp of hair behind her ear. "I rode like hell to rescue you from the Comanches, and now that I have, I've got nothing to give you. You were better off with Esatai. At least he had a home to give you, shelter from the storm that's coming."

"Oh, Dev," she said, feeling helpless. "Everything will work out, you'll see."

He nodded, but she knew he didn't believe her. Reaching behind him, he unrolled the blanket tied behind the saddle and draped it over her head and shoulders. Only then did she notice that the sky was rapidly turning black. There was, indeed, a storm coming.

"You take it," she said, starting to remove the blanket. "I've got your coat."

"Keep it," he said gruffly. He pulled the blanket over her head again with a firm but gentle hand. "You need it more than I do."

Toklanni urged the gray into a lope, his narrowed eyes scanning the land for refuge, but there appeared to be only miles and miles of flat ground.

He pushed the horse hard for the next hour, his concern for Sarah growing with each passing mile. The baby was due in less than three weeks. He wasn't a doctor, but he was pretty sure that spending hours on the back of a horse in the pouring rain wasn't good for a woman in her condition, or for the child she carried.

Oh, God, please don't let anything happen to this

baby, or to Sarah. Please, let this child be strong and healthy. Please . . .

It was near dusk when they found shelter in the lee of a rocky overhang in a small canyon. Toklanni lifted Sarah from the back of the horse, heard the small groan she tried to stifle as her feet touched the ground.

Moving quickly, he stripped the saddle from the horse, spread the blanket on the ground beneath the overhang, and helped Sarah to sit down. There was no dry wood for a fire, nothing to eat but jerky and pemmican, but she didn't complain.

"Come sit beside me," she urged. "It'll be warmer if we sit close."

"You're a remarkable woman, Sarah Dennehy," he remarked, putting his arm around her and holding her close. "Why aren't you complaining about the cold and the rain and the lousy food?"

"I don't mind the cold, and I like the rain," she said, smiling up at him. "And lousy food is better than no food at all."

"True enough," he muttered, remembering times past when the Apache had been close to starving, when they ate their horses and their dogs and anything else they could get ahold of. When the old ones went out in the snow to die so there'd be more food for the rest of the tribe.

Sarah cupped his cheek in her palm. "Everything will be all right, Devlin. I know it will."

"Yeah."

"Trust me, Devlin," she murmured, her eyelids fluttering down. "Just this once . . ."

At the first touch of her lips on his, all his

worries and doubts faded into oblivion. She was woman, the giver of life and solace, the bearer of sorrows. She was his wife, willing and able to stand beside him during good times and bad. *For richer, for poorer, in sickness and in health . . .*

He had chosen his woman wisely, he thought. He only hoped he would not let her down, that she would never have cause to regret choosing him as her husband.

"Sarah." He murmured her name, knowing that wherever they lived, he would always be at home in Sarah's arms.

Chapter Nine

It rained for the next two days. Sarah was cold
and wet all the time, but she never complained.
Her stoic attitude only made Toklanni love
her more. She had every right to be miserable and unhappy, but she was the one who
was unfailingly cheerful, who was constantly assuring him that everything would be all
right.

He'd managed to kill a rabbit the morning of
the second day. That evening, he'd found a handful of dry wood and they had a hot meal for the
first time in three days.

He watched Sarah carefully, worried by the
dark shadows under her eyes. She ate little and
fell asleep almost as soon as he lifted her off the
horse, but she assured him she was fine, just fine,
and he had no choice but to believe her.

Silently, he cursed the rain, which made traveling slow and treacherous.

Toklanni woke early the following morning, a strong sense of unease coursing through him. Sarah lay beside him, sleeping peacefully. For several minutes, he stayed where he was, keeping his eyes closed and his breathing slow and even. He could hear the stallion cropping damp grass, the chatter of a jay, and then, abruptly, there was only silence. The gray whickered softly and stamped its foot.

With an oath, Toklanni rolled to the left, away from Sarah, grabbing his rifle as he did so. He'd barely cleared the blankets when he heard the soft thwack of an arrow pierce the ground where he'd been lying only a moment before.

Toklanni sprang to his feet, rifle at the ready as he peered into the thick fog, searching for some sign of his attacker.

"What is it?"

He heard Sarah's voice, thick with fear, but he dared not spare a glance in her direction. "Stay down," he warned.

A second arrow hissed through the gray dawn, slamming into the ground at Toklanni's feet. He jerked around, the rifle swinging in the direction the arrow had come from, and the third arrow, meant for his heart, buried itself high in the fleshy part of his left arm.

He fired twice, blindly, instinctively, heard a harsh cry of pain, and then Esatai stumbled into view, his buckskin shirt sodden with blood.

"No, oh, no," Sarah murmured. She stared at

the Comanche warrior as he staggered toward her, one hand pressed against the dreadful wound near his heart, his other hand outstretched, reaching toward her.

Sarah shook her head, tears stinging her eyes, as he continued toward her. She slid a glance at Devlin, searching his eyes for . . . what? Understanding? Sympathy?

He had neither. His face was set in hard, implacable lines as he watched the deadly crimson stain spread across the front of the warrior's shirt, saw the strength drain out of the warrior's body.

Slowly Esatai dropped to his knees, his gaze fixed on Sarah's face. "My . . . woman . . ."

Unable to help herself, Sarah went to him. Kneeling beside him, she cradled him in her arms, her hand holding his.

"I'm sorry," she murmured brokenly. "So sorry."

With an effort, Esatai lifted his other hand, his fingers touching the gold of her hair, caressing her cheek.

"*Tu . . . su . . . naru . . . nue . . .* ," he murmured, and then the light went out of his eyes. His hand dropped lifelessly to his side.

Sarah was crying now, the tears running down her cheeks, unchecked and unnoticed.

"Why?" She stared up at Devlin, her eyes searching his for answers. "Why?"

"Don't you know?"

Sarah shook her head. "I was nothing to him, just a captive white woman."

"No. He loved you."

"He didn't even know me," she exclaimed, suddenly angry because Esatai had died needlessly. "He didn't know a thing about me."

"Some people are easy to love," Toklanni remarked quietly. "I think I loved you from the moment I first saw you, before I even knew your name."

Sarah shook her head, unwilling to accept the fact that a man she'd hardly known had died because of her. She looked down at Esatai. Why hadn't he stayed with his own people? Why had he come after her?

"What did he say, before he . . ." She swallowed hard. "Before . . ." She couldn't say the words. She'd seen death before, but she'd never had anyone die in her arms.

"I'm not sure. I think he said, 'Forgive me.'"

A wordless cry of sorrow escaped Sarah's lips as she buried her face in her hands. She'd known Esatai for only a few weeks, but he'd been good to her, in his own way. He hadn't shamed her, or hurt her. He had been patient with her ignorance and her shortcomings. And now he was dead.

She sobbed aloud as Devlin lifted her to her feet.

Toklanni held her close, wishing he could say something to comfort her, but every tear she shed for the Comanche was like a thorn pricking his heart, sharper and more painful than the arrow lodged in the meaty part of his arm.

"I'm sorry," Sarah murmured.

Drawing back, she wiped her eyes with the backs of her hands. "Oh, Lord, you're hurt! I . . ."

Guilt washed through her. How could she have forgotten that Devlin was wounded?

"It's all right, Sarah."

"No, it isn't, but I . . ." All the color drained out of her face. "I've never seen anybody . . ." She gazed into the distance, fighting the urge to vomit.

"It's all right," Toklanni said again. It was never easy, watching someone die, no matter if that someone was friend or enemy.

Gritting his teeth, Toklanni took hold of the shaft and jerked the arrow from his arm. White-hot agony speared him from shoulder to wrist, but he welcomed the pain. It was cleansing, somehow.

Kneeling beside Esatai, he removed the warrior's headband and wrapped it around the bloody gash in his own arm.

When he looked up, he saw Sarah staring at him, a gentle reproach in her eyes. "I would have done that."

"You've been through enough. We need to go."

"You're going to leave him here, like that?"

"I don't have the time or the energy to bury him. His people will find him soon enough."

It was in her mind to argue, but one look into Devlin's eyes changed her mind. But she couldn't just leave him lying there. Grabbing up one of their blankets, she draped it over Esatai's still form.

Wordlessly, Toklanni saddled the gray, then helped Sarah mount.

She heard him cuss under his breath as he

swung up behind her. "Are you all right?" she asked, risking a worried glance in his direction.

"Fine."

"Devlin, I'm sorry."

"For what?"

"I feel as though I've let you down somehow."

"You haven't," he replied curtly.

She studied his face for several moments, but his expression was closed to her.

With a sigh, she turned around, wishing she could heal the gulf that seemed to be opening between them, but then she felt his arm slip around her waist, drawing her back against his chest. His breath was warm against her neck, his chest was as strong and solid as the mountains.

"Rest, Sarah. Everything's all right."

His voice was deep and reassuring, filled with love and tender affection. Relief flooded through her as she settled against him. Overcome with a sudden weariness, she closed her eyes and drifted to sleep.

She woke to the feel of raindrops on her face. The sky had turned dark as night. Thunder rumbled overhead; in the distance, a slash of jagged lightning ripped through the clouds. There were teeth in the wind.

They were both soaked to the skin by the time they found shelter in a hollow formed by a pile of huge gray boulders.

They spent the rest of the day there, huddled beneath their blankets. Devlin held her close, warming her with the heat of his body, but he seemed far away, as though he had withdrawn from her. Was he angry because she had wept for Esatai? Could he be jealous?

The thought was oddly disturbing and yet satisfying. What woman didn't want her man to be insanely jealous once in a while? But Devlin had no cause. She loved him heart and soul. Surely he knew that?

Resting against his chest, she lifted her hand and let it slide down his scarred cheek. "I love you, Devlin."

He grunted softly as he lifted her hand away from his face. "I know."

"Don't shut me out."

"What do you mean?"

"I feel as if you're angry with me, and I don't know why."

"I'm not angry, Sarah."

"Then what?"

He shook his head. "Nothing." He said the word, knowing it was a lie, as all his old doubts came back to haunt him. "Get some rest. We'll be moving on as soon as it stops raining."

She wanted to argue with him, but her eyelids were heavy. Her body, too, felt heavy and lethargic. Capturing his hand, she placed it over her womb so he could feel their child stirring within.

Closing her eyes, she murmured, "I hope it's a girl," and then she was asleep.

A girl, Toklanni thought, with Sarah's golden hair and sky blue eyes. His daughter. She'd be a quarter Apache. Would life be different for her than it had been for him, or would people look at her with scorn because there was Indian blood in her veins? Boy or girl, he didn't want any child of his to be ashamed or ignorant of its heritage.

Resting his head against one of the boulders, his arms wrapped around Sarah, he closed his eyes, praying for a strong, healthy child.

Chapter Ten

She woke wrapped in the warmth of Devlin's arms. For a moment, she didn't move, only lay there, watching him sleep. Even at rest, his face was lined with worry. It grieved her that she was the cause of it.

Unable to resist, she reached out and lightly stroked his cheek, loving the touch of his skin, warm and smooth beneath her fingertips. Her gaze moved over his face, a face she knew so well, admiring the high-bridged, straight nose, the strong, square jaw, the high cheekbones, the sensual line of his lips, the color of his skin.

She brushed a lock of hair from his brow, smiling as his eyelids fluttered open. "Good morning."

"Morning."

"It stopped raining."

89

Toklanni grunted, wondering how she could be so cheerful. They'd lost everything they owned. They were miles from town, and she was smiling at him, her blue eyes bright, her hair like a golden cloud around her face.

"I'm hungry," she said, her hand gliding over his chest. "Do we have anything to eat?"

"There's some pemmican left."

"I'll get it."

"You stay put. I'll get it."

After a meager breakfast, Toklanni saddled the horse, and then they were riding again, heading southeast, toward Pepper Tree Creek.

It would be hard for her men, living in a town again, Sarah thought. Danny was used to the freedom of the ranch, of being able to come and go as he pleased. He liked fishing in the stream near the house with the Loomis boys. He liked having a yard full of animals. He even liked milking their ornery cow and prowling through the henhouse, outsmarting the chickens to collect the eggs.

Difficult as it might be for Danny to adjust to such a change, it would be twice as hard for Devlin. He'd told her his mother had taken him to live in Santa Fe when he was nine years old. She'd wanted him to meet his white grandparents, to learn how the white man lived. He'd hated it. It was there, he'd told her, that he'd first heard the word "half-breed," the first time he'd heard the word "squaw" used in a derogatory way. The people had been unkind to his mother, as well, mocking her, staring at the blue tattoo on her chin.

After six months, they'd returned to his father's people.

She couldn't ask him to live in a town again. Even though most of the people had accepted him, she knew he still felt like an outsider. Somehow, they'd find the money to rebuild the ranch, and if not . . .

Sarah took a deep breath. If not, she'd ask Devlin if he wanted them to live with the Apache for a while. He'd given up so much for her, it was the least she could do for him.

It was near midday when her back began to ache. Knowing it would only worry Devlin, she didn't say anything. She slept for a while, holding on to Devlin tightly, and when she woke, it was late afternoon.

Toklanni reined the gray to a halt. Dismounting, he lifted Sarah from the back of the horse. "Are you okay?" he asked.

"Fine."

He moved behind her and rubbed her shoulders and back for a few minutes, grinning at her soft sound of pleasure. Turning her in his arms, he kissed her cheek. "Stretch your legs a little," he said. "I'll see if I can't find a rabbit for dinner."

Sarah nodded, then sat down on a rock, one hand massaging her back.

It was nearly dark when Devlin returned, a couple of prairie chickens slung over his shoulder.

"Fresh meat tonight," he announced.

Sarah smiled, biting back a groan as the pain in her back slid around to the front.

Toklanni frowned. "What is it? What's wrong?"

"Nothing, just a little pain in my back."

Dropping the birds to the ground, he went to Sarah and knelt in front of her. "How long has it been hurting?"

"All day, off and on."

"Why didn't you tell me?"

"I didn't want to worry you. It's probably nothing," she said, and then gasped.

"Are the pains getting worse?"

Sarah nodded.

Wordlessly, he picked her up and placed her in the saddle.

"Where are we going?"

"There's a little Mexican village not far from here," he said, draping a blanket over her head and shoulders. "You're not having the baby out here. There's another storm coming."

Swinging up behind her, he lifted the reins and urged the gray into a rocking-chair lope, the need to get Sarah to safety pounding through him like an Apache war drum. She'd lost two children already. It would kill her to lose another.

It was dark when they reached the little Mexican village nestled in a range of low foothills.

Sarah was in labor now, of that there was no doubt. Toklanni stopped at the first jacal he came to. Dismounting, he knocked on the door.

A moment later, an aged woman dressed in black from head to foot opened the door.

"I need shelter for my wife," Toklanni said.

The old woman shook her head. "No room. Go away."

"She's having a baby."

The old woman shook her head again. "No."

Toklanni swore under his breath. He could hardly blame her for not wanting to let them in, he thought bleakly. His scarred face alone was enough to make the old woman wary. The fact that he was an Indian didn't help any. The Apache and the Mexicans had been enemies for generations.

Turning away, he took the gray's reins and walked down the dusty street to the next house. And the next. And the next.

No room. Go away. No room. It was the same at every house. No one was willing to open their door to a scar-faced Indian and his woman.

When they reached the end of town, he felt as if his anger would strangle him. Sarah needed shelter, and she needed it now. Try as she might, she couldn't hide the fact that the pains were coming harder, faster.

Muttering an oath, he swung up behind Sarah and reined the horse toward the foothills. He'd seen a cave up there on the way into the village. At least she'd be dry.

The cave was small. Toklanni went in first, making sure there were no animals inside, and then he carried Sarah in and made her as comfortable as he could.

"I'll be back in a little while," he said, taking up his rifle.

"Where are you going?"

"To get some blankets and something to eat. Don't worry, I won't be gone long."

He was gone before she could argue with him.

Toklanni rode hard for the village. He didn't bother to ask for help this time. Leaving the gray tethered in a copse of trees, he entered the town on silent feet, ghosting toward the ramshackle general store at the far end of the main street.

It didn't take much to break into the place. Finding a burlap bag, he stuffed it with food, a length of clean linen, another of flannel. To that, he added a half dozen fat candles, a box of matches, a couple of tin cups, forks and spoons, a blue enamel coffeepot, a ball of twine. Lastly, he grabbed three wool blankets.

He retraced his steps out of town, pausing only once in the shadows to let a couple of vaqueros go by.

The gray whickered softly at his approach. Tying the bag over the saddle horn, Toklanni vaulted into the saddle and rode hard for the cave.

The sound of Sarah's muffled groan reached him as soon as he stepped out of the saddle. Grabbing the burlap bag, he hurried into the cave.

"Sarah!"

"Devlin."

He heard the pain in her voice, the relief at his return. Moving quickly, he lit the candle, then knelt at her side. Her eyes were glazed with pain, her face and bodice damp with sweat.

He spread a blanket for her in the rear of the cave, then built a small fire to turn away the cold. When she was comfortable, he filled the coffeepot with water and made her a cup of tea.

"Where'd you get all this stuff?" she asked between contractions.

"I stole it."

"Devlin!" she exclaimed, shocked that he would do such a thing.

Toklanni met her gaze, his eyes dark and brooding. "The Apache don't think it's wrong to steal from their enemies."

"The people in the village aren't our enemies."

His expression hardened. "They are mine."

"Because of me?"

His silence was all the answer she needed.

He sat beside her through the long hours of the night, holding her hand, massaging her back, insisting she get up and walk a little between contractions.

He talked to her of his childhood, of his mother and father. And all the while the fear grew deep inside him—fear for the child's life, for Sarah's. He cursed the villagers for refusing to give his wife shelter.

At dawn, they heard the low, sweet sound of church bells.

"It's Christmas," Sarah said, panting between contractions. "This year . . . we'll have a . . . wonderful . . . present."

Toklanni nodded, squeezing her hand with a warm reassurance he didn't feel.

Christmas, he thought, the day the white man's God had been born. He remembered the story of the Nativity that Sarah had told him the first year of their marriage, how the people of Bethlehem had refused to give shelter to the mother of the Christ child, forcing Mary to give birth to the savior of the world in a stable.

Sarah clutched at Toklanni's hands, her fingernails digging into his palms, as a sharp pain knifed through her. For the first time, she began to be afraid. She'd been in labor so long. What if something was wrong? Oh, Lord, what if this baby died, too? She knew how much Devlin wanted a child. She couldn't fail him again.

Toklanni grimaced as her nails cut into his hands. Such strength for such a small woman, he mused, and wished he could absorb her pain into himself. Her cries sliced into his heart like an Apache skinning knife. She had been in hard labor for hours now. He didn't think he could bear to see her agony if this child didn't survive.

"Devlin, if anything happens to me, take care of Danny."

"Sarah . . ."

"Promise me."

"I promise."

She grasped his hands as her body strained to expel the child. "Something's wrong!"

He fought down the panic aroused by her words, by the terrible fear in her eyes. "What can I do?"

"See . . . if . . . it's breach."

She groaned low in her throat, her fingernails digging into the hard-packed earth as Toklanni washed his hands, then probed inside her womb.

Sweat broke out across his brow as his fingers encountered a tiny foot. The baby was coming feet first, one leg bent so that it blocked the birth canal.

Swearing softly, fervently, Toklanni straightened the tiny leg, then took hold of both of them in his hand and gave a gentle tug, timing it to coincide with a contraction.

Moments later, a scrap of pink flesh topped off by a mop of damp black hair slid into his hands.

It was a girl, tiny and perfect, with dark blue eyes and a turned-up nose. She took one look at him and let out a loud wail.

Grinning broadly, he placed the baby on Sarah's stomach. "We have a daughter," he said, his voice thick with unshed tears.

And then, seeing the look of love and relief on Sarah's face, he did cry, his heart sending a prayer of thanks to the Great Spirit as he cupped Sarah's sweat-sheened face in his hands and kissed her with all the love in his heart.

Chapter Eleven

In the flickering light of the fire, Sarah gazed at her daughter, marveling at how pretty she was, how small, how perfect, from her dimpled fingers to her tiny toes. Love swelled in her heart as the baby's hand curled around her finger. It was worth it, Sarah thought, all the waiting, all the pain, it was all worth it.

Sarah's gaze moved over her husband's face. The lines of worry were gone, replaced by an expression of peace.

Earlier, they'd bent over the baby, checking her from head to heel, a little awed by the miracle they had wrought between them.

Now, her gaze drifting from father to daughter, she thought about Danny. She hoped her son wouldn't be too disappointed to have a sister instead of the brother he'd been counting on.

Danny. She wondered how he was getting along, though she wasn't really worried about him. Mary Kate Loomis would take good care of him.

Beside her, Devlin stirred. His hand, resting on her now flat belly, moved slowly upward to cup her breast, now heavy with milk.

"Morning," he murmured. His voice was deep and low, husky with sleep. "How're my girls?"

"We're fine. Hungry for a kiss."

Sitting up, Toklanni pressed a feather-light kiss to his daughter's brow; then, his arm slipping around Sarah's shoulders, he kissed her, slowly, deeply.

"You sure you're feeling all right?" he asked, drawing back a little so he could see her face.

"I'm fine, Dev. Honest."

He had to admit she looked fine. Terrific, in fact. Her eyes sparkled with happiness, her lips were curved in a smile that was hers alone, her hair framed her face like a golden halo.

"You look like the Madonna in that Bible picture you showed me," he remarked.

His compliment brought a warm flush to Sarah's cheeks.

Devlin insisted she rest while he prepared breakfast, then went out to check on his horse.

He swore under his breath as he saw a trio of horsemen riding toward the foothills. They weren't Indians, but out here, strangers of any kind could mean trouble. A village this close to the river was a great place for outlaws to hole up. Comancheros, con men, gamblers on the dodge, lawmen gone bad, sooner or later they all seemed to head for the safety of the Mexican border.

He tethered the horse closer to the mouth of the cave, then ducked inside, careful to keep his expression impassive.

Sarah was nursing the baby, and for a moment Devlin forgot about the possibility of trouble heading in their direction. She was so beautiful, sitting there with his child at her breast, her hair falling over her shoulder, her expression filled with tender affection for the new life in her arms.

"Is everything all right?" Sarah asked as Devlin entered the cave.

"Why do you ask?"

Sarah shrugged. "I don't know. You were gone for a long time." She frowned as he reached for his rifle. "What is it? What's wrong?"

"Probably nothing."

"*Probably* nothing?"

"There's some riders heading in this direction. They'll probably ride on by."

"But they might not?"

"I just want to be ready." He bent toward her, his hand caressing her cheek. "Don't worry." He pressed a kiss to the top of her head. "Stay inside."

"Devlin—"

"Do as I say, Sarah."

She swallowed the lump rising in her throat as she watched him leave the cave. She wasn't afraid for herself. Devlin would die to protect her and their child, of that she had no doubt. But what if he was killed? What would she do without him?

Wrapping the baby in one of the blankets, Sarah rummaged through Devlin's saddlebags, looking for the spare Colt that Joe Loomis had given him.

She lifted the gun, surprised by its weight. She wasn't familiar with handguns, had never even fired one. Vern had insisted she learn to fire a rifle. On occasion, she had even hit what she aimed at.

Hefting the gun in both hands, she moved toward the mouth of the cave.

She could see the riders now, three men wearing the loose cotton pants and shirts of Mexican peasants. Broad-brimmed hats shaded their faces.

Her heart began to pound a quick tattoo as they approached the cave.

She heard the sound of a rifle being cocked, saw Devlin walk forward to meet them.

"That's far enough," he said. "What do you want?"

The man in the middle removed his sombrero. "We mean you no harm, senor. My brothers and I returned to our home late last night. Our grandmother told us an Indian had come looking for shelter for his woman. Our grandmother is old and easily frightened. She watched you leave town, no doubt to make sure you had gone. We are sorry for her inhospitality, and we have come to make amends."

"We have brought food," the young man on the left said.

"Blankets and clothing for you and your wife."

101

"And a bottle of tequila to celebrate when the child is born," added the first young man.

"My thanks," Toklanni murmured.

"It's a girl," Sarah said, stepping out of the cave.

"Congratulations, senor. Senora," exclaimed the three brothers.

"Step down," Toklanni invited.

The men, Pedro, Juan, and Carlos, gathered around Toklanni and Sarah, admiring the baby, apologizing profusely for their grandmother's behavior. As one, they invited Toklanni and Sarah to come and share the meager wealth of their home, but Sarah declined. She was anxious to go home, anxious to see Danny.

"Are you sure you don't want to rest a few days?" Devlin asked.

"I'm sure."

"The night, at least," Pedro insisted. "You should have a hot bath, a good meal, and a good night's sleep before your journey."

"Thank you," Devlin said. "We accept."

Maria Juanita Bautista welcomed them with a hesitant smile. Her eyes, as black as olives, were wary as she followed Toklanni and Sarah into the kitchen, but one look at the baby melted the last of her distrust. The father might be a scar-faced Apache, the mother might be a *gringa* dressed as an Apache woman, but the baby was an angel.

After preparing them a hearty meal, the old woman took the baby from Sarah. Cooing softly, she sat down in an old wooden rocker and sang to the child, leaving her grandsons to entertain the parents.

Sarah went to bed early. There were only two bedrooms in the small *casa*, one for Maria and one that was shared by the brothers. Sarah felt guilty for turning the three young men out of their room, but they insisted and she knew it would be rude to refuse.

Toklanni entered the room a few minutes later. He grimaced as he eyed the three narrow beds.

"Looks like I'll be sleeping alone," he muttered.

Sarah looked at him over the baby's head. "We'll make room."

He chuckled softly, trying to imagine the three of them in one narrow bed. "I guess I can tough it out alone for one night."

"I don't know if I can."

"You need the rest, Sarah."

"There's something else we need."

"Oh? What's that?"

"A name for our daughter."

"Yeah." So much had happened, he'd forgotten all about that. "Got any ideas?"

"What was your mother's name?"

"Christine."

"How about Christine Marie, after your mother and mine?"

"Christine Marie," Toklanni murmured. "I like it."

Sarah yawned. "Christine Marie it is, then," she murmured agreeably.

Devlin smiled down at her as her eyelids fluttered closed. A moment later, she was asleep.

Chapter Twelve

They left the Bautista spread the following morning, laden with gifts and supplies.

Sarah looked forward to going home with mixed emotions. She couldn't wait to see Danny again, to assure herself that he was well. She'd be glad to see Pepper Tree Creek again, but it would be hard to go home and see only a pile of charred rubble where their house had been.

They traveled leisurely, stopping often so Sarah could rest and nurse the baby. Toklanni never tired of watching the two of them, his heart brimming with love and gratitude. The Great Spirit had been kind. Each day, he gave thanks to the gods, both red and white, for blessing them with a healthy child, and for the good weather that followed them home.

It was midafternoon when they reached the

Loomis place. Mary Kate hurried out to meet them, her face wreathed in smiles.

"Welcome home," she gushed, hugging Sarah. "Oh, look at the wee one. Isn't she a precious thing! What's her name?"

"Christine Marie."

"Makes me wish for another one myself," Mary Kate mused.

"Where's Danny?" Sarah asked, glancing a-round.

"He's over at your place with Joe and the boys."

"Our place?" Toklanni frowned. "What are they doing there?"

"Oh, just cleaning up a few things," Mary Kate replied with a mysterious grin.

Toklanni's frown deepened. "I guess I'll go over and look around. Is it okay if Sarah stays here until I get back?"

"I think she should go with you."

"Yes, Dev," Sarah said, laying her hand over his arm. "I want to see Danny."

With a nod, he lifted her onto the back of her horse.

"Thanks for looking after Danny for us," Toklanni said, his tone formal, polite.

"Anytime," Mary Kate said, her eyes twinkling. "Anytime."

"Is it my imagination, or was she acting a little strange?" Toklanni asked as they rode out of the yard.

Sarah shrugged. "I don't know. I thought she'd ask me to stay, but it doesn't matter. I'll bet Danny's grown a foot since we've been gone."

Toklanni grunted softly, wondering at Mary Kate's behavior. He knew she still felt a little awkward around him, perhaps more so now when he was dressed in buckskins.

He put the thought from his mind. He had more important things to worry about, like where he and Sarah were going to live, and what they were going to do for money until he could find a job. The little they had saved wouldn't last long.

"I've been thinking," Sarah said. "I know you don't want to live in town. And I know Danny won't be crazy about the idea, so I thought maybe, if you want to, we could go live with your people for a while, until we decide what to do."

Toklanni turned to stare at her. "You'd do that?"

"If you want."

"It's a hard life, Sarah. They don't always have enough food to eat. The winters, especially, are hard."

"But you'd rather live there than in town, wouldn't you?"

"Yes."

"Then, if Danny has no objections, I think that's what we should do." She smiled at him. "You could be Toklanni again."

He grinned a little sheepishly. "I've been Toklanni ever since I left the ranch."

"Have you? I wondered what was different about you."

"Different?"

"I can't explain it. It's a subtle difference, nothing I can put my finger on."

"Do you mind?"

"No," she replied with a grin.

"Which one do you want me to be?"

"It doesn't matter. I love you both, but I have gotten used to Devlin. Still, Toklanni has a lot to offer, too, so I . . ."

She broke off, her eyes widening, her mouth forming an "O."

Devlin tensed, his hand reaching for his rifle. "What is it?" he asked.

"Look!" Sarah pointed down the hill.

Devlin stared in the direction she pointed and knew he looked every bit as surprised as Sarah, for there, where the old house had been, stood a new house built of peeled wood and stone. New corrals. A new barn with a peaked roof and a weather vane.

Sarah looked at her husband. "When? How?"

"I don't know."

Too stunned for words, they rode up to the house.

"Ma! Dev!" Danny ran out of the house, his smile as wide as the Missouri. "Welcome home!"

Devlin dismounted, then helped Sarah from the saddle, taking the baby from her arms so Sarah could embrace her son.

"I was afraid, Ma," Danny confessed as he wrapped his arms around her. "Afraid I'd never see you again."

"I know, I know." Sarah held her son tight, silently thanking God that her son was well, that she had a husband who had been willing to risk his life to bring her home.

"Not bad, huh?" Joe Loomis remarked as he stepped outside. He wiped his hands on a big red bandanna. "Got two bedrooms, and a loft for the boy."

"You did this?" Devlin asked.

"I had lots of help from the townsfolk."

"But why?"

"Just being neighborly," Joe said. "We all pitched in. Frank Nellis, Bill Murphy, Jim and Jack Howell. Everybody. It needs some finishing up on the inside, but I'll be glad to come over and help with that."

Devlin stared at Loomis as if he'd never seen him before. "I don't know what to say."

"Do you like it, Ma?"

"It's lovely, Danny," Sarah said, hardly able to speak past the lump in her throat. "Just lovely."

"I helped build it, too," Danny said proudly.

"So did we," Brian Loomis said.

"We cut wood for days," Brent Loomis added with an exaggerated groan. "I got blisters on my hands as big as Texas."

For the first time, Danny noticed the blanket-wrapped bundle in Devlin's arm. "What's that?"

"Your baby sister," Devlin replied, his voice tinged with pride.

Squatting down on his haunches, he peeled back the blanket so Danny could see the baby's face. "Her name is Christine Marie."

"A girl," Brian Loomis said, obviously disappointed.

"A girl," Brent echoed sympathetically. "Too bad."

"Shut up, you two," Danny warned. "She's . . . she's kinda pretty. And so tiny. Hi, there, Christine." He reached toward the baby, then grinned when she took hold of his finger. "Look, Ma, she likes me!"

Devlin glanced up at Sarah. She was smiling brightly, her eyes shining with tears of love.

"Well, welcome home, you two. Ah, three," Joe Loomis said, clearing his throat. "Come on, boys, let's go see what's for dinner. I reckon Sarah and Dev would like a chance to look around."

"Okay, Pa," Brian said. He took a last look at the baby. "I guess she is kind of cute, for a girl."

"See you tomorrow, Danny," Brent called. "Bye, Mr. and Mrs. Dennehy."

"Good-bye, boys," Sarah said. "Thanks for everything."

"There's some venison in the root cellar," Joe said, taking up the reins of his horse. "Mary Kate said if you didn't feel like cooking, to come on over for supper."

"Thanks, Joe," Devlin said. He handed the baby to Sarah, then put one arm around her waist, his free hand resting on Danny's shoulder. "I don't know how we'll ever repay you."

"No need, Dev. Just being neighborly. See you in church."

Devlin nodded, his throat tight.

"Can I hold the baby a minute?" Danny asked when Brian and Brent were out of sight.

"Sure, son." Sarah handed Christine Marie to Danny. "Be sure to hold her head."

Devlin smiled at Sarah, then swung her into

109

his arms. "Well, Mrs. Dennehy, shall we go take a look at our new home?"

"I'd love to," Sarah said. Leaning forward, she pressed her mouth to his ear. "I promised Danny a little brother for Christmas next year."

"I'll do my best," Devlin promised as he carried her over the threshold into their new home.

Wrapping her arms around her husband's neck, Sarah gave herself up to the joy that flooded every fiber of her being.

Loving Devlin, and being loved by him, was the greatest gift of all.

ELIZABETH CHADWICK
THE FOURTH GIFT

To Matthew and Sheila who came home for Christmas.

Special thanks to Carol and Mike Eastman, our hosts in Flagstaff; to the helpful Special Collections librarians at Northern Arizona University; and to Joan Coleman, good friend and hometown editor.

Chapter One

Jonathan inhaled the cold, thin air with that heady anticipation he always felt at the beginning of an adventure. Wet snowflakes were drifting singly out of the blue-black sky above Flagstaff in the Arizona Territory. The San Francisco Mountains filled the horizon, dark with their huge pines, a jaunty cap of snow glistening against the night sky. Storm clouds, rolling in from the northwest, hastened to engulf an icy moon. Beside him in the street, Jonathan's new acquaintance, Uncle Burden Fox, was slamming a gnarled fist against the office door of a lawyer.

"Wake up, Hiram," Fox bellowed. "Git your butt down here." They were on Railroad Avenue, several doors from Sandy Donahue's Mineral Belt Saloon, where Jonathan had just played the most interesting poker game of his life, not that he had won so much, but Uncle Burden seemed to think it a considerable amount to lose.

The two men listened to heavy footsteps thumping down the stairs inside the building, to low-pitched muttering, to locks snapping open.

"Burden, what the hell?" grumbled Hiram Apple, appearing in his nightshirt at the door to his office, above which were his just-vacated sleeping quarters.

"Hiram," said Uncle Burden exuberantly, "I'm on my way to San Fran-cisco." He broke into a phlegmy cough that had interrupted the dozens of sheep-raising adventures with which he had regaled Jonathan during the course of their evening at the Mineral Belt. "I aim to spend my last years surrounded by fallen women with big bosoms an' dimpled knees, all awearin' satin an' feathers an' asquabblin' amongst themselves over my company."

"You drunk again, Burden?" asked Hiram Apple.

"I am Jonathan Forrester, sir," said Jonathan, cutting into Burden's dreams of Arabian splendor in the brothels of San Francisco. "Mr. Fox has just sold me—for the consideration of a poker debt, a ticket to San Francisco, and five thousand dollars—his share in the F & F sheep ranch."

"You old fool," said Hiram Apple to Burden. "Merrill's gonna kill you."

"Merrill won't git the chance," said Uncle Burden. "Merrill don't git back till week's end, an' I'm headin' for Californy soon as we sign them papers."

Hiram Apple slanted a worried glance at Jonathan. "Merrill's not gonna take to a new partner," he warned. "Might kill you too."

"Oh, I hardly think so," said Jonathan cheerfully. What a piece of luck—that he'd been so taken with the beauty of the mountains as his train made the trip between Santa Fe and San Francisco that he'd decided to stop at Flagstaff. He considered the night's transaction a great bargain, as Mr. Fox had assured him that the F & F ranch was not only profitable but included a large, sturdy log house, cool in summer, warm in winter. What situation could be more ideal, Jonathan reasoned, for research on his next book, which would be about sheep raising in the magnificent mountains of northern Arizona?

Jonathan was an author of some renown, his Western adventure books popular all over the Northeast and Middle West. His publisher would be delighted with this new one. As for the formidable Merrill Fox, over whose reaction lawyer Apple was still fretting, Jonathan foresaw no difficulties. He and his new partner would have a fine time the next year or so, and then Jonathan might or might not retain his rights to the F & F spread. He'd been thinking of settling down, giving up his roving life, and he'd seen no place more beautiful than this one.

"I have a good feeling about this venture," he said to the lawyer. After the hot, dusty plains of Texas and Oklahoma, the locale of his just-published epic, *The Last Cattle Drive*

North, the mountains of the northern Arizona Territory would be a welcome change.

"I'm easy to get along with," he added, glancing politely away from spindly arms and twiggy hands resting on the generous paunch that ballooned under the lawyer's nightshirt. "No matter how grumpy an old codger he is, your Merrill Fox will find me pleasant company."

"Merrill ain't exactly old," said Hiram Apple.

"Mr. Forrester, this is Merrill Fox, best flockmaster in Arizona, just back from trailing four or five bands of sheep down to winter pasture."

"My pleasure, Mr. Fox," said Jonathan, holding out his hand.

"Merrill, meet Jonathan Forrester. He's a—"

"What the hell is this about, Hiram?" interrupted Fox, ignoring Jonathan's outstretched hand in favor of quieting a short-haired, black and tan sheepdog that was snarling at the lawyer. "Sit, Boss," snapped the flockmaster. The dog immediately slapped its rump onto the lawyer's Turkey carpet, but it remained on guard, ears alert, teeth bared. "I was over at Doc Brannen's place getting some Beschee's German Syrup for Boss here, who's been coughing some," said Fox. "Hadn't hardly passed over the money when one of the Daggs brothers came in and said I'd better head for your office fast."

The lawyer, backing away from the dog, fell into his rolling desk chair. "Well, Merrill," he stammered, "seems like your Uncle Burden got it in his head that he wanted to spend his gray-haired years surrounded by harlots with big bosoms and dimpled knees. Those are his words, not mine."

"Old fool," muttered Fox. The dog cocked its head sideways to study its master's face.

"A-yah. Well, for a consideration of five thousand dollars, a poker debt, and a ticket to San Francisco, where he doesn't expect to see another flake of snow to his dying day—"

The rancher, who was brushing snow from the sleeves and shoulders of a sheepskin jacket, glared. "Just what'd my stupid uncle give for this windfall?"

"Half the F & F spread."

"What?" The voice was sharp and indignant. "Why, that skunk-brained, lazy, good-for-nothing, ugly, unwashed . . ."

Jonathan could see that lawyer Apple had been right. Young Merrill Fox was not happy to hear that his uncle had sold half of the ranch to a stranger.

"Now, Merrill," said the lawyer as he scooted his chair nervously away from the paper clutter on his rolltop desk, "you can't blame me for this." He was eyeing the dog warily, for the creature's attention had returned to him. "Money had changed hands before the deal ever showed up at my door. Five thousand dollars! Plus the gambling debt forgiven. An' a ticket—includin' a sleepin' car."

"Private compartment," corrected Jonathan.

"Soon as I catch my donkey-brained uncle, I'll put a shot right through the hand that signed away my ranch."

"It's not your land only," the lawyer protested. "Burden owned the half your pa didn't leave you."

Jonathan studied the angry young man, who wasn't a whit better dressed than the uncle had been—same dusty, rumpled trousers; heavy sheepskin jacket; well-worn, once-brown, broad-brimmed hat. The dog looked better groomed than either Fox, and the only difference in uncle and nephew was that Merrill was a short, slightly built young fellow and clutching a heavy Winchester rifle in his left hand as if he did indeed plan to use it if he caught up with his uncle.

"Since Mr. Forrester here's a writer," said Apple, "it's not likely he'll want to interfere with the way you run the ranch."

"A writer?" groaned the young man as if he'd just been told that his new partner was an outlaw wanted all over the territory.

"Yep, Western adventure books for Yankees. Reckon his next adventure's going to be sheep ranching with you."

"It should work out conveniently," said Jonathan. "For instance, we won't have to change the name. F & F will do as well for Fox and Forrester as for Fox and Fox."

Merrill Fox made a low, snarling noise, which was echoed by the dog. Then the young man jerked his hat down over his eyes and, hands on hips, scowling at his boots, muttered, "Uncle Burden's no great loss, I reckon. I'll buy you out, but I haven't got any five thousand dollars. You'll have to settle for—"

Jonathan shook his head. "My thought is to be a working partner," he interrupted.

"That right?" Fox looked insufferably smug. "You know anything about sheep?"

"Well, I'm a man who appreciates a good lamb roast," said Jonathan, who was beginning to enjoy himself. "Especially with mint jelly and a fine, thick gravy." This young fellow was easy to provoke, thought Jonathan, grinning as he watched the boy's scowl deepen. Fox acted a lot tougher than he looked. No doubt the boy was trying to compensate for his youth, small stature, and not very manly voice.

"You wouldn't like sheep ranching," said Fox.

"Oh, but I would," Jonathan insisted.

"Not with me, you wouldn't!" The young man whipped off the battered hat and tucked one thumb pugnaciously into the waistband of his trousers right above a holstered pistol tied with a thong to his upper leg. Merrill fox gave every indication of a mean-spirited satisfaction when Jonathan's mouth dropped open.

However, Jonathan recovered quickly from the shock dealt him by the sight of the long, honey-haired braid that tumbled loose from under the brown hat. Having been fooled by the clothes and the belligerence, he took his time studying Merrill Fox's tanned, delicate features, not to mention the thrust of a small breast revealed under the flannel shirt when *Miss Fox* brushed aside her jacket to tuck her little thumb into the band that enclosed her slender waist. His new partner was a girl, all right.

119

Jonathan's face lit with a delighted smile, and he bowed politely. How good could a man's luck get? he asked himself. He was going to team up with the only female flockmaster in northern Arizona, probably the only female flockmaster anywhere. His next book ought to sell better than umbrellas in a rainstorm.

Merrill Fox sat hunched glumly on the seat beside the miserable, stubborn, ass-eared Forrester, who insisted that half her house, as well as half her land and stock, was now his. He had refused to be dissuaded from accompanying her back to the ranch, even though snow fell silently all around them, muffling the thud of the team's plodding gait and nipping at her skin like a cloud of tiny ice insects.

Behind her the sleigh was piled high, not only with the supplies she had bought from Brannen's Pioneer Store for the sheep camps she would visit next week, but with Jonathan Forrester's many trunks and boxes. He'd even had crates of spirits loaded onto her sleigh from Lowenthal and Meyers, the wholesaler who supplied local saloons. She'd evidently traded a drinking uncle for a drinking writer. Merrill sighed and muttered encouragement to the reluctant horses. Boss, who occupied the driver's seat between her and Forrester, nuzzled Merrill's elbow consolingly.

"That was a big sigh for such a pretty young lady," said Jonathan Forrester. He had been looking this way and that through the snow as if he expected something interesting to happen any moment, something beyond their imminent danger of running off the road and getting stuck if the storm worsened.

Merrill gritted her teeth. Her looks were not a subject to which she gave much thought, but she did resent being made sport of by this dandified Yankee. Pretty young lady, huh? She wasn't even particularly young. And Merrill knew what the women and the young men of the area said about her—that she rode like a man, dressed like a tramp, and smelled like a sheep. She'd never much cared what people thought of her, but the last, about the smell, was unfair. Merrill bathed every few nights, not a pleasant pastime when the facilities were a wooden tub filled with water that went from hot to cold before you'd hardly got the first layer of dirt off. Also Merrill saw to it that Mrs. Oblati washed the clothes regularly, so unless she was out there working with them, Merrill figured she *didn't* smell like a sheep. But she wasn't anyone's idea of a *pretty young lady* either, while Forrester, who had obviously been making fun of her, was just about the handsomest man she'd ever seen—tall, broad-shouldered, well dressed, with thick, dark hair and a storybook hero's face.

Not that Merrill had ever read a storybook. Her mother had been the reader in the family and had provided many a fine bedtime tale before the books got burned up in a tent fire. Unfortunately, Mama had died in the California gold fields before she could pass the ability to read on to Merrill. In later years when Merrill, Pa, and Uncle Burden—damn him!—had given up prospecting and gone back to sheep ranching, there'd been no time and nobody to teach Merrill to read. Finally drought had forced them to drive their flocks across the Mohave to the Arizona Territory, where they founded the F & F Ranch, by which time Merrill was too old and too embarrassed over her illiteracy to attend school in Flagstaff when the first one opened. Now she'd never learn.

And that was the worst of Jonathan Forrester. Not only was he handsome, while she was homely, but he could read, and she couldn't. And the man didn't just read books; he wrote them. The very idea filled her with awe. And sadness. And humiliation. What if he found out her secret? Unhappily, she slapped the reins onto the horses' necks. Well, she'd never let him find out. Even old Apple, her lawyer—that traitor!—didn't know that Merrill couldn't read the papers he drew up for her, that she had to trust to his honesty.

And look where that had got her. Her no-good uncle had run off, leaving this Eastern dude to claim half the ranch she and Pa had sweated to make profitable these ten years since '76. What she had to do was get rid of Forrester. Make him want to leave. Want to sell out to her. For some amount she could afford, and that wasn't much.

"Do you usually travel in snow this heavy?" asked Forrester.

"Why, this isn't heavy," Merrill drawled. "We're having a real mild winter so far. Only had ice once, and this is the first snow since last April."

She nodded emphatically. "Real mild. The heavy snow won't start for a week or two. Might even hold off until December." That ought to give him something to think about.

"I'll look forward to seeing it," said Forrester, laughing. "The harder the winter, the better the book."

Merrill turned to glare at him. Nobody wished for a hard winter. Only a fool. And a fool would be harder to scare off than a sensible man. She shifted uncomfortably on the seat, half frozen. Why wasn't *he* shivering? He had an inch and a half of snow on the shoulders of his gray wool coat, and he sat there radiating heat, keeping her Forrester side warm, although the dog was between them and snuggling up to the author with her nose poked into his armpit.

"Boss," hissed Merrill, and the dog reluctantly sat up straight. Since when did Boss take to strangers? Merrill asked herself resentfully. Heretofore, the dog had never liked anyone but Merrill and sheep. Merrill shivered again, but not from the cold. It was that blasted Forrester so close to her on the seat. She had to get rid of him. He was too tempting—even for a sensible woman like her.

"I suppose you think you're going to make more money out of this than a Mexican horse thief," said Merrill, who had always imagined that the wealthiest folk among the nonworking must be Mexican horse thieves, those who didn't get hung, and even then they died rich.

"Well, your uncle led me to believe that there were profits to be made in sheep ranching," said Jonathan mildly. "Investments doubled in only one year."

"We never did that," she protested.

"He said the cost of raising sheep is minimal what with the low wages of the herders and the free grass."

"Humph," said Merrill, and she rattled off what it had cost them to raise an ewe in northern Arizona for the last ten years, what the average clip had been, the price of shearing, the cost of freight to market, and the price of wool paid per pound in markets they had and hadn't used. Merrill might not be able to read, but she had a head for figures and remembered everything she ever heard. "Now maybe that sounds good to you, but you ought to remember that a Western flockmaster needs to bring through eighty to eighty-five percent of the lamb crop to break even and ninety to make a profit."

"The best investment a man can make," said Jonathan, "is a knowledgeable partner," and he smiled at her so warmly through the falling snow that she couldn't miss the compliment in his words and the pleasure it gave her. Boss evidently felt the same, for she snuggled her nose back into his armpit and gave a low woof of friendship.

"Boss!" admonished Merrill. The dog removed her nose and faced forward again on the sleigh seat. "And of course, those profits," said Merrill, staring with disapproval at her fickle companion, "have to be put back into the herd and into land.

Just this year I bought a hundred crossbred rams from Daggs Brothers at twelve dollars a head. That's twelve hundred dollars," she pointed out. "The Daggs paid between one hundred and six hundred in '82 for Vermont merinos and bred them to their best range ewes. Now, you get a forty-pound clip from a purebred, which I can't afford to buy, naturally, and twelve to fourteen from a crossbreed, whereas an ordinary range ewe won't yield you more than six to eight."

"I could put up the money for merinos," said Jonathan. "Then we could breed and sell our own crossbreeds."

Damn, thought Merrill. She'd reasoned that the twelve-hundred-dollar expenditure would shock him. How much money did a man make on a book about Western adventure, and why in the world would he see running a sheep ranch as an adventure? She enjoyed it, wouldn't do anything else, but lots of folks hated sheep. Shaking her head, Merrill fell into a gloomy silence. So far the campaign to discourage Forrester didn't seem to be accomplishing much, and Boss was snuggling up to him again, while Merrill thought wistfully of owning her own purebreds. Suffering sheep scab, but the man was a tempting devil!

"Pay six hundred dollars for a ram and then lose it to sheep scab or lupine!" she exclaimed disdainfully, just to let Forrester know that she hadn't been softened up by his cunning ways. "That would be a fool move."

"Well, you're the boss," said Jonathan.

Elizabeth Chadwick

Merrill blinked. Uncle Burden had never said that to her, although she *had* been the boss since Pa died. "Been buying land from the railroad too," said Merrill. "Pa started that before he passed on. *He* saw the catsclaw hiding in that free grass."

"I'm afraid your metaphor escapes me," said Jonathan as he fondled the dog's ears. Boss's whole body wiggled with delight.

"Boss, get in back," muttered Merrill. The dog cast one longing look at Jonathan and scrambled over the low seat as Merrill tried to figure out what a metaphor was. Didn't Forrester know about catsclaw? Lord, it tore up a sheep's fleece something terrible. "The free grass won't last forever, you know," she said cautiously. "There's sheep and cattlemen driving in flocks and herds from everywhere. Must be 150,000 sheep in the area, most of them not worth more than $2.75 a head. Ranges'll be overstocked in no time, and the big cattle outfits—Hashknife and A-1 Bar—are buying up the land. If I don't buy too, I'll end up without grass—summer or winter."

"Very wise," Jonathan agreed. "The same thing's happening in Texas, and smart ranchers take the long view."

Merrill nodded smugly. Uncle Burden had never understood that, but this man—good Lord, what was she thinking of? She wanted to drive Jonathan Forrester off, not make a friend of him. The F & F was *hers*. And she had to get it back.

"Look at that snow, will you?" exclaimed Jonathan. "If it's this heavy in early November, we should be able to count on a white Christmas."

"A white what?" asked Merrill, jerked out of her resentful thoughts.

"Christmas. A white Christmas."

"Don't celebrate it," said Merrill, hoping once again that he'd be disappointed and go away. If he was looking for festive holidays, he'd bought into the wrong outfit.

Chapter Two

Innocenta Oblati, massive-bosomed and lightly mustachioed, was a railroad widow. Her husband, along with several others, had been killed in an explosion, his body catapulted into the top of a pine tree beside the A & P tracks. Since that time, Mrs. Oblati had been the housekeeper at the Fox ranch.

"You gonna live in sin, I gonna leave," she said, placing great clenched fists on ample hips.

"Who said I was going to live in sin?" Merrill demanded. "Do I look like the kind of woman who would live in sin?"

"He gonna stay here, I gonna leave."

"Mrs. Oblati," said Forrester, "since I'm a partner now . . ."

Mrs. Oblati was already on the way to her room to pack.

"Look what you've done," cried Merrill. "On top of everything else, they're going to say I'm a fallen woman." To herself she admitted that she didn't really care what *they* said. The real point was that, with Mrs. Oblati gone, Merrill might starve to death, her clothes would go unwashed, and there'd be nobody to keep the place clean or to heat her bathwater in the reservoir built into the left side of the wood stove. Furious, she turned on her new partner. "I'm a sheepwoman," she said fiercely. "I don't cook, I don't clean, I don't—"

"Now, Merrill," said Forrester calmly, "there's nothing to cooking. You just read the recipe . . ."

Merrill hardly heard the rest of his reassurance because his large, warm hand, resting on her shoulder, caused her to feel very peculiar, very skittery, and what had he said? All you had to do was read the recipe? Merrill shook off his hand and the hot tingles it caused along her shoulder, her heart plummeting at the reminder that she couldn't read. "Then you do it," she snapped.

"Do what?" he asked.

"Cook."

Jonathan smiled at her.

Drat the man. Didn't he ever get angry?

"I'm a fine cook," he assured her. "You mustn't worry about a little setback like this."

"You must have donkey brains between your ears," she shouted at him and stamped out into the storm to begin unloading the sleigh. First, she dumped Forrester's trunks and boxes into the thin coating of snow that had accumulated in the yard. Second, she dragged out and saddled the

129

mule Mrs. Oblati insisted on riding to town that very afternoon—stubborn woman! Merrill could just imagine the gossips twittering, "Did you hear what Merrill Fox is up to now? Her housekeeper says she's living in sin with some Yankee. Land sakes!"

Gritting her teeth, Merrill tethered the mule to the hitching post in front of the house, then drove the sleigh on to the barn, where she'd store the provisions and put up the horses, she and Teofilo, a retired Portuguese shepherd who acted as her handyman. Teofilo was so accustomed to the solitary life and open spaces that he refused to eat or sleep in the house or even the barn, which meant she couldn't claim him as a chaperon.

And Forrester, that sissy, hadn't even come out to help. Some partner he'd make. Cooking and writing books. What kind of man occupied himself with things like that? Well, she admitted uneasily, a very handsome one. And he looked as if he could unload the sleigh more easily than she if he wanted to. Oh Lord, what was she going to do? Until now Merrill had never seen a man that interested her in any way other than his connection with sheep raising. Could she, sensible, hardworking Merrill Fox, be infatuated? Maybe she was suffering from indigestion. Forrester had made her try oysters when they'd had a meal at Coulter and Gale's Chop House. Nasty, slimy things. No wonder she felt peculiar.

Jonathan discovered that Merrill had flung his baggage out of the sleigh into the snow. He hoped that she wasn't so angry she'd stay away from the house overlong and endanger her health. He hauled in, first, his clothes, then his books and writing materials, and finally his supply of wine. How had a little thing like Merrill managed to lift that heavy trunk of books out of the sleigh and dump it on the ground? he wondered. Now there was a woman! She was as interesting as her house—*their* house.

It was a massive, two-story log structure with a steep, split-shake roof and huge native stone chimneys at either end, the whole thing as seemingly indestructible as the mountains that surrounded it. Inside, one end of the first floor had been walled off to form the kitchen and the housekeeper's quarters, both warmed by the right-hand fireplace. Giant logs driven down through the floor, to bedrock for all he knew, supported a second-floor balcony that ran the length of the house and was reached by an open stair of halved logs. It looked as much like a slanted ladder as a conventional staircase. One could glance up and see the bark on the underside of each step or mount on the flat side, polished smooth by ten years of Fox boots.

Large, comfortable chairs fronted the left-end hearth. On the kitchen side of the room were a massive oak sideboard and a round oak table with four straight chairs. Otherwise, the spaces were empty, no desk, no books—didn't the Foxes read or keep accounts?—no decorations except two handsome Indian rugs and some fine, old pots of archaeological interest on a rude shelf in the eating area.

131

All this he discovered before seeing Mrs. Oblati off on a mule slung with various bundles and bags. The woman, quivering with moral indignation, absolutely refused to reconsider her decision, even temporarily, although she would have to ride into Flagstaff through the snow. What a difficult person, he mused as he boosted her atop the already overburdened mule.

Once she had departed, he went upstairs to explore and found three bedrooms off the balcony-hall that fronted the staircase. Two were now unoccupied, and he chose the room on the left for its proximity to chimney warmth. The small, disgustingly dirty middle room would be cold and tedious to make habitable. The right-hand room, warmed both by its chimney and the kitchen below, was, he assumed, Merrill's—not because any dresses or petticoats hung on its pegs, but it did contain a dressing table with a mirror. He wondered if Merrill ever looked into it. So smoky was its glass that she must have looked to herself like some ephemeral mountain wraith.

As he unpacked, he called to mind his first real sight of her, when she'd whipped off her disreputable hat. Given the length of the honey-colored braid, her hair must be knee length. How he'd like to see it undone. He'd certainly need a photograph of her for his book. And her eyes—oval and tipped up slightly, with smoky blue-gray irises, long lashes, and brows darker than her hair. And her skin—not the sickly white of fashionable ladies in the East, but a satiny pale color like *café au lait* with an extra dash of cream,

132

stretched tightly over those lovely, austere facial bones. And her body—

At that point Jonathan, having built a pyramid of empty trunks, was shelving his books on the ledges he had created. The body—he fantasized what it would be like under her comical masculine clothing. All he had seen was a slender neck and the thrust of one small breast, but her hands were delicate, calloused no doubt but delicate, as he imagined the rest of her would be.

He couldn't think of another woman who had so taken his fancy, except perhaps for the picture of a medieval noblewoman he had seen once in a museum in Europe, a childlike miss wearing a ludicrous headdress instead of a sensible hat like Merrill's. What a character Merrill would make for his book! What an opportunity to become friends with such a woman!

Humming to himself, Jonathan slotted the last volumes of his library onto his makeshift shelves and strode to the kitchen to see what delicious thing he could prepare for her dinner. By the time he had finished feeding her, she'd never want him to leave. Ten minutes later, having reconnoitered the kitchen, he was wondering how impressed she'd be with mutton stew. Still, the spice selection was a pleasant surprise, not what one would expect on a wilderness sheep ranch. Mrs. Oblati's doing, no doubt.

It was full dark when Merrill finished in the barn and started toward the house. The snow had ceased, the wind picked up, and the sweat she'd worked up stowing crates of supplies and rubbing down the horses, now turned cold on her skin beneath her heavy clothing. Boss rubbed against her legs as she latched the barn door, then turned toward the house. Forrester's trunks and boxes were gone from the yard, and lamplight flickered in the second-floor window of her father's room.

Dang, she thought miserably. She didn't want anyone in Pa's room, though she knew why Forrester had chosen it. Uncle Burden's room was a pigsty, a place Mrs. Oblati had refused to enter more than once a year. Merrill could see through the first-floor windows that Forrester had built up the fires on the hearths and lit lamps in the kitchen and in the big room—that was what they called it. It was there they ate and sat a spell before bedtime, conducted business, and did whatever else a body had to do that didn't involve sleeping, cooking, and washing. He'd made himself right at home.

She pushed open the heavy door and staggered under a smell so enticing that it brought saliva rushing to her mouth. She'd been thinking that, just to discourage him, she wouldn't eat much of whatever he cooked, but she knew as soon as that smell infiltrated her nostrils that she'd eat. Whatever could he have prepared that smelled so good? Then it occurred to her that he must have used Mrs. Oblati's spices.

When the Italian housekeeper first came to them, Pa had said, "None of that foreign Eye-talian stuff for us—just plain old meat and potatoes," and Mrs. Oblati had obliged. They'd had years of "plain old meat and potatoes." Sometimes Merrill got sick of them, but then she'd feel disloyal to Pa, who had liked his food bland and plentiful. But, suffering sheep scab, if Forrester had used those old spices, he'd probably poison them both. Like as not, spices went bad as fast as anything. All the more reason for her not to eat, although resisting would be hard. Boss, who was not allowed in the kitchen, seemed to be tempted too. She was sidling in that direction, tail wagging.

As Forrester came through the kitchen door, Merrill called her dog back, then clamped her own mouth shut lest she drool onto her chin.

"It's a relief to see you home safe and sound," he said. "If you want to wash before dinner, I've got water heated."

"You saying I'm dirty?" she snapped.

"No need to take offense, Merrill. I'll put the stew right on and open a bottle of wine."

"I don't drink," said Merrill.

"Well, you'll have to try some of this. I was surprised to find such an adequate selection at that wholesaler's you have in town."

Merrill was thinking of hot water and interrupted him to say, "Stay out of the kitchen while I wash." Then she tramped in. He nodded agreeably and made for the stairs.

Relieved, Merrill hustled to the sink and stripped out of her sheepskin jacket, then pulled down her suspenders and whipped off her flannel shirt and the top of her long johns. There wasn't time for a full wash, but, by golly, the hot water he had heated would feel good on her upper body and face. She grabbed her washrag and towel.

Jonathan hastened down the steps with the candles he'd retrieved from his room. Planning to make it a really festive dinner, he put them into holders on the table and lit them, then opened the wine he'd purchased in Flagstaff, a bold red that, if it hadn't turned, should go well with his highly spiced mutton stew. Assuming she'd have finished washing her hands and face, Jonathan started for the kitchen to bring his creation in to the table. He'd no more than got the door open a few inches when he backed out hastily, but not fast enough to miss the sight of a slender, naked back, a thick, honey-colored braid bisecting it, and then a flash of a small, rounded breast as she reached for a towel.

Jonathan felt stunned. As interested as he'd been in her body, he'd not expected to see so much of it. Obviously there wasn't an ounce of excess flesh on her, except for the womanly areas, yet her spine wasn't knobby as you'd expect in a slender woman because her back was so well muscled. And her arms—he'd never really pictured muscles on a woman. They didn't bulge like a man's, but for all that, he could now understand how she'd lifted his trunks and boxes down. She was sleek and strong, not soft or bony as were females with whom he had been intimate now and then in years past. How would it be, he wondered, to make love to a woman like Merrill—a woman full of stamina and power, as well as beauty?

Jonathan thrust those thoughts abruptly from his mind lest his body betray him when she returned to the room. If they were to get along, if she was not to drive him crazy without ever meaning to, he had to think of her as a partner, not a desirable woman.

"All finished?" he asked with false good cheer as she entered, her blue plaid shirt catching the blue of her eyes, her honey hair curling damply around her face. "I'll put the food on." He practically leapt through the door to the kitchen and hustled out with his stew, which smelled pleasantly appetizing considering what he'd had to work with.

"Candles?" she asked. "We've got coal oil lamps."

"Well," said Jonathan, pulling out her chair and then pushing her into it when she didn't seem to know how to respond, "I thought the candles would be more festive to celebrate our partnership."

He poured the ruby wine into a strange, fragile tumbler that sat like a glass flower on a glass stem. He must have brought it with him, Merrill decided. The Foxes had never owned anything like that.

Before seating himself, he ladled out a steaming heap of his stew onto her plate, then a helping for himself. "Do you want to say grace?" he asked.

"What?"

"Guess not." He raised his wineglass to her and said, "To a profitable and happy partnership."

"I don't drink," mumbled Merrill, miserable at how ungracious she sounded, yet terrified to drink with this man. She'd be sure to make a fool of herself if she did. Instead and in self-defense, she popped a piece of mutton into her mouth. It tasted so wonderful that she hardly wanted to chew lest in swallowing she lose that flavor.

At that point Boss emerged from under the table and eyed them reproachfully. "What does the dog eat?" Jonathan asked.

"Whatever I do." Merrill was embarrassed that she had forgotten all about her dog, not to mention her handyman. "Except for beans. Boss has to be pretty hungry to eat beans. Did you feed Teofilo?"

"The old fellow? He came to the door for a plate." Jonathan went to the kitchen and found a bowl for Boss, who wolfed down her portion and headed for the other end of the room and a nap by the hearth.

"Where were you born?" asked Jonathan conversationally when Merrill was halfway through the first helping. "Here in Arizona?" He was pleased to note that she had drunk some of the wine without seeming to notice and was mopping up gravy with a hunk of leftover bread he'd discovered in the bread box.

"During nooning," she said. At his puzzled glance she added, "Nooning. My folks and Uncle Burden were driving a flock to California from New Mexico. I was born when we stopped to rest the sheep at noon."

"Convenient," he murmured.

Merrill nodded. "It was that. Once you get sheep moving, they don't stop till nooning or till they get to bed ground, just keep right on traveling, and you have to chase after them if they go the wrong way, which isn't much fun because you miss breakfast.

Sheep aren't too smart," she added, remembering that she wanted to discourage him. She took another sip of wine and a mouthful of stew, then said around it, "If you've got a thirsty flock, they can be right on the river's edge, and they won't drink. They just run around bleating. Have to use the dogs to drive them into the water."

"Uh huh." Jonathan refilled her glass and plate.

"Why, if one of your ewes falls down in a little depression, she's not smart enough to turn over and get up. You won't like sheep," warned Merrill, digging into her second helping. "Sheep are dumb!"

"I'll look forward to watching their antics," said Jonathan, grinning.

Merrill shot a suspicious glance at him, wondering whether he was laughing at the sheep or her. Then to cover her confusion, she took another sip of wine and sopped up more gravy with her bread. Finally to divert his attention from the fact that she was eating so much, she asked, "Where were you born?"

"In New York City," he replied.

Merrill sighed. That was, as she'd heard it, the biggest, most sophisticated city in the world, or at least in the United States. Like as not, he thought she was a hopeless country bumpkin.

"My father owns a stevedoring company on the New York docks. They unload ships from all over the world and freight the goods out."

That sounded wonderfully exotic to Merrill, who asked wistfully, "Have you ever been on a ship?"

"Oh, yes. Once I graduated from Princeton, I spent a year in Europe—England, France, Spain, Italy, Germany."

Merrill didn't know what Princeton was, but she realized that he must be naming foreign countries, some across the ocean. Italy, now— why would he want to go there? It was such a terrible place that Mrs. Oblati couldn't wait to leave it.

"While I was in Europe, I wrote letters back to my friends, and one of them sent a communication of mine to a newspaper. There was money waiting for me when I got back, which gave me the idea of being a writer."

Think of that! she marveled, taking a big gulp of the red wine and eating the last of her second helping. He not only wrote letters, but they were so good that newspapers wanted to publish them and give him money. He could probably get things published in the *Arizona Champion*, the Flagstaff newspaper, which she'd never been able to read. Her heart plummeted, and to console herself, she dug into the third helping he'd just given her.

"That's when I came out west," he said. "Always had a fascination for the West. Guess I read every book ever written about it."

"Nothing special about the West." If he liked it out here so much, she'd never get him to leave.

"Oh, you say that because it doesn't seem new and exciting to you. You've known it all your life. What did your family do once they got to California?" he asked.

"Sold the sheep," Merrill replied. "Same sheep that go for $2.75 today, and they sold them for sixteen dollars a head! Can you imagine that? Then they tried their luck in the gold fields—California and Nevada. Didn't do too bad till Mama died."

"I'm sorry," said Jonathan sympathetically. "What happened to her?"

"Bad water," said Merrill. "If she'd drunk whiskey like Uncle Burden or water with a little whiskey like Pa, she'd be alive today, but she was a teetotaler like me." She caught the flash of a smile on his face and glanced guiltily at her wineglass, which was again half empty. "Mining towns were bad for Uncle Burden too, full of saloons, you know. If there was a saloon around, that's where Uncle Burden wanted to be. As long as Mama was alive, she used to go in and drag him home. After she passed on, I did it myself a time or two." She had almost finished her third helping.

"I remember once in Bodie maybe a year after Mama died. I was walking to the dry goods store when I heard someone in a saloon shouting, 'Burden Fox, I'm gonna kill you,' so of course, I rushed right in. This big Irish miner had Uncle Burden backed up against the bar with a pistol in his belly. I had to shove in between them and grab the gun." Merrill took another gulp of wine and wiped her mouth with her towel-sized napkin. They got one napkin a week—that was Mrs. Oblati's way. No telling what they'd wipe their mouths on now that she was gone—their sleeves probably. "Pa was really mad at me about that gun business. He said I like to got myself shot, and besides that

141

someone spilled beer all over my pinafore. Did get my own firearm out of it 'cause I kept the one I took off the Irishman."

"How old were you?" asked Jonathan.

"Oh, seven, I guess."

"And you've been going armed ever since?"

"Well, of course," she replied. "Now and then you have to threaten someone. Maybe even shoot 'em. I shot a cowboy last year who was fixing to run some of my sheep over a cliff. Those cowboys are rough characters."

"I wouldn't argue," said Jonathan. "I've been a cowboy myself."

She stared at him, open-mouthed.

"My last book was about a trail drive from Texas to Kansas. Would you like to read it?"

Merrill flushed and said, "No, I wouldn't. Why would I want to read a book about cowboys? A more worthless bunch of people never lived. I'd as soon shoot a cowboy as—"

"I didn't say you *had* to read it," Jonathan interrupted, looking a little hurt, "but I will say it's too bad your Uncle Burden doesn't have your head for alcohol."

"What do you mean by that?" demanded Merrill.

"Between us," he said, "we've just finished off two bottles of wine, and it doesn't seem to have affected you a bit."

She stared, aghast, hardly able to believe what he had said, but there they sat, two empty bottles and just a sip or two left in her flower glass.

"I guess you were teasing me about being a teetotaler," he said.

Merrill shook her head wordlessly, wondering how she was supposed to be feeling now that she had indulged in so much alcohol. He was wrong about it not affecting her. It had made her loquacious, friendly when she should have kept her mouth shut and glared at him. It was going to be a hard task, getting rid of Jonathan Forrester. She'd really have to work at it.

Chapter Three

"In case you didn't realize, this is an unusual catering arrangement," said Jonathan. "I serve a retired shepherd recluse out the back door, a picky dog under the table, and two meals on top of it."

"If you don't like the way we do things, you can always leave," said Merrill.

"Nonsense," Jonathan replied. Boss was nudging him for another helping of sausage and flapjacks. "I can't figure out why a dog this hungry passed up a second helping at dinner last—"

"Too spicy," said Merrill.

"It wasn't too spicy for you. I thought he ate everything you eat."

"She. Boss is a she, and she likes more syrup on her flapjacks."

Jonathan grinned and applied the syrup more

liberally to the dog's third serving before he slid the bowl back under the table where Boss began to lap up the molasses with noisy appreciation. "Never heard of a dog with a sweet tooth," muttered Jonathan.

"Uncle Burden had one too." Merrill was staring at her own breakfast, the sight and smell of which made her feel queasy.

"So it runs in the family, does it?" Jonathan unfolded his newspaper. "Want part of the *Champion*? I picked it up yesterday before we left Flagstaff."

Merrill shook her head, which was aching abominably. So much for his idea that she was an accomplished drinker. She never wanted to taste wine again, much less be offered a newspaper she couldn't read.

"It says here that Samuel F. Bullock, who shot Ferdinand G. Hatch during a political dispute, has been acquitted. I wonder whether the jury agreed with Mr. Bullock's politics or his plea."

Bad as she felt, Merrill realized that she'd just been offered a ripe opportunity to discourage him, one she couldn't afford to pass up. "Juries don't hang too many white men," she said. "They always figure it was self-defense, this being a violent area. Cattlemen killing sheepmen and vice versa. Indians killing white men and vice versa. We got the Apaches and the Navahos raiding here in the territory. They massacred twenty or thirty whites at a time last year. And of course, there are the cowboys—obnoxious lot, swaggering around town, picking fights, driving cattle right through the middle of Flagstaff. They did that last July. If they don't shoot you, likely they'll kill you in a stampede. And the trains are always wrecking and getting held up by bandits, folks getting killed—both trainmen and passengers. Fellow named Frank Warner shot conductor Peagram—that trial's coming up. Yes sir, must seem pretty uncivilized to you." She sneaked a look at him over the rim of her coffee cup and discovered that he didn't seem at all alarmed. He wasn't even looking at her.

"I couldn't help but notice the pots you've got on that shelf, Merrill," he said. "Wonderful pieces. Who's the archaeologist in the family?"

"The what?"

"The pot collector."

"There's Indian cliff dwellings in Walnut Canyon," she admitted. "When I get a chance, I like to go digging."

"You have a feel for it," he responded. "Don't know when I've seen so many fine specimens, some of them very old."

Forgetting her campaign to run him off, Merrill nodded enthusiastically. "I never go over there but I wonder who they were and how long ago they lived in those caves, what their lives were like. It's a real shame it's so hard to get down to the dwellings in winter when I have the time to do it."

"Maybe you'll take me with you next spring," suggested Jonathan. "I'd not only like to see the ruins; I'm pretty sure I could sell an article on the subject back east. We'd co-author it."

Now there was an irony, thought Merrill. He wanted her to co-author an article, although she could neither read nor write. She couldn't even get rid of an unwanted partner. The enthusiastic gleam in his eye told her that he'd be here at least until spring.

In mid November Jonathan insisted on making the supply rounds to the sheep camps with her. She spent the travel time telling him a hundred distasteful things about sheep, but he said, as they approached yet another flock, "Even so, a pastoral scene has a certain biblical charm, don't you think?"

Merrill turned a puzzled glance his way.

"Well, after all, King David—"

"Who?"

"Merrill," he asked, grinning, "are you a heathen?"

She scowled at him.

"King David was a shepherd—in the Old Testament. And among those who came to pay reverence at the birth of the Christ child in the New Testament were shepherds. With Christmas so close now—"

"We don't celebrate Christmas at the F & F," said Merrill. She didn't really see the application to modern sheep raising. Obviously King David's time and even the Christ child's were long before hers. "I don't imagine you'd be too charmed by a flock with scabies," she said smugly. "Did King David's sheep have scabies?"

"Would that be sheep scab? I noticed in the

147

newspaper that the Daggs brothers are calling for stronger sheep scab laws in Arizona."

"Oh, sure," said Merrill. "The Arizona Sheep Breeders and Wool Growers Association. Been meeting since '84, complaining about low wool prices and high freight rates, and the big cattle companies taking over public lands—much they've been able to do about it. You want to represent us, you're welcome. They sure wouldn't take to a woman turning up."

"I don't see why not," said Jonathan. "Apple said you're the best flockmaster in northern Arizona. They ought to welcome you."

Merrill sniffed cynically.

"Of course, I'll attend the meetings if you want me to," he added. "I'd be honored."

She knew immediately that she'd made a mistake in showing any dependence on him, although what she said was true: the association would never welcome her.

"Now tell me about scabies—just so I don't make a jackass of myself in front of the other flock owners."

"The name says it all," she replied, planning to make scabies sound as disgusting as possible. "First your sheep start rubbing themselves against trees or posts, frazzled as a dog in heat." Then she flushed, realizing what she'd said, and hurried on. "They've got itching blisters under the fleece and break them by rubbing. That's what forms the scabs. Pretty soon you've got a sheep getting skinnier and more miserable, bald as an eagle's head in places, wool hanging off the skin in tatters like a shirt that's been through barbed wire. After a while your whole flock's infected, you got no wool clip, and they start dying like coyotes at a poisoned spring."

"Well, Merrill, you do have a way with words. You should be a writer yourself."

After that Merrill shut up, flattered and saddened because she'd never be a writer or even a reader.

"I'd be obliged," he said, "to have you read one of my books. Wouldn't have to be the one about cowboys. For instance, I wrote one about a madam in a—"

"You want me to read a book about a fallen woman?" she demanded, angrily defensive. She wished he'd stop offering her books and newspapers. She couldn't keep her secret long if he did that. And the strangest thing was that every time she refused to read one of his books, he looked as if she'd hurt his feelings.

"Have you had much trouble with sheep scab?" he asked.

"Some," she replied. "I keep a sharp eye out for it."

"Maybe when you see that a sheep's got it, you could kill the animal and sell it for meat before—"

"We don't stock the Rambouillet or any of the heavy meat animals."

"Then maybe we should."

"Bad idea. The feed's not plentiful enough here, and they don't have the flocking instinct that the Vermont merinos and the native sheep have. Oh, there are folks trying foreign breeds, but it's not going to work."

"I'll take your word," said Jonathan.

Merrill had to bite her tongue to keep from thanking him for his confidence and yelling at him because no matter what she said, she couldn't seem to discourage him. He acted like he was going to spend the rest of his life sleeping in Pa's room, cooking up fine dishes for her and Boss and Teofilo, and entertaining her on her rounds between sheep camps when she was used to being by herself, bored with her own thoughts and worries.

Jonathan—he insisted she call him Jonathan—was reading the newspaper to her again, and she—weak-willed female that she was—couldn't resist listening.

"Says here William McCullum's recovering from being rolled over by logs."

"Lucky him," said Merrill bitterly. "That's what happened to Pa, but he never recovered. He was bossing a gang of tie-cutters for the railroad, making a little extra money." She was sitting in Pa's chair, toasting her stocking feet on the big stone hearth. First time they'd been warm all day.

Jonathan nodded. "I know what you're going to tell me. This is a dangerous place. Paper says C. P. Stanton was shot by three Mexicans at Antelope Springs."

"Good Lord, that's real close to Flagstaff."

"And Cista Lucero was killed," he continued.

"That one of the Mexicans that shot Stanton?"

she asked. "Never know who's going to get killed next. Could be you."

"I could get killed just as fast crossing a street in New York," he pointed out. "Ah hah! Sheep news. W. J. Hill has moved his flock to winter range north of the San Francisco Mountains."

"He's leaving it a little late," said Merrill. She had the passing realization that she and Jonathan, sitting in front of a roaring fire, were like two old married folks. Quickly Merrill admonished herself not to think that way. No chance that an educated, handsome man like Jonathan Forrester would ever marry a homely, illiterate—

"Here's some good news. The San Juan Saloon's going to have an old-fashioned rodeo dance. Reckon you'll want to go in for that."

"Look," she said, "I don't have time for dances at the San Juan." *Time or a dress,* she thought. "Neither do you." Maybe if he never had any fun, he'd want to leave.

"I don't see that we're so all-fired busy we can't—"

"Maybe *you* aren't," she interrupted. "You're always sitting around the table, scribbling, but I'm out there doing real work every day. Maybe you ought to try it. In fact, it won't be a bad thing to have a man with big teeth on the job." She'd just had an inspired idea.

"Big teeth?" He looked puzzled. "You want me to bite someone?"

"Most of the rams have to be castrated, you know. How do you think it's done?"

"With teeth?" he asked, surprised. "I've castrated

cattle, but we used knives. Only place I've ever heard they use their teeth is in Australia."

"Where?"

"Australia. It's west of California. Across the Pacific Ocean. They raise a lot of sheep there. Got kangaroos and—"

"What's a kangaroo?"

"Well, they carry their babies in a pouch."

"Like possums?" How was it he always managed to derail her conversational attacks and catch her interest at the same time?

"Right, but a kangaroo looks more like—oh, maybe a giant squirrel. Big tail. Short front legs. Not so furry. They travel in huge leaps, but on the ground, not through trees."

"You know the damnedest things," said Merrill. "Imagine a giant squirrel with a little squirrel in a pouch."

Jonathan smiled at her. "You know what I like about you, Merrill? There isn't a thing you don't know about your own world, and a thing you don't know about the rest of the world that you're not interested in learning. Now, that's what I call true intelligence."

How was she going to discourage a man who, no matter what she said, seemed to admire her?

"Have a little more wine?" he asked.

She held out her goblet. "Might as well."

"I notice we've got some fine fat squirrels around here. I'll have to get out my rifle and make you a squirrel stew."

"Didn't know you could shoot."

"I'm a crack shot. Now let's get back to that San

Juan Saloon and the rodeo party. Even if we don't go, it sounds to me like there's a lot of money to be made investing in a place like that."

Merrill felt a flash of panic. If he was going to start buying into things in town, she'd never get rid of him. "You don't want to do that. Flagstaff's always burning down. Half the town went up in flames last February. They were rebuilding for months."

"Well," he said thoughtfully, "you have to admire their spirit. That's the kind of town a man *wants* to invest in."

Merrill sighed and gave up. She'd have to think of some new way to discourage him.

Merrill viewed the Mexican who came to her door with hard suspicion. Except for the two *Californios*, who had come with them over the Mohave, she suspected that all Mexicans were horse thieves. This fellow, with his long hair and black clothes, certainly looked like one, but the flood of excited Spanish that issued from underneath his flowing *bandito* mustache doused her suspicions.

"What is it?" asked Jonathan, coming up behind her.

She ignored him in order to question the visitor. When he had finally exhausted his information, Merrill said to Jonathan, "Got to head for the sheep camps."

He gave her a sour look. "Tomorrow's Thanksgiving," he protested. "Why did I bother to shoot that turkey if we're not going to be here?"

"Well, stay home and eat it yourself," said Merrill. "I'm leaving."

"Maybe I will," muttered Jonathan, looking distinctly sulky.

Merrill almost grinned. He certainly took his cooking seriously. The Mexican let loose another barrage of Spanish.

"*Lobos?*" said Jonathan. "That means wolves, doesn't it?"

"Joaquin sends word he's lost four sheep to wolves and needs some fire power." She spoke to the Mexican again. He shook his head, answering.

"What's he saying now?" asked Jonathan.

"He says he doesn't have time to stay and eat Thanksgiving dinner with you but thanks me for the invitation."

"Oh, I see." Jonathan looked even angrier. "I'm supposed to stay home cooking turkey while you go out wolf hunting. Forget it. I'm as good a shot as you."

Merrill raised her eyebrows but didn't argue. Instead she reached into her pocket to give the messenger a coin for his trouble and, when he had left, went first to the gun rack to lift down her Winchester, then to retrieve a supply of ammunition, and finally to the kitchen to assemble food supplies.

"Is this wolf hunt going to take till Christmas?" Jonathan asked. "Or maybe we're going to restock the camps while we're hunting wolves?"

"It's a week to restocking time," said Merrill, "but wolves move on. It may take a few days

to track them down, and the weather's bound
to turn nasty on us sooner or later."

"I notice you speak Spanish," he said, following
her into the big room.

"Got shepherds that speak Spanish," she replied.
"They'd never have left California if they thought
they had to learn English. Same with the Portuguese and my Basque, Sanxi Ferrieres."

"Good lord, you speak English, Spanish, Portuguese, and Basque? What else?"

She gave him a sharp look because he was smiling as if he didn't think, one, that she really spoke
all those languages and, two, that she'd have any
others at her command. "Some Chinese," she said.
"I don't hold much with Celestials as shepherds.
They're not too reliable, but still—"

"You never forget anything, do you?" Jonathan
interrupted.

She glanced at him, puzzled.

"Not too many people pick up four extra languages in passing, as it were. I assume you didn't
have grammar books for any of these languages."

She narrowed her eyes at him, wondering if
he'd finally realized that she couldn't read.

"And then there's the figures. You remember
every number pertaining to sheep for ten years
back."

"Further back than that," she said huffily.

"My apologies." He grinned. "And you can do
figures in your head that would take me five
minutes to do on paper. Did you think I hadn't
noticed when you calculated what we might make
on the spring clip at three or four different prices?

155

I redid the figures on paper after you went to bed, and you hit it right every time."

"Why wouldn't I? Numbers are numbers. They don't change."

"Your memory is phenomenal, girl. Sometimes I think you don't know how smart you are." He turned toward the stairs to assemble a wolf-hunting wardrobe, leaving Merrill astounded. She'd never thought of her abilities as anything unusual, especially considering that she couldn't read.

After a long ride, they shot two wolves, one each, between Joaquin's camp and Sanxi's, the Basque shepherd who was the closest thing Merrill had to a grandfather. She loved the old man dearly and had always told him her secrets and relied on his advice. Merrill hoped he'd live forever. Given his seamed brown face and thin white hair, he looked as if he already had, yet the old man could still lift a stranded ewe, and his eyes were sharp.

When they arrived, he'd killed another of the wolf pack. "How many sheep did you lose?" she asked in Basque, and he answered, "Three," and pointed them in the direction where he thought the pack was traveling.

She and Jonathan did not tarry but went tracking, which is to say Merrill tracked on foot and Jonathan followed on horseback. Tracking was not a Western skill he'd acquired during his years of adventure. Nor was he an ardent walker. They caught up with and killed three more wolves, then returned to Sanxi's camp, now a full day away from headquarters. Merrill decreed that they spend the night where they were.

As he prepared dinner, Sanxi studied Jonathan closely, and Merrill's attempts to distract the shepherd with conversation met little success. "It is not courteous of you," he said to her finally as he passed roasted mutton to Jonathan, "to ignore your partner and speak without translating in a tongue he does not understand."

"It is my hope," she replied, "that he will become unhappy with Arizona and go away." She bit into her own share of the dripping meat and added, "This was my ranch and still would be if it were not that my miserable uncle sold half without asking me."

"Burden never liked sheep," said the old man. "It is surprising to me that he stayed as long as he did."

"Probably no one made him an offer before now," she retorted bitterly.

"His betrayal may turn out well. Tell me of this man who is your new partner."

"He writes books."

"Ah, a learned one." Sanxi nodded, an expression of respect lighting his dark eyes under their wrinkled lids.

"And travels all over the world. Even across the ocean. He has seen both France and Spain."

Sanxi beamed at Jonathan, who asked Merrill, "What did you say to him?"

"I said you had been to Europe."

"I imagine even at his age and after so many

years, he misses his homeland," Jonathan murmured. "And a beautiful place it is."

Merrill scowled at him.

"What did he say?" asked Sanxi.

"That your homeland is beautiful," she mumbled.

The old man smiled and nodded to Jonathan, then proceeded to question Merrill closely, ascertaining everything she knew about the writer and every interaction between them, chuckling with amusement at Merrill's failures to discourage her partner from staying in Arizona. "You might as well give up," said Sanxi when she had finished. "This one will stay and marry you."

Merrill's mouth dropped open. "Old age is turning your brain to sheep dip," she muttered.

"What did he say?" asked Jonathan curiously.

"None of your business."

"Do not speak to your future husband with such disrespect. It is not seemly," said the old man.

"He's not my future husband," snapped Merrill, who knew all the reasons why he never would be. "He is, as you say, learned, and I can't read. He's not even as old as I."

"How old is he then?" asked Sanxi.

"Twenty-eight."

"Ha! That is nothing. You are only twenty-nine, and he has seen more of the world than you. He will enrich your life. Also, it's time you bore a child. If not, who will follow you and inherit all this?" He waved his arm to encompass the sheep who had bedded down for the night, the surrounding mountains and valleys, some of which

Merrill owned, some of which she grazed and hoped to buy when she had the money.

Yes, she thought downheartedly, who would come after her? She had tried for years to find her father a woman so that he could marry and have a son to help Merrill run the ranch when Pa was gone, a brother who would in turn marry and have sons to keep the name alive and the ranch in Fox hands. But there had never been another wife or any brothers. Pa had loved Eleanor Merrill Fox to his dying day and would look at no other woman. Merrill had even tried to marry Uncle Burden to a widow who was still in her child-bearing years, but no sensible woman would have Uncle Burden. That left Merrill, the last of the Foxes. Suffering sheep scab, what was she to do? Jonathan would not want to marry her so that she could produce her own heir, and she knew of no other man who would, especially now that the ranch was only half hers.

She felt Jonathan's hand touch her shoulder and looked up. "What did the old man say to worry you so?" he asked.

"Nothing. Nothing," she mumbled, more unhappy than ever at the kindness Jonathan always showed her. "We'd best turn in," she added, reaching for her bedroll and heading toward the herder's wagon, under which Jonathan and Sanxi would sleep while Merrill took the bunk inside.

"What? Are we not to play together?" asked the old man. "Are you so bemused that you have forgotten to bring your flute?"

Merrill glanced over at her friend, sitting stubbornly beside his fire. Then she went to her saddlebags and took out the flute that Sanxi had carved for her and taught her to play when she was eleven and her father and uncle had given up on the gold fields and gone back to raising sheep. That was before the drought had driven them out of California in '76 and back across the desert to try their luck in the Arizona Territory. For another half hour she and Sanxi played the mournful and the merry songs of the Basque shepherds, their separate parts intertwining with the beauty of those who have played together for many years. As long as the music lasted, Merrill forgot her worries and gave herself to the joy of it.

"Now we sleep," said Sanxi and tucked away his flute.

"Tell him for me," said Jonathan, who had listened to every note floating out into mountain air that bathed their cheeks and fingers like ice water, "that I have heard the finest musicians the world has to offer, both here and abroad, and never have I heard anything more beautiful, nor music that spoke more tellingly to my heart."

Merrill stared at him for a moment, horrified that tears had come to her eyes. She blinked them back and turned to Sanxi, for she would not deprive the old man of such a fine compliment. Sanxi nodded and smiled at Jonathan, revealing both his missing teeth and his acceptance of a new friend.

Merrill sighed and climbed inside the wagon, bedroll under her arm. Always Jonathan said the right thing to make friends, to fit in. No doubt he had done this everywhere he went and, when he was finished here, would move on and find new friends somewhere else. The prospect made her heart sore. She no longer knew what she wanted of Jonathan Forrester, and Sanxi's prophecy, that she and Jonathan would marry, had not eased her confusion. She knew that a marriage between them was impossible.

Chapter Four

"Bruce Rosson got lost in the snow and died. That would be two years ago January."

"He didn't have you with him," said Jonathan. They were huddled side by side with Boss between them in a herder's shack, knees drawn to their chins, horse blankets around their shoulders, their mounts shifting and snorting not four feet away.

"Fellow named Prentice went snow blind two months later," said Merrill.

"I'd say we're safe from that peril," Jonathan replied, "seeing as this shed is black as a railroad tunnel."

He had a point; snow blindness hadn't been much of a scare tactic under the circumstances. In truth, Merrill wished she hadn't insisted on leaving Sanxi's camp when the snow was falling so heavily. She'd just meant to convince Jonathan that they were lost and in danger of freezing to death—as another lesson on the perils of life in northern Arizona. She certainly hadn't meant to actually die out here, which might now happen with the snow piling up and the temperature dropping like an eagle swooping down on a spring lamb. Unfortunately, there was no way to heat this miserable shack.

"Not that I don't appreciate your warning me of the danger, but I have every confidence in you, Merrill. You're the most knowledgeable woman I know."

Merrill gritted her teeth. The man would go to his grave, frozen solid but believing that she'd save him.

"Now, why don't we share a can of beans and pass the time telling stories?" Which they did, except for Boss, who hated beans and couldn't talk. Jonathan drove his knife into a can, and they shared Merrill's spoon as he told her about trailing cattle to Kansas and she responded with tales of herding sheep across the Mohave to Arizona when drought forced her family to leave California. They swapped mining tales, hers about California and Nevada, his about New Mexico. By late afternoon they were eating canned peaches, which Boss did enjoy, and Merrill was telling Jonathan about hauling the spring clip by ox team over Raton Pass to Trinidad, Colorado, before the railroad came to Flagstaff in '83 and made their lives simpler. "'Course that's when the range started filling up," she concluded ruefully. "By the '90s the sheep and cattle'll be haunch to haunch all over the San

Franciscos, and there'll be enough corpses from the range wars to make the countryside smell like buzzard heaven."

"By God, Merrill, you're wonderful company," said Jonathan, laughing as he hugged her.

Merrill, who had been shivering, froze up, bemused at the feel of his arm around her. Boss, caught between them, wiggled irritably.

"I didn't mean to offend you," Jonathan said, hastily removing his arm.

"I wasn't offended," she mumbled. While she was turning into a human icicle, he was still radiating heat; his arm had felt good.

"You were shivering, weren't you?" he asked. "I don't want to seem ungentlemanly, but I think we'd get through the night better if we curled up spoon fashion with the blankets wrapped around us." So after sharing two more cans of beans, Boss again turning up her nose, they curled together and shared their warmth, Merrill sandwiched between Jonathan and the dog.

Jonathan, who had been lusting after her, managed to keep himself under control by solving the most difficult mathematical equations he could remember from his years at Princeton. Since he'd hated math, that cooled him off faster than the temperature of the air around them, which he estimated was going to drop below zero. Maybe he should have paid attention to her warnings about danger this time, not that there was much they could do about their situation, other than what they were doing. Merrill must find him singularly unattractive, he mused as he was dropping off to sleep with her slight, strong body tucked against him. She hadn't hesitated in taking up his offer to snuggle.

Merrill, although as toasty as a flea on a live dog, didn't sleep for some time. She had thinking to do. First, she concluded that she was not going to frighten Jonathan. He wouldn't leave until he was good and ready. But he would, she was sure, leave someday. Then the ranch would be hers, and, as Sanxi had said, she would need an heir. *Why couldn't I have been a boy?* she wondered. *Then I could just get me a wife and take care of the problem the easy way.*

Bearing a child wasn't going to be easy at all. How was she to tend to business, all blown up like a horse with colic? And with Mrs. Oblati gone, who would tend the baby while Merrill was tending the flocks? Not to mention what folks would say about an illegitimate child, for Sanxi was wrong; Jonathan wouldn't be proposing marriage. Sanxi had spoken from love, something Jonathan would never feel for Merrill, not in a million years.

Still—she savored the warmth of his strong body against hers and experienced a flash of inspiration. Jonathan Forrester was prime breeding stock— big, strong, smart, even brave, and as stubborn as an overburdened mule. Any child of his and hers would be a top-grade crossbreed. If she had to produce her own child, she couldn't do better in the stud department than Jonathan. Of course, the problem was getting him to sire a child. She recollected that Pa had always said a ram would mount any ewe in heat and that men were no better. If she could send Jonathan a signal that she was available, maybe he'd take her up on it. And likely as soon as he discovered that she was with child, he'd run for his life.

Then she'd have at least two of the three things she wanted out of life—her own ranch in her own hands and someone to inherit it. The third thing, learning to read, was beyond her grasp. But how in the world did a woman signal that she was available? Wake him up and say, "I'm in heat"? She supposed that, in some ways, she'd never have a better opportunity than this one, since they were marooned together in this shack. On the other hand, they weren't alone, and she didn't much like the idea of losing her virginity with Boss and the horses looking on. Conception, at least among humans, ought to be a bit more private. On that thought Merrill allowed herself to drift into sleep. If they got out of this fix, she'd think more on the problem. No use seducing a man, only to freeze to death before her womb had a chance to ripen.

Merrill stood in her room staring into the cloudy oval mirror that hung between two raised sections of the dressing table. Pa had bought it for her when she was nineteen. He'd said it was about time she started taking some interest in her appearance. "Fellas like a well-turned-out girl," he'd told her, "and girls, no matter how handy around the ranch, gotta marry." Here she was, twenty-nine and needing a child, but with no more idea than she'd had at nineteen of how to be "well turned out." In the struggle to establish the ranch, Pa had neglected to provide any practical advice.

Downstairs Jonathan, unaware of her ill-formed plot, was still reading the newspaper he'd picked up in Flagstaff, which had told them what they'd discovered for themselves during the hard going from that shack to ranch headquarters: two feet of snow had fallen, after which the temperature had dropped to seventeen below zero, causing stock losses to both sheepmen and cattlemen. Merrill figured the F & F had lost sixty head, not counting the wolf kills. Looking up from his newspaper, smiling at her, Jonathan had said, "Didn't I say you'd get us home? You're a hero, Merrill."

Merrill had noticed that he didn't say *heroine*. A man wouldn't want to bed a *hero*, even if she *had* got him home through two feet of snow. Then he'd read aloud about the Walters' little girl being saved with milk and eggs after she drank a bottle of corrosive sublimate, thus reminding Merrill of her need to bear a child. A girl would be nice, she'd thought wistfully. So now she was studying herself in the mirror, seeing, as through a heavy winter fog lying over a mountain valley, herself— a skinny female rancher, not white-skinned, not soft and womanly, all bone and sinew.

Would a dress help? she wondered. The only dress in the house was one of her mother's, a pretty blue thing that Pa had got out every year on the anniversary of Mama's death. Merrill went to the trunk in the corner and lifted the dress from its muslin wrappings, shaking out the folds of the skirt, then holding it up in front of herself as she peered once more into the mirror. She had Mama's eyes, so the blue silk was a match. Without much hope, Merrill stripped out of her shirt and trousers and her long johns. She didn't have any female-type undergarments, and the goose bumps were already rising on her skin, so she pulled the dress quickly over her head and tried to settle it in place.

Then she looked at herself again and shook her head at what she saw. It was hopeless. Mama must have been her height but carrying a lot more flesh. The round, low neck of the dress dropped off Merrill's shoulders and barely covered her nipples. The upper halves of her little breasts were exposed as if she were some skinny whore at one of the brothels in town. Pathetic, she thought, staring at her reflection. Because she didn't fill out the bodice, the waistline hung down around her hips.

The knock at her door didn't surprise her at all. When luck was running against you, there was no use trying to swim upstream. "Come right in," she said bitterly, having abandoned all thought of seducing Jonathan. If he stood to stud for anyone, it would never be her.

Jonathan pushed her door open, saying, "Donahue's got a new billiard table at the Mineral Belt. Says so right here. If he can get one, so can we." He looked up from the paper, smiling, and then his eyes widened as he caught sight once more of the beautiful lines of her back.

"We could put a billiard table in the big room downstairs," he continued, his voice trailing off because he was mesmerized by the smoky reflection of her delicate collarbones and the rounded curves above her neckline. She looked like an ethereal wood nymph, or maybe one of those ballet dancers he'd seen in Paris, so slender yet, like Merrill, agile and strong. He was drawn across the room to her like a compass needle to true north. Curving his hands over her bare shoulders, he bent and touched his lips to her neck. Then he lifted the long braid aside, dropped it over her shoulder between her breasts, and kissed her again.

Evidently any dress would do, thought Merrill wonderingly as she trembled under the second touch of his mouth, which now moved over the curve of her shoulder, brushing the dress off and revealing her left breast as the blue silk slipped to her elbow.

"Merrill?" he whispered, and he turned her around, wrapping her closely in his arms.

Merrill had never been kissed on the lips before and found it surprisingly pleasant. His mouth was coaxing and his breath sweet with wine. Before he'd finished kissing her, the dress had fallen off completely, and she hadn't tried to stop it happening, although he seemed surprised to find her naked under the blue silk. He drew in his breath sharply and tightened his hold on her, his hand moving up to touch her breast. That was another surprise. Having her breast touched was a little like being stung by a fire ant, only nicer. *It surely did send a shock right through you, a shock that headed straight down and just about melted your female parts,* she marveled. While he was stroking that breast, Merrill was suffering from wobbly knees.

She didn't know exactly how human females were bred, something like ewes she supposed, but Jonathan, kissing her again, had picked her up and was heading for her narrow bed. Like as not he was cold and looking to warm himself by the chimney stones and wrap up in the quilts. Merrill herself was in a fever and not bothered at all by the cold air. Still, he laid her down on the bed and came down beside her, not bothering with quilts. Maybe he was in a fever too. Hard to tell when he always gave off heat like a good fire on the hearth.

She supposed he meant to take her. He certainly was busy, touching her breasts, her hips, even between her legs, all the time kissing her, and she kissing back. She liked it all, although she'd never expected to take such pleasure in getting herself with child.

Then Jonathan rose and stripped his clothes off. Suffering sheep scab! thought Merrill. She'd never imagined a human organ would be that big, and looking at him, somewhat alarmed at the prospect of him pushing that thing inside her, she felt as skittery as an ewe at her first breeding, which, of course, she was.

He must have noticed her alarm, because he said, "Merrill?" again in that questioning way. Well, she wasn't going to back out. If getting pregnant hurt, then it would just have to. She reached for his hand, and Jonathan, kneeling beside the bed, cupped her face and kissed her lovingly. He must like her a little, she decided as he stretched out and rolled his weight onto her, sliding a knee between hers. Or maybe he just liked what they were doing.

Merrill wrapped her arms around his shoulders to encourage him. Couldn't have him back off because he took her for some scared little chipmunk. She wasn't really scared. Her body was telling her that it wanted him, there between her legs, where he was pressing into her, front to front, surprisingly. She barely had time to realize that it wasn't going to be like sheep or horses when she felt something inside her give way with a sharp pain. Jonathan said, "Oh, sweetheart," in a rueful voice as she bit her lip and held her breath.

Sweetheart? Merrill felt a thrill of happiness, and then he began to move and she to tremble, soaring, her heart pounding and her legs wrapped around him as if to let go would be to lose the most lovely, frighteningly exciting feeling in the world. When he withdrew after what seemed like hours and hours of splendor, she was still throbbing.

"Good Lord, Merrill," he said, as breathless as she, "I wish I'd known that you'd never—ah—that is, I hope I didn't hurt you too much."

"Well, it was no worse than getting tangled in barbed wire," she replied, beginning to catch her breath. Then she added, "Barbed wire's no big problem anymore. The territorial legislature passed a law in '85 that folks can't put up wire without their neighbor's—*What are you laughing about?*"

Jonathan, who was still holding her in his arms and chuckling against her neck in little puffs of breath that tickled her, said, "Well, most men hope they're a little more pleasurable to a woman than barbed wire."

"I didn't mean to say it wasn't enjoyable," Merrill replied defensively. "In fact," she admitted, "this is one of the few times I can think of that being a woman was worth all the trouble."

Jonathan pushed himself up on his elbow and gazed down at her. "Sweetheart, I do think that's the nicest thing anyone's ever said to me. You make me all the sorrier that I didn't have the sense to anticipate your—well, inexperience, that I wasn't gentler."

"I suppose you mean you should have realized that a homely woman wouldn't have attracted any men, and you've got that right."

"Homely!" he exclaimed. "Merrill, you're beautiful."

She pulled away from him, scowling. "If there's anything I hate, it's a liar," she said and gave him a push. "Why don't you go on back to your own room now?"

"Merrill—"

He looked shocked—at her rudeness, she supposed. But what did he expect? To stay all night and have another go at her? Once ought to do the job, and any idiot knew she wasn't beautiful. "Go on," she ordered, sadness settling in. If he hadn't lied to her, she wouldn't have minded doing it again, although she supposed all those church folks in town would say it was immoral, bedding with him just for the fun of it now that she'd got her baby started.

"I hardly meant offense by saying you're beautiful," he murmured, having risen from her side. Merrill whipped a quilt up. She didn't want him looking at her skinny body. He'd turned to leave, giving her a fine view of *his* body with that long, powerful back and muscular rump. She'd be having a fine, strong child, and Jonathan, if he stayed long enough to find out, would be on the train to San Francisco before you could say "Put out that fire" to a Chinaman. With that thought, she turned over and cried because she was in love and likely to make a fool of herself if she didn't get rid of him fast. The worst of it was that she didn't want him to go.

How could she not know how beautiful she was? Jonathan wondered as he settled into his own bed. He'd never met a woman like her—intelligent, although he'd never seen her open a book; completely self-sufficient, although she had that sweet touch of vulnerability that never failed to soften his heart; and ardent—Lord, but she was a hot-blooded woman. How could she have kept

herself untouched all these years when that kind
of passion simmered underneath her practical,
hardworking exterior? Making love with Merrill
was like being caught up in a tornado.

He wished she hadn't kicked him out of her
bed, that he still held her in his arms. Just thinking of it made him ache to possess her again.
And again. Jonathan opened his eyes wide in the
darkness, for it had suddenly occurred to him that
he might be in love. He loved women, certainly.
But *in love?* And with a woman who was, at this
moment, if she hadn't sensibly gone off to sleep,
madder than hell at him because he'd told her she
was beautiful. Well, she'd have to get used to it. If
she thought he'd allow her to continue her funny
little campaign to get rid of him, she was in for
the fight of her life. Then, uneasily, he admitted
to himself that Merrill was one tough lady. What
if she won?

Jonathan was washing his clothes in the big
wooden washtub. He didn't mind cooking, but
he *hated* washing clothes. As he fished his long
johns out of the steaming water, Merrill stamped
into the kitchen, snow falling off her boots in
dirty clots. Well, he wasn't mopping the floor after
her. If she expected maid service, she could think
again.

Jonathan was peeved. For two nights since their
encounter in her room, he'd lain in bed burning
for her, while she treated him like a leper, hardly
speaking to him by day and locking her door at
night. "You must have the biggest wardrobe in

northern Arizona," he muttered as she put on the coffeepot to heat. "I haven't seen you wash clothes yet."

"I'm going to town," said Merrill, madder than ever for some reason he couldn't fathom. She stamped out of the room.

As he flung the wash water out the back door and poured more into the tub so that he could rinse his laundry, he heard Merrill tramping up and down the stairs, saw her dumping sacks of something or other into the wagon. Stupid woman! Going into town on such a cold day. The snow was wearing away, but not the low temperatures. She'd freeze her pretty nose before she got to Flagstaff. And he'd freeze his long johns.

He knew from experience that they'd turn into flat-bodied ice figures by morning if he hung them outdoors. With Merrill gone, maybe he'd string a line in the big room. Housewifery was hell! He should have sweet-talked that mustachioed Italian woman into staying on. And where was Merrill going anyway? Getting away from *him* probably. He supposed that, just like a woman, she was regretting their night together. While he was dying to lure her back into bed.

Jonathan's remark about the size of her wardrobe had made her wonder if she smelled bad. Merrill had worn her way twice through her own clothes, her Pa's, and even the clothes Uncle Burden had left behind, which just went to show how much attention Jonathan paid to her appearance.

He'd never noticed that her working clothes kept getting looser and longer until she looked like a scarecrow in a potato field. Beautiful was she? Even Burden Fox hadn't looked good in his own clothes. Not likely she did. And now she hadn't a half-clean thing left, so, hating dirty clothes, she'd bundled up the three Fox wardrobes to carry in to Charlie Kee, the Chinese laundryman.

She sure hoped they hadn't run him out of town again. Ever since the fire started in Sam Kee's restaurant last February—Sam was some relation to Charlie—and burned down half of Flagstaff, the folks in town had been running the Chinese off. 'Course, the Chinese came right back. If she were lucky, she'd get her clothes washed between one exodus of Celestials and the next.

"Reaving town. Wash own clothes," said Charlie Kee. His face was expressionless as he bundled up his belongings.

"They chasing you off again?" asked Merrill. What was she going to do with all those dirty clothes out in the wagon?

"Fragstaff not rike Chinee."

Merrill nodded sympathetically. The townsfolk didn't care much for her either. They were glad to take her money, but they snickered behind her back, and the women tut-tutted, especially now that Jonathan was living at her place. No doubt, everyone in town believed that she and Jonathan were up to no good, which would be the truth after her successful seduction of him. Or had it been the other way around?

Whichever, she really had to get rid of him. Undoubtedly, she was pregnant now. She'd got out of bed the next morning and hobbled over to her mirror sure of it. He was a lusty man. She doubted that many men could have left her with muscles as sore as a shearer's at clipping time. Her body had recovered, of course. Her mind was the problem. She couldn't stop thinking about him. When she should be plotting how to drive him off, she was thinking about how much she enjoyed his company, in bed or out.

"Where you heading, Charlie?" she asked. He shrugged, and just as she began to feel sorry for the Chinaman, she had an idea. "Say, Charlie, I know you're good at washing, but can you cook?"

"Arr Chinee cook." He tied the knot off on another bundle.

"How about keeping house? Dusting. Floor mopping. That sort of thing." She remembered Jonathan's scowl when she tracked dirty snow into the kitchen. What had he expected? That she'd mop the floor? "How about coming out to the ranch and working as my housekeeper?" said Merrill. She knew that folks who worked for Ayers in Mill Town had Chinese household help.

Charlie squinted his narrow eyes at her, considering the offer. Merrill held her breath. Jonathan was so proud of his cooking. How would he like being replaced by a Chinaman? Anyway, having Charlie Kee in the house would keep Jonathan from getting any ideas about coming back for seconds, keep her from thinking that way too.

"Pay good?" Charlie Kee asked.

Merrill nodded and named the amount she'd paid Mrs. Oblati. She hoped he wouldn't ask for more.

"Buy Treasure Tea at Pioneer Store?"

Merrill nodded. She had an account there but hoped the tea wouldn't be very expensive.

"Name Chun Kee, not Charrie." The Chinaman then picked up his four bundles and carried them out to her wagon.

Merrill sighed. She was on her way to getting rid of Jonathan, and Charlie—no, Chun Kee—ought to be able to take care of the baby that would come along nine months from now.

Chapter Five

Chun Kee was out in the kitchen talking to Boss in Chinese, which Boss seemed to understand— or maybe the dog would listen to anything as long as she was allowed in the kitchen. Merrill certainly couldn't understand Chun Kee. His Chinese wasn't like any she'd ever heard or spoken in California. Jonathan said it was a dialect from the Pearl River Delta in China, just one of hundreds, most of which she couldn't expect to know. Merrill hadn't been much pacified to hear about all those different varieties of Chinese. Why couldn't the new housekeeper—Jonathan kept saying to call him a house *boy*—speak some ordinary brand of Chinese that *she* understood? When bad luck sank its talons into you, she reflected morosely, it just wasn't going to let go, unless maybe it dropped you into a freezing lake during a blizzard.

"We've been invited to a dance at Lockett's on December fourth," said Jonathan after he'd drained the last of his morning coffee. "Want to go?"

Sure enough, she'd make a fine sight at Lockett's in her herder's clothes. "Lockett is selling sheep and buying cattle," said Merrill, as if it were a sin rather than a diversification strategy being followed by many sheepmen. She'd have considered it herself if it hadn't meant employing cowboys. *That* would be an irritation Merrill felt she didn't need added to her life.

"What you're saying is that you won't go to Lockett's," muttered Jonathan, "there or anywhere." He slapped the book he'd been reading down on the table and headed for the stairs, back stiff with frustration. "I'm of a mind to dance with a pretty girl, so if you won't go with me, maybe I'll find someone else."

"Do that," she shouted after him. "I don't care." But she did, and she couldn't seem to formulate a plan these days that worked out. Jonathan hadn't been outraged to be replaced as cook by Chun Kee. He'd just chuckled when she told him how dangerous the Chinese were—that they started fires, and smoked opium, and might even poison you with their cooking, not to mention the fact that as sheepherders they weren't worth a flock of raggedy Navaho ewes at clipping time. Not a day after Chun Kee arrived, she'd heard Jonathan out in the kitchen discussing recipes with the Chinaman. Darned if they weren't talking about co-authoring a book on Celestial cookery.

The Fourth Gift

Merrill had always wondered why the Chinese were called Celestials. She didn't see anything heavenly about a short man with slanted eyes and a pigtail. Jonathan said it was because China was called the Celestial Kingdom. Her partner had an explanation for everything—damn him. And he seemed to have forgotten all about the article he'd planned to co-author with her on the Indian cliff dwellings in Walnut Canyon. But there was no use in worrying about that. She had more immediate concerns, having awakened this morning to discover that she wasn't pregnant. Every ewe in her flock started to swell after one encounter—well, except for the old ones. Was that it? She was too old to conceive? What a disheartening idea! She might be twenty-nine, but she didn't *feel* old.

So where did that leave her? She'd brought the Chinaman into her house to keep Jonathan away, and now she needed to get back in bed with him. Merrill figured she had to give it one more try before declaring herself sterile; after all, it was possible that women didn't conceive as easily as ewes. But how was she to manage it? Surely not with Chun Kee in the kitchen at all hours of the day and night, talking to himself and the dog in his incomprehensible dialect, running around upstairs grabbing dirty clothes to wash before you'd hardly got them off your back and jerking the sheets out from under you before sunup. She'd outfoxed herself. When she realized the inadvertent play on words—out-Foxed by Merrill Fox—she had to laugh.

Jonathan, coming back down the stairs, said, "Did I hear a laugh, Merrill? Let me guess. You've thought up some new, more fiendish plot to get rid of me."

Merrill looked up, her smitten heart in her eyes. Had her efforts to drive him away been so obvious? she wondered.

Seeing that soft look for the first time since she'd said that making love with him made it almost worthwhile being a woman, Jonathan felt somewhat cheered, but he surely did wish that he knew what went on in her head. He understood perfectly why she'd brought Chun Kee home and come up with all those crazy tales about Chinamen, but obviously she'd hired a man she knew nothing about. Chun Kee was the most careful, least dangerous person Jonathan had ever met, besides which he'd taken over the washing, and Jonathan would have hired a convicted arsonist to get the washing done.

"Sure you don't want to go to the dance at Lockett's?" he asked.

She shook her head, ducking so he couldn't see that she was wondering what it would be like to dance with him. As wonderful as talking to him? Or making love with him?

"Man ride in, say cowboys on rand. She take many guns, ride out. You stay to eat?" Chun Kee pointed his large wooden spoon at a concoction bubbling in a large pot on the stove. Jonathan had just returned from the dance and a couple of days spent in town avoiding Merrill, whose very presence was beginning to drive him crazy. He armed himself and left, badly shaken, riding as fast as he could to catch up with Merrill. Why the devil had she gone without him? She knew he'd be home by noon; he'd sent word. Was she bent on getting herself killed? His heart clenched with fear at the thought of Merrill shot down, or worse, by those rowdy cowboys she was always complaining about. He kicked his horse to get the last ounce of speed. At least he knew what pasture she'd headed for.

There were six of them, what outfit she didn't know because they'd tethered their mounts in a clump over among the trees. One swaggering fellow with a shaggy, tobacco-stained mustache had Joaquin's dog tied to the wheel of the herder's wagon and was preparing to set fire to it while the shepherd screamed at him in Portuguese. Merrill shot the torch from the man's hand. "The next one'll be a belly shot," she warned, pulling a second pistol from her waistband. She favored a rifle, but two pistols would give her eleven shots, not that she was very accurate with her left hand.

"Well, well," drawled a cowboy with stringy yellow hair while the shot fellow nursed his bleeding fingers. She'd seen yellowhair staggering around drunk in town on Saturday nights, pursuing whores. "Ain't got your partner with you, honey?" he asked, leering, one hand inching toward his gun.

"Any one of you draws gets killed," said Merrill,

turning her right-hand pistol toward the blond's chest.

"Sure you don't figger to take us all on? You're jus' one lil gal."

"One of me's worth six of you any day," said Merrill, who was almost as angry as she was scared. "I saw ewes shot dead in my pasture. I figure that's the same as rustling, so I've got a perfect right to string you up."

"One lil gal gonna string up six armed men?" That cowboy was laughing so hard he choked on his own spit. As he ha-haed and coughed, the man to his left was edging sly fingers toward his holster. Before Merrill could reaim her right-hand gun, a shot rang out, and the would-be shooter howled a curse and clutched his elbow.

From across the clearing Jonathan had stepped out of the trees, drawn a pistol from his holster, and fired. To Merrill the flash of his gun had seemed almost simultaneous with the first movement of his gun hand.

"One little girl who's a crack shot, and one big partner who's another," said Jonathan, his lathered horse ambling in behind him.

None of the cowboys had yet managed to draw weapons, and they were beginning to look worried with Jonathan's arrival. "Just in time," said Merrill, weak with relief.

"It's real satisfying to know that you're glad to see me for a change," he replied dryly.

"You keep a gun on them, Jonathan, while I start stringing them up," said Merrill.

The cowboys turned pale. Joaquin retrieved his rifle. "Back off my dog," he said to the rider who had planned to burn dog and wagon. Killing a sheepdog was, to Joaquin, a capital crime.

"Why string them up now?" Jonathan asked reasonably.

"They killed some of my sheep and were about to set fire to the wagon and Amador, Joaquin's dog. Figuring to drive me off my own land— that's what they had in mind. Wouldn't be the first time someone tried. I told you about range wars and—"

"Well, I think we should respond in kind," Jonathan interrupted. "I say we shoot their horses and then walk these cowboys from here to the jail in Flagstaff."

"That must be three-four miles," cried shaggy mustache. "I'd rather git hung."

Merrill grinned. There'd be trouble if she actually hung them, so Jonathan's suggestion presented a satisfying alternative. "Six sheep for six horses. That's a trade that appeals to me," she answered.

"You wouldn't shoot a horse over a smelly old sheep!" exclaimed the fellow whose elbow had caught Jonathan's bullet.

"I would, but I'll give you a choice. It's shoot the horses or hang you."

Five cowboys, looking downhearted, opted to lose their horses. The sixth, who felt that walking was a fate worse than death, voted to hang.

"It's a democracy here in the territory, so you're outvoted," said Merrill. "Too bad." She didn't really, now that she was faced with it, want to kill six innocent horses either, so she counted up her sheep losses and drove the horses into town to see if the sheriff would let her sell them and take the money in reparation. The cowboys were roped together and started on their long walk, neckerchiefs tied around the hand and elbow wounds of those who had been winged. They complained endlessly as their high-heeled boots raised blisters and their pointed toes pinched.

"Shut up," said Merrill. "You ought to be saying a prayer of thanks. This meadow's closer to town than most of my winter pastures." Then she and Jonathan conversed more amiably than at any time since they'd fallen upon one another in her bedroom. "You handled that six-shooter like a gunslinger," she said, glancing admiringly toward him at one point in the conversation. "A real killer."

"I'm no killer," said Jonathan. "I'm just proficient with a revolver. It happens I wrote a book about gunmen. Must have ridden with ten or twelve at one time or another. Naturally, I took a few lessons, but I don't kill people. You want to read my book?"

He could see the flare of interest in her eyes, but she said, "Not me. I'm not interested in gunmen."

Usually her refusals hurt his feelings. Why, he mused, would she never read a book of his? Was there something operating here other than rejection of *him?*

"Ah'm bleedin' agin," said the cowboy whom Jonathan had shot. "Ah'm gonna drop right over, an' you'll have to gimme a horse." The threat was made hopefully.

"We'll just leave you where you fall," said Jonathan.

"Only another half mile to go," added Merrill. "The sheriff can pay for doctoring you if you make it."

"We're one hell of a team, Merrill," said Jonathan, sounding particularly pleased.

Merrill could hardly disagree. She'd never been so glad to see anyone as when Jonathan had stepped out of those trees and saved her hide.

It was nightfall by the time they'd filed charges against the cowboys and returned to the ranch. The men who had killed her sheep were from a small cattle outfit, newly come to Arizona and trying to muscle in on her range. The sheriff arrested them with no qualms since they'd been on land that Merrill and Jonathan actually owned. He also took charge of the horses, promising to sell them and return her the money once he'd checked out her dead "critters."

As they rode into the ranch yard, Teofilo, their reclusive handyman, told them, highly offended, that no dinner awaited them in the kitchen because the Chinaman had gone off to visit newly returned relatives in town and to replenish his supply of Treasure Tea.

"Suffering sheep scab," muttered Merrill. "That tea is expensive. He's running me into debt at the Pioneer Store."

"Hell," said Jonathan, "I'll pay for the tea as

long as he keeps doing my washing. Bringing him home was a fine idea on your part, Merrill."

"Will Chun Kee be home tonight?" she asked Teofilo.

"Mañana," said Teofilo.

She and Jonathan would have the house to themselves, she realized with a stirring excitement.

Jonathan had fixed her a fine dinner. His cooking tasted much better than the Chinaman's, who put strange things together in what he thought of as American dishes. And Jonathan had been friendly and talkative. She couldn't have shut him up if she'd wanted to because he was determined to discuss the confrontation with the cowboys, an event that he'd enjoyed immensely and intended to put in his book. "In a year or two you'll be the heroine of North America," he promised, embarrassing her no end. And she hadn't missed the word "heroine." Last time he made a remark like that, he'd said "hero." Did the change mean he saw her as more womanly?

Now she stood irresolute in her room. If she wanted to have a child, this might be her only chance at the privacy to conceive one, but she'd have to go to him, an idea that embarrassed her. What if he said, "Go away"? She hadn't been very friendly since the last time. Still, what other option had she, unless she found some orphan child to adopt? Some waif whose parents wouldn't have been good breeding stock at all, while she and Jonathan—well, the truth was that, if she went to the trouble of having a child, she wanted it to be Jonathan's. She wasn't ever likely to fall in love again, so at least she'd have his son or daughter to remember him by.

Having made up her mind, she revisited the trunk that contained her mother's things—the blue silk dress, which she rejected as too unsightly on her skinny frame; a worn baby quilt her mother had pieced (she couldn't go to him wrapped in the quilt; it wouldn't cover her up); her china doll with the chipped nose, for which her mother had sewn a more feminine wardrobe than Merrill had had since early childhood (well, she couldn't wear doll clothes); her mother's nightgown, sheer and embroidered at the neck. The nightgown would have to do, she decided, although she'd be half frozen wearing that flimsy item down to the end of the hall. Still, it was pretty and, being shapeless, wouldn't be so obviously meant for a more curvaceous woman.

With a sense of life repeating itself, Merrill stripped quickly out of her shirt, trousers, and long johns. She whipped the nightgown over her head, hardly pausing this time to glance at herself in the mirror lest she lose her nerve before she got to his room. "Sit, Boss," she hissed when the dog tried to follow her. Merrill drew her door closed as silently as possible, hoping that Boss wouldn't manage to pull the latch string and escape. Wouldn't that be fine—Boss outside Jonathan's door, whining to get in while Merrill was—oh well, no use borrowing any more trouble than she already had.

She slipped into Jonathan's room without

knocking, somewhat taken aback that his light was out. Usually he lay abed with his lamp burning, reading for an hour or so before he slept. She hoped their scrap with the cowboys hadn't worn him down so much that he couldn't or wouldn't be interested in her. The sound of his breathing led her across the room. "H-s-s-t. Jonathan. Are you awake?"

"Merrill?"

Fumbling for the covers, she crawled into Papa's big bed beside Jonathan, who was astonished to find himself graced once more with her presence. Her conduct had been a source of confusion to him since their one amorous encounter. Here he, for the first time in his life, was thinking of marriage, while she, having given herself to him so ardently, had gone right back to her less-than-subtle efforts to drive him away. He'd about come to the conclusion that she didn't want to marry; perhaps she simply hadn't wanted to die a virgin. Women, as he'd often observed, were curious creatures, and this one was snuggled up to him, all swathed in some voluminous piece of clothing. "I thought you were mad at me," he said.

"I was," she replied defensively, "but—ah—I liked the last time."

Jonathan laughed, thinking how often Merrill managed to surprise him. She was a woman of "infinite variety" like Shakespeare's Cleopatra, but probably more fun in bed.

"Well, if you don't want to, just say so," Merrill snapped, "but I don't see that there's anything to laugh about."

The Fourth Gift

"Don't want to!" Jonathan groaned and pulled her over on top of him. "Sweetheart, this time you're in my bed, so you can't make me leave, and I don't intend to let you loose until the sun comes up."

"Then you're going to be listening to a howling dog all night," said Merrill, who had just realized that her dog was loose and whining at Jonathan's door.

"I've got more staying power than Boss," Jonathan promised. "She'll give up and go away."

"Maybe I ought to—"

"—stay right where you are," Jonathan finished for her, rolling, bending his head, and touching his lips to her breast. "In the time that you've been keeping me at arm's length, I've thought of a thousand things I want to do to you—all of which you'll like."

Given what he was doing at the moment, Merrill believed him, and somehow one moment melted into the next, Boss forgotten in the hall as Jonathan taught Merrill things about coupling that she would never have dreamed of in her years of experience as a northern Arizona flockmaster.

When she staggered out of his bed the next morning, she had no sore muscles, as she'd had after their first coupling. Times two, three, and four had left every inch of her glowing with pleasure, although she hadn't got enough sleep to see a body through the day, and her dog, waiting beside the pile of clothes she'd stripped out of the night before, gave her a resentful "woof" when she walked barefoot and naked into her room, trailing Mama's nightie behind her. That dainty tent, Merrill recalled, giggling, had been disposed of about three minutes into the night's activities. Catching herself in the giggle as she pulled up her suspenders, she realized, uneasily, that she was turning into a lovesick fool.

"Oh well," she said to Boss, "everyone has to have at least one silly season. Pa always said so. I'm just late coming to mine—and lucky." She hurried cheerfully down the stairs, listening to the sound of Jonathan humming in the kitchen as he shaved and fried up bacon. *I'll just pretend,* she told herself, *for this one morning, that I'm having breakfast with my husband, just the two of us. With a baby coming.* She patted her stomach, sure that Jonathan must have planted his seed this time. He'd certainly tried hard enough and often enough.

"Morning, sweetheart," he said, turning from the sink with a smile.

She loved it when he called her sweetheart— even if it didn't mean anything long-term. After all, she'd had more happiness from him than she'd ever expected to find in a man. It didn't do to let your wish list get out of hand. Pa always said that.

"Want to go hunting with me after breakfast? I've got a mind to bring down a deer and teach Chun Kee to cook venison."

"Be sure to save him the liver," said Merrill. "He asked me just the other day if I could get him one. Said he wanted to make an aphro—something— aphrodisiac?" Merrill never forgot a word, even if she didn't know what it meant. "Offered to give me some and share the profits when he sold the rest in town. Probably some nasty Oriental dish."

"No doubt," said Jonathan, grinning, "but I don't think we need any. Are you coming with me?"

Merrill sighed. "Guess not. I'm meeting the sheriff out at Joaquin's pasture this morning. Don't you remember?" She sat down as he scooped eggs and bacon from the frying pan and put them on her plate.

"Tonight then," he agreed cheerfully and sat down across from her.

He was going to be hard to say no to, Merrill told herself, and why should she, after all? "Tonight," she agreed, smiling. Then she remembered Chun Kee. Oh well. At least he slept downstairs.

Merrill rode into the yard just before noon after a satisfying chat with the sheriff—satisfying and profitable because six cow ponies were worth a lot more than her six dead sheep, and the sheriff had once again promised her the proceeds from the sale. "Teach them newcomers a lesson about causin' trouble in Yavapai County," he'd said smugly, and Merrill wondered whether she'd fare so well if any of the original San Francisco Mountain cattle outfits tried to co-opt her land and kill her sheep.

Then she reined her horse to an abrupt stop because a vision of childhood elegance confronted her, climbing down off the wagon with Chun Kee's help. The little girl was wearing an elaborately ruched green velvet bonnet with a lace ruffle edging the underside of the brim. Dangling beneath the bonnet strings were glossy black curls that rested on the matching green velvet coat. Beneath the coat peeked a froth of petticoat ruffles as the girl alighted, her pretty kid slippers with green velvet rosettes contrasting oddly with the packed gray snow under her feet.

"Thank you, Mr. Kee," she said politely, then turned to Merrill. "Good morning, ma'am. I'm Abigail Mirabelle Forrester, and—" she curtsied in midsentence "—and I presume that you are my Uncle Jonathan's new partner, Miss Merrill Fox."

Merrill gaped at her.

"Do you think we might go into the house? Your Arizona climate is bracing, but quite cold. Don't you find it so?"

"Actually, we're having a warm spell," said Merrill, glancing at the bright sunlight and blue sky. "May not be another snow till week's end." She followed the little girl into the house, not knowing what to make of the situation. Jonathan's niece? What was she doing here? Who had she traveled with? Besides Chun Kee? Behind them the housekeeper was talking to himself in Chinese, as usual.

"Mr. Kee is quite a conversationalist, isn't he?" said Abigail. "Unfortunately, I couldn't understand a word he said. He spoke no English from the time we left Flagstaff to the time we arrived here. I suppose you're surprised at my arrival, but you see I've come to live with Uncle Jonathan." She removed her gloves and nodded brightly. "My mother ran off with a wealthy manufacturer of fine buggies when I was very young, and my father died just recently. Has Uncle Jonathan received word yet of his passing?"

Merrill shook her head, mute under this flood of information. The child planned to *live* with Jonathan? Here at the ranch? Occupying the only bedroom left—Uncle Burden's? So much for the nighttime rendezvous she and Jonathan had planned. Abigail Mirabelle Forrester upstairs would be more inhibiting than Chun Kee downstairs. Of course, if the older brother had died, Jonathan would have to return to New York. Merrill bit her lip hard to control the sudden, unhappy emotion that thought aroused.

"Oh, you mustn't look so stricken," said Abigail, tucking her hand into Merrill's and giving it a consoling squeeze. "I have come to terms with my loss. What an absolutely, marvelously *pioneer-y* room!" Abigail let go of Merrill's hand with a second friendly squeeze and proceeded to remove her bonnet and coat, hanging them neatly on the pegs set into the wall by the door.

She had to go up on tiptoe to manage, and Merrill wondered how old she was. She looked like a little girl, but she talked like a society belle, not that Merrill had ever heard a society belle talk, but she'd heard a woman who ran a boarding house in Flagstaff accusing her next-door neighbor of acting like one. "Who do you think you are?" Mrs. Botts had screeched. "Some hoity-toity society belle?"

"I suppose you're wondering why I didn't stay at home with Grandmother and Grandfather after the death of my remaining parent." Abigail had hastened to the banked fire and was warming her hands at its embers. "The reason is quite simple, really. After Papa died, Grandfather said there was no one to inherit his business, so he sold it. Now he's home every day telling Grandmother how to run the house and conduct her affairs. Unfortunately, family relations have become very strained since then, and I did not think it a proper environment for a girl my age, approaching the verge of her young womanhood. Therefore, I had Uncle Jonathan traced and came here to Arizona."

"By yourself?" asked Merrill, astonished. "How old are you?"

"Eleven," replied Abigail. "Quite old enough to manage the trip. Obviously. Here I am." She spread her arms in proof of her safe arrival and sent Merrill a smile of such childlike sweetness that Merrill felt overwhelmed. "Now you and Uncle Jonathan can be my family. Won't that be nice?" asked Abigail, showing every confidence that Merrill would agree.

Chapter Six

Once he had heard her story, Jonathan chuckled, hugged his niece, and said, "You and I must be chips off the block of some buccaneer ancestor, Pippin."

"Uncle Jon," Abigail replied severely, "I'm no longer a rosy-cheeked baby, so I think you should stop calling me Pippin. It's undignified. Abigail will do nicely."

"Won't you at least allow me to call you Abbie," he asked, "and congratulate you on managing to track me down?"

"Oh, that was simple. I went to your publisher and explained that we needed to contact you about Papa's death. I didn't mention that Papa died three months ago, or about Grandfather making everybody miserable in his retirement from the stevedoring business. I hope you don't feel that I'm selfish and disloyal in leaving them alone to fight it out."

Jonathan grinned. "I can hardly criticize you for what I did myself eight years ago."

"My thoughts exactly. I was following in your footsteps, although I do think it's fortunate that you've settled down, Uncle Jon. I might have enjoyed adventuring with you, but it would hardly have advanced my formal education."

Merrill, who had been observing the reunion with amazement, shuddered at the mention of education. Where did Abigail think she was going to continue it? At Merrill's knee? Or in town? Flagstaff hadn't had a school until 1883, and then Mrs. Marshall had closed it down because she said all the gunfire in Old Town was endangering the children. It took the town eight or nine months to build her a new school—frame, one-room, spacious, between New Town and Ayers Mill—but Merrill doubted that either Jonathan or Abigail would find it as desirable an institution as Merrill did, looking at it wistfully from afar. "I suppose you'll both be going home to New York now," said Merrill.

Uncle and niece turned and stared at her reproachfully. "We *are* home," they assured her.

Jonathan looked downright smug, as if to say, *You surely wouldn't try to get rid of me and my poor little orphaned niece?* He looked a lot less smug when, after dinner, he whispered to Merrill, "Shall we meet in my room or yours?"

"Neither," said Merrill, shocked that he'd even suggest such a thing. "Abbie will be sleeping in

Uncle Burden's room. Right between yours and mine."

"You're a hard woman, Merrill," Jonathan complained, looking indignant and disappointed.

"Sh-sh!" she hissed back.

"But I'm not giving up." And he shot a merry smile at Abbie, who was observing them closely. Merrill blushed.

Abbie was a source of continuing amazement to Merrill. She had arrived with more baggage than Jonathan—crates of books, trunks of clothes, hat boxes, furniture she had bought in St. Louis in case the comforts she was used to weren't available on the frontier, and even a sidesaddle and riding habit with sweeping skirts. Jonathan informed her that she'd break her neck if she tried to ride sidesaddle in the mountains of Arizona. Abbie replied that, as she did not have a western saddle or proper clothing to wear with it, Jonathan would have to make arrangements for their purchase.

The little girl made friends with Teofilo and lured him into the house to put up a rod for her clothes and shelves for her books and to rearrange three times the placement of her new bed, chiffonier, and dressing table. She announced that since Merrill was uninterested in running the house, she would be glad to assume that responsibility, part of which involved long menu discussions in the kitchen with Chun Kee. The results as they arrived at the table were mixed at best, since Chun Kee listened respectfully to everything the child said and then interpreted her instructions to suit himself.

Merrill's questions about Abbie's education were answered when the girl set up a study program, after minor consultation with Jonathan, and pursued it daily, except Sunday, when she insisted on being taken to church. She wanted Merrill to go with her.

"As soon as the new Methodist-Episcopal Church is ready we shall go there, naturally," she explained. "Completion is expected by Christmas according to the November twenty-seventh issue of the *Arizona Champion*. However, no mention was made of the subject in the December fourth issue." Abbie had been reading Jonathan's newspapers to "familiarize herself with issues of local concern." "So we can assume that the new church may not be ready for some time."

"If ever," Merrill said under her breath.

"Otherwise, there would have been articles on its progress. If they can mention a duel in which a Mr. Charles Spencer was killed," said Abbie, looking indignant, "they can certainly give news of the new church. Therefore, I think we should visit various churches as a way of introducing me to the society of the town. You absolutely have to go with me, Merrill."

"There aren't all that many," said Merrill, "and I don't go to church."

"Well, you should!" exclaimed Abbie. "After all, you need to set a proper example since I intend to take you as my model so that I may become a useful Western woman." Then she giggled, hugged Merrill, and said, "Do come." Merrill's heart turned to mush. However, she still refused to go to church, although she did allow the child to follow her everywhere, asking millions of questions to which, and much to Merrill's dismay, Abbie wrote down the answers. Couldn't she just remember them? Merrill wondered as she explained what they did with the manure from the stables.

"Manure is disgusting," said Abbie, "and I'd really hate to eat anything that was grown in it, but if the potato farm man is willing to haul it away for you, I can see the advantage. We don't buy his potatoes, do we?"

"I've brought the mail," said Jonathan, shuffling through a stack of envelopes. "Letters for me from my publisher, two requests for articles from newspapers, one in Boston, one in St. Louis, and a nostalgic missive from a lady friend in Fort Worth." Grinning, he sniffed the last letter, pink and saturated with enough perfume to reach Merrill's nose across the width of the table. Jonathan had just returned from town, where he had been ordering a saddle for Abbie. "Then here's two for you, little Abbie," he said, sailing them across the table toward his bespectacled niece, who was doing a geography lesson as they waited for Chun Kee to serve the evening meal, "and one for you, Merrill." He flipped a creased envelope with a smudged address in Merrill's direction. "Not to mention the *Champion* for December eleventh, late but always full of exciting news."

Merrill stared at her letter as if it were a rattler, coiled to strike.

"Let's see. The paper says—" Jonathan dropped his coat onto the fourth chair at the table—the one Teofilo refused to occupy—and sat down in the third, opening the newspaper. "—ah, here's the *good* news. Ayers is looking for tie choppers, and Hawks has moved his boarders to a two-story brick building, which is marginally better than the old place. I stayed there. In my opinion, Flagstaff needs a good hotel."

"It certainly does," Abbie agreed, removing her eyeglasses from the end of her nose. "I had to stay in a very *plain* room in some lady's house, and she gave me long lectures about the dangers of girls my age traveling alone, although I imagine I'm the first she ever encountered, and I *did* pay my bill promptly." She opened and read one of her letters, then glanced toward Merrill. "Aren't you going to read your letter, Merrill? Mine is from my grandparents, who are angry with me, of course, because I didn't tell them I was leaving."

"You didn't mention that to me," said Jonathan sharply.

"Well, I sent them a wire from St. Louis." She opened the second envelope and glanced rapidly over the text. "My second letter is from Cardinal John Henry Newman of England and Ireland. He says that he was very sorry to hear that I disagree with some of the opinions advanced in his book *The Scope and Nature of a University Education*, but he thanks me for my letter.

"Grandfather fired my tutor, made me stay in my room for three days, and cut off my allowance for a month when he learned that I had read a book written by a Roman Catholic who deserted the Church of England." Abbie then inspected her letter from England more closely. "I think Cardinal Newman's reply was written by a secretary. Who is your letter from, Merrill?"

Merrill had no idea since she couldn't read anything on the envelope but her own name, which her mother had taught her to write when she was four.

"It's from her Uncle Burden, Abbie," said Jonathan, "and I suppose she won't read it because she's still mad at him for selling me the ranch."

"Half the ranch," Merrill corrected. Uncle Burden? She hadn't even known that he could write.

"Now for the *bad* news," said Jonathan, taking up his newspaper again. "It's been discovered that the Wells Fargo treasure box is missing from the westbound train."

"What treasure was in it?" asked Abbie, her eyes lighting with interest. "Pieces of eight? Precious jewels belonging to a noblewoman traveling—"

"Nothing so glamorous, Pippin. Ah, listen to this. Mr. Cohen has been discharged as having acted in self-defense. Wasn't he the fellow who killed someone named Spencer in a duel?" He looked up. "Good Lord, Merrill, go ahead and read your letter. You know you're dying to hear what the old reprobate has to say."

"I am not," said Merrill self-consciously and flung the envelope right back at Jonathan. "I'm not reading anything from Uncle Burden."

"Is having me in the house really that awful?" he asked with that wistful, charming smile that always turned her heart over.

"I haven't forgiven him. That's all," she mumbled.

"Well, *I* want to know what's happened to him. I'll read it to you." Jonathan used his letter opener to slit the envelope, then shook out the folded sheet of paper.

"The only reason I'm staying is that I'm hungry, and Chun Kee's about to bring in supper," said Merrill, who was eaten up with curiosity to know how the old fool was getting along.

Dear Meril,
    This leter is bein writ by a hore who is a grat frind of mine. Hope you an the shep an yer new pard are doin well ha ha. I am fine an walowin in hi clover.

                          Yer unkl Birdun

"Writes a fine letter, doesn't he?" said Jonathan, "but I must say his scribe lacks something in the spelling department."

"Oh, can I see it?" cried Abbie, snatching the sheet from her uncle's hand. "What a funny letter! Is that the way to spell whore? I've never seen it written down."

"I'd like to know where you *heard* it," muttered Jonathan.

Abbie, having perused the letter, giggling, passed it back to Merrill. "I'd love to meet your uncle," she said. "Is he a funny old man? Why did he go off and leave you? I should think you'd be a lot happier to have *my* uncle for a partner than yours. Don't you like Uncle Jon?"

Before Merrill could answer, Jonathan said, "Not much. She won't even read one of my books, much less forgive Burden for selling out to me."

"Why, Uncle Jon's books are wonderful!" cried Abbie. "All the best people read them, not to mention people who are practically illiterate and have to sound the words out letter by letter. And of *course*, Merrill likes you, Uncle Jon. Don't you, Merrill?"

Merrill's face, which had turned pink at the mention of illiteracy, turned pinker. She could feel the heat in her cheeks. And what could she say to the demand that she admit to liking Jonathan? "Maybe I do," she mumbled, but she'd only gone that far so as not to upset Abbie, who was a lovable child—if somewhat pushy and intimidatingly well educated.

Jonathan caught Merrill just outside her door and pinned her to the wall as if he'd been lying in wait for her. "We need supplies from town," he whispered. "Why don't we send Abbie in with Chun Kee?"

"Merrill!" Abbie's clear, sweet voice drifted up the staircase from the big room. "Hurry up. This is the morning you give me my lesson on the mathematics of sheep raising."

Merrill raised her eyebrows pointedly at Jonathan and ducked under his arm. Jonathan muttered, "Looks like I'm the one who's going to town with Chun Kee." They didn't like to send the Chinaman in by himself for fear irate townspeople would decide he was responsible for the latest fire and drive him out of Yavapai County before they could rescue him. His last Treasure Tea run had resulted in the accusation that he had somehow managed to set a fire, quickly extinguished, in a house rented by one of the Daggs brothers to a Mrs. Jacobs.

Jonathan dragged Merrill back for a quick kiss, and then they both went down to breakfast.

"What's this crunchy stuff in the flapjacks, Chun Kee?" Jonathan asked after taking his first bite.

"Secret ingredient," said the housekeeper.

"Very interesting," said Jonathan.

"But not meant for human consumption," Abbie whispered, grinning, to Merrill.

Merrill stifled a giggle. Much as she tried not to become too involved with the girl, since she still believed that Jonathan and Abbie wouldn't last out the January-to-April blizzard season, Merrill already adored Abbie. She was so much fun—and a fountain of information. Knowing Abbie was almost as good as getting to attend school—or at least so Merrill imagined. Between Abbie and

Jonathan, Merrill had learned a million interesting things. Sanxi had been right about that; the Forresters enriched her life. Too bad he couldn't be right about—oh well, there was no use thinking of marriage. She and Jonathan couldn't even couple anymore.

"Merrill, do you realize that you're hurting Uncle Jon's feelings by refusing to read his books?" asked Abbie before Merrill could begin on flock mathematics, as Abbie had dubbed the lesson. "Now, I've chosen the book I thought you might enjoy most, *Mining Misadventures*. It's about a silver boomtown in New Mexico. I just want you to read two or three pages. Is that too much to ask?"

When Abbie passed the book over, opened to what were presumably the first pages, Merrill realized that she'd have to pretend to read. What if Abbie asked her questions? Oh, this was terrible, embarrassing, dishonest. How long did it take to read a page? she wondered desperately, staring at the strange letters without really seeing them. She had to turn the first leaf sooner or later but had no idea how long to wait. Well, fast. She flipped the page. If she seemed fast and was asked a question, she could say, "Oh, I must have missed that."

She ran her eyes over the next page, taking a little more time since the first page had stopped short of the bottom. "There you go," she said, handing the book back to Abbie. "I mean no disrespect to your uncle, but I've *been* a miner. I know about mining, and I'm *not* much of a reader. Too busy, you know. Dead tired when I get in at night. I don't know when I've had time to read a whole book."

Abbie, looking up from the opened pages of the returned book, asked, "Can you read at all, Merrill?"

"Why, I—why would you—"

"Your grammar is quite good," said Abbie. "Better than most I've heard in Arizona, so I wouldn't have believed you were illiterate."

Merrill had turned bright red. "Why do you then?" she stammered defensively.

"Because I handed the book to you upside down, and you didn't reverse it."

Merrill hung her head, knowing she was caught, hoping Abbie would keep her secret. "Mama taught me to speak properly," she explained, "although I'm not always sure I still remember what she said. And she was going to teach me to read—as soon as we made our fortune in the gold fields and she could afford to replace the books that burned up when our tent caught fire. Only she died."

Abbie was out of her chair and hugging Merrill before you could say, *Shoot that coyote before it brings down another lamb.*

"I just knew it wasn't because you didn't like Uncle Jonathan, which is a great relief to me. Now there's no reason you can't marry him."

"What?"

"Marry Uncle Jonathan. I need a mother and father, and you two will do very nicely. I'll get right to work on it."

"Abbie, your uncle—he—he wouldn't to want to marry me," gasped Merrill, anticipating all sorts of horrible embarrassment and hurt if single-minded Abbie pursued her scheme.

"Why not?" demanded Abbie indignantly. "Uncle Jonny's not one of those men who only like loose women. He's just been waiting for the right lady and the urge to settle down somewhere. You and Arizona are perfect."

"How can you say that? I'm—I'm homely, and—and old, and illiterate," she finished miserably.

"Old?" Abbie fastened on that one aspect with dismay. "How old?"

"Twenty-nine."

"Well, goodness gracious, he's twenty-eight. What's a year? As for homely, you'll dress up well. I'll have a gown made for you and fix your hair, and he won't know he's looking at the same woman. Although he seems to like you fine the way you are, which says something. I've seen better-looking clothes than yours on panhandlers in New York City, on poor immigrants just off the boat, on—"

"You don't have to go on," said Merrill crossly.

"Well, I didn't mean to hurt your feelings, but you aren't well dressed, Merrill," said Abbie. *She* was wearing a red and green plaid wool dress with green moire ribbons and green-trimmed petticoats. Merrill was wearing a brown-faded-to-spring-mud-colored wool shirt with a hole in the elbow, her black and mold-colored suspenders, baggy trousers, and heavy boots decorated with manure spots.

"As for reading, I can teach you to read—just like that!" Abbie snapped her fingers and warmed a saddened Merrill with her innocent, eager child's smile.

Oh, the confidence of the young, thought Merrill sadly. "I'm too old to learn now, Abbie," said Merrill, "although it's sweet of you to offer."

"Hogwash," said Abbie crisply. She was picking up the language of the frontier at a frightening rate. "Uncle Jon told me you speak four or five languages. I know for a fact that you're some kind of numbers genius. Well, don't look so shocked. How many people do you think can do huge sums in their heads the way you do? And you have a memory like an elephant."

"What's an elephant?"

"We'll get to that later. We're going to have your first reading lesson right now—just to prove that you can learn to read." She grabbed her slate and a piece of chalk and drew a squiggly line. "Look at that," she commanded. Merrill wanted to run. "And this. What do they look like to you?"

Merrill stared hard, fascinated in spite of herself. She *knew* it was too late for her to learn reading, but she couldn't resist the offer of a lesson. "A snake and a chair," she said.

"Good. Anytime you see those two together, they say, 'sh-sh,' like you say to Uncle Jonathan when he's been whispering to you and you don't want me to hear."

Merrill blushed.

"Say it," Abbie demanded sternly, suddenly a no-nonsense schoolmarm in a rich child's dress.

"Sh-sh," said Merrill obediently.

Abbie wrote 'ee' on the slate after 'sh.' "Look at those two. What do they look like?"

"I don't know," said Merrill, squinting at them. "But they're the same."

"Right. Every time you see them together, they say 'e-e-e,' like a woman who sees a mouse."

"Why would anyone say 'e-e-e' to a mouse?" asked Merrill.

Abbie sighed. "Actually, I don't suppose *you* would. Just remember—two of those say 'e-e'."

"E-e-e," said Merrill.

Abbie wrote 'p' on the slate. "This letter says—" and she puffed into Merrill's face.

Merrill puffed back.

"Now make the sounds one after the other, run them together, and see what the word says."

Merrill stared at the mysterious letters. "Sh—ee—p. Sheep?" She felt a rush of exultant wonder. "Sheep!"

"Now you've learned to read your first word," said Abbie smugly. "As soon as you accept Uncle Jon's proposal of marriage, I'll teach you all the rest of them."

"But, Abbie—" Merrill's heart fell. Her smile disappeared.

"Don't bother to argue. It'll be your wedding present from me."

"Couldn't we do just one more word?" asked Merrill wistfully, looking at the letters to *sheep* as if she were Moses looking at the original Ten

211

Commandments engraved in stone. She felt that the magic skill was within her grasp if it weren't for that one condition she could never meet.

"Not even a short one," said Abbie firmly. "But don't you worry. I'll take care of everything. Now I'm going out to see Teofilo about building me a desk. It's ridiculous that I should have to do my lessons on the dining room table."

Abbie would take care of everything? Merrill shuddered to think of what that meant. Abbie was a dear girl but *not* subtle. There'd be broad hints, outright demands that she have her way. Merrill would be humiliated. Jonathan would run for his life. Had Jonathan been back with the supplies, Merrill would have left immediately and alone for the sheep camps and stayed away for two months.

"Oh, one last thing, Merrill," said Abbie, popping her head, encased in its green velvet bonnet, back in the door. "Christmas is coming. What would you like for Christmas?"

"We don't celebrate Christmas."

Abbie looked shocked. "You don't go to church. You don't celebrate Christmas. Merrill, are you a heathen? No, don't answer that. I'll just have to save your soul too. But at least you can tell me what you'd like for a Christmas present."

"Nothing. I've never had one."

"Oh, goodness." Abbie looked profoundly sympathetic. "Well, do think about it, because Uncle Jon and I will certainly be giving you Christmas presents. Think of three things, so you'll be surprised at which two you get."

Did that mean she'd have to reciprocate? Merrill wondered without an idea in the world of what one gave or received at Christmas. Three things? What three things would she ask for if her wishes could be granted? She stared at the slate where Abbie had written the word *sheep*. Well, to read, which was, to her amazement, possible, although not likely. And to keep her ranch all her life. She thought she could do that; it had always been her wish, but now, having had Abbie and Jonathan living with her, she'd be lonely when they left. So her last gift wish would be Jonathan's baby, but unless she turned up pregnant, that wish wasn't likely to be granted, not with Abbie sleeping in the room between them.

Merrill sighed and rose from the table. Christmas gifts! What a waste of time! She had more important, more practical things to do than daydream about gifts and wishes and Christmas, the story of which she remembered only dimly from the time when her mother was still alive.

Chapter Seven

Jonathan returned in high spirits from Flagstaff with a wagonload of provisions. He calculated that restocking the sheep camps might be stretched out to allow him three, maybe four days alone with Merrill. Therefore, he was extremely irritated to discover that she felt one or the other of them, in this case he as the blood relation, should remain at home with Abigail.

"Chun Kee can look after her," Jonathan protested. "Hell, if she can go into town and protect Chun Kee from the local bigots, he can damn well take care of her for a couple of days here in the house."

"Fire follows Chinamen like a buzzard follows death," said Merrill, her mouth set in a stubborn line.

"Charming imagery, Merrill," he snapped.

Her eyes narrowed. "So now you've decided

you don't like the way I talk. Is that what you mean?"

"I never said—"

"Well, fine, Jonathan. You've got Chun Kee to help you with your fancy Celestial cookbook—"

"What's that got to do with—"

"So you don't need me with my country-bumpkin imagery to take you to Walnut Canyon. You can stay home with Chun Kee and burn my house down while you're writing—"

"Don't be ridiculous, Merrill. You act like the man's a pyromaniac."

"I don't even know what a pyromaniac is. You probably made the word up so I'd be embarrassed that I don't know what it means. It's just like you to be such a snob and . . ."

Jonathan closed his ears to her tirade. Good Lord, the woman was supersensitive! And she had a temper, and a tongue sharper than a buffalo skinner's knife. "All right, go by yourself," he muttered, knowing that was what the argument was really about.

"I intend to."

Why was she so anxious to get away from him? She ran hot and cold, hot and cold, but mostly cold. Trying to get along with Merrill was a difficult endeavor, but challenging.

"Uncle Jonathan, it's so fortunate that we have this time alone together." Abbie was hopping down the ladder staircase on one foot, a sport she'd invented and one that frightened him half to death. Although he'd appealed to Merrill for support in his objections, she had shrugged and said, "She's surefooted."

"And why are you so glad to get rid of Merrill?" Jonathan demanded. He himself had started to miss his irascible partner before she disappeared over the hill.

"I didn't say I wanted to get rid of her," Abbie replied, coming over to snuggle beside him in the big chair that had been Ben Fox's before the logs killed him.

Good Lord, what was coming? Jonathan wondered. Whenever Abbie climbed into your lap, she had some outrageous request to make. Maybe she wanted him to buy her the town of Flagstaff, or lure Cardinal John Henry Newman across the ocean so that she could debate with him.

"It's about Christmas, Uncle Jon. Did you know that Merrill has never had a Christmas present? I think that's the saddest thing I ever heard."

"Yes, it is," Jonathan agreed.

"So you have to buy her something really wonderful."

"And I suppose you're going to tell me what," he responded, chuckling. "Have you been pumping her for suggestions?"

"She won't say a thing except that she doesn't celebrate Christmas. But that's probably just as well because she might ask for something dull and practical."

"Whereas you have—what in mind?"

"A beautiful gown that she can wear to the Christmas Eve ball."

Jonathan shook his head, face gloomy. "Merrill refuses to go to dances."

"You've invited her?" asked Abbie eagerly.

"Repeatedly. I'm not sure whether she doesn't know how to dance or she just doesn't want to be seen on my arm. And even if Merrill were interested in dancing, Pippin, she's *not* interested in clothes. I'm surprised you haven't noticed that comic wardrobe of hers."

"Well, of course I have. That's why—"

"So buying her a dress would be a waste of time. She might even consider it an insult. I think I'll buy her—let's see—a purebred merino ram. Now, that—"

"You'll do no such thing," cried Abbie indignantly. "I've never heard such an unroman—ah—insensitive suggestion in my life."

"Why do you say that? She'd give her eyeteeth for a merino ram."

"Maybe, but she can't wear it to the Christmas ball. And a merino ram isn't going to convince Merrill that she's pretty. Maybe you don't realize it, Uncle Jon, but Merrill thinks she's homely. Can you believe that? Why, she could be a beautiful woman."

"She already is."

"And her hair. It would be gorgeous if I could get my hands on it."

"It *is* gorgeous."

His niece squinted at him. "How do you know? It's always in that rag-tag braid."

Jonathan cleared his throat. "I still don't think—"

217

"If Merrill ever saw herself all dressed up in a beautiful gown with her hair fixed, she'd realize that she's not just some homely old sheep rancher."

"Well." His niece might be on the right track. If he could get Merrill to see herself as he saw her, it might make a world of difference in their relationship. "But a dress—I'm afraid she'd throw it at me."

"We should go into town today. There's not much time left till Christmas."

"You give her the dress," said Jonathan, "and I'll pay for it."

"No, I have something else in mind. If you don't give it to her, no one will, and then you won't be able to take her to the Christmas Eve ball."

"Where every man in town will fall in love with her, and I won't—"

"Oh, but you'll dance every dance with her, Uncle Jon. Won't that be roman—fun?"

"Are you up to something, Abbie?" he asked suspiciously.

"I just want to make Merrill happy," the little girl said, an irresistible smile lighting her pretty face.

"Oh, all right," said Jonathan, wondering if Merrill would agree to award her dance card to him exclusively. "We'd better head for Flagstaff while she's away."

The best dressmaker in Flagstaff was acquainted with Merrill Fox and very dubious at the idea of making her a fancy ball gown. "If Merrill's ever wore a dress, I'd be surprised to hear it," said Mrs. Crandell. "An' she ain't here. How'm I s'posed to measure it to her?"

Jonathan and Abigail stared at one another, momentarily stymied. "You've known her longer than I have, Uncle Jon," said Abigail. "How big is she?"

"Well, she stands about so tall." He touched himself under the chin, remembering the first time he'd held her in his arms. "And her waist's about this size." He circled his hands, leaving about an inch between thumbs and fingers. "Does that help you any, Mrs. Crandell?"

The woman glared at him. "I can't be held responsible if the dress don't fit."

"I told you this was a bad idea," said Jonathan to Abbie.

"Oh, stop arguing. We need to pick out a design."

"That ain't no way to talk to your uncle, child," said Mrs. Crandell.

As Jonathan and Abbie looked at fashion magazines, the dressmaker said, "This here satchel bustle is real stylish—handy too. If'n the lady is agoin' to an overnight dance, she can pack her nightclothes into her bustle."

"What a peculiar idea," said Abbie, "and the satchel bustle is a year out of date. Goodness, is this magazine—"

"We'll take it," said Jonathan.

"Uncle Jonathan," wailed Abbie.

"That way she'll have a place to stow her gun."

"Gun!" cried Mrs. Crandell, scandalized.

"Did you ever see Merrill Fox without a gun? Not likely she'd agree to attend anything, even a fancy dress ball, unarmed. Now, can you make a dress with this skirt and neckline, plus the satchel bustle?" he asked, pointing to a different picture.

They quickly settled on the style, the blue velvet, the embroidered trim, and, most important, the satchel bustle for the well-armed lady who would wear the dress—he hoped. "No one in Flagstaff, least of all Merrill, will know the bustle is out of style," Jonathan consoled Abbie as they left the dressmaker's.

"I'll know," she retorted.

Merrill delayed her return as long as possible and got back to the ranch to discover Jonathan dragging a huge tree through her front door. "What do you think you're doing?" she demanded. "If you're going into the lumber business, you can't do it in my house."

"*Our* house, and this is the Christmas tree. Abbie picked it out. Teofilo and I cut it down."

"Christmas tree?" Merrill looked astonished. "I told you we didn't celebrate—"

"We do now," Jonathan interrupted.

"We'll string popcorn tonight," said Abbie, clapping her hands with excitement, although Merrill said they had no popping corn in the house.

"Oh yes, we do. When we went Christmas shopping—" the child bubbled with mysterious glee "—we bought yards and yards of colored ribbon and candles so I can make bows and other pretties—oh, we'll have a lovely tree. You'll string the popcorn, Merrill, and I'll make bows and rosettes, and Uncle Jon will set up and decorate the tree. Then we'll have hot chocolate and Christmas cookies just as we did before Mama ran off with the carriage maker."

Merrill hadn't the heart to protest further. Perhaps the poor child's Christmases had disappeared with her mother, just as Merrill's had, for Merrill remembered now that the china doll with the chipped nose had been a Christmas gift from her mother.

Chun Kee found popping corn, which he had never seen before, an alarming foodstuff and, sulking, retired to his room. Merrill wished fervently that he'd taken his Christmas cookies with him. They seemed very peculiar to her. Mrs. Oblati had made cookies for Uncle Burden, who'd had a sweet tooth, and her cookies had never contained unidentifiable chunks of crunchy stuff. Nor had they been sprinkled with red powder that burned your mouth. Abbie had inspected them and declared them "very festive," but she'd turned pale when she tasted one. Jonathan liked them.

He would! thought Merrill, wincing as she jabbed her finger again. After Mama died, Pa had done what darning and patching needed to be done, then Mrs. Oblati. Stringing popcorn was a difficult and painful business, although Merrill supposed Abbie would declare the popcorn strings "very festive" since they were sprinkled with red, Christmasy dots, the result of all the times Merrill jabbed the needle into her finger instead of the popcorn.

Boss certainly liked the decorations. She was caught leaping and snapping at the popcorn strings on the middle section of the tree, having quietly devoured all those on the lower branches. She had to be locked in the barn. And Jonathan kept referring to an article he'd read in the paper about local folk planning to celebrate New Year's in Albuquerque because the railroad was offering special holiday rates. Who did he think was going to run the ranch if the three of them went gallivanting off to Albuquerque?

"You and Abbie go," said Merrill, thinking that would probably be the last she'd see of them.

In the increasing holiday excitement, Merrill's spirits fell. She hadn't forgotten Abbie's comment that she and Jonathan had been Christmas shopping in town, buying extravagant presents, no doubt. And how was Merrill to reciprocate? She didn't know what to give a wealthy child or her wealthier uncle. They both had accounts at the Bank of Flagstaff, whereas Merrill had very little cash money. She could use credit at the Pioneer Store, but that didn't seem a good place to buy gifts unless she wanted to give someone a gallon of coal oil with a potato stuffed in the top as a plug.

To escape the problem, she left the ranch again and stayed away several more days without anyone complaining or offering to go along. Obviously Jonathan had lost interest in getting her off by herself.

Merrill was home the Saturday when Jonathan announced that he and Abbie were driving into town. "I'm taking Abbie to see Santa Claus at O'Neill's store."

"Really?" Merrill had never seen Santa Claus and invited herself along. While she was there maybe she'd find a present or two that she could afford.

"Sorry, Merrill," said Abbie, "but we're staying over for church, and I know you wouldn't want to do that."

Abbie's words hurt. Was she really so upset at the idea of living with a heathen that she didn't want to be seen in Flagstaff with Merrill?

When Abbie and Jonathan arrived in town to pick up the dress, they found that it wasn't ready. "I've had a real rush of business, and you weren't the first to ask for my services," said Mrs. Crandell. "I'll promise it to you on the morning of Christmas Eve day. That's the best I can do."

"Good heavens," complained Abbie as they rode home. "We'll have to come in, get the dress, go home, open the presents, talk Merrill into wearing it, and come right back for the dance. We'll be worn out before the music starts. Did you see that handsome Fenton boy? The one singing in the choir. Do you think he'll ask me to dance?"

"He's too old for you," said Jonathan, realizing

that in a few years he'd be fending off Abbie's suitors, just as Christmas Eve he'd be fending off Merrill's—if she agreed to attend the dance. He counted on Abbie to persuade her.

"Here's the Christmas turkey," announced Jonathan, coming in out of the cold, carrying a thirty-pound wild turkey. "Pluck it, stuff it, and roast it, Chun Kee."

"Stuff?" Chun Kee stared at the bird, obviously perplexed.

Jonathan scratched his two-day beard as he considered how to explain turkey preparation to a Chinaman. "Fill up the inside with bread dressing. What's in dressing, Abbie, besides bread?"

"How should I know? Cook always made Christmas dinner," said Abbie, who was doing a last set of lessons before she declared school out for the holidays. Abbie turned questioningly to Merrill.

"Don't look at me," said Merrill. "I told you we never celebrated Christmas. Anyway, I have to visit Sanxi's camp."

"Why?" asked Jonathan suspiciously.

"I realized that I forgot to leave him his holiday tobacco bonus."

"There, I knew you did *something* for Christmas," said Abbie. "And Merrill, if you're not back by noon on the twenty-fourth, I'll never forgive you."

Merrill hoped that Abbie didn't have any silly ideas about that Christmas Eve dance in town. The girl had been talking about it and reading newspaper articles about it for two weeks now.

The Fourth Gift

"I mean it, Merrill," said Abbie. "If you're not home for Christmas Eve, I'll cry till New Year's, and I'm a loud crier, lots of tears. You'll hate it."

Merrill thought about staying away, but she couldn't do that to Abbie, so on the morning of the twenty-fourth she was riding home through light snow, wondering what in the world she'd give as gifts. She'd have to have something ready in case they'd bought presents for her, and her only resource was Mama's trunk. It contained the china doll, whose nose was just a little bit chipped, and the doll had a wonderful wardrobe. Abbie would probably love it.

But it had been a gift from Mama, and Merrill's heart sank at the thought of giving it away. And Jonathan. What could she give him? The only possibility was Pa's watch. She'd hate to see that watch leaving the ranch forever when Jonathan left, but still . . . she loved them—both Abbie and Jonathan, just as she'd loved Mama and Pa.

Maybe it was the right thing to do. She didn't know anything about gift giving, but it felt right. It wasn't as if she'd be playing with the doll herself or passing it on to a daughter. Merrill had discovered that again she'd failed to conceive. Evidently it just wasn't meant to be.

As for the watch—well, she didn't know how to tell time—except by the sun—and she wouldn't be giving the watch to a boy child of hers, so Jonathan might as well have it to remember her by. She, on the other hand, wouldn't need anything to remember him by. He was engraved in her heart, just like those letters engraved on Pa's watch. Merrill knew what they said, even if she couldn't read them. "From Ellie to Ben with love. 1855." Mama had given him the watch.

"Well, where are they?" demanded Merrill, who had slipped into the house, fetched her gifts from the trunk, and wrapped them in material from an old shirt of Uncle Burden's. It was plaid—green and red, which seemed to be Christmas colors.

"Fragstaff," said Chun Kee irritably. He'd already told her three times during the afternoon.

Merrill opened the kitchen door and peered out. The snow now fell heavily.

Chun Kee thrust under her nose a bowl of cranberries that Jonathan had brought back from Jim O'Neill's store when he took Abbie in to see Santa Claus. "What for these?" Chun Kee asked. "Trim tree or stuff bird?"

"Well, I'm not stringing anything else for that tree," said Merrill. "I've got a hundred holes in my fingers from the popcorn." They weren't coming home, she thought with a painful wave of disappointment. They'd probably decided to stay in town for that dance Abbie kept talking about. They'd probably forgotten all about insisting that Merrill get home for Christmas. "I should have stayed with Sanxi," she muttered.

"Then who eat giant devil bird?" asked Chun Kee.

"I even changed my clothes." She had put on her best blue wool shirt and a clean pair of trousers. She'd even wished, for just a minute, that she had a dress to wear for the occasion. Wouldn't that have been fine—her all gussied up in a dress, eating the giant devil bird by herself at the big table. It was such a silly idea that she had to blink back tears—from trying not to laugh, of course.

Chapter Eight

They probably wouldn't have liked her second-hand presents anyway, Merrill thought. Just as well they hadn't come home. She was sitting in Pa's big chair with her stocking feet on the hearth when the door flew open and slammed against the wall. Abbie's voice rose over the wind's hollow boom. "Our plans are ruined," she cried. "We'll never get back to the dance."

"The snow's slacking off some," said Jonathan. Merrill rose and turned to stare at them. Abbie clutched a square box to her chest, arms extended along the sides, holding the green bow that decorated the top in place with her chin. Jonathan carried two large boxes, one rectangular and flat, one deep, both with large red bows. The wind snatched the bow from the second box and whirled it away into the dark tumult of the yard.

"I—I thought you two'd be staying in town for the dance," Merrill stammered as Jonathan said, "Damn, there goes my bow."

"Without you?" cried Abbie. "How could you even think such a thing, Merrill?" She kicked the door shut, hurried to the table, and released her burden with a thud. "Why, we risked our lives, driving through snow and ice, buffeted by—"

"Oh hush, Abbie," Jonathan ordered. He'd returned from the yard but without the missing bow. "The wind didn't come up until just the last stretch, and as long as Merrill agrees to go, we may yet make it to town for part of the dance."

"I'm not risking my life again in that storm," cried Abbie as Merrill protested, "I never said I'd go to any dance."

"Stuffed berries in bird," said Chun Kee from the kitchen doorway. "Now red juice dripping out."

Jonathan swore under his breath. Abbie said, "Merry Christmas," and, pressing an icy cheek against Merrill's, hugged her. "Isn't this exciting? Uncle Jon can use it in his book—an adventurous uncle and his courageous niece brave a mountain blizzard to make the first family Christmas on the wilderness Forrester-Fox sheep ranch. I get to open my presents first." She was removing layers of expensive clothing that had made her look more like a small green bear than a slender eleven-year-old girl. "Chun Kee, I want hot chocolate and fried donuts."

"For dinner?" asked Merrill, scandalized.

"What about bleeding devil bird?" asked Chun Kee.

"We'll have to hope that by tomorrow noon it will have stopped bleeding," said Jonathan. "The thing is, you shouldn't have put the cranberries inside the turkey."

"I ask. You say I decide. Missy Merrir say she not hang berries on tree." Chun Kee stamped out to the kitchen.

"Hot chocolate and fried donuts, with lots of sugar," Abbie shouted after him. "Which present is mine, Uncle Jon? We have to hurry in case the storm does slack off."

"The bowless one is for you." He too had divested himself of bulky winter clothing as Abigail tore into her gift.

"Oh, you got them," she cried. "See, Merrill, the complete works of Charles Dickens. He writes the most wonderful novels. They make you laugh and cry. You'll just love them."

Merrill gave her a reproachful look and mumbled, "I have a gift for you too, Abbie." She brought out the knobby package wrapped in Uncle Burden's red and green plaid shirt. "I didn't have a bow."

"Oh, I do love presents, but we should be sitting by the Christmas tree." Abbie carried her gift to the tree, Jonathan muttering and transporting his rectangular package after her. Merrill followed nervously because Abbie was already seated on the blanket she'd spread around the Christmas tree, pulling Uncle Burden's shirt off her gift and staring. "It's a doll," she said as if she'd never seen

230

one. "But I'm too—" A hard look from Jonathan cut her off. "Wherever did you get it, Merrill?" she asked instead.

"My mother gave it to me. At least, that's what Pa said." Merrill wished with all her heart that she had given Abbie something else. Probably Abbie was too old for dolls. She hadn't brought any with her.

Probably—Merrill noted with dismay that tears were rolling down Abbie's cheeks. Then the little girl hurled herself into Merrill's arms and said, "I'll play with it every day. We'll share it. We'll use it in our lessons. Oh Merrill, it's the lovingest gift anyone ever gave me. It'll be like sharing your mother."

A doll with a chipped nose was the lovingest gift Abbie had ever received? Merrill felt thoroughly confused as she hugged Abbie back, patting her awkwardly on one thin shoulder and wondering how the two of them could share her mother, long dead.

"Here, Pippin, use my handkerchief," said Jonathan. "You're crying all over Merrill's shirt."

Merrill tugged the plaid-wrapped watch out of her pocket and handed it to Jonathan. "This is for you," she mumbled, not looking at him.

Jonathan unwrapped it, ran his thumb over the worn case, and opened the lid to read the inscription. Then he leaned forward and brushed his mouth lightly over hers. "You've given me the gift of your past," he said softly, "and I'll always treasure it."

Merrill wasn't sure exactly what he meant, but

she did know he was pleased, which gave her a warmth of heart that overcame any sadness she might have felt as she watched Jonathan tucking her father's watch into his waistcoat pocket.

Abbie was beaming at them like a benevolent bishop. "Now mine for Uncle Jon," she said and pulled another rectangular box from behind the tree. "I brought this with me from New York."

Jonathan opened it and discovered a blue velvet jacket with satin lapels. "A smoking jacket?" he asked. "But, Pippin, I don't—"

"Oh, put it on, Uncle Jonathan. You'll look absolutely smashing." Jonathan obliged, and Abbie said to Merrill, "Isn't he beautiful? Isn't he just the handsomest man you ever saw?"

Merrill was staring at him, wide-eyed. He did look beautiful, although she had no idea what occasion would warrant such a coat.

"Now put your hand in the left pocket, Uncle Jon," Abbie instructed, fidgeting with excitement.

Jonathan drew out a small velvet box and opened it. Inside were three gold rings, one larger than the other two, each etched with an elaborate scroll of leaves and flowers, one of the small-sized rings set with a sapphire surrounded by diamonds. Jonathan glanced at his niece, an eyebrow lifted in wry inquiry. He knew the sapphire ring had passed to Abbie from her maternal grandmother. The other two she must have bought.

"In case you should need them," said Abbie, giggling.

What could have been in the box? Merrill wondered, for Jonathan had returned it to his pocket without comment. Merrill looked questioningly to Abbie, but no answer was forthcoming.

"Now yours, Merrill." Abbie hauled the square box with its green bow from the dining room table and placed it in Merrill's hands, which immediately dropped a foot with the weight. The box was full of books. "Just remember what you have to do," Abbie whispered conspiratorially.

Merrill scowled at the child, which was possible because Jonathan couldn't see Merrill's face. Her back was to him. "Thanks," she muttered ungraciously.

"The idea, Abbie," said Jonathan, "is to give people things they'd like to receive. You know Merrill isn't interested in reading." Abbie giggled, and Jonathan, looking uneasy, handed his box to Merrill. "I'll get you something else if you don't like it," he said.

What had he got her that she wouldn't like? Merrill wondered, undoing the bow. Not more books. The package wasn't heavy enough. She considered Abbie's gift a cruel jest since she had no hope of meeting the child's conditions and earning the lessons. Still, she didn't suppose Abbie was old enough to realize that one couldn't always have what one wanted from life—like marriage to a handsome, intelligent man in Merrill's case, and a ready-made family in Abbie's. They'd both be disappointed.

Merrill lifted the box lid and stared in confusion at the beautiful blue velvet gown.

"We meant for you to wear it to the Christmas

ball tonight," said Abbie, "but the snow ruined our plans."

"But I couldn't have—I mean I've never—" Merrill was speechless. The gown seemed meant for a princess, not for a sheep rancher. If she touched it, it would probably flinch away from her work-roughened fingers.

"Still, you can wear it for Christmas Eve," said Abbie. "Come on. I'll help you put it on."

"I can't," Merrill protested, knowing she'd look a fool in the dress. It wouldn't even fit her. She was too skinny for a dress like that. She looked toward Jonathan to rescue her and saw that he too wanted to see her in his gift. So she'd put it on. It would be the final proof to them that they were from another world and should leave her to her own place.

"Oh, here's my chocolate and donuts," cried Abbie. "I'm starved." She ran to the table where Chun Kee had just deposited hot sugar-coated donuts, a steaming pitcher, and cups. Merrill breathed a sigh of relief, set the dress box aside, and joined them at the table, but not for long.

"One's enough," declared Abbie. "Keep my chocolate hot," she sang out to Chun Kee through the kitchen door, "and don't eat my share of the donuts, Uncle Jon. We'll be as quick as we can." With the dress casually bundled up under one arm so that it wouldn't drag, Abbie waved Merrill toward the stair. "You bring the petticoats, Merrill, and Uncle Jon, you'll have to carry the chemise and drawers."

"What?" exclaimed Merrill, horrified at the idea

that Jonathan would see ladies' undergarments, especially undergarments meant for her. She forgot for a moment that Jonathan had already seen the body they'd cover. When she remembered, halfway up the stair, her cheeks turned pinker than before.

"Oh, and the slippers, Uncle Jon. Don't forget them. Getting a pattern of her foot was *so* much trouble. I had to push her into some mud and then trace the imprint, which was really messy and disgusting. Can't you climb faster, Merrill? You act as if you don't want to try on Uncle Jon's dress. Well, not *his* dress." Her giggles floated up after Merrill. "Wouldn't he look smashing in it?"

"Better than me," Merrill muttered.

"What was that?" called Jonathan, who was behind Abbie with a load of silk, lace, and ruffles.

"No arguing," Abbie ordered, having reached the top of the stair two steps behind Merrill. "Not on Christmas. I'm going to fix your hair, Merrill. Chun Kee, I need a bucket of coals for the curling iron." She leaned over the rail. "Chun Kee, did you hear me?"

"You're not putting hot irons on my hair," said Merrill, blushing as she accepted the undergarments and slippers from Jonathan.

"Oh, don't be a sissy," Abbie retorted.

Descending the ladder in a dress that was long in front and longer in back, when you never wore dresses at all, with soft little slippers on your feet, when you were used to heeled boots, was, Merrill felt, one of the trickiest things she'd ever

235

done, especially with Abbie behind her on the stairs, hopping up and down and crying, "Look at Merrill, Uncle Jon. Look at Merrill!"

And he was looking. By the time she reached the first floor, Jonathan was staring at her with much the same expression she herself had worn when she first looked into the mirror and saw an unfamiliar lady. The mirror image had thick blond hair arranged in elaborate loops and rolls and wore blue velvet that draped across the hips, making her waist look like nothing at all and her breasts look like—well—a lot bigger than Merrill had ever thought of her breasts as being, also a lot more exposed. They were sort of squeezed together by an uncomfortable garment that pinched her waist and pushed her bosom up so that she bulged above the low, gold-embroidered neck of the dress. Thank goodness the sleeves were long and warm, not that she felt cold. How could she, with Jonathan looking at her as if he'd just seen a beautiful stranger that he wanted to make a grab for?

Feeling decidedly uncomfortable, Merrill tried to kick into some sort of order the folds of the skirt that dropped from under the draperies. Then self-consciously she poked that huge, silly bundle in back, which was the only ugly thing about the dress.

"She doesn't like the bustle," said Abbie smugly. She'd just jumped down the last two steps to land beside Merrill. "I told you she wouldn't."

"It's so you'll have a place to put your gun, in case you want to carry it to a dance."

"Oh," said Merrill. She stopped scowling and smiled, appreciating his thoughtfulness. Without any weapon, she'd certainly have felt uneasy, and she knew a holster would look ridiculous with the dress.

"Unfortunately, the snow's got heavier," Jonathan added ruefully. "I'm afraid we won't be able to attend the dance."

"I told you so," said Abbie. "Didn't I say we'd never make it back to town? But I brought my music box down, so you can dance to that." She turned a small key on a pretty enameled box. Much to Merrill's amazement, music tinkled out as if there were a tiny man playing inside. "Now I'm going to bed," said Abbie.

"Now?" Merrill echoed. Jonathan always had to drive the child upstairs, and Merrill, acting on her own, rarely got Abbie to bed without telling at least two stories about mining for gold or stalking mountain cats or freighting fleece with Uncle Burden drunk on the wagon seat and the oxen balking all the way to Colorado. Abbie's favorite story was about Jonathan and Merrill shooting cowboys and making them walk to town all roped together.

"Yes, I'm completely tired out," said Abbie. "You look beautiful, Merrill." Then she hissed in Merrill's ear, "Just remember to say yes, or you won't get your lessons, and I'll tell him you can't read." Then Abbie scooped a handful of donuts off the table and hopped up the steps.

"You do look beautiful." Jonathan was still staring at her. He rewound the music box and, bow-ing, asked, "May I have this dance?" as if she were a real lady.

"I don't know how," Merrill whispered.

Jonathan put one hand at her waist, placed her hand on his shoulder, wrapped his other hand warmly around hers, and exclaimed, his eyebrows shooting up, "You're freezing!"

"I am not," Merrill retorted. Actually, she felt almost feverish, as she had the first time he'd kissed her. Only her fingers were freezing. Jonathan smiled at her in a way that made her breath catch, and then he taught her to waltz. They rewound the music box seven times before they stopped dancing, breathless, and Jonathan pulled her down on his lap in Pa's big chair by the hearth.

"Do you like waltzing?" he asked.

She nodded shyly, biting her lip to keep from saying that it ran a close second to making love.

"Will you marry me?"

Merrill stiffened on his knee. "What?"

"I want to get married," he said patiently. "To you."

"But—"

"Now that you know you're beautiful, you have one less reason to say no—unless, of course, you really don't like me."

"Of course I like you." She loved him. "But we can't get married."

"Why not?"

She thought of spending the rest of her life with Jonathan, spending each night in his arms and each day in his company. "I'm older than you are.

Men don't marry women who are older than they are," she said reluctantly. "I'm almost thirty."

"If you were almost forty, I'd still want to marry you."

"Why?"

"Because I love you."

Merrill couldn't really believe that. Even after seeing her in this beautiful dress, he couldn't love her. He might think he did, but as soon as she got back into her ranch clothes, he'd change his mind. The ranch must be what he wanted—all to himself. "It's always been the Fox ranch," she said. "If we married, it would be the Forrester ranch, and under law you'd probably own the whole thing, and I'd be just a female nobody."

Jonathan thought about that, holding her firmly in place on his lap and in the curve of his arm when she tried to edge loose. "You're a hard woman to please, Merrill, but I'll tell you what. We'll take both names like those fancy English families do. We'll call ourselves Jonathan and Merrill Forrester-Fox. There's probably some legal way to do that. And we'll sign an agreement saying the ranch is half yours, half mine, legal partners, even after we're married. Apple can take care of it."

"You'd do that? Change your name for me?"

He nodded.

"How about Fox-Forrester?" she suggested, an impish gleam lighting her eyes.

Jonathan roared with laughter, and they heard Abbie's voice piping down from the head of the stair. "You're not supposed to be laughing," she called reproachfully.

"Go back to bed," Jonathan shouted, then whispered to Merrill, "I wonder what she thinks we're supposed to be doing."

"Dancing," said Merrill absently, knowing and dreading the one last impediment to the marriage, the thing she'd never wanted to tell him. "Jonathan," she said, staring down at her hands, "I'm illiterate. A famous writer shouldn't marry a woman who can't read."

He tipped her chin up so that she had to look at him and said, "What a relief! I thought you just didn't want to read my books."

Merrill shook her head sadly. She'd love to have read his books.

"Well, if that's the problem, sweetheart, I'll teach you to read. Or Abbie—by God, she knew, didn't she?"

Merrill nodded, then giggled. "She's been blackmailing me."

Jonathan's brow furrowed, and his mouth turned hard. "To do what?" he demanded.

"Say yes if you asked me to marry you. But I told her you never would."

"Well, do what the child wants. That minx has obviously known all along that I was in love." He reached into his pocket for the velvet box. "And what about you, Merrill? Are you in love, or just tempted to marry me so that you can learn to read?"

"Both," said Merrill promptly.

"Humph. I'd like to ask which is more important to you—me or the reading lessons, but I won't push my luck." He opened the box and slipped the sapphire ring onto her finger. "Abbie's Christmas gift to the two of us. We'll go into Flagstaff and use the wedding rings tomorrow," he added, showing them to her. "Tomorrow or as soon as the weather clears and Hiram draws up the contracts. Then we'll move Abbie into your room down the hall and you into my bed, because this is, my dear future wife, the very last night I intend to set a good example for Abbie by sleeping alone. *Then* we'll honeymoon in Albuquerque over New Year's."

Merrill, who had been staring in wonder at the beautiful ring on her finger, looked up, frowning, when he mentioned Albuquerque. "It wouldn't be sensible to—"

She'd been about to say "leave the ranch with nobody to watch over it," but Jonathan interrupted her, sounding disgruntled. "Of course, you're right. Albuquerque might be more fun, but the *proper* thing is for me to take you home to meet my parents."

"To New York?" cried Merrill. She could just imagine what his rich, snobbish New York family would think of *her!* And it would take weeks to get there and return. They might not be back in time for lambing, if any of the sheep survived her absence.

"I've always wanted to see Albuquerque," she said cautiously, hoping he'd change his mind about his family obligations.

"Me too," called Abbie from the top of the stairs.

"Go to bed this instant," Jonathan roared.

"Oh, all *right!*"

They heard the door to Abbie's room slam. "You've made me a very happy man, Merrill," said Jonathan, "and I hope to do the same for you. I want to give you everything you've ever wished for."

"I think you have," said Merrill, smiling a secret smile as she remembered her three Christmas wishes—a lifetime on her own ranch, the ability to read, and a baby to inherit the land. Now she'd have them all, plus the fourth wish, for which she had never allowed herself to hope, a life with Jonathan.

NORAH HESS
CHRISTMAS SURPRISE

To Patrice,
my very French son-in-law.

Chapter One

Upper Peninsula, Michigan, 1887

Jassy Jeffers closed the door to the chicken house and dropped a heavy bar across it. She bent slightly to pick up a pail of milk and a basket holding seven eggs she had taken from a hay-lined lay-box. Then, the pail in her hand and the basket on her arm, she stepped onto a path that had been shoveled clear of snow and walked briskly toward the sturdy cabin from whose chimney smoke drifted lazily in the cold air.

Part way to her warm home, she heard her name called and turned her head and smiled. Two neighbor children, Lela and Amos Anderson, were approaching her astride a mule so old his face had grown white. But he was still strong enough to carry the two youngsters and drag a pine tree behind him.

"Ain't our Christmas tree a beaut?" a rosy-cheeked Amos exclaimed proudly, bringing his elderly mount to a halt. "We picked it out last summer one day when we was bringin' the cows in from the pasture."

Jassy made a big thing out of looking over the tree, then said admiringly, "It is indeed a beaut. It's the most handsome tree I've ever seen."

A pleased smile split Amos's freckled face, and Lela smiled shyly. "Are you going to have a tree this year, Jassy?" she asked.

"I don't think so," Jassy answered. "I can't seem to get the Christmas spirit since Ma and Pa passed away. It doesn't seem worthwhile for just one person."

"But there's Luke," Amos pointed out. "I bet he'd like a decorated tree for Christmas."

Yes, there was Luke, Jassy thought as the boy kicked the mule with his heel and he and his sister rode off with waves of their hands. But who knew what Luke Slater liked or disliked? He was like the hills and the valleys, silent and unfathomable.

As Jassy walked briskly on in the arctic cold that had hung on for the past two weeks, her mind went back to last July when Luke had come into her life.

The day had been hot and humid, not a leaf stirring in the stand of birch back of the cabin as she carried water from the lake to her scorched and dying garden. She was determined to at least save her string beans and tomatoes.

She was carefully pouring water onto a tomato

plant, admiring its large firm fruit, when Digger, the old hound, growled a low warning sound. She spun around and gasped.

Three bearded, motley-looking men leered down at her from the backs of rib-thin horses. Two of them were leaning toward each other, talking in undertones.

"What do you men want?" she asked coldly, camouflaging the fear that shook her insides, regretting that she hadn't brought the rifle with her. "If you're hungry, I can give you some meat and bread."

The biggest and dirtiest of the lot, evidently the leader, sneered, "Our bellies are hungry, but we've got another appetite that needs appeasing." He made as if to dismount, and Digger walked stiff-legged toward him, his lips drawn back in a snarl. The bearded one put his hand on the butt of a pistol, shoved in his belt, and warned, "If you don't call the hound off, he's dead meat."

Jassy's fear grew, making her heart pound. These men meant her harm, harm of the worst kind. She shot a glance at the cabin. Could she run fast enough in her long skirt to beat the men to the door, get inside, and drop the bar in place?

As though the man had read her mind, he grinned wolfishly and said, "You'd never make it, gal."

Stiffening her spine, Jassy determined that she wasn't going to stand there like a frightened rabbit and wait for the men to drag her to the ground without a fight. At the same time she knew it wouldn't be much of a battle, pitting her puny strength against three strong men.

Then, as she stood there, a hand clutching Digger's collar, a cold, deadly voice ordered curtly, "Stay right where you are, men."

Simultaneously, she and the riders turned their heads. A man had ridden quietly out of the fringe of the forest and sat watching them.

He was a big man, broad-shouldered, lean-hipped, and dressed in buckskins. Hard-faced, he lounged loosely in the saddle, his hand resting on his thigh only inches from a large knife shoved into its sheath.

There was a dangerous glint in his eyes as he asked in icy tones, "Are you men scaring my wife?"

Jassy somehow managed not to betray her surprise that the stranger had claimed her as his wife. She was so relieved, however, she wouldn't have cared if he had referred to her as his horse.

The three men were shaking their heads, vehemently denying that they had any intention of scaring the lady. "We only want to water our horses," the bearded one muttered hastily.

"If I believed that, I'd believe it was going to snow today." The stranger jerked a thumb over his shoulder. "There's a big lake only a few yards away. I'll give you two seconds to get the hell away from here."

"I guess we didn't notice the lake." One of the men tried to laugh but it came out like a croak.

The big man astride the stallion made no response to the obvious lie, but just sat waiting for them to leave. When they had ridden out of sight, in the opposite direction from the lake, Jassy let her breath out in a relieved sigh.

"I can never thank you enough for putting the fear of God in those lowlifes." She gave the stranger a wobbly smile.

He gazed down at her a moment, then asked quietly, "How do you know that I'm not looking for the same thing those men were looking for? Maybe I drove them away because I want you all to myself."

For a moment uneasiness gripped Jassy. Was that why he had seen to it that the others had left? Did he too have rape in mind?

She looked into his clear blue eyes and knew that he would never do violence to a woman. For one thing, he was so handsome he'd never have to resort to forcing himself on a woman. Most would probably be more than willing to make love with him.

Jassy shook her head and said with conviction, "You don't have that in mind."

"How do you know?"

She dropped a hand to Digger's head and said with a grin, "My dog isn't growling at you. He's a good judge of character."

The man grinned back. "I am hungry, though. If you'll give me and my mount a bite to eat, I'll do some work in payment." He ran his gaze over the cabin, then the barn.

Jassy knew he was appraising the run-down condition of the two buildings. She paused but a moment before saying, "Take the stallion to the barn, then come on up to the cabin. I have a pot of venison stew on the fire. It should be done right about now."

He nodded, lifted the reins, and rode toward the building that housed her mule and cow. "The name is Luke Slater," he called over his shoulder.

"Jassy Jeffers," she called back.

He lifted a hand and said, "Glad to meet you, Jassy Jeffers."

Inside the cabin, Jassy swung the crane that held an iron kettle over a bed of red coals to where she could reach it. As she ladled meat and vegetables into a large bowl, she thought of all the things that needed taking care of and wondered which of them she should ask Luke Slater to do in payment for his meal.

So many things had fallen into disrepair over the past two years. There were shutters to be tightened. Some of the stones in the chimney should be recaulked, as well as several places between the cabin's log walls. There were rails to be replaced in the fence that surrounded the pasture and her garden. And the yard gate was hanging by one hinge. She had to lift it up every time she opened or closed it.

The big barn door sagged a bit also. And a couple of rungs were missing from the ladder to the hay loft. Then there was the chicken house. Its roof leaked in a couple of places every time it rained, and the fenced-in area where the chickens were let out in the daytime needed a few sapling poles replaced. Wood creatures had almost clawed through in half a dozen places.

Jassy shook her head. There was so much to be done, so many repairs that her woman's strength couldn't handle. As she sliced bread from a loaf she had baked that morning, she wondered if this Luke Slater would stay on a few days, take care of all those pressing things for room and board. She couldn't pay him anything; she had only enough money put aside for necessities.

A shadow loomed in the doorway and Jassy looked up, pleased to see Luke wiping the dirt off his feet on the small rug in front of the door before stepping onto her clean floor. It showed he'd had a good upbringing. A fast glance at his face showed that he had stopped at the water trough and washed his face and hands. The front of his hair was damp and curling.

He smiled at her, and she motioned him to sit down at the table. "Help yourself, and there's more in the pot if you want it," she said before leaving the cabin to resume watering her plants.

She had debated sitting with him while he ate, to bring up the subject of his working for her a couple of weeks. She figured that a man as proud as he seemed to be would have to be pretty hungry to ask for food and would want to forget nice table manners as he filled an empty stomach.

Jassy had made two trips to the lake with her pail, and had watered the last bean plant when Luke came out of the cabin rubbing a full stomach.

"You're a fine cook, Jassy Jeffers." He grinned at her. "I hope you don't mind, but I helped myself to a cup of coffee. I hadn't had any for a couple weeks."

"That's quite all right." Jassy placed the dipper into the empty pail. "I should have thought and poured you some."

"I'm not one of those men who have to be waited on. I know my way around a kitchen." This last was said with a thin smile.

"My father was like that," Jassy remembered out loud. "When I was little and Ma didn't feel well he'd do the cooking, and even housework if necessary."

"I take it your parents are dead." Luke had seen the sadness in the hazel eyes behind the steel-rimmed glasses perched on her nose.

"Yes. A little over two years ago. Typhoid fever took them within two weeks of each other. They drank some bad water from a neighbor's well, the Johnsons. That couple died from the same fever also."

"So you've been carrying on alone."

"I've been trying to, but there's so much I can't take care of."

"Your cabin and barn look relatively new. You haven't lived here long, have you?"

"Only about two years. We came here from Minnesota to get away from warring Indians." Jassy waited for Luke to volunteer where he came from. When he didn't offer any information, she asked, "Are you from around here?"

After a moment Luke shook his head and answered, somewhat reluctantly, "No. I'm from Vermont. I'm also escaping a sort of war." He paused before adding, "A battle that made me end a marriage to a cheating wife."

Jassy looked at his stony face and said sincerely, "I'm sorry to hear that. I hope you don't feel too badly about it."

"I don't feel at all bad about it." Luke's face darkened. "I'm only sorry I didn't cut the strings two weeks after I married her instead of waiting over eight months."

"Now," he said in a tone that indicated he wasn't going to say any more about his past, "what can I do to pay for such a good, hearty meal?"

"Well," Jassy laughed, "there's so much that needs fixing around here I don't know what to choose. I feel like a youngster with a penny looking at an array of candy, trying to decide which piece would last longest."

"What about if I fix the shutters on the windows? If a grizzly should come along and decide he wanted to get into the cabin, those broken shutters wouldn't keep him out."

Jassy shivered. That very thing had happened at the Johnsons'. Luckily, they had not been home at the time, but the bear had made a shambles of their cabin. He had come in one window, torn open bags of flour and cornmeal, swept shelves bare, and broken furniture in his rage at not finding anything to eat. He had then left the cabin by breaking through another window.

"Where do you keep your tools?" Luke broke into the thoughts that had taken Jassy back to the past. "If I get started right away, maybe I'll have time to fix the hinges on the barn door. I noticed it's sagging pretty badly. Your animals would be right tasty to a grizzly or a cougar."

"I'd appreciate it if you could," Jassy said, leading the way to the shed where the tools were stored. "I've worried about my mule and cow. There are claw marks from a big cat all over the barn walls. I worry about my chickens too. Their house needs some work done on the roof."

"Jassy Jeffers," Luke said humorously, "you need a husband to keep this place up."

"Well, I don't have one and I'm not looking for one," Jassy snapped and stamped away, leaving her annoyance hanging in the air.

Luke watched her until she went into the cabin and slammed the door, a big grin on his face. Jassy Jeffers was as prickly as a hedgehog, he thought. No wonder she didn't have a husband. She was as plain as a rail fence to begin with, and a bristly disposition wouldn't endear her to a man looking for a wife.

But later as he began hammering at the first shutter, he thought to himself that he had never seen a more beautiful complexion than that of Miss Jassy Jeffers. It was so smooth and creamy-looking, completely flawless. His ex-wife Nell, although unusually attractive, had a coarse-grained skin, marred with several scars left from chicken pox.

He wondered idly if Jassy's skin was soft all over.

Every shutter on the cabin needed work. There were two with hinges so weak he'd had to replace them. Fortunately he found three in the shed, rusty but solid. From the accumulation of odds and ends piled in a corner, Luke guessed that Jassy's father had never thrown anything away.

By the time Luke finished mending the window coverings, the sun was almost ready to set. He had hoped to head out with a couple of daylight hours left so he could find a suitable spot to camp overnight.

His belly rumbled and he said to himself, "I wonder if Miss Prickly will offer me supper before I leave. There was a lot of stew left in the pot."

Luke had just climbed down the ladder when Jassy spoke behind him. "The shutters look good and tight. You've done a fine job. I'll sleep much more comfortably at night from now on."

"I'm sorry I didn't get around to fixing the barn door."

"I've been wondering," Jassy said with a slight hesitation, "if you'd be interested in staying on for a while, shaping the place up for me and chopping some firewood for this coming winter." Her perfect white teeth flashed in a smile. "I must warn you, though, that the winters are bad here in northern Michigan and it takes a lot of logs to keep the cabin warm.

"Also, I want to tell you up front, I can't pay you. I can only feed you and give you a place in the barn to sleep."

Luke thought a minute, then decided, why not? He had no particular destination in mind. He half planned to go on up to Canada and trap during the winter. A month's delay wouldn't make that much difference. And though Jassy wasn't much to look at, she was a damn fine cook.

He smiled at her and said, "It's a deal. I should be able to whip the place into shape within a month."

Jassy stepped up on the porch and turned to wave at the children one last time. They waved back and she paused a minute to wipe the snow off her shoes before hurrying inside where it was cozy and warm. Luke had gone all round the cabin outside, caulking between the logs, then had done the same thing inside. Not a breath of winter wind could get inside and set one's teeth to chattering. He had worked on the chimney until it now drew better than it ever had for her father.

Inside the cabin she set the egg basket on the table, then removed her shawl, shrugged out of her jacket, and hung them on a peg. She put the eggs with three others in a large gourd she had cured purposely for that use. Placed in the cool larder room with the lid placed tightly over them, the eggs would stay fresh for weeks.

She went to the fireplace where she poured herself a cup of coffee from the pot warming on the hearth. She sat down in a rocker to drink it.

As she sipped, her thoughts returned to Luke. She didn't know how it had come about, but Luke's month had stretched into two months, then another, and then another. It was now December and he was still here.

It seemed that every time he planned to move on, something always came up. First, he had insisted that he had to help her harvest the wheat, claiming that it was too much for a woman to do. Then it was time to gather the dry corn and take the yellow ears to the miller to be ground into cornmeal. He had loaded them into the wagon, along with bags of hulled wheat, and driven off to the mill alone.

That day when he returned home he looked a little cross and hadn't said a dozen words all through supper. When later, sitting in front of the fire, she asked him if anything was wrong, he answered brusquely, "Why should anything be wrong?"

She shrugged and fell silent. But her mind was still full of questions. Was Luke wanting a woman? After all, he was young and virile, had been married and used to the comfort that only a woman could bring a man.

She felt a stab to her heart when that thought entered her mind and she was tempted to throw away the ugly glasses with the plain glass, let her dark red hair fall into its natural curls, and once again wear the colorful dresses hidden away in her wardrobe. She was sick to death of the drab grays and browns she'd worn since her parents' deaths.

But she had felt that the alteration to her looks was neccessary as she lived life alone. Not that her plain appearance would keep her safe from some types of men, like those three last summer, but at least she wouldn't be drawing attention to herself, tempting men to come out to the cabin in hopes of sharing her bed for a while.

Jassy gave a small sigh. She guessed it was fortunate after all that she had looked so dowdy that July day when Luke rode into her life. Before two weeks had passed she had learned that he had no use for pretty women. In his words, he wouldn't trust one to give him the right time of day. Had she looked her normal self that day, he would have taken care of her shutters and then ridden away. Chances were, actually, he probably wouldn't have asked her for something to eat in the first place. She knew, however, that regardless of what she might have looked like, Luke would have saved her from those terrible men. He was a very honorable man.

And a very dour one lately, she thought, rising and going to the window to gaze out on the cold, white world. Where had Luke gone today? she wondered. Had he gone hunting, or to the small fur post to kill some time with male friends or female company?

Chapter Two

Jassy awakened to the sharp scent of pine. She frowned, confused. Was a window open in the cabin? Surely not. She'd heard no noise of a cat breaking into the cabin. And even if she had missed that noise, she certainly would have heard the report of the rifle if Luke had shot it.

"Oh, for heaven's sake," she suddenly exclaimed, turning over on her back. She had remembered why the pine scent was so strong in the cabin.

Luke had brought home a Christmas tree yesterday afternoon. That was why he had disappeared for a while. She had been stunned when she glanced out the window to see Luke riding across the bare wheat field, his stallion, looking very insulted, dragging the pine tree behind him.

She had thrown a shawl around her shoulders and stepped out onto the porch just as Luke pulled Prince to a halt. He had looked at her, an uncertain smile on his handsome face, and said, "All our neighbors have their trees up, I figured it was time we did the same."

Christmas spirit rushed through Jassy. This Christmas would not be like the last two. She would have someone to share it with. Someone special. Someone she had fallen in love with, she realized in that second. That knowledge so stunned her it took a moment before she could say breathlessly, "It's a lovely tree, Luke."

Luke's smile widened, giving him an almost pleased, boyish look as he untied the pine from the singletree he had fastened on to the stallion.

"Lean it up against the cabin so I can sweep the snow off before you bring it inside," Jassy said, stepping back inside to fetch the broom.

When she came back, Luke took the broom from her. "I'll do it. Do you have a stand for it?"

"There's one somewhere in the storage shed. It's two thin boards crossed and nailed together."

Luke nodded, then said, "You'd better get back inside now before you catch cold."

"Yes, I believe I will," Jassy agreed, but she had never felt warmer in her life. It had been so long since anyone had cared about her welfare.

As she put supper on the table she softly hummed the tune of a song she used to sing with her mother at this time of year.

She was slicing bread when Luke opened the door and carried the tree inside. "Set it over there opposite the fireplace," she directed him when he looked at her questioningly. "That's where we always put our tree."

Luke stood the tree in the corner as told, turned it a few times so that the best side faced the room. "How's that?" He stood back so she could get a clear view of the pine.

"Beautiful!" Jassy exclaimed. "I think it's the nicest tree this cabin has ever known. I can't wait to trim it. I'll pop a big pan of popcorn after supper."

"To string and wind around it." Luke grinned. "That brings back some good memories."

"For me too," Jassy said quietly, then made herself smile brightly as she added, "Supper is ready if you are."

The evening meal had a festive quality, conversation flowing easily between Jassy and Luke. Luke spoke of the holidays spent with his parents in Vermont, how he and his sister had always looked forward to Christmas.

Jassy learned that the sister was married and still lived in the same village where they had grown up, and that Luke had a niece and nephew.

Then, as they drank their coffee, Luke spoke of his ex-wife. "Nell was the prettiest girl in our village. She had long black hair, laughing brown eyes, and teasing red lips. Every single man, and some married ones, chased after her, including me.

"She had always favored red-headed Mike Sullivan over the rest of us. Then one day the Irishman slipped away in the middle of the night and was never heard of again.

"It was then Nell turned all her attention on me. I thought I was the luckiest man in the world when she agreed to marry me."

Luke's face took on a grim look. "From the beginning it was pure hell living with that woman. My first disappointment was finding that she wasn't the virgin she pretended to be. I could have dealt with that had I known which man, or men, had been there before me. But not knowing, every time I talked with a friend I couldn't help wondering if he had been with Nell and was secretly laughing at me.

"On top of everything else, a week after our marriage I realized I was tied to a shrew. She was always complaining, never took an interest in the small cabin Pa and I built for her. It was always a mess, the table was never clear of dirty dishes, the bed never made up. The meals she served were unbelievably bad. I finally ended up cooking most of the meals."

Luke paused to refill his cup from the coffeepot sitting on the table as though he needed its bracing effect to go on. Jassy wondered if she should stop him from continuing the story that had made his face so stony. But she had the feeling that telling it was cleansing his mind of the woman he'd married, so she sat quietly and listened as he continued.

"We'd been married about a month when Nell started having morning sickness. At any rate, that was the first I was aware of it. At first I was happy she was in a family way. I told myself that with a baby to take care of she would settle down, not be so restless, that just waiting for its arrival would make her more content."

Luke shook his head. "She only grew worse as the child grew inside her. As her swollen stomach distorted her figure, and her face and ankles swelled, she became sullen and carped day and night, blaming the little one for causing her to lose her looks.

"It was the worst eight months I ever spent in my life."

Jassy gave him a startled look. "Eight months? You're saying that she had an early delivery?"

"When she went into labor that's what I thought." Luke's lips curved in a mirthless smile. "But when she birthed a strapping baby boy with brick-red hair, I knew, as did everyone else in the village, that it was a full-term baby and that Mike Sullivan had sired it."

Luke turned his head to stare into the fireplace. "It was the last straw. I had already lost any feelings I'd ever had for Nell, had realized early on what a shallow, selfish woman she was. To learn that she had never cared for me, had only used me to give her child a name so that she could keep up the pretense of respectability, was just too much." His lips twisted wryly. "I guess it hadn't occurred to her that her child might have its father's hair.

"At any rate, I'd had enough and I went to the preacher who had married us and had the marriage set aside. The papers are in my saddlebag. The most important thing I own. I saddled Prince then, and here I am, a wiser man. I'll never go near a pretty woman again."

"It's not fair for you to take that attitude," Jassy objected indignantly. "I know a lot of women who are very pretty and are good, decent people. You mustn't compare every attractive woman you meet to your ex-wife."

"Here's the way I look at it," Luke broke in before Jassy could go on. "When a woman has more than her share of good looks, men are always eyeing her, hanging round her. In time she's going to weaken from all that attention and she's going to cheat on her husband."

"You're wrong, Luke Slater," Jassy said, anger in her voice. "My mother was a beautiful woman who men always stared at, and she never looked at another man with romantic notions on her mind."

"Maybe there are rare cases," Luke finally agreed, but Jassy didn't think he meant it. She had heard doubt in his voice.

What were his plans for the future? she wondered. Did he intend to remain single for the rest of his life, or was he going to seek out a plain woman to marry next?

Possibly herself? Jassy's heartbeat picked up at the thought. She smiled inwardly. If so, he'd feel duped again. For beneath her skinned-back hair and wire-rimmed glasses she was the image of her mother, and she was tired of her camouflage. She longed to once again wear her pretty dresses, let her hair fall into its natural curls around her shoulders, and throw away the ugly glasses.

Stop your fanciful thoughts, Jassy Jeffers, she told herself. *Luke will never have such feelings for you. When he looks at you he sees a dried-up old maid. You've outdone yourself in looking plain and unattractive.*

After giving herself that advice, Jassy stood up and began scraping the table scraps into a pan for Digger. "In time you'll change your mind, Luke," she said. "You'll want a wife and home again. As you said, you're a wiser man now. You'll be able to see beyond a facade, read any falseness that may lay hidden beneath the skin."

Luke cocked an eyebrow at her. "Do you have someone in mind, Jassy?" he asked with a wicked, teasing smile, but there was a seriousness deep in his blue eyes.

Jassy became flustered, and in her agitation she knocked a cup to the floor. She hated the red flush she felt rising to her cheeks and prayed that Luke wouldn't notice.

"Of course not," she finally managed, "but there are some very nice women in the area."

"I know," Luke said, finishing his coffee and standing up to go sit before the fire. "It might interest you to know I've got my eyes on one."

Jassy felt as if all the blood had left her body. Luke was already interested in someone to replace his wife. She wondered in dull misery which of the young women in the area Luke had set his sights on.

When she had popped the corn and Luke had helped her string the white kernels on long strings, they talked of inconsequential things. Luke's mood was light and contented, Jassy's dispirited and pensive.

*   *   *

Jassy put aside her painful thoughts when she heard Luke moving about, then smelled the aroma of fresh-brewed coffee.

After he'd moved into the cabin they'd fallen into a comfortable routine. He rose before she did, built up the fire, and put on a pot of coffee. It was so nice for Jassy, getting up in a warm room and having a cup of coffee before starting breakfast. A ragged sigh escaped her. She was going to miss that, and him, when he married the woman he had his eye on.

She scooted off the bed, yanked the gown over her head, and hurriedly stepped into her underclothes, then dressed in one of her drab dresses. She left her hair in its braid, and put the hated glasses on her nose. She stepped from behind the blanket that cordoned off her bed, anxious to get breakfast out of the way. There were yards of stringed popcorn to drape on the tree, a box of homemade ornaments under the bed. Some were quite old, going back to the time when she was a youngster.

Luke greeted her with his usual warm smile, then picked up the milk pail. When he left the cabin to milk the cow, Jassy thought, *We're almost like a married couple.*

But as she washed her face and hands her little inward voice niggled, *Except for one thing you are. He isn't sharing your bed, and it doesn't look like he wants to. He's got someone else in mind for that.*

"Shut up!" Jassy hissed, and went about preparing breakfast.

*   *   *

"Some of these are very beautiful, Jassy," Luke said as she handed him an embroidered baby Jesus to hang on the tree. "Did you help your mother to make them?"

"A few of them, I did. But Ma made most of them herself. She was very handy and creative with needle and thread." She held up a white lacy crocheted star. "I think this is her finest piece of work. It goes on the very top of the tree. It's supposed to be like the star that guided the three wise men to the baby Jesus."

Luke carefully took the fragile article in his hands. "How did she get it so stiff? It almost feels like wood."

"She soaked it in sugar water, then stretched and pinned it on a towel to dry."

She grinned at Luke. "I always got to hang it."

"Well," Luke said, grinning back, "this seems to be the last thing to hang on the tree. Pull a chair over here and put your star up there."

Jassy had to stretch a little on the wobbly chair to reach the top. The tree was about eight inches taller than all the others had been. But by standing on her toes she managed to secure the little treasure on the topmost branch.

She ran into trouble when the chair began to totter on one uneven leg and she lost her balance, falling sideways. Luke shot out his hands and caught her around the waist before she hit the floor. She stood facing him a moment, calming her nerves, then started to pull away.

Luke did not lessen his hold on her. Instead he drew her closer and closer until her body rested against his, his sudden arousal pressing against her stomach. She looked up and grew weak at the darkening look of passion in his eyes.

He's going to kiss me, she thought, her pulses racing, and stood on her toes, her lips parted invitingly.

The kiss didn't happen. Luke released her, saying in a cracked voice, "I'm sorry, Jassy, I don't know what came over me."

But I wanted you to kiss me, Jassy almost cried out. Instead she righted the chair. Before she could say anything, a knock sounded on the door. Jassy's hands went to her flushed face, and Luke shoved his hands into his pockets.

"You'd better get it," he said with a humorous grin, sitting down in the rocker and resting an ankle on his opposite knee.

Jassy rubbed her damp palms over her hips, and willing her face not to show the turmoil going on inside her, crossed the floor and opened the door.

The settlement's gossip, Emma Coulson, and her daughter, seventeen-year-old Jemma, stood smiling at her.

"Good morning." Jassy's welcoming smile included both visitors. "Hurry in by the fire." She opened the door wider.

"It sure is cold out there," Emma said, stamping the snow off her boots. Jemma followed her mother's example, craning her neck for a glimpse of Luke, who now stood up.

"Good morning, ladies," he said, coming to help Jemma off with her coat and scarf, sending the plain-faced girl into flustered giggles.

Emma's fat face beamed as he led her daughter to the fireplace and settled her in the chair he had just vacated. A tiny frown etched its way across Jassy's forehead. Was Jemma Coulson the one Luke had his eyes on? The girl was plain enough, although pleasant-looking. She was on the plump side, and after a couple of babies would probably be as fat as her mother.

Once the visitors were settled before the fire, with Luke entertaining them, Jassy set about pouring coffee and placing a platter of cookies on the table. When she had added a bowl of sugar and a small pitcher of milk, she called out, "If you ladies are thawed out, come have some refreshments."

Jemma went into another fit of giggles when Luke assisted her from her seat, keeping a hand on her elbow as they moved to the table.

How can he stand that silly tittering? Jassy thought irritably, taking her seat at the table. She mused later that she might as well have not been there for all the attention she got. Every word and look from her visitors was directed at Luke.

Emma fired so many questions at Luke, he couldn't eat a cookie or take a sip of coffee he was so busy answering her. Where did he come from? she asked. Were his parents still alive? Did he have any brothers or sisters? Did he plan on staying in the settlement?

The three women grew quiet at this question, each waiting eagerly for his reply. Jassy had wondered many times what his plans were. Did he intend to stay on in the settlement, and marry whomever it was he had set his sights on? And if he did, could she bear seeing him with a wife and children?

Neither she nor the others saw the look that Luke shot her before he answered, "I'm not sure yet whether I'll stay or move on. I'll make up my mind after Christmas."

He stood up. "Now, if you ladies will excuse me, I'm going to step outside for some fresh air."

"Stop by for some coffee and cake," Emma invited as Luke pulled on his jacket. "Jemma makes a delicious pound cake."

"I'll bet she does." Luke smiled at the blushing girl. "I'll have to stop by and sample it someday."

When he left with a wave of his hand, it was hard to tell who was more pleased, the beaming mother or simpering daughter.

There was no elation on Jassy's face. Had either woman looked at her she'd have seen pain in Jassy's shadowed eyes.

Her companions left shortly after Luke's departure, and Jassy was glad to see them go. If Jemma giggled one more time, Jassy was afraid she might slap her.

As Jassy went about clearing the table, washing and drying the cups and spoons, her mind was on Luke, re-creating the way he had held her. It had been plain that he wanted her, had meant to kiss

her there for a moment. What kept him from it?
The woman he intended to marry? He was the
type of man who would be true to a woman he
cared about.

What could he be doing outside so long? she
wondered, hanging up the dish towel. He had
been gone for at least an hour. When another half
hour passed, she realized he had gone off somewhere. Where? To visit the unknown woman?

Chapter Three

The cold wind knifed through Luke's fur-lined jacket as he reined the stallion onto the snow-packed trail that would lead him to the post. He welcomed the silence that was broken only by Prince's hooves clipping along on the frozen ground. If he'd had to stay another second in the company of Jemma Coulson and her nervous, silly laugh, he would have ordered her to shut up.

I shouldn't have led her on, he thought, feeling a little guilty, *but I had to do something. That gimlet-eyed Emma would have noticed right away that something had just happened between me and Jassy. The only thing I could think to do was to throw her off the scent by showing interest in her daughter.*

He smiled. Jassy hadn't liked it one bit. She had tried to hide it, but he had seen the tightening of her soft lips when he'd made a big to-do of helping Jemma off with her coat and then leading her to a chair.

Jassy had welcomed the kiss he had almost given her. Reason had come to him only a second before he lowered his mouth to hers. If he had kissed those sweet, red lips, he knew he would sweep her up and carry her to the bed behind the blankets.

And that would have put him only one step above the three men who had meant to rape her last summer. His taking her would be wrong, too. She was ignorant of every aspect of lovemaking. His experienced, stroking hands would have her surrendering to him in minutes.

"And how she would have hated me afterward," he thought out loud. No, Jassy Jeffers's first introduction to lovemaking must be in the marriage bed with a man she loved.

And he wanted to be that man so badly it was driving him half crazy. But did Jassy Jeffers love Luke Slater?

A pair of scampering chipmunks darted across the trail, startling the stallion and causing him to snort and rear up. Luke left off thinking of Jassy as he fought Prince back to the ground.

When the animal calmed down, Luke noted they had arrived at the shallow end of the frozen Sunset Lake. He steered Prince out onto the beaten path across the ice, thinking that Jassy's father had chosen wisely when he bought his tract of land. In the winter when the ice was a foot deep a man could ride straight across the lake instead of traveling halfway around as one had to do in summer.

Of course, when the lake was thawed out a man had only to jump into a boat and row across. That was if he was lucky enough to live at the narrow end of the water. If he happened to live dead center in one of the many stump-dotted clearings, he would have a hard row of it, crossing a hundred-acre lake.

But no matter where a man chose to settle in this vicinity, the land itself was very fertile in this untouched wilderness. He and Jassy had raised and harvested an abundance of food, plenty to see them through the winter.

And as for fresh meat, the deer were so numerous a man didn't have to go far before he could bring one down. He had only one thing to worry about in the winter: getting lost in a sudden blizzard.

Luke hunched his chin in his collar, telling himself that this great white north was a man's paradise. Anything he could desire was here. He could fish and farm in the summer, trap for furs in the winter.

Furs were the reason he was making this cold ride today. A couple of weeks ago he had gone through the beaver hides he had trapped along the lake and had laid aside the thickest and softest of them. He had then taken them to an old woman in the Indian village about a mile away. He'd arranged with her to make them into a jacket for Jassy. It was to be a Christmas gift. That holiday was only a week away, and the old woman had promised she'd have the jacket at the post today.

How would Jassy accept his gift? he wondered. With coolness? With pleasure? Or would she accept it at all? She was a deep one.

Damn, he wished he knew how she felt about him. Sometimes she smiled at him with real affection, other times she held herself aloof, chilling him with her coolness. Her actions today told him that he could arouse her passion.

He wondered if she knew her neighbors were talking about her; about them both. Claiming that they were living together in sin.

As Prince stepped along, Luke wished he and Jassy were living together in the way the gossips meant. He had wanted to share her bed for a long time. Only recently had he wanted it to be in an honorable way, though, as man and wife.

At first he had scorned the idea of ever marrying again. He had tried wedded bliss once and suffered because of it. A man who stumbled over the same stone twice was a fool. It wasn't long, though, before he was arguing with himself that there was no way to compare Jassy with Nell. Nell was loud and selfish and man-crazy, whereas Jassy was a lady in every sense of the word. She was gentle and soft-spoken, her movements graceful even in those awful clothes she wore.

Luke's loins suddenly stirred. Those old-woman clothes Jassy wore hid the most beautiful body he had ever seen.

He had been at the farm a couple of months when one sweltering hot day he decided to go down to the lake and swim to cool off. There was a spot where some willows grew close to the bank, their branches extending out over the water, a perfect place to swim in privacy, stripped to the skin.

When he arrived at the shaded area, he was startled to see that Jassy had had the same idea and was there before him.

She stood with her back to him, in water a little past her ankles, a bar of soap in her hands. She had come to the lake to bathe. He told himself to turn around and leave, but he couldn't take his eyes off the slender back, the narrow waist that flared into gently rounded hips and long, shapely legs. He watched her soap her back and delightful little rear, then gasped when she turned slightly and he saw the profile of proudly jutting breasts.

God! he thought, *they're just right to fit in my hands.*

He had finally come out of his trance and told himself that it was a shameful thing, watching in secret while Jassy took a bath. He had slipped quietly away, but since then, every time he looked at her he was seeing what lay beneath the drab dresses. The sight of her beautiful body was branded on his mind, a fire in his blood.

He had thought to quench that fire with one of the tavern women at the post, but had never done so. After living with Jassy, who was so clean-smelling, so fresh and flower-scented, the stench of the post women revolted him now, made him wonder how he had ever used their kind in the past.

Luke remembered that Nell hadn't always smelled all that good either. She wasn't one to bathe very often, and in the summer one was aware of it.

As the stallion moved along, Luke thought back to the night he had moved from the hayloft in the barn to his present spot, the loft room in the cabin. The room Jassy had called hers before her parents passed away.

The late November day had been cloudy and windy, the temperature dropping fast. That evening as he walked to the barn after supper the first snowfall of the season roared in. And though he buried himself deep in the hay, and had left all his clothes on, he couldn't stop shivering. When his teeth began chattering, he knew he had to go ask Jassy for some extra covers.

She hadn't gone to bed yet when he rapped on the door, and he saw her peek through the heavy window covering before letting him in. Jassy never took chances.

"What is it, Luke?" she asked anxiously. "Is there a cougar prowling round?"

"No," he answered, grinning wryly. "It's too cold out for beast or man to be out. I was wondering if you could loan me a couple quilts. That cold wind is finding every crack in the barn."

"Of course. Go stand by the fire and warm up while I get them."

He was standing in front of the fireplace, gazing down into the flames, wishing that he could curl up in front of them for the night, when Jassy turned from her linen chest, a thoughtful look on her face.

"You know, Luke, it's only going to get colder in the barn as winter wears on," she said, and he had held his breath, afraid that she was going to say that maybe it was time he left her and sought work with a farmer who would give him a warm bed in his cabin.

Her next words left him weak with relief. "Maybe you'd better sleep up in the loft room. I should have thought of it before. It's my old room and has a very comfortable bed. Let me light a candle and get some linens and we'll go make up the bed."

As they climbed the ladder that was almost flush against the wall, his eyes remained glued on her hips. It was all he could do to keep his hands off them.

When he stepped up on the hewn wide-plank floor, he discovered a full bedroom. There was a wide bed with a small table beside it, a chest of drawers, a rocking chair, and a waist-high bench on which sat a basin and a pitcher. On the bed lay a ticking woven of cotton and tow, stuffed with hay, and on top of that a ticking filled with feathers.

Together they smoothed on sheets and slipped cases over the pillows. Jassy had gone to her chest of drawers and pulled out the bottom one, taking from it a comforter filled with soft goose feathers.

Jassy had smiled at him and said, "You'll be toasty warm under this."

Luke's lips curved in a humorous grin. She had made him hang blankets around her bed the next morning, giving her some privacy. Miss Jassy Jeffers was a very proper lady, and he would have her no other way.

Just when he had fallen in love with Jassy he couldn't pinpoint. It had happened gradually as they worked the farm together, she right along beside him, doing her share, so unlike Nell who was downright lazy. He had found that it was relaxing, being round Jassy. She never chattered like most women, going on and on about some trival matter. Sometimes an hour would pass with no words spoken between them. It was a comfortable silence, as each thought his own thoughts. And she, like himself, liked her private time.

Jassy wasn't a dour person, though. She had a quick wit, could always see the humorous side of things. He recalled her sparkling laughter the time he slipped in mud and landed hard on his rump. And she was so gentle with youngsters and old people. As he watched her with the little ones, he'd think what a good mother she would make, always adding that he would like to give her a baby.

How much longer, he wondered, could he continue sleeping under the same roof with her and keep his hands to himself? It was gut-wrenching to watch the shadow of her body that the candle-light cast on the blankets as she prepared for bed. He could see her every movement as she pulled her dress over her head, then shed her underclothes and laid them in a neat pile on the chair. It was all he could do not to groan aloud his frustration when she stood bare a moment, every lovely curve silhouetted, before she pulled a gown over her head, hiding her lush body in its soft folds. He knew that she had no idea what she was revealing to him.

The stallion snorted and came to a stop and Luke came out of his reverie. The post stood in front of him.

It stood in an isolated clearing about a hundred yards from the lake. It was a long, low building made of logs, and was divided into two parts. The front of the building held general merchandise that a farmer or a trapper might need. It was also where Bill Dimmer, the owner, bartered with trappers and Indians for the furs they brought in.

A door led into the back part of the building where a man could drink and chat with friends, and if he so desired, accompany a whore to the log house a few yards behind the post.

Luke rode the stallion around to the back of the post where Dimmer had erected a stable of sorts so that a man's mount wouldn't have to stand out in the cold while its owner stayed inside where it was warm. He even provided hay for the animals. Luke dismounted and dragged open the solidly built stable door, one that could withstand a charging cougar.

As he pitched Prince a forkful of hay, he recognized two horses and a mule that belonged to his neighbors. A couple of dogs curled up in a corner opened their eyes to look at him, then went back to sleep.

When Luke entered the post by the front door, Bill Dimmer, short and squat and balding, gave him a genial smile, then motioned toward a dark corner. "She's been waitin' for you since I opened up early this mornin'."

Luke crossed the floor and hunkered down beside an old woman who looked as ancient as primeval rock. "You have finished the jacket, Little Deer?" he asked softly.

Little Deer nodded and reached behind her. She brought forth a beautifully fashioned garment. As Luke took it from her, she gave him a toothless smile and said, "Your woman will not feel a breath of cold air when she wears it."

Luke ran his hand over the soft fur, inspected the seams, ran a gauging eye over the hood, making sure it was big enough to fit over Jassy's heavy head of hair. He smiled at the anxious-looking old woman and said, "You've done a fine piece of work, Little Deer. My woman will be well pleased." He handed her the money agreed upon, plus an extra dollar.

A pleased smile deepened the many wrinkles on the weathered face; then Little Deer jumped to her feet and hurried to the counter behind which Dimmer stood. As Luke went through the door and on to the tavern, she was arguing price on the items she was purchasing. He smiled wryly. That one would get her money's worth.

He was welcomed warmly by the six men leaning against the rough plank bar. He had gotten to know Jassy's neighbors over the summer and liked the hardworking family men. They were always ready to pitch in and help each other, which was the only way a man with a family could survive in this beautiful, harsh land.

However, the four men sitting at a table in a corner didn't greet him with friendly voices. They only directed sullen looks at him. They were trappers who had been drinking since early in the morning and were most likely looking for trouble, Luke thought as room was made for him at the bar.

And it will be me they'll try to release their spleen on, he told himself after ordering whiskey from the burly bartender. He had tangled with one of them a couple of weeks back when he caught the man robbing one of his traps. In fact, the trapper still wore a bruise on his cheekbone where Luke had hit him. He could hear them muttering among themselves, their words salted with obscenities.

Luke and three other men were talking about getting up a pinochle game when the one he had fought with slurred out loudly, "Hey, Slater, we've been wonderin' just how good that skinny, prim and proper Miss Jeffers is in bed. Could you enlighten us? If you give her a good recommendation, maybe we'll go give her a visit."

A burning rage stiffened Luke's body. How dare they say Jassy's name in a tavern? The pewter cup that had been raised partway to his lips was slammed back onto the bar. As the whiskey sloshed out of it, he spun around, facing the drunk.

"You bastard," he ground out, his lips thin and his eyes icy cold. "You're not fit to say her name, let alone in here. I'm going to wipe the floor up with your ugly face."

"Is that right?" The trapper jumped to his feet, his chair going over backward sending the tavern women scampering out to the safety of Dimmer's store.

Raw hatred for each other galvanizing both men into action, they rushed toward each other, their intent to hurt, to maim. The fight didn't last long. When the trapper drew a knife from the top of his boot, Luke ducked beneath the down-plunging blade, and bringing his fist up from his knee, landed it on the point of the trapper's chin.

Disappointment gripped him when his opponent crumbled to the floor, his eyes rolling back in his head. "Damn," Luke swore silently. "I wanted to beat the bastard to a pulp. How can I pummel an unconscious man?"

As he stood over the fallen man, his fists still clenched, Bill Dimmer came rushing into the room, the slatterns crowding behind him. Fixing a fierce look at the fallen man's companions, he ordered, "Get him the hell out of here and all four of you keep goin'. When you learn how to act like decent folk you can come back."

Their faces dark with resentfulness, two of the trappers hauled their limber companion to his feet and dragged him out of the tavern.

"Come on, Slater." Dimmer clapped Luke on the back. "Finish your whiskey and calm down.

Not that you ain't got good reason to be upset," he added.

Luke pushed his way through the men who had gathered to watch the fight, and finished his drink. He ordered another and took it with him when he and three others moved to the table where the trappers had sat and set up a pinochle game.

Guilt gripped Luke so hard he could hardly concentrate on his cards, even found it hard to count points. It was his fault that Jassy's name had been bandied about in a tavern. That day in July he should have ridden away after fixing her shutters. What had kept him there? Had he felt sorry for the plain, bespectacled woman who had so many things that needed repair, things that she couldn't do? Had he immediately liked the little farm and cabin and wished that they were his, or had he, even then, unconsciously felt attracted to the quiet-spoken woman who had hidden her fear from the three men who undoubtedly meant to rape her had he not come along?

Most women would have been crying and begging the men to leave them alone. But she had stood there, fire in her eyes, ready to pit her fragile strength against their brute force. He admired spunk, whether it be in humans or animals.

Luke sighed inwardly. He had to make up his mind about Jassy. Either he had to ride away, or ask her to marry him. Of the two options marriage was what he wanted in the worst way. But did Jassy? If she turned him down, he didn't know how he could handle his disappointment, be able to ride away from her. She had become a neccessary part of his life.

When the other players twitted him about not having his mind on the game, he forced his unsettling thoughts of Jassy from his mind and put all his attention on the cards in his hand. He became so deep into the game that when Dimmer came into the tavern and mentioned that a blue norther was raging outside, he didn't even hear him.

The hanging overhead lanterns were lit and the men played on, intent on the game. Night had come on when the storm quickened and the wind grew to a howling gale.

"What the hell," one of the men swore when a gust of wind blew the side door open. Finally aware of the storm raging outside, they all jumped to their feet, exclaiming in unison, "I've got to get home."

The bartender closed the door and dropped a bar across it. He gave them a grim look and said, "You men ain't goin' anywhere tonight. You wouldn't get ten yards in that white curtain out there before you'd be lost. And if you were lucky enough to find your way, your lungs would be frozen before you reached home."

Each man there knew the bartender spoke the truth. They had heard of such things happening in the frozen north.

As the men stood with worried faces, wondering if their families were all right, Dimmer entered the tavern, a pile of blankets in his arms. He unloaded them onto a table and said, "Feel your way along the wall out there and cover your mounts with these. When you come back, I'll have some venison stew on the bar for you, and more blankets to make pallets with. All you'll have to do is keep the fire going all night and you'll be warm enough."

They thanked the big man, and with Luke carrying a lantern, they felt their way to the stables. In the freezing cold they hurriedly tossed some hay to their mounts, then spread a blanket over each of their backs. When the men fought their way back inside the tavern, the two dogs were at their heels.

Very little was spoken between the men as they ate the tasty stew. Their minds were on their families, wondering if they were all right. Good nights were said, and each man rolled up in a blanket before the fire.

Luke was a long time falling asleep. Was Jassy frightened of the raging wind and blowing snow? She must have lived through blizzards before. He didn't fear for her well-being. She had food in the cabin, and he had stacked almost a cord of wood on the porch. And he'd be home as soon as daylight arrived.

Chapter Four

The sky became overcast around noon and Jassy started making trips to the window, staring down the trail that led to the post. She imagined that was where Luke had gone, since she had discovered that the stallion wasn't in the barn.

She admitted to herself that it wasn't any of her business when Luke left the farm, nor where he went. She did feel, however, it would only be a common courtesy to at least say he was leaving.

She contented herself with the thought that he always came home in time to milk the cow and tend to the animals before he ate a meal. He had a hearty appetite, being such a big man.

Taking a long string of dried beans from a rafter, she placed it in a basin of water to soak up the moisture the sun had dried out of the vegetable. They would go well with the pork roast she planned to serve for supper.

Two hours later the sky was dark and ominous-looking, with great black clouds roiling overhead. The temperature was dropping and a cold wind had risen. Jassy knew beyond a doubt that they were in for a blizzard, a bad one.

With one last look out the window, and seeing no big stallion coming up the trail, she pulled on her heavy jacket, tied a scarf around her head, and stepped outside. She might as well fasten the lead rope that stretched from the porch to the barn while she was thinking about it.

Every farmer had such a rope. During a snow-storm it could be the lifeline between the two buildings. Many a man and woman had become turned around in a blizzard and frozen to death only feet away from their cabin.

Fighting the gale-force wind that sometimes took her breath away, Jassy managed to run the rope to the barn and secure it to the big door. On her return she carried enough wood inside to see her through the night and dumped it in the woodbox.

It was three o'clock when Jassy crumbled dry sage leaves over the piece of pork, added salt and pepper, and slid it into the oven that had been built into one side of the large fireplace. The third time within an hour, she looked out the window hoping to see Luke riding in. She only saw the frozen white pellets of snow that was beginning to fall. She told herself that surely Luke would be home soon.

Christmas Surprise

Four o'clock arrived and the snow was coming down in earnest, and still no sign of Luke. She was becoming concerned. Another hour and he'd be unable to see his way home. As she turned from the window, the lowing of her cow drifted on the wind. She knew that the animal was in pain from a full udder and that she must be milked.

Bundled to her eyes, a wooden pail in her hand, and Digger at her heels, Jassy fought the wind to the barn. She tossed some hay to the mule and put a good amount of shelled corn in the cow's trough. The animal chomped on it contentedly as the milk was drawn from her.

When Jassy opened the barn door, the pail half full of milk, she gave up her plan to feed her chickens. The snow was falling so thick and heavy that all visibility beyond a foot ahead was shut off. She grabbed hold of the rope, thankful that she'd had the foresight to string it between the two buildings.

Jassy felt that she was halfway to the porch when Digger lifted his head and sniffed, his nose pointed to the right. Just when she thought it might be Luke returning home, Digger's hackles rose; then a deep growl rumbled in his throat. She stared intently in the same direction, then gave a frightened gasp. She could make out the dim shape of a large cougar.

His eyes shone red and his tail lashed from side to side as he inched toward them. She couldn't move until he stopped and crouched on his belly ready to spring. Her muscles were released then and she was yelling, "Come on, Digger," as she ran as fast as she could, the rope sliding through her gripping hand.

In seconds she was on the porch, her cold fingers fumbling with the latch. It readily lifted and she was inside, pulling the furiously barking Digger behind her. She had just slammed the door shut and dropped the bar when she heard the large cat bounce onto the porch. He lunged against the door, screaming his anger that his prey had gotten away.

The raking of his great paws against the door didn't frighten Jassy. She had no fear that it would give, for it was made of heavy wood and hung on strong hinges.

"But what about the shutters?" she asked herself fearfully. Luke had mended them all, but would they hold against the large animal? He was one of the largest she'd ever seen.

Jassy tried to hush Digger, but the hound was in a rage that equaled the cat's and continued to jump against the door, the cabin ringing with his fierce barking.

She suddenly began to laugh hysterically. She still gripped the milk pail in one hand. Some milk had splashed out in her mad rush to the cabin, but most of it was still inside.

She commanded herself to calm down and placed the pail on the table, thinking with relief that the cow and mule were safe from the cat. She had shrugged out of her jacket and hung up her scarf when the beast started clawing at the shuttered window over the drysink. Her fingers trembling, and a prayer on her lips that

290

the shutter would hold, she lit the two candles on the table with a flaming twig she carried from the fireplace. The candlelight still didn't push back the darkness enough to please her, so she lit two more and placed them on the mantel.

Hurrying to the door, she took down the rifle that hung above it.

The cat had moved to the window next to her bed and was still screaming his fury as Jassy sat down in a rocker, the loaded rifle lying across her lap. If he did get in, she hoped that she could kill him with one shot. For there was nothing more dangerous than a wounded cougar. He could claw her to death before she could get off another shot.

As she sat on, the wind continued to howl and the snow to hiss against the windows. Digger continued to bark and the cougar to scratch at the shutters. Jassy leaned her head back and thought of Luke. Was he lost out there in that white world, trying to find his way home?

She somehow doubted it. He was the type of man who could take care of himself in any kind of situation. She felt pretty sure that he was holed up somewhere waiting for the storm to pass, or until daylight arrived.

But holed up where? An aggravating little voice inside her reminded her of the niggling question she asked herself every time Luke went to the post. Did he go there to spend some time with menfolk, or did he make that ride to visit one of the tavern women in the cabin behind the post? Was he in bed with one of them right now, cozy in her arms?

She'd had glimpses of those women a few times, their hair all frizzed, their faces painted and their dresses scandalously short, showing their knees, as well as a lot of bosom. Their eyes said they were wise in the ways of pleasing a man in bed.

A thought that Jassy had been pushing to the back of her mind all day wouldn't be denied any longer. Maybe Luke hadn't gone to the post at all. Maybe he had ridden to visit the woman he'd said he had his eye on. Maybe he was bundling with her, warm and cozy beneath a heavy quilt.

Bundling was a winter custom when couples were courting. Of course, they were supposed to keep all their clothes on, which was laughable. Almost every spring there was a young female with child when she took her wedding vows. One needn't strip to make a baby.

Jassy pictured in her mind all the single women in the settlement, trying to decide which one Luke might be interested in. Jemma Coulson's round face kept returning to her. She couldn't believe that Luke would have any serious thoughts about that simpleton.

Jassy jumped to her feet, tired of trying to figure out what Luke's plans were. She had to strain the milk and store it in the cold larder room. Although Digger was still barking, the cat had ceased scratching at the windows. Jassy hoped he had given up and gone away.

A couple of minutes later, the milk in a cloth-covered crock, she opened the storage door and dropped the crock with a scream. The cat had discovered the small window near the top of the ceiling and had broken through the thin sheeting of wood that covered it in the winter. The window was only about ten inches by twelve, just large enough for the cougar to get his head through. He saw her and hissed his frustration that he couldn't pull the rest of his huge body through the opening.

Jassy saw her chance to shoot the animal and darted back into the cabin, almost tripping over the hound who had gone into a frenzy at the sight of the cat. She grabbed up the rifle and dashed back into the larder. The animal was still intent on getting into the small room. She raised the firearm to her shoulder, took careful aim, and squeezed the trigger.

A round hole appeared between the eyes that glared at her; then a split second later the window was empty.

Jassy slumped back against the wall, her legs trembling. As though he knew there was no more danger from the cat, Digger had stopped barking and was now lapping up the spilled milk. She picked up the crock that had broken neatly in half and tossed the pieces into the trash can next to the sink.

Relieved of her fear, Jassy was suddenly hungry. She thought of the roast she had put into the oven at three o'clock and glanced at the clock. It was a little past seven. The pork had been in the oven for four hours and would now be unfit for consumption. She shook her head, remembering the spilled milk. She had certainly wasted a lot of food today.

She put half a pot of coffee on the coals to brew, then fried a slice of ham to make herself a sandwich. She gave Digger a thick slab as well.

After eating the light supper, Jassy opened the door, holding her hand up to shelter the candle against the wind as she stared intently into the white night.

There was no sound, nothing to see but the driving snow. A mood of depression settled over her as she closed the door. She added a log to the fire, changed into her gown, and went to bed, leaving the two candles on the table burning as a guide to Luke if he was lost out there.

She pulled the covers over her head, praying that he was all right wherever he was.

Luke awakened to a gray dawn. His three companions slept on, two of them snoring loudly, as they had done all night. Jassy came immediately to mind. Was she all right? Had she worried when he didn't return home?

He threw back his blanket, rose stiffly to his feet, and walked to the window and looked outside. A smile lit up his face. The storm had blown itself out. However, it had left at least a foot and a half of snow in its wake. There would be drifts up to his waist in some places, and he'd have one hell of a time getting home.

And that he must do as soon as possible. Seeing how much snow had fallen, he had visions of Jassy in dire need of him. Not knowing the purpose of the coiled rope tied to one of the porch's supporting posts, a horrible thought gripped him.

What if she had gone to the barn to milk the cow and tend her mule and then couldn't find her way back to the cabin? What if a cougar or a pack of wolves had come along and attacked her?

Suddenly he couldn't wait to get home. Home. How wonderful the word sounded.

He shook awake his three companions of the night, saying, "Come on, men, the storm is over, let's get going."

The men were immediately awake and on their feet, anxious to get home to their families. They were folding the blankets they had slept on when Dimmer entered the room, a steaming coffeepot in his hand.

"Here's some coffee for you fellers. Can I make you somethin' to eat before you take off? It's colder than billy-be-damned out there."

All four men agreed that a cup of coffee would set well, but that they would wait until they got home to eat.

The bracing brew was quickly drunk, then the men were ready to leave. Dimmer laid four pairs of snowshoes on the bar. "Strap them on, men, you're gonna need them."

With the shoes clamped on their boots, the men thanked Dimmer for his hospitality, then clomped through the door, out into the icy air.

They found their mounts stamping their feet against the cold, white vapor escaping from their nostrils. They saddled their horses and led them outside. They separated then, each man going his own way.

Luke found it slow going at first. Prince floundered several times in drifts up to his chest. At such times Luke had to break through the barriers and pull the stallion through them.

When Luke had fought his way across the frozen lake for about half a mile, he came to a spot where the wind had swept the surface of the ice clear of snow. He peered ahead, and as far as he could see, the ice was clear all the way across the lake. He drew Prince to a halt, unstrapped the clumsy webbed snowshoes, and swung onto the stallion's back. Half an hour later he was emerging from the forest and gazing at the little cabin sitting in its small clearing.

Smoke rose from its chimney, and relief whistled through Luke's teeth. Jassy was all right!

He rode on past the cabin, headed for the barn. There he stabled Prince, gave him and the mule a fork of hay and some corn to the cow. When he had secreted Jassy's Christmas gift up in the hayloft, he began mushing his way through the snow, anxious to get in front of the fire and thaw out.

He was almost there when he saw the cougar tracks. His heart skipped several beats. Was Jassy all right after all? He tried to run in the knee-deep snow but it was impossible. It seemed to take forever to reach the porch and fling open the door.

Jassy awakened at the first pale light of dawn. She lay quietly, listening. There was no howling wind, no hiss of snow against the cabin's walls. The storm had passed sometime during the night.

She leaned up on an elbow and pulled aside

one of the blankets that hid her bed from the rest of the room. Her gaze went straight to the wall where outer garments were hung on pegs.

Luke's jacket was not hanging beside hers.

She dropped the blanket and lay back down. She had hoped that maybe he had come home and gone to bed without disturbing her. That would have been hard to do, she reminded herself. Her sleep had been so light and restless she'd have heard the slightest sound. Between worrying if he was lost somewhere in the storm, and wondering who he was sleeping with if not trying to get home, and the image of the cougar's head stuck in the window, she had had very little sleep.

Jassy stared up at the rafters vaguely visible in the semigloom of the room. What should her attitude toward Luke be when, and if, he finally came home? Should she be her normal self or should she greet him the way she wanted to . . . throw herself into his arms, pull his head down, and press her lips against his?

Her lips curved in a wry smile. She'd shock his boots off if she did that.

One thing she was sure of, she must hide her suspicions that he had spent the night with some woman. That would expose her jealousy, an emotion she had no right to have. It was going to be difficult, though, she knew.

She sat up and reluctantly left the warm covers, and in her bed stockings hurried to the fireplace. Kneeling on the hearth, she raked the dead ashes off the red coals that lay beneath them and added small pieces of wood on them. When they took fire, she added several split logs and soon had a roaring fire going, sending heat out into the room. She went back behind the blanket wall and got dressed in a heavy muslin petticoat and a dark gray woolen dress.

Back in front of the fire, Jassy stripped the stockings she had slept in off her long, smooth legs and drew on black ribbed ones. She was lacing her mid-calf shoes when Digger whined and went to the door, his tail wagging eagerly. He probably has to go outside and lift his leg against a tree, Jassy thought, although that wagging rear end could also mean that Luke had finally come home.

She tied off the laces, hurried to the window, and opened the shutter. She was in time to see Luke leading the stallion into the barn. She hurriedly washed her face in a basin of cold water, catching her breath from the shock of its iciness. She made sure that her hair was skinned back in its usual fashion, then perched the glasses on her nose. Next, she hastily put a pot of coffee to brewing.

Jassy was slicing bacon when Luke burst into the cabin. His eyes wild, a day's whiskers darkening his firm jaw, he looked like a madman as he demanded anxiously, "Are you all right, Jassy?"

Jassy stared at him. He seemed genuinely concerned about her. Would he be that upset about her welfare if he intended to marry another woman?

After telling herself that naturally Luke would care whether or not she was all right, they were friends, weren't they, she smiled at him and answered, "Yes, I'm fine, Luke."

Luke pulled a chair away from the table and plopped down on it, some of the pallor fading from his face. "I saw cougar tracks out there and I was scared to death the beast might have gotten into the cabin. I didn't know what I'd find in here."

Jassy wanted to ask if he'd have cared had he found her with her throat torn out but knew it would be an inane question. Of course he'd care. He'd care regardless of who might be killed by a wild animal.

She smiled at him again and said, "As you can see, I'm quite all right. But I did have an awful scare. When I was coming from the barn yesterday afternoon, that beast chased me into the cabin, then tried to get inside. The shutters held, thanks to your good work. Then he tried to come through that little window in the larder room."

"That's when I shot him between the eyes."

"You didn't!"

"Yes, I did. You'll find him out there dead in the snow." Her eyes twinkled behind the ugly glasses. "Do you think you could skin him and tan the pelt? He'd look and feel real good in front of the hearth."

"I can skin him and I know an old Indian woman who can cure the hide. I don't know how to do that. I'll take the knife to the critter as soon as I've had breakfast and done the milking."

He looked up at Jassy, apology in his blue eyes. "I'm sorry I wasn't here last night to tend to the animals and to keep you from being frightened by the cat. I only intended to play a few games of pinochle with our neighbors. We got so involved trying to beat each other, the first thing we knew the sun had set and a blizzard was raising hell outside. There was no way I could get home."

"You must be starved," Jassy said, not daring to look at him for fear she'd blurt out, "Where did you sleep?"

Luke nodded. "I am a bit. Dimmer gave us some stew for supper and blankets to sleep on in front of the fire. He offered us breakfast before we left this morning, but all we'd take was a cup of coffee. We wanted to get home."

Relief almost rendering her speechless, Jassy managed to get out, "Bill Dimmer is a fine man, feeding you men and letting you sleep before the fire."

"Well, it was a humane thing for him to do, but wouldn't most men do the same thing?"

"I guess so." Jassy felt foolish making such a big to-do over something that any of her neighbors would have done. She hid a tickled grin when he grumped, "I didn't get much sleep. Two of the men snored all night. One on each side of me."

"Maybe you can catch a nap later. You can use my bed."

"I might as well. I sure can't do anything outside."

When Jassy carried the skillet of bacon to the fire, Luke's loins stirred as he watched her bend over the fire. He sure wished that she'd be napping with him.

Chapter Five

Jassy smiled contentedly as she sat before the fire, the knitting needles in her nimble fingers flashing in the firelight as they purled and knit in fashioning a scarf from a ball of dark blue yarn.

She feared the throat protector meant to be a Christmas gift for Luke wouldn't be finished in time. There were only four days left until that holiday, and only a little over half of it was finished.

It had been difficult to knit in secret since Luke was in the cabin most of the time since winter had set in. Almost always she went to bed first. Before Luke retired he liked to see to the banking of the fire for the night, check that the shutters were fastened tight, and let Digger out to visit his favorite tree.

Again Jassy thought how like a married couple they were in so many ways as she carefully untangled a piece of yarn. The only thing missing, as the aggravating little voice inside her delighted in pointing out, was that they didn't sleep together.

Her lips twisted wryly. Luke was sleeping in her bed now. Had been since early this morning.

She glanced at the clock. It was a little after one. He should be stirring pretty soon. She hoped so as she put the yarn and unfinished scarf in her knitting bag. She wanted to bake another batch of cookies for the holiday. She already had two big crocks filled with them in the larder room, plus two mincemeat pies and a fruitcake, all tightly sealed with a plate on top of them. She would slice the cake and serve it to her neighbors when they started stopping in to wish her a merry Christmas. It was the custom in the settlement to visit each other during this time of year.

As Jassy stood up she wondered if Luke would accompany her when she returned her friends' visits. But should he? she wondered. Maybe the neighbors might put some importance to it. As if there were a romance between them.

As she amassed flour and sugar and spices on the table, then went to the larder to get the small crock of butter, it occurred to Jassy for the first time that her neighbors might be talking about her and Luke. A thoughtful frown creased her forehead. They didn't know that Luke slept upstairs in the loft room, did they? Didn't they think that he still slept in the barn?

She thought back, trying to remember if she'd had company who might have seen some evidence that Luke now shared the cabin with her.

She couldn't think of a time, but she'd be careful from now on that none of Luke's clothes were lying around when someone stopped in. Although she knew that she and Luke were perfectly innocent of any wrongdoing, others might not think so.

Jassy was briskly stirring the cookie batter when Luke stepped from behind the blanket, stretching and yawning. He had removed his boots and shirt before lying down on her bed, and she admired his broad shoulders in the close-fitting undershirt. Her gaze traveled up to his hair-tousled head and she grinned. He looked like a big overgrown boy.

"Why did you let me sleep so long?" Luke glanced at the clock.

"I figured there was no point in waking you up since there's nothing you can do to spend the time."

Luke's blue eyes twinkled teasingly. "I could be talking to you. Or," he went on, "I could go visit Jemma and have a piece of the cake her mama says is so delicious."

Jassy felt that Luke was talking in jest, but wasn't too sure. She slid a quick sideways glance at him and found his face perfectly sober.

She didn't respond to his remark right away as she spooned the spicy dough onto a cookie sheet. But inside, pain and jealousy were building.

Then, as though her inner voice was directing her words and actions, she slammed the spoon into the empty bowl and said through clenched teeth, "Why don't you do that? I'm sure I don't care. You can bundle with her until the spring rains for all that it matters to me. And you can go to the post and sleep with a whore for all the difference it would make to me."

Luke's lips drew into a tight line as Jassy's skirts swished angrily as she strode to the fireplace, shoved the dough into the oven, and slammed the door. When she returned to the table and started clearing it, he gave her a hard smile and said, "Maybe I'll just do that! Maybe I'll bundle with Jemma a couple hours first and then go on to the post and sleep with all the whores there."

"Fine! I'm sure it won't be the first time."

"The hell it won't! I've never touched one of those tavern women yet."

Both were out of control now, their voices raised and shouting, when Jassy yelled, "Well, don't let me keep you from doing it now."

Luke opened his mouth to cut back at her, then closed it when a loud rapping sounded on the door. When he spun and went to sit before the fire, Jassy brought a semblance of calm to her face. Whoever was out there, had they heard her and Luke quarreling? she asked herself as she went to the door. And what must they think of the words angrily yelled?

She opened the door and wished it was all a dream. Her neighbors Jake and Sue Ellen Anderson and a stranger stood smiling uncertainly at her. Of all the people in the settlement, this pair was the last she'd want to hear the shouting match that she and Luke had engaged in.

Sue Ellen wasn't one to preach the Bible to a

person, but she was a firm believer in people doing what was right. Jassy liked and respected her. She swallowed, to bring some moisture to her mouth that had gone dry, and opening the door wider, she smiled and said, "How nice to see you and Jake, Sue Ellen. Come by the fire."

"We can't stay long, Jassy," Sue Ellen said as she took off her jacket and head scarf. "I don't like to leave the younguns home alone very long. Lela and Amos tend to get into arguments which sometimes lead to hitting each other." She grinned. "And that leads to Jake doing some hitting on their seats."

Sue Ellen turned to the stranger who had taken off his heavy black coat and stood waiting to be introduced. Jassy's eyes widened a bit when she saw the white clerical collar fastened around his neck. A reverend! Where did he come from? There was no preacher among the residents of the settlement.

With a proud smile, Sue Ellen said, "Jassy and Luke, I want you to meet my brother, John Donner. He came for a short visit which has been lengthened because of the blizzard, and we are very happy about it. We don't see him nearly often enough."

John Donner gave Jassy a warm handshake and smile, then turned and offered his hand to Luke, who had risen to his feet.

"Do you have time for a cup of coffee and a slice of my fruitcake?" Jassy asked, her nerves settling a bit.

"Yes, we have time for that," Sue Ellen answered, sitting down at the table. "Then we want to bring up a delicate subject."

Jassy knew intuitively what the delicate subject was. She and Luke living together. But how did they know that Luke now slept in the cabin? They had to be guessing.

Even as she told herself that, however, she saw Sue Ellen looking pointedly at Luke's undershirt, then at his boots lying on the hearth. She knew that next her neighbor would see his razor and shaving mug on the shelf under the small tin mirror. That, if nothing else, was a dead giveaway that he was sharing the cabin full time.

When her company was seated and Jassy was putting out the cake and pouring coffee, Luke pulled up a stool to sit on, leaving the extra chair for Jassy.

Although the Andersons were their normal friendly selves as they drank their coffee and praised the fruitcake, Jassy felt her nerves tightening up again. She glanced at Luke and knew by his taut features that he was uneasy also. He evidently guessed what the delicate subject Sue Ellen had referred to would be.

When the cake was eaten, Jassy pressed her company to have more, putting off as long as she could hearing what was coming. She was sure that Sue Ellen was going to say that it wasn't right for a single man and woman to live together and that Luke should move on.

Would he agree? she wondered. In all likelihood he would. There was Jemma, after all. He'd be welcomed with open arms at the Coulsons'.

Her heart seemed to drop to her feet at the thought. She was so deep in misery she scarcely heard Sue Ellen when she said, "Well, what do you think, Jassy?"

Jassy could only stare at Sue Ellen a moment, the thought of losing Luke still gripping her mind. "I'm sorry, Sue Ellen, but I didn't hear your question."

"It wasn't a question, girl," Sue Ellen said impatiently, "It was a statement. I said that you and Luke should get married."

"Get married!" Jassy exclaimed, her tone so sharp that Digger rushed to her side as though she was in danger. As Luke watched her through eyes that had suddenly narrowed, she asked, "Why should we get married?"

Sue Ellen looked at her reproachfully. "Jassy, you know it's not right for you and Luke to be living together without benefit of marriage. Your mother and father must be spinning in their graves."

"But we're not living together," Jassy denied.

"That's right," Luke spoke up indignantly. "Who says that we are?"

"Only half the settlement, Luke." Jake spoke up for the first time. "Several men have passed by the cabin at night and seen a candle burning in the loft room. Common sense told them that Jassy wouldn't be lighting up an empty room."

There was a long strained silence as Jassy and Luke accepted the fact that their secret was no longer secret.

While Luke cursed inwardly that Sue Ellen had

ruined his plan of courting Jassy awhile, then asking her to marry him, Jassy wanted to curl up and die of embarrassment. Luke was a gentleman. Even though his heart was set on another woman, he would do what he thought was right. To marry Jassy Jeffers, save her reputation.

I mustn't let that happen, she thought to herself. *I must say firmly that I don't want to marry him.* She started to speak, to say she had no desire to get married at the time, but Luke spoke before her.

Taking a long breath, Luke said, "I'll leave in the morning."

Jassy felt as if a fist had been delivered to her chest. Those were the last words she had expected to come out of Luke's mouth. She knew now that above everything else in the world she wanted to be his wife, no matter how she got him. But he must never know that, she added as she forced her features not to show their dismay.

She waited for the Andersons and the preacher to rise, put on their jackets, and say good-bye. She badly needed to get to the privacy of her blanketed corner and let the tears that were choking her run down her cheeks.

But Sue Ellen wasn't satisfied with Luke's announcement. Looking at him, she shook her head and pointed out, "It's too late for you to leave now. The damage is already done. If you go away, Jassy's reputation will be in shreds. She'll never be able to marry a decent man. If you respect Jassy, you must marry her."

Jassy shot a glance at Luke and felt chilled to the bone. His jaw clenched tight, he looked like a cornered animal not knowing which way to jump.

Her pride shattered, she asked herself if marriage to her was that distasteful to Luke. Well, she thought determinedly, no one would ever know how torn up she felt.

"Look," she said sharply, her eyes flashing, "that decision isn't entirely Luke's to make. I have some say in the matter. I would rather remain an old maid and be talked about than to enter into a marriage where there is no love."

"Jassy, what are you saying?" Sue Ellen sounded scandalized. "A woman's good reputation is the most important thing she can own. Love will come to your marriage in time. I can tell that you and Luke like each other, and that's very important."

Jassy wanted to cry out, *But Luke has already chosen the woman he wants to marry. He'll end up hating me.* She glanced up at Luke to say again that she didn't want to marry him, and caught her breath.

Luke was smiling at her. When he said, "I think we would suit, Jassy," she could only stare at him a moment before muttering, "I suppose we could muddle through somehow."

"Good!" Sue Ellen exclaimed, her eyes sparkling. "What about having the wedding on Christmas Eve? Doesn't that sound romantic?"

Romantic? Jassy bit out to herself. Sue Ellen could say some outrageous things sometimes. Here she had just practically forced two people to marry each other against their will and had the nerve to make off that it was a love match.

Not to be completely rolled over by Sue Ellen, Jassy tried to take some control. "Christmas Eve is only two days away. I need more time to get ready."

"Time for what?" Sue Ellen demanded, then teased, "Do you want to sew yourself a white wedding gown?"

When Jassy shook her head and looked at the floor, though that had always been a dream of hers, Luke said in a cold, clipped voice, "Jassy has every right to wear white when she stands up with me."

"Oh, Jassy, I didn't mean that to sound the way it did." Sue Ellen left her chair to come hug Jassy's shoulders. "I was just making a joke. You know as well as I do that no one here in the settlement has ever been married in a special white dress. It would be a waste of hard-earned money to buy the material even if we could get it."

Jassy smiled at her friend, knowing that she truly meant her apology. Sue Ellen often spoke before thinking. But how nice of Luke to set them all straight about her right to wear white when she took her vows with him.

"So," Sue Ellen said with a grin, "what is your excuse not to get married on Christmas Eve? Tell the truth, don't you have all your holiday baking done?" She looked toward the corner where the shapely pine stood. "You even have your tree up. What's so pressing that you can't be ready in two days?"

Everything that Sue Ellen said was true, so

Jassy could only give in and say, "Christmas Eve it is."

"Good. Now, what time should we be here, and do you want any of your other neighbors to come along with us?"

Luke answered before Jassy could. "Just you and Jake and the preacher will be fine. I'll be nervous enough with just you folks looking on."

The preacher grinned, and Jake slapped Luke on the back and said with a laugh, "It's hard to give yourself over to a woman's rule, ain't it, Luke?"

Luke would have liked to say that it would be no hardship giving himself over to the gentle Jassy. If only she loved him, he added.

Finally Sue Ellen was ready to go home. She was still talking about the wedding as she drew on her jacket. Jassy didn't know if she was relieved or disappointed when Luke donned his jacket, picked up his rifle, and without a word to her followed their guests outside.

The four of them passed from her view as they went around the corner of the cabin, leaving her with no idea what direction Luke had taken.

Was he going to the post? The sun would set in another hour. Or had he gone to tell the other woman that he was getting married in a couple of days?

Her teeth worried at her bottom lip. If Jemma was the one he had chosen to marry, there would be hard feelings when he married someone else. The Coulsons would probably never speak to her again.

With a long sigh Jassy began to clear the table of the cups and plates and flatware, still pretty much in a daze. She was going to get her heart's desire.

As she went and sat down in front of the fire and picked up Luke's unfinished scarf, she wished that it was Luke's desire to be married to her.

She took up the knitting needles and began knitting and purling. He would be her husband when she gave it to him on Christmas Eve. A rueful smile curved her lips. When she had started the woolen length, she never dreamed that one day she would become Mrs. Luke Slater.

Would she be a wife in name only, she wondered, or would Luke claim his conjugal rights? She knew that men, and some women, didn't have to love the person they made love to. Luke didn't love her, but she remembered she had aroused him that day when he had swept her up against his hard body. She had felt the evidence of it.

Yes, Jassy thought, Luke would want to consummate their becoming husband and wife. She didn't quite know how she felt about that. If Luke loved her, she would look forward to their wedding night as eagerly as he. But knowing that there was no love on his part, she feared she'd feel used.

The knitting needles clicked away, the blue yarn sliding through her fingers. Another four inches and the scarf would be finished.

Luke parted with the Andersons and preacher Donner at the barn. It was with relief that he watched the three walk single file along a narrow, snow-packed trail leading through the forest. Their cabin and holdings were a scant mile away.

Finally he could relax, he told himself as he saddled Prince and led him outside. He didn't think he could have gone on much longer, pretending that Jassy's reluctance to get married didn't bother him. It bothered the hell out of him. He wanted her to want it as much as he did.

And dammit, he felt confident that had he been given time to court her she would have accepted him when he proposed. A closeness had been growing between them, a warmth that he had been nurturing toward the time he'd ask her for her hand.

Now, thanks to Sue Ellen's meddling, Jassy was being forced to a commitment she wasn't ready for. She was bound to resent it, resent him.

Luke swung onto Prince's wide back and nudged him to move out. The thought hit him that there was nothing to say he couldn't court Jassy after they became man and wife. His spirits lifted somewhat, and he put his mind to the reason he was taking this cold ride. He wanted to find and shoot a wild turkey for his and Jassy's Christmas dinner.

Half an hour later Luke pulled Prince in on a small rise at the fringe of the forest. He had an unparalleled view of the valley below. He had picked up on turkey tracks right away and had been following them all this time. He had begun to wonder if he'd ever catch up with them. The sun would set soon and he wanted to get home before darkness came on. Wolf packs would be running then, and Prince would look awfully good to the hungry animals.

He stood up in the stirrups suddenly and stared off to his right. He had heard the gobbling call of a turkey. "Ah ha!" he exclaimed under his breath, sighting several big birds feeding on the seeds of tall grass that rose above the snow. He was close enough to see the red wattles under their necks.

He ran his gaze over the flock a minute, pulling his rifle from its saddle sheath, and gripping the stallion's sides with his knees, signaling it not to move, he brought the fire-piece up to his shoulder. Taking careful aim at a good-sized hen, he squeezed the trigger. She fell over on the ground, her head shot off. The rest of the wild ones ran awkwardly toward a stand of pine, making a raucous noise. A pleased smile on his handsome face, Luke guided Prince down the incline to retrieve his trophy. It would make real good eating on Christmas day. The beginning of his life with plain, sweet Jassy.

Jassy folded and smoothed the blue finished scarf, thinking how warm it would keep Luke's throat. The one he had been wearing had seen better days.

She glanced out the window and was startled to see that the red ball of sun was beginning to sink below the timberline. In another fifteen minutes darkness would be setting in.

She placed the Christmas gift in the sewing

basket at her feet and covered it with a small white tea towel. She didn't want Luke to see it until she gave it to him on Christmas Eve.

Rising, she walked to the window on the kitchen side of the room, thinking that Luke had better return soon or he'd be caught out in the dark.

As she stood and gazed through the glass pane, watching a pair of squirrels scurrying about looking for their supper before daylight faded, she began to wonder if Luke even planned on coming home tonight.

A dismaying thought struck her. Maybe Luke wasn't ever coming back. It was possible he had left the area for good in order not to marry her.

Jassy was so convinced that she would never see Luke Slater again, a rush of hot tears glimmered in her eyes. "Accept it, Jassy Jeffers," she whispered fiercely, rubbing her eyes. The first words that came out of his mouth when Sue Ellen was badgering him was that he would leave. The rest of the time he just pretended to go along with the meddling neighbor.

She squared her shoulders, reconciling herself to going back to her lonely existence, doing all the chores on the farm besides. Milking the cow was the first in order. As she turned from the window, a movement in the woods caught her notice. She spun back around, her lips parted in a wide smile of thanksgiving.

Luke was riding in, a wild turkey tied to his saddle. He had gone hunting for their Christmas dinner.

Chapter Six

The night before their wedding was to take place, Jassy and Luke sat before the fire, their stockinged feet propped on the hearth.

They had sat this way countless evenings during the winter, but tonight was different. Both were deeply aware that this time tomorrow night they would be man and wife.

The same question was on the minds of each. Would they be sharing the bed in the corner? Would the blankets that had been hung for Jassy's privacy be taken down, folded and put away?

I shouldn't press sharing her bed right away, Luke said in his mind. *We haven't even kissed yet.* There had been only that one act of intimacy between them, and that had been on his part when Jassy had started falling off the ladder and he had grabbed her, then lost his head and obeyed the dictates of his body to snatch her softness into his arms. She had felt so good, so right, pressed against him. It had been all he could do not to kiss her.

He had known, however, that a kiss wouldn't be nearly enough and had had the good sense to release her while he could still keep his hands from stroking all over her.

Luke wondered now if he should have listened to his conscience that day. If he had followed the urging of his body, they might already be married and there wouldn't be this uneasiness between them.

He came to the conclusion that he would follow Jassy's lead tomorrow night. He would know by her actions whether or not he was to join her in bed.

As Jassy sat beside Luke, gazing into the flames, she thought of what tomorrow would bring and looked forward to it with excitement and reluctance. Although a thrill ran through her every time the thought of marrying Luke crossed her mind, there was the knowledge that he didn't love her.

Was she making the mistake of a lifetime binding herself to a man who wanted to marry another? Damn Sue Ellen Anderson for sticking her nose into something that wasn't her concern. Luke was having the same doubts she had, for she had sensed him looking at her several times and had expected each time for him to say that he had changed his mind about marrying her tomorrow.

A sigh drifted silently through her lips. She was so tired of thinking about it, worrying the whole thing through her mind. When the clock struck nine she pretended a sleepy yawn and stood up. "Good night, Luke," she said in his direction, not looking at him. "I'll see you in the morning."

"Good night, Jassy," Luke answered quietly, and as was his habit before retiring, sat and watched the shadows cast on the blankets as Jassy undressed and changed into her gown.

Would she do that in front of him tomorrow night? he asked himself, hoping fervently that she would.

The first part of the day went pretty much in the usual fashion. Luke rose from bed before Jassy, stirred up the fire, and put on a pot of coffee to brew. Then he picked up the milk pail and went to the barn.

As usual, Jassy waited in bed until the room warmed up a bit before rising and getting dressed. And as the day wore on, though each appeared their normal self on the surface, inside they were a bundle of nerves with the unanswered questions running through their minds.

In the early afternoon Jassy baked three loaves of bread and checked a half dozen times on the refreshments she would serve the Andersons and Reverend Donner after the ceremony. There was a platter of thinly sliced ham that she had baked the day before, covered with a cloth so that it wouldn't dry out, and flanking the meat was a dish of sweet pickles she had put up in the summer and a small dish of homemade mustard.

And for her company's sweet tooth there were the cookies, of oatmeal and spice and nuts, plus the fruitcake and mincemeat pies. There would be buttered rum for the men and sweet cider for her and Sue Ellen.

Around three o'clock Luke saddled Prince and disappeared for close to an hour. Jassy immediately began to wonder if he had ridden off to visit Jemma, and to ask herself if that would continue after they were married.

What would she do if that happened? Would she demand that he stop? And would he if she did? When he returned to the cabin whistling softly to himself, she wanted to slap his face. How could he go about, seemingly carefree, while she was so miserable?

At four o'clock Luke milked the cow, fed all the animals, and gathered the eggs. When he had brought in the wood for the night, Jassy put out a light supper of beans and cornbread. They would be having sandwiches later.

By the time supper was eaten and the table cleared, it was time to get dressed for the event that Sue Ellen had insisted upon. She and her husband and brother would be here at five o'clock. Luke lit a candle and carried it up to the loft room, and Jassy carried a lighted one into her makeshift bedroom.

Inside the narrow enclosure Jassy placed the tallow on the bedside table next to the white pitcher and basin, then dithered over her two

Sunday-best dresses, trying to decide which to wear. Both were of fine woolen worsted that fitted perfectly her upper body before falling in a soft gathering at her waist.

She gazed at the sky-blue one with its white lace edging on the small collar and cuffs, then switched her eyes to look at the green one with a wide collar of lace which she had crocheted. She had worn neither dress since her parents' passing. Since then it had always been the drab, shapeless dresses she pulled over her head each morning.

She finally decided on the dark green one. It would bring out the green in her hazel eyes. She left it hanging on its peg while she undressed and took up the pitcher and poured water into the basin. Picking up a soft piece of flannel and a bar of rose-scented soap she had made last summer, she began her sponge bath.

Upstairs in his room, Luke found it easy to choose what he would wear. It was his black trousers and snow-white shirt with a black string tie, or a pair of clean buckskins. The Indian garb was out. He wanted to look his best when he stood up with Jassy. He wanted their marriage to be as special to her as it was to him.

He could only vaguely remember marrying Nell. All he had been able to think about that day was to get it over with and get her in bed.

Luke sat down on the edge of the bed to draw on the black boots he had polished yesterday. His feelings for Jassy were so different from what he had felt for Nell. Since falling in love with Jassy, he now knew that he had never loved his first wife. What he had mistakenly thought was love had been only lust. There had never been any quiet times with her, when they sat before the fire talking and laughing together. It had never been as it was with him and Jassy. They enjoyed each other's company even when they had nothing to say.

He stood up. All he had left to do was go downstairs, brush his hair, and wait for the preacher.

In her room, Jassy smoothed the skirt down over her shoe tops and buttoned up the five white bone buttons. She took up her brush then and swept it through her hair until the russet-colored tresses fell into deep waves past her shoulders. She hated pulling it back into the knot she'd worn for more than two years, but she was going to keep up her pretense of looking plain until after the marriage. If Luke demanded his rights tonight, her hair would be released and her phony glasses thrown away forever. She was tired of pretending to look so plain when she knew that she wasn't. Her mother and father had always claimed she was the prettiest girl in the settlement.

As she settled the glasses she smiled wryly. Of course they would think so. Emma Coulson probably thought the same thing about their plump daughter, Jemma.

She took a deep breath, parted the blankets, and stepped into the room. Luke raised his head from staring into the fire and glanced at her, then really looked at her.

By God, he thought, Jassy might be plain of face, but her shape could knock a man's eyes out.

He had seen the back of her the time she bathed in the stream, but faced with a front view of her in a dress that fit her almost took his breath away.

Jassy tensed under Luke's close appraisal. Didn't he like her dress? Did he think it too plain for the occasion? He looked so handsome in his black pants and white shirt. He looked a little more tamed somehow.

Then Luke lifted his gaze to her face, and as he thought that she looked almost beautiful despite the severe dressing of her hair and the ugly glasses, his face broke into a slow smile, and Jassy relaxed. He stood up and walked toward her, his hand held out.

"You do me proud, Jassy Jeffers," he said softly.

Jassy smiled up at him as he led her to a chair, but before she could compliment him on his good looks, a rapping sounded at the door. Luke grinned and remarked as he walked to open it, "They're early. Sue Ellen can't wait to see us hitched, to make an honest woman of you."

He swung open the door and Jemma Coulson giggled and said, "Hi yah, Luke."

While Luke gaped at Jemma and her mother, Emma said, "Since you ain't been over to see us, we decided to drop in and say Merry Christmas to you and Jassy."

"Well . . . that's nice," Luke managed to say. "Come on in."

Jassy stood beside the chair where Luke had led her, nervously twisting her fingers in the gathers of her skirt. Of all the times for those two to come visiting, she thought. The Andersons and the preacher would be here any minute. What would Emma and Jemma think when they learned that Luke was going to marry Jassy Jeffers instead of Jemma?

"Why are you two all fancied up?" Emma asked as she struggled out of her jacket. "Are you goin' to a party we don't know about?"

Luke looked at Jassy to see if she was going to explain why they were all dressed up, and when she didn't speak but only stood there in confusion, he walked up to her, put an arm around her shoulders, and said, "Jassy and I are getting married this evening."

"Gettin' married?" Jemma's voice was shrill and her eyes wide. "To each other?"

Luke felt a stab of guilt at the dismay in the young girl's voice. By flirting with her that one time to make Jassy jealous, he was now hurting Jemma. He took a deep breath and said gently, "Yes, Jemma, to each other. We'd like for you to be happy for us as we will be for you when you marry one of the young men who eye you every chance they get." He asked God his forgiveness for the lie he'd just told.

"They do?" Jemma looked mollified. "I never noticed any of them lookin' at me." She gave Luke a coy look. "Do you think I'm pretty, Luke?"

Luke grinned at her and told his second lie. "You're as pretty as a speckled pup, Jemma."

Emma, however, wasn't so easily soothed. She'd never noticed any of the young men looking at her daughter. Her lips finely drawn, she bristled, "When Jemma does get married it won't be a have-to case." She shot Jassy a spiteful look. "She won't have a babe started in her belly."

Luke scowled and Jassy paled at the thinly hidden insult. Jassy looked down at her clasped hands. It was only natural that Emma would think the way she did. Everyone else probably thought the same way.

Jassy lifted her head and stiffened her spine, her chin held proudly. Time would prove Emma and everyone else wrong in their thinking. She'd just have to weather their gossip for a while.

While Jassy had been reconciling herself to her situation, Luke had composed himself and now told his third lie. "That's the way it should be. I'd never marry a woman who let me sleep with her before marriage."

Emma's eyes were still snapping angrily, but before she could respond to Luke's statement, Sue Ellen's laughing voice was heard outside on the porch. Jassy gave a sigh of relief and rushed to open the door.

"You two all ready to tie the knot?" Sue Ellen asked gaily, stepping inside, her cheeks rosy from the cold. As her husband and brother followed her, she spotted Emma and Jemma. Her face showed her surprise as she said, "I didn't know you had been invited to the wedding, Emma. Jassy said she didn't want a big to-do made over it."

"We wasn't invited," Emma huffed, and taking Jemma by the arm she hustled her toward their jackets hanging on the wall. "We'll be goin' now."

"Now that you're here, Emma, why don't you stay?" Jassy followed the irate woman across the floor. "We're going to have refreshments after the ceremony."

"Thank you, but no." Emma refused to be appeased. "We just stopped in for a minute."

"Well, Merry Christmas," Jassy said. "Maybe we'll see you tomorrow."

Emma didn't say yes or no, nor good-bye as she stamped outside. When Jassy closed the door behind mother and daughter, she looked at Sue Ellen. That sprightly woman shrugged her shoulders indifferently as if to say, "Let her go, who cares." She, like all the other women in the settlement, didn't overly care for the Coulson women.

There was a warm glow in Jassy's breast as she helped Sue Ellen off with her hip-length coat. Luke hadn't left her to deal with Emma alone. His warm presence beside her, the gentle pressure of his hand on her shoulder, had given her the courage to lift her head and proudly look Emma in the eyes.

Did she dare hope that Luke cared for her? Something told her that she should.

When everyone had rid themselves of their heavy outer garments and had warmed themselves before the fire, Reverend Donner smiled and said, "Will everyone take their places please."

Sue Ellen moved to stand beside Jassy, and Jake aligned himself beside Luke. The reverend opened his worn Bible and began the often spoken words. "Dearly beloved, we are gathered here . . ."

When she looked back on it later, Jassy felt sure that it had been a lovely service, but it was all like a dream to her while it happened. She couldn't believe that she was getting her heart's desire. It was almost too much to grasp, that the rest of her life would be spent with the man she loved so dearly.

Evidently she said all the right words at the right time, for suddenly she felt a ring being slipped on her finger and the preacher saying, "You may kiss your bride, Luke."

Luke's kiss was short and gentle, but she knew she had been kissed.

"There, it's done." Sue Ellen pratically rubbed her hands together in satisfaction. She kissed Jassy on the cheek, but kissed Luke on the mouth, then laughingly said, "Let's eat now."

Everyone echoed her laugh and sat down at the table. A toast was drunk to the newlyweds; then everyone helped themselves to the ham.

As Jassy nibbled on her sandwich, she looked down at the gold band on her finger. It wasn't new and she wondered where Luke had got it. Sue Ellen saw her examining the ring and with a wide grin reached a hand across the table.

"It's mine, Jassy," she said. "Luke borrowed it until he can buy you your own. The post ran out of them last spring and Dimmer didn't get around to ordering more."

"I wondered where it came from." Jassy smiled and, stripping the ring off her finger, laid it in Sue Ellen's palm.

"It doesn't make you any the less married, wife," Luke teased, putting an arm around her shoulders and hugging her. "Don't go getting any ideas you can kick me out."

Jassy joined in with the following laughter and found herself relaxing. By the time Sue Ellen and the men prepared to leave, she was laughing as heartily as the rest at the bantering.

Her face was flushed and her eyes were sparkling as she said Merry Christmas and good night to the departing Sue Ellen and her menfolk. Luke walked out with them, saying that he would be right back.

Jassy used his absence to hurriedly wrap his Christmas gift in brown paper. She had just laid it on his chair when he returned, carrying a cloth-bound package.

"Merry Christmas, Jassy," he said softly, handing it to her. "I hope you like it."

"A Christmas gift, Luke?" She laughed delightedly, then like an excited youngster pulled at the cloth until the beaver jacket rolled out of it. "Oh, Luke, it's beautiful!" She grabbed the garment up and buried her chin in its softness.

A pleased look on his face, Luke started to sit down in his chair, then saw the package lying there. When he picked it up to set it on the floor, Jassy said, "That's my Christmas gift to you."

"It is?" Luke's face showed that he was touched. He hadn't received a gift of any kind since the death of his parents.

Jassy watched him unwrap the scarf, holding her breath, wondering if he would like it.

His rapt expression told her he was very pleased. He stood up and, wrapping the scarf around his neck, smiled and said, "I expect you noticed I needed a new one."

Jassy returned his smile. "Just like you saw that my jacket was looking pretty worn."

Luke slipped his fingers into his shirt pocket and brought out a sprig of greenery. Holding it up, he asked, "Do you know what this is?"

"Yes, it's mistletoe."

"Do you know what it's used for sometimes?"

Jassy knew that custom had it that if a man could catch a woman standing beneath the plant, he was allowed to kiss her. However, she shook her head no, pretending to be ignorant of the practice.

Luke held it over her head. "It means that I can kiss you since you're standing under it." He pulled her into his arms. "That kiss you gave me before was as cold as charity. Let's try it again."

As he brought her softness up against his hard body, his mouth came down to cover hers. The kiss deepened, sending Jassy's pulse to racing, and her hands unconsciously gripped the front of his shirt as she pressed against him.

Breathing hard, Luke put Jassy away from him and whispered hoarsely, "I've wanted you for so long, Jassy. I think I fell in love with you that first day when you were standing up so bravely, defying those three men."

"Really, Luke?" Jassy looked up at him through love-drugged eyes. "It's been that long for me too."

Luke pressed his forehead against Jassy's. "What a pair of fools we've been. Wasting all this time." When Jassy nodded agreement, he said huskily, "I'm going upstairs to get out of these trousers and shirt. Will you be changing clothes also?"

"Yes." Jassy stepped out of his arms, her eyes luminous with happiness. Luke loved her.

Behind the blankets that would come down tomorrow, she quickly changed into her prettiest nightgown, then lifted her hands to release her hair from its tight knot. She started to braid it as she did every night, then dropped her hands. She would let it curl around her shoulders and down her back. Furthermore, she would wear it that way from now on. Luke might as well get used to it. She took off the glasses and threw them against the wall, laughing softly when she heard the tinkling of broken glass. Never again would she wear those ugly things. Something else Luke would have to get used to.

She was lying in the darkness when Luke slid in beside her.

Luke came slowly awake, his arms around his new wife's soft, warm body. He lay quietly, thinking that he was a wiser man than the one who had gone to bed last night. He had learned that making love was so much better when done with someone you loved.

Jassy stirred and turned over on her back. Luke leaned up to gaze at her face in the pale morning sun coming through the window. Wonderment grew inside him as he saw the russet curls spilling over the pillow. When she opened her hazel-green eyes and gave him a slow, slumbrous smile, he said accusingly, "You tricked me, Jassy

Je . . . Slater. You're not plain. You're downright beautiful."

"Do you mind awfully?" Jassy ran a finger around his lips. "I'm still the same woman you fell in love with. I'll always be true to you, you don't have to worry about that."

Luke looked deeply into Jassy's eyes and knew it was true. She was no Nell. She would never bring him shame.

Just before he lowered his lips to hers, he whispered softly, "You are the best Christmas surprise I've ever received."

CONNIE MASON
CHRISTMAS STAR

*This story is dedicated to my eight
beautiful grandchildren.*

Chapter One

Williamsburg, Virginia, December 1786

His name was Jedidiah Wells.

Charity deliberately crossed the street so as not to encounter him face-to-face. She had seen him a time or two in Williamsburg, but the reclusive cripple usually avoided people. One couldn't miss his shuffling gait as he limped along the street. Jed Wells had returned home from the war in 1780, bearing wounds so severe and repulsive his fiancée had promptly married another. The townspeople were in an uproar when he brought home a newborn Indian baby, widely assumed to be his daughter.

There was plenty of speculation concerning the child's mother, for no one had ever seen Jed Wells with a woman—Indian or otherwise—after he had returned to his home several miles west of Williamsburg. Nor had anyone caught more than a fleeting glimpse of his Indian daughter during the following years.

Charity Fairchild suppressed a shudder of revulsion. She hated Indians. Man, woman, or child, they were all savage heathens, responsible for her parents' death and making her an orphan. As a result she was little more than a servant in the large Kincaid household. The strict Quaker family had been persuaded to take her in after her parents' untimely deaths, and her role in the family had evolved into that of servant. She was nineteen now, and if she'd had somewhere else to go she would have left long ago.

Turning into the dry goods store, Charity looked over the array of laces displayed on rolls. She had been sent into town on an errand this cold bleak December day to purchase white lace to trim the collar on Mistress Kincaid's new black dress. And if she didn't hurry, the impending storm would unleash its fury before she reached home. The prosperous Kincaid farm was three miles west of Williamsburg, and Charity didn't relish the thought of making the walk home in a raging storm.

"Can I help you, Mistress Fairchild?" The storekeeper addressed Charity by name since she was often sent on errands into town. Normally Charity enjoyed the three-mile walk to town, but today the darkening skies made her anxious.

"I'd like four yards of white lace, Mr. Cromley," Charity said, handing him the roll of lace.

While Mr. Cromley measured the lace, Charity

was distracted by the tall, unfashionably dressed man who had just entered the shop. Jed Wells didn't wear knee breeches and hose like most men, or cover his hair with a wig. Instead, his legs were encased in long trousers and his light brown hair was worn long and clubbed in the back. Charity grew flustered and looked away when she found his dark, inscrutable eyes on her. She had no idea he'd be so handsome up close. If not for his limp and whatever horrible disfigurement that lay hidden beneath his clothes he looked as normal as any other man. Unfortunately, his involvement with an Indian woman made him a virtual outcast.

She dared another glance at him and saw that he was still staring at her, his dark eyes hooded. She flushed, embarrassed by her unaccountable interest in Jed Wells.

"Shall I charge this, Mistress Fairchild?"

Marshaling her wayward thoughts, Charity nodded, aware that Jed Wells was limping toward a section of the store that displayed children's wear. She turned sideways to watch his slow progress, wincing when his step faltered to accommodate his awkward gait. He restored his balance easily, as if accustomed to compensating for his disability. He looked like a strong man despite his crippled leg, Charity thought, her eyes traveling the length of his muscular torso. If hideous scars did indeed lie beneath the layers of his clothing, she saw no sign of them.

Suddenly Charity realized her thoughts were traveling along dangerous channels, and she pulled her eyes away from the mysterious Jedidiah Wells. Mistress Kincaid would no doubt faint dead away if she saw Charity ogling a man, especially a man like Jed Wells, who had obviously gotten a daughter on an Indian woman. Shameless, that's what Mistress Kincaid would call her. The Kincaids wore their morals like a badge.

"Good day, Mr. Cromley," Charity said as she left the shop.

"Good day to you, Mistress Fairchild. You'd best get on home if you're walking. Looks like a storm's brewing."

"I have just one more errand," Charity answered as she stepped outside. A blast of cold wind billowed her cape around her slim form as she hurried across the street to the bakery.

Jed Wells felt the loss of her presence the moment she left the dry goods store, though he didn't see her leave. She was young, no more than nineteen or twenty, he calculated, thinking his own twenty-eight seemed ancient in comparison. Maybe not so much in years, but in experience. He felt like a bitter, disillusioned old man, dragging a useless leg behind him.

If he were a whole man he would be married to the lovely Mistress Hilda Appleby now instead of living the life of a recluse. He'd be able to give his daughter everything a child should have: the companionship of her peers, a mother to love her, respect. Fortunately, Star had a father who loved her, for she had little else. Since his mother had died, little Star had become the most important person in his life. At this time of the year he was more aware than ever of how much he loved her. She would be six years old on Christmas Eve.

Jed's thoughts returned to the woman who had just left the store. She had an exuberance about her that spoke of life, and hope, and happiness such as he could never bring any woman. Hilda hadn't been able to deal with his grave injuries, and he knew better than to expect any other woman to overlook them. Yet something in the young woman's eyes—the storekeeper had called her Mistress Fairchild—gave hint of an inner strength that Hilda hadn't possessed.

Jed muttered a curse and shook himself. He had no business thinking of a woman when he knew how his appearance repelled feminine sensibilities. Yet he could recall seeing no pity or revulsion in those soft honey-brown eyes. If he closed his eyes he could still see the vivid color of her hair. Dark auburn, with rich red highlights. He'd noticed it when she'd pulled off her hood. He hadn't really looked at another woman that closely since he'd returned from the war with a useless leg and disfiguring scars. And a baby daughter he'd named Star.

On his rare visits to Williamsburg he sometimes stopped in at the King's Inn where a coin bought him an hour with an accommodating tavern wench. But he never completely removed his trousers, and once his bodily urges had been satisfied he paid his coin and left. His emotions were in no way involved, and that was the way he wanted it. For Star's sake he could ill afford to become attracted to a woman who would not tolerate his Indian daughter.

Jed presented his purchases to Mr. Cromley, paid his coin, and left the shop, pulling his collar up to ward off the wind's chilling bite. Across the street, Charity stepped from the bakery at the same moment. She tried not to stare at Jed, but she couldn't help it. He held several awkward bundles in his arms, and as he stepped off the wooden boardwalk, his right leg seemed to crumple beneath him. The packages went flying every which way and for a frantic moment he clutched at thin air. She watched in growing horror as the ground came up to meet him.

"Oh, no!" Charity was flying across the street before she had time to think about what she was doing. She saw several people pass him by with no more than a fleeting glance, offering neither help nor comment. But that wasn't surprising. One hard glance from the recluse's steely dark eyes was enough to frighten the hardiest soul.

Rubbing his lame leg, Jed scowled fiercely and spit out a curse. He knew his limitations, but being humiliated in public was beyond human endurance. Before going off to fight the British, no man had been stronger than he, no man more outgoing or forthright. Now look at him, half a man, living like a hermit because of his scars and his refusal to expose his Indian daughter to the town's prejudice. Cursing again, he tried to lever himself to his feet.

"Here, let me help."

Before Jed realized what was happening, someone had placed his arm around shoulders so slim he doubted they had the strength to offer much assistance at all. He swiveled his head, stunned to see the young woman from the dry goods store. Her face was strained as she tried to lift him with her meager strength. Her bones felt so fragile beneath Jed's huge forearm, he wanted to laugh. Instead, he grew angry, mostly from embarrassment, but partly because he was too proud to accept help from a woman. Jed's features turned to stone as he jerked his arm from Charity's shoulders.

"I don't need your help."

His voice was almost a snarl, cold and hostile. She pulled back in surprise, so flustered she could only stare at him.

"I—I—didn't mean—that is . . ."

"You heard me," Jed repeated, sending her a glare that would make most women swoon from fright.

But Charity wasn't most women. Few things frightened her, although this man came close. The only thing she truly feared was Indians. She wasn't even afraid of Mistress Kincaid's heavy hand, for her guardian wasn't really cruel, just strict and insensitive. Charity appreciated the home the Kincaids provided for her despite her lowly position in the household.

Charity stood aside as Jed struggled to his feet. When she bent to retrieve a package he had dropped, he literally tore it from her hands. She couldn't recall when she'd met a man as disagreeable as Jedidiah Wells. It was small wonder that folks distanced themselves from him. His churlish manner discouraged their friendship.

By now Jed was on his feet and had gathered up his parcels. Barely acknowledging Charity's presence, he turned his back on her and limped away. Charity didn't realize she was staring until she acknowledged to herself that he was the finest-looking man she'd ever seen. Despite his limp, the rest of his body appeared perfect in every way. His broad shoulders and upper torso stretched the limits of his jacket. Abruptly Charity looked away, embarrassed by her unaccountable interest in a man who had dismissed her without so much as a glance.

Jed stomped away with as much dignity as he could manage under the circumstances. Six years ago his body would never have failed him as it had today. Six years ago he was strong and whole, a man women admired and men envied. His disability had changed him, made him a different person, not one he personally liked but one he had accepted after years of difficult adjustment. If not for Star, he wasn't certain what would have become of him. His daughter made life worth living.

Charity cast a wary glance at the lowering sky. She feared she wouldn't make it home before snow started falling. The wind howled through the trees and she shivered, pulling her cloak tighter around her as she trudged down the road from Williamsburg. She knew how unpredictable the weather could be in Virginia in December. When she had left home the sky had been cloudy, but not particularly threatening. A gust of wind filled her cloak and whipped it around her slim figure, and Charity felt an icy blast of wet snow spray her cheeks. A halfhour later it was snowing so hard she could barely see the road stretching ahead of her.

Jed made an unscheduled stop at the inn, engaging the services of Polly Greene. It wasn't something Jed had planned today, but after his brief encounter with Mistress Fairchild he became aware of an urgent need he couldn't ignore this time as he had done many times in the past. Fortunately, Polly had no qualms about pleasuring a cripple, as long as she received the promised coin. An hour later Jed drove his wagon from Williamsburg, his body sated but feeling strangely unfulfilled. The whole time he had strained over Polly he was seeing the young, innocent face of another woman. A woman with warm brown eyes, auburn hair and pert features—a woman with a kind heart. The kind of woman who would offer sympathy to a stranger.

The driving snow chilled Charity's bones as she trudged through the rapidly failing light of late afternoon. Her boots offered little protection against the cold as she made her way through the drifted snow. Her knees quivered from the exertion of putting one foot in front of the other, and her feet were numb from cold. She knew she must be close to home, but landmarks were barely recognizable in the heavy snowfall, causing her to miss completely the branch in the road that led to the Kincaid farm.

*　　*　　*

Jed made a disgusted sound deep in his throat when he realized he had nearly missed the fork in the road. One direction led to his small farm and the other to farms of neighbors he had made no effort to meet. Most had bought their farms while he was off fighting the British, and after his return he had kept mostly to himself. It was bad enough having to guide his horse and wagon down a road he could barely see, let alone ending up miles from home, Jed reflected, aware that few of his neighbors would appreciate his dropping in unexpectedly.

Who would have thought when he left this morning that a storm was brewing? It had just started to snow when he left Williamsburg, and if he hadn't had Star waiting at home, he would have taken a room at the inn and waited out the storm. He had lived in the area long enough to know the capriciousness of the weather at this time of year.

Jed would have missed the snow-covered hump in the middle of the road if his horse hadn't shied away and refused to move forward.

"Giddap, boy," he growled, annoyed at the skittish behavior of his horse. "There's a nice warm barn at home, and hay. Don't stop now." But no matter what he did, the horse refused to budge.

Hauling himself awkwardly from the wagon, Jed walked around and grasped the horse's bit, tugging him forward. The stubborn animal stomped, snorted, and backed away. Realizing that something was spooking the horse, Jed made a cursory search of the road. He thought the snow-covered hump in the road hardly worthy of inspection until it moved. Dropping to his good knee, he frantically brushed the snow away, uncovering the still figure of a woman. Her lips were blue, her eyes were closed, her face was as white as the falling snow.

Jed stared at the woman in stunned comprehension. It was the same woman who had tried to help him earlier. What in the hell was she doing on this deserted road in the middle of the worst snowstorm of the season? Who was she? Where did she live? Where was her family? Though he had little to do with his neighbors, there weren't that many and he'd recognize their names when he heard them. Fairchild wasn't familiar to him.

He shook her shoulder, hoping to elicit a reply. He needed to know where she lived so he could take her home. He was rewarded by a low moan, but nothing recognizable as coherent speech. He spit out a curse, realizing that she was in no condition to give him the information he sought. She needed to be thawed out before she froze to death. Dammit, why did he have to be the one to find her? Bringing a woman to his home was a complication he didn't need. If there was any alternative . . . There wasn't.

Bracing himself with his good leg, he lifted Charity in his arms, amazed that she weighed so little, and carried her to the wagon. After laying her in the wagon bed, he pulled a canvas over her and climbed onto the driver's seat. This time the horse set out at a brisk trot when Jed slapped the reins smartly against his rump.

Chapter Two

Charity resisted the urge to awaken. She felt so warm and safe in the fuzzy dream world where life held no threat. Funny, she thought curiously, but she couldn't recall arriving home. The last thing she remembered was walking against the icy wind and growing panicky when drifting snow reached her ankles and then her knees. Storms like this were rare in Williamsburg, but they did happen upon occasion, and she had gotten caught smack dab in the middle of one.

Charity assumed that one of the Kincaids had come looking for her in the wagon. She remembered nothing after stumbling in the knee-deep snow and falling. But the throbbing pain in her head told her she must have struck her head on a rock. Thank God the Kincaids had found her when they did. She could have frozen to death had she lain there long enough.

"She's waking up, Papa."

The high-pitched voice of a small child brought Charity into full awareness.

"It's about time," came the disgruntled reply.

Charity stirred restlessly, vaguely aware that she had heard that deep, rumbling voice before. The child's voice could belong to little Sophie Kincaid, but the man's voice definitely wasn't that of any Kincaid she knew.

"She's pretty, Papa."

"I hadn't noticed." Jed Wells nearly bit his tongue over the outright lie. Truth to tell, he had noticed. Mistress Fairchild was fairer than any woman he'd had occasion to look upon, including Mistress Hilda Appleby.

That voice! Reality intruded upon the protective haven where Charity had sought refuge as she recognized the throaty growl and was jolted from sleep. She didn't know the why or how of it, but she knew that the voice belonged to Jedidiah Wells! Her lids rising slowly, she hoped she was hallucinating and feared that she wasn't.

Fear shot through her when she found herself nose to nose with a doe-eyed Indian child, and there was no way she could stifle the scream that ripped from her throat. The child recoiled in alarm, her eyes wide with fright as Charity's scream went on and on.

"Papa, why is the lady screaming?"

"What in the hell is wrong with you?" Jed cried, grasping Charity's shoulders and shaking her roughly. "No one here is hurting you."

"In-Indians," Charity managed to gasp between rattling teeth.

"Are you crazy or something? This is my daughter, Star."

"Daughter?" Charity squeaked on a rising note of panic. The child's features were pure Indian. Hair as black as a raven's wing framed a round little face with high cheekbones and skin a rich dusky brown. The child stared at Charity through chocolate brown eyes that tilted at the corners and appeared too large for her face.

Drawing the covers up to her chin, Charity looked from Star to Jed. "What am I doing here?"

"Believe me, it's not because I want you here," Jed complained sourly.

So much for hospitality, Charity thought.

"I found you unconscious in the road, and since I had no idea where you lived, I carried you home. Couldn't let you die," he added, sounding as if that was exactly what he would have liked to do.

"How long have I been here?" She hoped it wasn't too long and that he'd be willing to take her home.

"Since late yesterday afternoon. You must have been exhausted, for you didn't awaken all night. Of course, the bump on your head didn't help."

Charity groaned in dismay. "Oh, no, it can't be! The Kincaids must be frantic with worry."

Jed frowned. Kincaid. He'd heard the name before. If he wasn't mistaken they owned a farm several miles to the south. "I heard the storekeeper call you Mistress Fairchild. Are you related to the Kincaids?"

"No, they took me in when my parents were killed. They'll be shocked to learn I spent the night with . . ."

"Me," Jed said grimly as he completed Charity's sentence.

"Exactly," Charity dared to say. "They're Quakers, and very strict."

"Would they rather you'd frozen to death on the road?"

"Probably."

Star couldn't take her eyes off Charity. Never had she seen such a pretty lady. She rarely left the farm. The only other person besides her papa with whom she was familiar was Songbird, the old Indian woman who lived nearby in the forest and came during the day to care for her when her papa was out trapping or hunting. Intrigued by Charity's auburn hair, she reached out and rubbed a vibrant tress between her thumb and forefinger.

From the corner of her eye Charity saw Star reach out to her, and she jerked back violently. "Keep her away from me!" She pulled the covers over her head, aware that she was behaving abominably, but unable to help herself.

Startled, Star retreated, hurt by Charity's reaction to her innocent gesture. A small sob escaped her throat. "What's wrong with the pretty lady, Papa? I wasn't going to hurt her."

Jed slanted Charity a furious glance. "I'm sure Mistress Fairchild knows you won't hurt her, sweetheart," he said with more gentleness than Charity thought him capable of. "It's just that she's not herself yet. Why don't you put a kettle of water on the fire for tea? I doubt Songbird will come today because of the weather."

Charity heard the child leave the room but wisely decided to remain beneath the cocoon of blankets. She knew from the tone of Jed's voice that he was furious with her, and she didn't relish the thought of facing his formidable anger. Unfortunately, Jed didn't allow her the luxury of retreat. He ripped the blanket aside, forcing her to look at him. Charity gasped in shock when she realized that her dress had been removed and she was wearing only a flannel shift, worn thin from constant washings and patched in many places.

It might have helped Charity to know that Jed was even more shocked when he saw her wearing so little. Yet it didn't stop him from looking his fill. His gaze traveled the length of her body, noting how the high peaks of her taut little breasts poked impudently against the fragile material, and the way her hips swelled enticingly below her narrow waist. Before she yanked the covers up to her chin, he saw the mysterious dark shadow between her thighs, and his loins leaped in violent reaction. Deliberately he turned away.

"Who took my dress off?" Charity asked shakily. If he said he had done it, she knew she'd faint dead away. He wouldn't dare, would he? But she knew he would. A man like Jed Wells would dare anything.

"Songbird. I left you in her care after I brought you home."

"Who is Songbird?"

"An old Indian woman who spends her days taking care of Star. She lives in a shack in the woods not far from here. I found her shortly after my mother's death. She was starving and would have died if I hadn't discovered her hiding in the woods. She was sick, and her tribe had left her behind when they migrated west. I nursed her back to health, and she stayed on to help raise Star."

Charity shuddered in revulsion. "You let an Indian touch me?"

Jed's expression hardened. "Do you have something against Indian women and children?"

"I—I'm frightened of Indians. They killed my parents. I can remember—never mind, it's too painful to recall. But I'll never forget their dark faces, or the hatred in their eyes. Thank God they've been driven from the area."

"Not all of them," he told her. "There are still small bands scattered around the countryside. They rarely come close to town, though, unless the winter has been exceptionally hard. Then they come begging for food."

Charity blanched. "To my knowledge none have ever appeared at the Kincaid farm."

"They're there, you just haven't seen them," Jed told her.

An awkward silence ensued as Jed and Charity stared at one another. Mesmerized by Jed's dark, compelling gaze, Charity forced her eyes away and said, "If you'll leave I'll get dressed. I'd like to go home immediately. My guardians must be worried sick about me."

"I'll leave so you can get dressed, Mistress Fairchild, but you can forget about leaving, at least for the time being. The road is all but impassable."

"Oh, no! I can't stay here."

He scowled at her. "I'm afraid you have little choice. When you've finished dressing, come out to the kitchen and I'll fix us some breakfast." Without waiting for her reply, he turned and stalked out the door. Charity stared at him as he limped away, so enthralled by the wide expanse of his back and the incredible strength of his shoulders and forearms that she hardly noticed his limp.

"Is the pretty lady going to stay, Papa?" Star asked as she watched Jed slice bacon and place thick slabs into a frying pan to sizzle over the open flame of the hearth.

"Unfortunately, she has no choice," Jed complained.

"Why doesn't she like me?" Her innocent question thoroughly unsettled Jed. He kept forgetting how astute his daughter was.

"She does like you, sweetheart, how could she not? I fear Miss Fairchild is overwrought after her ordeal yesterday with the storm."

Star's round little face screwed up into a thoughtful frown. "Do you think she'd like to be my mother?"

Jed went still. Star's question had caught him

off guard. He didn't realize she missed not having a mother. Lord knows he'd tried to be both mother and father to her. He bent and swung the little girl high in his arms, planting a kiss on her plump cheek.

"I didn't know you were looking for a mama. Isn't having a papa enough for you?"

Star giggled happily. "I love you, Papa, but a mama would be nice."

"Don't get any ideas, little one. To be perfectly honest, I doubt any woman would want a husband who's half a man. Besides, I'd rather have you all to myself."

Wrapping her dimpled brown arms around his neck, Star hugged him tightly.

Charity chose that moment to walk into the kitchen, stunned to see the man she and everyone else in Williamsburg considered a surly hermit actually smiling. It changed his entire appearance. Once the scowl was removed from his face, he looked younger and less forbidding.

The moment Jed saw her watching him, his lips turned downward and the scowl returned. Setting Star on her feet, he turned back to tend the sizzling bacon.

"Sit down, Mistress Fairchild," he said without inflection. "I don't cook as well as Songbird, but Star has survived on my cooking with little complaint." He set the bacon on the table and added biscuits left from the night before and leftover beans.

Charity sat obediently. After Jed dished out the food, she did not begin eating immediately but bent her head in prayer, as was the custom in the religious Kincaid household. Jed had the spoon halfway to his mouth when he saw Charity silently saying grace. Flushing, he set the spoon down, realizing that he had been remiss in his instruction of Star.

Raised in a religious household himself, he had fallen out of the habit of performing this important ritual. He tried, despite his own bitterness, to instill in his daughter a healthy respect for God and his teachings, and each Christmas he dutifully recited from memory the story of the Nativity. Yet the small courtesy of reciting a prayer at meals had fallen into disuse in the course of everyday living.

He waited until Charity finished her silent prayer and picked up her spoon before resuming his own meal. But he remained thoughtful. Having Charity at the table made him realize how much Star was missing by not having a mother to guide her. He glanced at Star, wondering if her exotic Indian features would prevent her from having the kind of life she deserved, with a man who would love her for herself and not judge her by the color of her skin.

After the meal, Charity cleared her throat and said, "Mr. Wells, I really do insist you take me home."

"Have you looked out the window, Mistress Fairchild? There's nearly two feet of snow outside and it's still snowing."

"Nevertheless, it's not proper for you and I . . ."

A becoming flush crept up her neck. "Your daughter is hardly a proper chaperon."

If Jed hadn't been so annoyed he would have laughed. "You've no need to worry on that score. You don't interest me. And I'm sure, after getting a good look at me, that I don't interest you." His voice sounded so bitter, Charity felt a twinge of pity.

"It's not that," Charity tried to explain. "You just don't know the Kincaids. They're bound to think the worst."

"Mistress Fairchild," Jed ground out, exasperated. "You may leave anytime you like. I brought you here in the first place because I couldn't let you die out there in the snow and cold, but if your life means so little to you, it's no concern of mine."

"Don't go," Star begged. "You might fall down in the snow again." She reached out and gave Charity's hand a comforting pat.

Charity jerked her hand away as if burned.

Jed shot to his feet, his chair banging to the floor behind him. "Perhaps it's best you do leave, Mistress Fairchild." His expression was so fierce, Charity paled, bravely trying not to cringe in the face of his fierce anger.

"I—I'm sorry," she stammered. "I can't seem to help myself."

She rose quickly and walked to the window, certain that Jed was exaggerating about the weather. Unfortunately, he wasn't. It was every bit as bad as he had said. She'd be lucky if she got out of here within the next two days. Meanwhile, she was virtually marooned with a recluse most people thought a little strange, and his Indian daughter.

"Would you like me to get your cloak, Mistress Fairchild?"

Resentment welled up inside Charity. He knew she couldn't leave. He was deliberately goading her. She turned to glare at him. "I might be foolish but I'm not stupid, Mr. Wells. No matter how badly I want to leave, it would be suicide to venture out on a day such as this. I believe I'll accept your hospitality for a while longer."

"Very wise of you, Mistress Fairchild, to accept my humble hospitality," he said, executing a mocking bow. He limped to the hearth to refill his plate, turned abruptly to say something to Charity, and saw her staring at his crippled leg, an odd expression on her face. "Hasn't anyone told you it is rude to stare, Mistress Fairchild?"

A dull red crept up Charity's neck and she lowered her eyes. "I'm sorry."

"It doesn't matter," Jed tossed back harshly. "I'm accustomed to women staring at me with revulsion. I don't need your pity, Mistress Fairchild. Star and I will get along just fine without your sympathy."

"No, it's not that!" Charity denied vehemently. How could she tell him that she barely noticed his disability? That except for his limp he was perfect in every way? She couldn't. It was not permissible to say such things to a virtual stranger.

"No need to lie, Mistress Fairchild. I told you it doesn't bother me anymore."

"Would you like to see the new dress Papa bought me in town, Mistress Fairchild?"

Charity stared at Star, surprised to finding her tugging at her skirt. The child had been so quiet that Charity had forgotten she was still seated at the table eating breakfast. She had slipped from the bench and stood beside Charity now, her huge chocolate eyes round with excitement. Charity decided that anything was better than remaining in the same room with the rude, overbearing hermit. He was too intimidating, too forceful, too male, and his dark, compelling eyes frightened her. She was unaccustomed to the company of men, especially men like Jedidiah Wells.

She turned to follow Star. Suddenly she felt herself jerked roughly aside. Jed was glaring at her, his expression fierce.

"If you say or do anything to hurt Star, I'll kick your butt out in the snow so fast you won't know what hit you."

"How dare you?" Charity hissed, pulling away from the cruel bite of his hard hand. Never in her nineteen rather sheltered years had she heard such rough language.

"I dare anything in my own home. Now go with Star, but you damn well better behave."

Charity turned and ran as if the devil were after her.

Chapter Three

"I really think you should take me home, Mr. Wells," Charity said with quiet desperation. She was seated at the breakfast table, eating the thin oatmeal Jed had prepared.

Circumstances had forced her to remain with Jed Wells and his daughter a second night, sleeping in his bed while he rolled up in a blanket in front of the hearth. During the entire day yesterday the snow had fallen without respite, piling up outside the door and drifting across the yard. Jed left the cabin briefly to attach runners to the wagon, converting it into a sleigh, but when Charity suggested that they leave for the Kincaid farm immediately, he balked, maintaining that to venture out now would be both foolhardy and dangerous.

Now Jed sent Charity a look that said he was

just as eager for her to be gone as she was to leave. He had awakened early and looked out the window, marveling at the silent white world whose beauty was unsurpassed by anything man could have created. The sun had made a belated appearance, sparkling like diamonds on the pristine whiteness of the snow. He knew from past experience that the storm was spent and they could expect the normal mild temperatures of a Virginia winter to return.

"Finish your breakfast, Mistress Fairchild, and I'll be happy to oblige. Having a woman guest in my home isn't something I'd care to do very often. Unfortunately, there are times when necessity forces us to act contrary to our wishes. I know this has been unpleasant for you, but I assure you it has been equally unpleasant for me."

Unpleasant wasn't exactly the word Charity would have used. Frightening, perhaps. Trying, certainly. Being alone with a man was disconcerting enough without the man being Jed Wells. He was something of a mystery. She could feel his bitterness intensely, and through those layers of disillusionment she sensed a tortured soul. Did it have anything to do with his being a cripple? she wondered. Or did it concern Star's mother? She couldn't help but be curious about the Indian woman Jed had loved.

"I can't thank you enough for saving my life," Charity said sincerely. "I never wanted to be a burden to you and if I—I offended you or your daughter, I'm sorry."

"Don't let Mistress Fairchild go home, Papa,"

Star begged. Her big brown eyes regarded Charity sadly. "Why can't she stay here with us?"

She touched Charity's hand, and Charity jerked reflexively in spite of her effort to control her revulsion for Indians. Star was an innocent little girl, she told herself, disgusted with her involuntary response to the child's friendly overtures.

Jed's eyes narrowed to a hard glitter, and Charity recoiled in fear. His look was so filled with disgust and accusation that her guilt was enormous. If she was lucky, once she left here she'd never be required to set eyes on Jedidiah Wells again.

"Eat your oats, Star," Jed said tersely, refusing to answer his daughter's question.

Truth to tell, Star's innocent inquiry made him feel lacking. He should have given her a mother. Though Songbird had tried her best, she made an inadequate substitute. But it couldn't be helped. No woman wanted a cripple for a husband. One look at his unclothed body would send most women fleeing in terror.

Jed rose abruptly to his feet, intending to go outside and harness the horse to the sleigh before Star's questions became too probing. Suddenly the kitchen door opened and a woman stepped inside. Charity started violently when she realized the woman was an Indian, her wizened face so wrinkled it resembled a dried apple.

"Songbird!" Star cried, jumping from her chair and embracing the old woman. "We were worried about you."

The old woman smiled, revealing a mouth completely devoid of teeth. "It is not yet my time to walk the path of my ancestors. I cannot leave the earth until I know you and your father will be taken care of after I depart." Her bright, penetrating gaze settled disconcertingly on Charity. "It pleases me to see the maiden of the snow looking so well."

"This is Mistress Fairchild, Songbird," Jed said. "Thanks to you she has fully recovered. Now that the storm has passed I will take her home. I am glad you have come to stay with Star."

Charity gave Songbird a timid nod, realizing she was the woman who had undressed her when she first arrived. "Th-thank you for taking care of me," she said timidly.

Songbird merely stared at Charity, the expression in her dark eyes unreadable. Abruptly her mouth opened in a radiant smile, as if she saw something no one else did. "My dreams told me you would come one day," she said cryptically. "When the time comes to join my ancestors, I can do so in peace. I do not think it will be long."

Jed scowled fiercely. "I don't know what you're prattling about, Songbird." Annoyed, he turned to Charity. "Get your wrap, Mistress Fairchild, we'd best be going. I imagine your guardians are sick with worry by now."

"I've been telling you that for two days, Mr. Wells," Charity said plaintively.

A thick silence lengthened between Jed and Charity. From the time he had lifted her onto the seat beside him in the sleigh until the moment they spied the Kincaid farm two hours later, neither saw the need for pointless speech. If the deep snowdrifts hadn't hindered them, the trip could have been accomplished in a much shorter time, but being a cautious man, Jed drove carefully, safeguarding the valuable horse and equipment.

Once, when the sleigh lurched into a frozen rut, Charity slid solidly against Jed. Before she was able to move away to a proper distance, she felt a languid, drugging warmth uncoil inside her. The feeling was most unsettling, and she tried not to concentrate on the attractive, albeit surly man sitting beside her.

Jed guided the sleigh down the lane, reining in before the front door of a large white clapboard farmhouse. The door opened almost immediately, revealing a buxom middle-aged woman dressed in unrelieved black, her gray-streaked brown hair covered by a white mopcap. She stood on the threshold, arms crossed over her ample breasts, staring at Charity as if she'd just seen a ghost.

"We thought you were dead," the woman said tonelessly.

"I'm truly sorry, Mistress Kincaid," Charity said breathlessly. "I knew you'd be worried."

"What happened to you? Mr. Kincaid took the wagon into town to carry you home when it looked as if a storm was coming, but you were nowhere to be found. That was two days ago." She gave Jed an assessing look, recognizing him immediately. "And what, pray tell, are you doing with this man?"

Jed stepped forward, having developed an instant dislike for Mistress Kincaid. "I'm Jedidiah Wells, Mistress Kincaid. Mistress Fairchild has been with me. Evidently she took a wrong turn during the storm and became lost. When I came across her, she had fallen and would have perished had I not found her when I did. Since she was unconscious and unable to tell me where she belonged, I took her to my home."

"Your home!" Mistress Kincaid recoiled in horror, aghast at the implication of Jed's words. "You took her to your home? Without a proper chaperon?"

"It's not what you think, Mistress Kincaid," Charity said, rushing to Jed's defense. "I would have died if Mr. Wells hadn't found me. Everything was perfectly innocent. His daughter was there the entire time."

"Daughter! Are you referring to a child barely out of diapers? Pah, what does a babe know of such things?"

Jed was growing angrier by the minute. "'Tis senseless to argue with you, Mistress Kincaid. I've brought Mistress Fairchild back safe and sound and I'll be on my way." He turned to leave.

"And I have work to do," Charity said, trying to duck past Mistress Kincaid. But the outraged woman was having none of it.

"Wait!" Her arm shot out to block Charity's way. "You will not set foot inside my home to corrupt my children."

Charity froze, her face a mask of disbelief. "What? What do you mean? This is my home. The only home I've known since my parents' deaths."

"And a good home it's been, Charity. I'm sorry you saw fit to betray our kindness like this."

Halfway down the porch stairs Jed turned abruptly, staring incredulously at Mistress Kincaid. Mistress Fairchild had said her guardians were strict, but this narrow-minded view of the situation went beyond strict into the realm of ludicrous.

"If you don't intend for Mistress Fairchild to enter your home, what do you expect her to do?"

"She must find employment elsewhere." Mistress Kincaid gave Charity an austere look and added, "If anyone will have her now that you have corrupted her."

"She has done no wrong," Jed argued. "Why are you punishing her?"

"You don't understand, Mr. Wells. We are simple people who live by the Word of God. Our morals are above reproach, and we frown upon the barest hint of scandalous behavior. If you want my opinion, I would strongly advise you to marry Mistress Fairchild. Now if you'll excuse me, 'tis cold out here and I've no time to waste in idle talk."

Charity's face went white with shock. Marry Jed Wells? The suggestion was so outrageously ridiculous she could barely credit it. Yet she knew by Mistress Kincaid's implacable expression that nothing would change her mind. Nor could she appeal to Mr. Kincaid, for the man usually abided by his wife's decision in anything having to do with the house, children, or domestic matters.

"Mistress Kincaid, wait! Can I stay until I find other work?"

"Nay, Charity, you have broken faith and you must go. You may take your clothes. Wait here and I will bring them to you." She stepped back into the house and slammed the door in Charity's face.

Jed paused on the bottom step, cursing beneath his breath. He couldn't believe what he had just witnessed. Having experienced the dark side of people's natures for the past six years, he understood exactly how Charity felt.

"Perhaps you could appeal to Mr. Kincaid," he suggested hopefully. Though he was anxious to be on his way, he felt a certain responsibility to resolve this impossible situation.

Charity shook her head in vigorous denial. "It will do no good. Once Mistress Kincaid makes up her mind, no one can change it. Mr. Kincaid is not a forceful man and usually agrees with his wife's decisions. If you would be kind enough to wait, perhaps you could take me to town."

"What will you do in town? Do you know someone who wants domestic help? Or a shopkeeper needing a clerk?"

Charity had to admit she knew of no one wanting or needing the kind of help she had to offer, and she said as much to Jed. Jed said nothing, paralyzing her with his inscrutable look. He was staring at her with a strange intensity that was both frightening and intoxicating. He appeared to be angry with her, and she couldn't understand why.

"I will take you to town."

His voice was taut, barely civil, sending a shiver down Charity's spine. With humbling insight she had an inkling of just how much Jed resented her intrusion upon his life.

"Do you have the coin to pay for lodging?"

Charity's brow furrowed. "Coin?" Until now she'd had no need for money, since previously all her needs had been adequately met by the Kincaids.

Jed gave an exasperated snort. "The only other way for a woman to earn her keep is by . . ." His words fell off abruptly as he realized how stupid they'd sound to a woman who obviously knew little about worldly matters. "I suppose," he said cautiously, "you could apply for a job at the King's Inn." Lord knows she was lovely enough to attract customers should the proprietor choose to employ her, and it struck him that the man would be a fool not to.

"The King's . . ." Charity gasped, incensed by the outrageous suggestion. "I assure you, good sir, I would not consider such employment. Mistress Kincaid has been quite vocal in her condemnation of women who work in disreputable surroundings."

"Forgive me," Jed mocked with a hint of amusement. "I was only trying to acquaint you with your choices of employment." Why he even bothered escaped him. Given her attitude toward Star, he wondered why he felt sympathy for Mistress Fairchild, yet for some unexplained reason her plight stirred an obscure emotion deep inside him.

Just then the door opened and Mistress Kincaid appeared on the threshold, holding out a pitifully small bundle to Charity. "I included only what you will need," she said by way of an explanation. "You and my Suzy are about the same size, and she could use your good black dress since you will have little use for it in your new situation. We treated you as one of the family, Charity. I hope you will remember it when you are gone from here." She thrust the bundle into Charity's hands.

"If you cared for Mistress Fairchild, you'd reconsider," Jed growled, feeling no charity whatsoever for the woman.

Mistress Kincaid's lips thinned. "Go with God," she said, deliberately ignoring Jed's statement. "We have done our best for you, but obviously it wasn't enough."

"You have used Mistress Fairchild like a servant," Jed argued. He wasn't certain if he was angry because he felt his life slowly disintegrating or because he abhorred hypocrites like Mistress Kincaid who lacked Christian charity.

Jed's words made little impact on Mistress Kincaid, for she had already entered the house and slammed the door behind her. Horrified, Charity stared at the closed door, uncertain what to do next. She had been little more than a servant in the Kincaid home but at least she'd had a roof over her head and food. Being turned out for a moral lapse over which she had no control seemed completely unwarranted.

"No sense dawdling out here, Mistress Fairchild.

Get into the sleigh and I'll take you into town."
Jed's voice was harsh, startling Charity from her
lethargy. She wondered if he was angry because
she'd asked him to take her into town. She'd made
the three-mile walk many times in the past and
could do so again if necessary.

When Charity was slow to move, Jed grasped
her by the elbow, hauled her down the porch
steps, and hoisted her into the conveyance. "Pious
bigot," he muttered, meaning Mistress Kincaid.
He limped to the driver's side and hauled himself
up beside Charity.

"They're really good people," Charity murmured, still stunned by the turn of events. She
had known that Mistress Kincaid would be upset
with her, but she'd had no idea this would happen.
"They took me in when no one else wanted me."

Jed slapped the reins against the horse's rump,
wondering what in the hell he was going to do
with his unwanted baggage. No money, no relatives, no place to go. Mistress Kincaid had had
the effrontery to suggest he marry the girl. The
last thing in the world he needed or wanted was
a wife.

Her eyes downcast, her shoulders hunched
against the cold bite of the wind, Charity sank
deeply into despondency. She had no idea what
would become of herself. Perhaps she could throw
herself on the mercy of Reverend Sinclair, begging him to find a position for her. Maybe he'd
let her stay with him and his family until she
found employment, although that didn't seem
too likely, given his large family and meager

circumstances. No doubt he'd be as unbending as Mistress Kincaid and consider her a fallen woman.

Jed's brooding silence persisted during the ride to Williamsburg. The taut angle of his body, his scowling features and tight grip upon the reins made Charity aware of his great agitation. From time to time she slid him a surreptitious glance, wondering what he was thinking. She had no idea why he was so angry. She was the one who had lost her home. Nothing had changed for Jedidiah Wells. It was always the woman who paid the consequences, she thought, angered by the unfairness of it all.

Jed's gloomy thoughts nearly matched Charity's. By the time they reached the outskirts of Williamsburg, he still had no idea what to do about Mistress Charity Fairchild. Then unexpectedly he remembered his daughter, and how sad she had been when Charity left their home; how she had begged Charity to remain and be her mother. He knew the obstacles were nearly insurmountable, that he could never expect her to look at him with anything but loathing and revulsion, that she would have to accept Star despite the child's Indian blood. But because Star seemed to like Charity he was willing to ignore his instincts and make the sacrifice.

He turned the sleigh down the road leading to the church.

Charity knew immediately where he was taking her. "I'm not sure Reverend Sinclair will be any more understanding than Mistress Kincaid," she said on a trembling sigh.

Jed gave her a measuring look, his features so hard they appeared sculpted in stone. "His understanding isn't necessary. There is only one possible course open to you, Mistress Fairchild. We will be married immediately."

Chapter Four

Charity gaped at Jed in horror. "Have I heard you right, sir? Are you suggesting that we marry?"

The lines in Jed's brow deepened. "I don't like this any better than you do. Do you by chance have another suggestion, Mistress Fairchild?"

"But you don't even like me! We don't know one another well enough to marry."

"True. Don't you think I've told myself that? But since I have inadvertently damaged your reputation, I'm willing, albeit reluctantly, to make it right."

"I—I can't marry you." A shudder slithered down her spine and her lids came down to shutter her eyes. She stopped short of telling him he was too male, too much man for her. How could she explain that she feared wedding and bedding a harsh stranger she knew nothing about?

Jed saw her shudder and assumed she was expressing her revulsion for him as a man. He thought of his crippled leg and the scars on his body and knew he could never expose himself to her scorn. If they were to marry, it must be a marriage in name only, which he suspected would greatly ease Mistress Fairchild's mind.

"I would not ask you to accommodate me as a wife," Jed began slowly. He watched her expression change from disbelief to hope. "You need not share my bed, or suffer my—my . . ." He scowled and looked away. "Needless to say," he continued brusquely, "I expect you to be the mother Star never had. Lord knows the poor child needs a mother's gentle influence."

"What happened to Star's mother?" Charity asked curiously. "It's common knowledge that you returned from the war with a motherless newborn babe. Did her mother die? You must have loved Star's mother very much to want to raise your child alone. Especially an In—" Her words stumbled to a halt.

"An Indian child, is that what you intended to say?"

Charity nodded mutely.

"Star is my daughter, that's all anyone need know about her."

"But she must have had a mother," Charity dared to say.

"Everyone has a mother, Mistress Fairchild. It's growing late. I suggest we ask Reverend Sinclair to marry us."

"Do you really mean it?" Charity asked hopefully. Her soft brown eyes probed relentlessly into the dark depths of Jed's soul. "About not—not sharing your bed, I mean." Her deep flush gave hint of the difficulty she had in discussing things of an intimate nature with a male. She was so inexperienced in matters concerning relationships between men and women that she assumed the tingling, burning flush she felt when in Jed's company was merely fear of the dark, compelling recluse.

"I do not lie, Mistress Fairchild. You may share my home as my wife with no strings, except for the one previously mentioned. I have no interest in you as a woman. I find all women rather shallow creatures. I realize I repulse most women and have no desire to offend you or any other woman with my unwanted attentions."

"Oh." Words failed Charity. It amazed her that he actually thought himself repulsive. Didn't he know he was handsome? What she could see of him was handsome, anyway. She was certain if he had scars on his body, they wouldn't bother her as he suspected. Why didn't men understand that it was what was inside their hearts that counted, not what people saw?

"Are you agreeable to my terms, Mistress Fairchild?"

Jed's heart nearly stopped beating when Charity turned huge brown eyes on him. Lord, she was beautiful. He must be crazy to open himself up to the kind of torment that having Charity in his home would bring him. He wasn't a monk, though he had tried for the past six years to suppress his sexuality, aware of how he repelled gently bred women. Living with Charity would be the sweetest torture known to man. Denying he was attracted to her would be lying to himself. But he'd witnessed her pity when he'd fallen in the street that day in Williamsburg, and he had reacted characteristically, with vicious, snarling contempt. No wonder she was frightened of him.

Charity gnawed her bottom lip as she considered her options, which were precious few. She could throw herself on the reverend's mercy and try to explain why she'd been turned out by the Kincaids. But even if he did understand, she wasn't certain he'd offer her a place to stay. For the most part, the townspeople didn't employ many servants, and shopkeepers depended upon family members to work in their businesses. Seeking work at the King's Inn was unthinkable. That left only Jed Wells and his marriage proposal.

"I assure you, Mr. Wells, if I do accept your proposal, it will be because I have no other alternative," Charity informed him coldly. Regardless of the relief she felt when Jed said he held no affection for her, she was more than a little hurt that he found her lacking in looks and desirability.

Jed's lips thinned. "I am aware of that, Mistress Fairchild. I know my shortcomings and am reconciled to them. I am accustomed to being half a man. Now, if we have that settled between us, let us continue."

He snapped the reins, and the horse responded with an unaccustomed burst of speed. Within minutes the sleigh stopped before the modest rectory occupied by Reverend Sinclair and his family. Jed lifted Charity from the sleigh and they walked together to the door. She was given no time to reconsider her decision as he raised his hand and rapped briskly. The knock was answered within minutes by the reverend's short, plump wife.

"Why, Mistress Fairchild, what brings you to the rectory this time of week? Is someone ill at the Kincaid home?" She opened the door wider, spying Jed for the first time. Her eyes widened and she gaped at him in astonishment. "Is that Mr. Wells with you? Whatever are you thinking, child, keeping company with a man like Jed Wells?"

"Who is it, Hope? Do we have visitors?" Reverend Sinclair appeared at his wife's side, as tall and gaunt as his wife was short and squat.

"'Tis Mistress Fairchild, Reverend," Hope Sinclair said cautiously. "And Mr. Wells. As for their errand, I have yet to learn what brings them here."

Jed took her words as an invitation to step forward and state their mission. "We wish to be wed, Reverend."

Mistress Sinclair recoiled in horror. "Marry! I wasn't aware that you two were acquainted. Whatever are the Kincaids thinking to allow this? Everyone knows Jedidiah Wells is . . ." Jed was glaring at her so fiercely, the rest of the sentence lodged in her throat.

"Pray let me handle this, wife," the reverend said, inviting Charity and Jed inside. When they were all seated in his small office, he asked, "Now, what is this all about? I wasn't aware you were stepping out with a man, child. Do you have the Kincaids' blessing?"

"Mistress Kincaid suggested it herself before she turned Mistress Fairchild out," Jed bit out tersely. Charity groaned aloud, dismayed by Jed's candid statement.

The reverend's shaggy brows lifted in mute understanding. "Then I assume there is good reason for this hasty wedding. Strange," he said with harsh disapproval, "I would never have paired the two of you. But stranger things have happened. It grieves me, child, that you succumbed to this scoundrel's lust." He glared at Jed. "There is a place reserved in hell for men who corrupt innocent women."

"Oh, no, Reverend, it's not like that at all," Charity denied, unable to look Jed in the eye. Would the whole town assume she and Jed had—had . . . She couldn't even think it, let alone say it.

Jed gave a tight-lipped smile. "Regardless of the reason, we wish to be married. Today. Now."

Reverend Sinclair glowered darkly, his disapproval intense. His sour-faced wife gathered her indignation around her like a cloak and said, "I would have thought better of you, Mistress Fairchild. The Kincaids are God-fearing people; 'tis no wonder they turned you out. If you are indeed increasing, marrying a man like Mr. Wells is fit punishment for your disgrace."

Charity buried her face in her hands, mortified beyond reason.

"That is between me and Mistress Fairchild," Jed said in a tone that sent chills racing down the reverend's spine. "Must we go to another town to be wed? Or perhaps," he added slyly, "I'll just take Mistress Fairchild to my bed without benefit of marriage."

The reverend gasped in outrage, leaping to his feet. "I will not countenance such immoral behavior. I will marry you, and my good wife can act as witness. Come along to the church. But mind you, I do this under duress."

"I don't care how you do it, Reverend, just do it."

Charity thought she had never attended so grim a wedding. The ceremony was better suited to a burying than a marriage.

Jed sent a sidelong glance at Charity, surprised at the unexpected longing that engulfed him. She appeared petrified, sitting tensely beside him on the sleigh, he thought irritably. Did he repulse her so much? Was she frightened that he might break his word and insist upon marital privileges? Jed snorted in disgust. Did she think he'd inflict himself and his scarred body upon a woman who regarded him with revulsion? No, he told himself, he had some pride left. If only she wasn't so damn beautiful. Even in her prim, high-collared dark dress, she was desirable.

Filled with a nameless terror, Charity kept her eyes downcast. Married! Fate had conspired to give her a dark, brooding husband who cared nothing for her . . . a man who neither needed nor wanted a wife. Jed Wells was so private a man, he shunned society like the plague. And if that wasn't enough his body carried wounds that by his own admission were hideous. Suddenly she became aware that he was speaking to her. Her long lashes swept upward, revealing soft brown eyes slightly unfocused.

"Were you saying something, Mr. Wells? I'm sorry, my thoughts were elsewhere."

Jed frowned, well aware of the cause of her distraction. "I merely suggested that you call me Jed. We're married now, so it hardly seems proper to address me formally. And I shall call you Charity. I believe that is your name."

Charity merely stared at him, mesmerized by his strong, handsome features. "Charity is your name, isn't it?" Jed repeated.

"Y-yes," Charity said numbly. The dark intensity of his gaze sent a shiver down her spine. Why did he affect her this way?

A tense silence prevailed as Jed concentrated on driving the sleigh through the snow. From beneath lowered lids Charity slanted him an occasional glance, confused by the strange currents that whispered across her skin whenever the sleigh lurched and she was pressed up against his solid weight. Though she broke contact almost immediately, the tingling of her flesh persisted.

"We're almost home, Charity," Jed said in a tone that brought Charity instantly alert. He sounded anything but pleased. "Before we arrive I'll give you one last warning. Do anything to hurt my daughter, either by word or deed, and I'll not hesitate to turn you out. But if you behave in a proper manner and be the kind of mother

Star needs, you'll have a home for as long as you want it."

Charity gulped and nodded, recalling vividly Star's little coffee-colored face, her classic Indian features and large brown eyes. She knew she had reacted badly to the child, but hoped in time she would overcome her unreasonable fear of Indians. Jed Wells didn't strike her as a particularly patient or understanding man, except when it came to his daughter. She hoped she'd never experience the full extent of his anger.

Jed guided the sleigh down the lane leading to the isolated farmhouse and stopped before the front door. "Go on inside. I'll be in as soon as I unhitch the horse and rub him down."

Charity nodded and hopped to the ground before Jed could help her. She knew how awkward it was for him with his bad leg to lift himself down to the ground and thought to save him the trouble. As if surmising her thoughts, Jed frowned, but he said nothing, watching her through narrowed lids as she opened the door and stepped into the house.

When she jumped from the sleigh he'd caught a fleeting glimpse of trim ankle and the merest hint of slender calf. He wanted to look away but couldn't. He had a wife who wasn't a wife at all, one he could only look at and wonder what it would be like to bed. For he could never bed Charity. She had made it obvious that she was repelled by him. He could see the fear in her eyes, the revulsion, the utter terror of having to live in the same house with him. Why did she have to be so beautiful? Why did he feel a tightening in his loins, a shortness of breath whenever he looked at her? Why did his heart pound in a wild rhythm he didn't understand?

Unaware of Jed's jumbled thoughts, Charity stepped inside the house and closed the door softly behind her.

Seated on a bench before the hearth, Star worked diligently on a piece of cloth, weaving a needle in and out with childlike concentration. Songbird sat beside her, supervising her work. When Star heard the door open and close, she quickly thrust the cloth behind her back and looked eagerly toward the door, expecting Jed. When she saw Charity step into the room, a radiant smile spread across her face.

"Mistress Fairchild, you came back!" The cloth lay forgotten on the bench as she rushed toward Charity. Behind her, Songbird's mouth stretched into a knowing grin, her expression strangely complacent.

Star grasped Charity's hand and pulled her toward the hearth. "Sit down, you must be frozen. Where is Papa? I'm so glad you decided to come back. Are you going to stay?"

Charity looked down at the outline of the little brown hand against her white skin and stifled the urge to pull from the child's grasp. But she did not.

"Your papa is seeing to the horse," she said slowly. Charity didn't know how to answer Star's questions and hoped Jed would return soon.

"Are you going to live here with us? That would be wonderful, wouldn't it, Songbird?"

Songbird's obsidian eyes held the answers to the mysteries of the universe as she regarded Charity. "The maiden of the snow is welcome," she said cryptically. "For many moons she has been expected, but I wasn't certain this was the maiden revealed to me in my dream. The Great Spirit has brought her to us so that I may leave here with a peaceful heart."

"Leave? Did I hear you say you were leaving, Songbird? Will we see you tomorrow?" Jed had entered the house in time to hear Songbird's words.

A sad look darkened the old woman's wrinkled features, and Charity realized with sudden insight that the woman was older than she had at first thought.

"You will not see me again, Jed Wells. I am old. I want to die with my people around me."

Jed frowned in consternation. "How will you find them? Are they camped in the area?"

"There is a band camped not far from here, but they are not of my tribe. I have spoken with them, and they told me where to find my people. I go to them now."

"Why now, Songbird?" Jed questioned. "Why did you pick this time to leave?"

Songbird's intense gaze slid to Charity. "The maiden of the snow has come. I am no longer needed."

"What nonsense is this?" Jed scoffed. "We will always need you."

Songbird flashed him a toothless grin. "My dreams do not lie. It is good you have found

379

a young woman to warm your bed and raise your daughter. I am weary, Jed Wells. It is time to go."

"I love you, Songbird," Star said sadly. "I don't want you to leave. If Mistress Fairchild decides to leave tomorrow or the next day, we will be alone."

"Charity won't be leaving," Jed said with quiet authority. "We were married today. She is my wife now."

Star's face lit with joy as she threw her arms around Charity's waist, hugging her tightly. Songbird smiled and nodded sagely, as if she had known all along the outcome of Charity's unscheduled arrival two days ago. Jed seemed the least affected, his face inscrutable as he stared at Charity with an intensity that set her heart to pounding.

Chapter Five

Overcome with nervousness, Charity couldn't control her shaking hands as she shared the evening meal with Jed and Star. Songbird had prepared the meal and then slipped out the back door before anyone realized she had left. Charity was surprised that Jed had made no effort to stop her, but she supposed that Songbird preferred it that way. Farewells were always sad.

That evening Charity had never been more aware of Jed as a man. It was difficult to believe that she was his wife. This entire day had been like a dream—or nightmare—however one wanted to interpret it. Being turned out by Mistress Kincaid, her hasty marriage to Jed, and now the wedding night. She wanted to believe that Jed expected no intimacy from this marriage, but she had noticed the way he watched her when he thought she wasn't looking. Unfortunately, she wasn't well enough acquainted with him to trust him to keep his word.

And if that wasn't bad enough, she had problems of her own to deal with. Problems that intensified whenever she looked at Jed. One steely-eyed glance from him turned her all shivery and mushy inside and made her tongue-tied. Even more terrifying was her uncontrollable urge to view those terrible scars he spoke of and to ease the pain in his lame leg with massages and hot packs, as Mistress Kincaid had taught her to do for the children when they were injured. It amazed her that she could even think of a man's limb, let alone look at one. Her strict upbringing had severely limited her knowledge or understanding of the male anatomy.

More than anything, Jed wanted to look his fill at Charity, but he feared he would frighten her. He knew she was innocent and already terrified of him and what he would demand from her. She couldn't know that he was a man of his word. No matter how much he wanted her, he would never break his vow that this would be a marriage in name only. He couldn't bear the rejection when she saw his disfiguring scars and twisted leg. If not for a barrage of cannon fire, he'd be a whole man today.

"'Tis late, Charity," Jed said, scraping back his chair. His voice sounded harsh in the tense silence, and Charity started violently. "You've had a difficult day. You may as well retire. After I put Star to bed in the loft I'll turn in myself."

Charity stared at him dumbly. Was she reading more into his words than was actually there? Rising abruptly, she nearly ran into the small bedroom she had occupied the previous two nights.

"G-good night," she stuttered, not waiting for a reply.

"Mistress Fairchild must *really* be tired, Papa," Star said as she watched Charity rush from the room.

"She is no longer Mistress Fairchild, sweetheart," Jed said, his voice softening. He couldn't ever recall raising his voice to his daughter. "You may call her Charity, and in time, if you feel comfortable with it, you can call her Mama."

"Is Miss—is Charity really my mama now?" Star asked hopefully. Even though Jed had said so, Star had the feeling that Charity wasn't exactly pleased with the title.

"Yes, sweetheart, since Charity and I are married she is now your mama."

Star's pixieish features turned wistful. "I've always wanted a mama. Will Charity stay with us forever?"

Jed wanted to say she would, but it was still too early to predict the outcome of their unstable marriage. "I hope so."

"Will she be here for my birthday?"

Since Star's birthday was on Christmas Eve, only two weeks away, Jed felt safe in saying, "She will be here for your birthday. No more talk, little one, 'tis time for bed."

After Star was tucked into her snug little bed in the loft, Jed looked longingly at the bedroom door, wondering how Charity would react if he walked through that door and climbed into bed beside her. He snorted derisively, knowing he'd never allow her to see him without the protection of his clothing. Though the good Lord knew he'd give anything to see her without her clothing. He'd be willing to bet she was perfect in every way.

Sighing regretfully, Jed limped awkwardly to the hearth, piling on sufficient wood to last through the night. His right leg might be weak, he thought as he lifted a heavy log, but the strength of his upper torso more than compensated. Thick, corded muscles rippled beneath his firm flesh as he bent to his task.

Finishing his chore quickly, Jed searched the room for the blanket he had used the previous two nights and found it missing. Too late, he realized that Songbird must have folded it and put it in its usual place in the chest in his room.

Spitting out a curse, he glared darkly at the closed bedroom door. He had almost decided to spend a miserable night without a blanket when it occurred to him how foolishly he was acting. If he wanted a blanket to make his rest more comfortable, all he need do was open the bedroom door and get it.

Inside the bedroom Charity stripped down to her shift and folded her clothes neatly. Her movements were jerky, almost furtive. All the while she kept an eye on the door. She was uncomfortable with the knowledge that the door lacked a lock. After all, she knew almost nothing about Jed Wells.

He could very well be a liar, or a mean-spirited soul who enjoyed hurting others. Just because he was kind and loving toward his daughter didn't mean he'd treat his wife the same way.

Charity finished her task and turned to blow out the candle. Suddenly the flame flickered in the draft created by the open door and she froze, aware that Jed had entered the room. A thrill of anticipation slithered down her spine when she saw his massive shoulders filling the doorway. His intimidating presence set her blood to tingling in a most infuriating manner.

Jed paused in the doorway, stunned to find Charity clad in her shift and little else. He should have knocked, he realized as his gaze strayed from her face downward over the ripe curves of her body. He was right, he silently exulted, she *was* perfect. The points of her firm breasts strained against the cloth of the shift, and he could see the barest hint of the shadowy mystery between her legs. He closed his eyes, inhaling the heady scent of her skin wafting to him from across the room.

"What—what do you want?" She was panting, made breathless by the intensity of Jed's diamond-hard gaze. The sound of her voice brought Jed abruptly to his senses. If he told her exactly what he was thinking, she would probably run away screaming.

Realizing he was behaving like a besotted fool, Jed frowned and tried to direct his gaze elsewhere. His good intentions were forgotten when Charity inadvertently moved in front of the candle and the diffused light behind her made her

Connie Mason

shift transparent. A groan slipped past Jed's compressed lips. He was so aroused by the provocative display of her charms, he felt his loins fill and swell.

"You promised," Charity whispered, suddenly realizing she was standing nearly naked in front of a strange man. True, the man was her husband, but that hardly counted since she had known him less than three days.

"Don't worry," Jed said evenly. "I'm here for nothing more than a blanket. I should have knocked, I'm sorry."

His expression gave nothing of his thoughts away as he limped toward the chest at the foot of the bed and extracted a blanket. He was so anxious to leave that he turned sharply—too sharply—and tripped on the upraised corner of the braided rug. He fell to one knee. Charity gave a little cry and rushed forward. Without conscious thought, she reached out to help him. He shook off her hands, glaring at her fiercely.

"Don't ever do that again," he bit out with scathing contempt. "I don't need your help, Charity. I don't need anyone's help. I've managed thus far by myself and will continue to do so."

"I—I didn't mean . . . I can massage your leg if you'd like. I often did it for the Kincaid children when they hurt themselves. I—I was very good at it."

Jed looked at her as if she'd lost her mind. Did she actually think he'd expose himself to her ridicule? "Let's get one thing straight, Charity. I never wanted a wife, but now that I have one

I'd appreciate it if you confined yourself to the mothering duties women are so good at. I don't need you to massage my leg, or help me when I fall. Above all, I don't appreciate your pity." He walked out the door. "Rest well, Charity."

Her face burning, Charity watched him limp through the open door. She marched after him, slamming the door behind him. What a thoroughly disagreeable man, she thought sourly. Didn't he know she wished only to help him? Couldn't he tell that she felt no pity for him? He had given her a home and kept his word. He wasn't insisting on his marital rights, and the least she could do was ease his suffering. What was he afraid of? Certainly not her, she reasoned. She felt fairly certain she could look at his scars and not be repulsed, if that was what bothered him. What did a few scars matter when the rest of him was strong and nearly perfect?

And after spending the day with Star, Charity decided it wasn't going to be as difficult as she had imagined to accept the little girl for what she was—an innocent child who happened to have Indian blood. Of course, that didn't dispel any of the terrible fear she harbored for Indians. That fear would always be with her. But little Star hardly seemed like an Indian, having been raised the same as any white child. Well, almost the same.

Long after Charity went to bed she recalled the way Jed had stared at her, remembered the dark intensity of his eyes, and was strangely warmed by it. She knew he must be terribly uncomfortable sleeping on the floor, and guilt smote her. He had taken on her problems and was saddled with a wife he neither wanted nor needed.

Strange, she thought, moments before she fell asleep, but she no longer feared him. True, he could be fierce at times, but not once did she feel threatened by him. Infuriated, perhaps, intimidated certainly, but not frightened.

Jed tossed restlessly on his uncomfortable pallet. He couldn't stop thinking about how utterly provocative and feminine Charity had looked wearing naught but a shift, the sweet lines of her body illuminated by candlelight. He knew she had no earthly idea how maddeningly tempting she was, and he cursed fate for giving him injuries that made him repulsive to women. The only kind of intimacy he would ever attempt again was the kind he paid for.

When he had returned from the war, his fiancée had told him frankly that she knew of no woman willing to bed a man with fearsome scars like his. To make matters worse, he had earned the townspeople's contempt when he returned with a newborn Indian baby in tow. Yet no matter how he'd tried, he couldn't bring himself to give up Star. He had settled on the family farm with his widowed mother, who had taken care of Star for the first two years of her life. His mother had died peacefully in her sleep one night. Fortunately, he had found Songbird shortly afterward.

Before Jed fully embraced sleep, he made a wish he knew would never come to pass. He wished he were whole and perfect in every way and that Charity would learn to love Star as much as he did. He wanted their marriage to be a true one, based on mutual love and respect, not pity.

Chapter Six

During the following days Jed spent precious little time with Charity. If he wasn't feeding and taking care of the farm animals, he was checking on his traps. Trapping small game was a source of food and provided much-needed coin. Each evening he returned to the house to share supper with Charity and Star, and afterward he put Star to bed while Charity cleaned up. By then it was time for Charity to seek her own bed, and after a curt goodnight Jed usually curled up before the fire. When Charity awoke in the morning he was always gone, having built up the fire and fixed his own breakfast.

With marked reluctance Charity took over the duties relinquished by Songbird. She was surprised to find the larder well stocked with flour, cornmeal, dried beans, sugar, and a small amount of precious salt. The root cellar beneath the house held potatoes, onions, squash, turnips, and several bushels of apples. Further inspection revealed cured hams, bacon, and sausage in the smokehouse. If nothing else, Jed was a good provider for his family.

Charity spared a glance at Star, who was painstakingly embroidering her father's initial on a handkerchief for Christmas. Her shiny black head was bowed as she concentrated on her work, her stitches uneven but surprisingly good for a child approaching six. As if aware of her gaze, Star looked up at Charity and grinned.

"Do you think Papa will like it? Songbird taught me how to embroider. It's not really very good."

Charity laid down the knife and turnip she was peeling and walked over to Star to inspect her work. "It looks fine to me, Star. I'm sure your papa will love it." The stitches were crooked and far from perfect, but Charity knew that Jed would think it quite wonderful.

"I don't have anything to give you, Charity," Star said soulfully. "When I started Papa's gift I didn't know I was going to have a mama."

The little girl's words tugged at Charity's heart, and she reached out to caress her soft brown cheek. Charity was surprised that she no longer felt the quivering sickness that had assailed her whenever she looked at Star at first. Star's cheek was smooth and downy, the same as a white child's, and her dark eyes regarded Charity with the kind of trust she had never experienced before. Within a very short time she had stopped thinking of Star as an Indian, seeing only a sweet little girl.

"I don't expect a gift, Star," Charity assured her. "The Kincaids didn't celebrate Christmas with gifts. They thought it a sinful extravagance and concentrated on the religious aspect."

"Every year Papa reads me the Nativity from Grandma's Bible. I almost know it by heart," Star said proudly.

Charity was stunned. She couldn't imagine Jed Wells being a religious man, this bitter, reclusive man who seemed to have little use for society or religion.

"I'm glad you're here this Christmas to share the story." Star flashed Charity a shy smile. "Did you know Christmas Eve is my birthday?"

"Why, no, I didn't. That makes Christmas a very special occasion, indeed. I will cook something that day in your honor. What would you like?"

"Something sweet," Star said, her dark eyes dancing. "Sometimes Papa brings me sweets from town."

"Then something sweet it shall be," Charity assured the child. Then and there Charity decided to make this birthday really special for Star. Returning to the paring knife and half-peeled turnip, she searched her mind for an appropriate gift for the little girl.

Distracted as she was by her thoughts, she didn't hear Star's question until the child repeated it. "Why does Papa sleep on the floor instead of in his bed?"

The point of the knife jabbed painfully into Charity's thumb and she cried out in dismay. "What! What did you say?"

"Until you came, Papa never slept on the floor. It's so hard and uncomfortable, it can't be good for his bad leg."

Charity's already considerable guilt intensified. To make matters worse, she had absolutely no idea how to answer Star's innocently posed question. She glanced out the window, trying to compose her thoughts. She let out a piercing scream when she saw a hideous brown face peering through the window.

"Charity, what is it? What do you see?" Frightened by Charity's ungodly scream, Star rushed to her side, hiding behind her skirt.

A minute later the door opened and two Indians stepped inside. They were tall and gaunt, and their clothing, crudely sewn from animal hides, hung on their lank frames. Each man was wrapped in a blanket and armed with a bow and quiver of arrows. They walked into the room without being invited, looking around curiously. One man spied the turnip Charity was peeling and popped it into his mouth.

Shaking in terror, Charity could do little more than stare at the two savages who had invaded her home. One man stepped forward, rubbed his stomach, and pointed to his mouth. When Charity appeared not to understand, he said something in a guttural tongue and repeated his motions.

"G-get out," Charity said, too frightened to heed what the Indian was trying to convey.

Suddenly Star, who had been hiding behind Charity's skirts, stepped forward. "I think they want something to eat. If Papa was here I'm sure he'd give them some food."

The Indian looked down at Star, seeing her for the first time. His eyes widened and he cried out, babbling in his own language as he motioned wildly to his companion. Both men stared at Star with growing horror. They looked as if they had just seen a ghost. They spoke rapidly to one another while backing out the door. Then they turned and ran as if the devil were at their heels.

Charity could not move, could barely breathe as she watched the two Indians disappear into the gray dusk. She recalled vividly the day Indians had attacked her home near Jamestown. She was nine years old. That day the Indians wanted more than food. Her mother had hidden her in the root cellar beneath the house during the attack, and Charity could still hear the sounds of the massacre that had occurred just over her head.

"Charity, are you all right?" Star had no idea why Charity was so frightened. Indians had come to the house before, looking for handouts, and nothing bad had happened. Though Star did not recognize these Indians, she wasn't unduly upset by them.

Once the Indians were out of sight, Charity started shivering violently. Her teeth were still chattering when Jed stepped through the open door a few minutes later.

"Why is the front door open? Don't you know it's cold outside?" Then he saw Charity's white face and Star's worried expression and his heart plummeted down to his toes. "My God, what happened?"

"Indians, Papa," Star piped up. "They came to the house looking for food."

His relief was stabbing and immediate. He turned to Charity. "Did they hurt you?" Charity shook her head. "Did you give them food?" Charity merely looked at him, her eyes unfocused, and Jed knew she was in shock.

Grasping her shoulders, he gave her a little shake. Then, without conscious thought or volition, she was in his arms and he was holding her close, rocking her, telling her he'd protect her, that he'd not allow anyone to hurt her. He kissed her hair, her temple, savoring the way her body fit snugly against his, wishing it would always be like this.

"Papa, why is Charity so scared?" Star's plaintive little voice brought him to his senses. He released Charity abruptly.

"I don't know, sweetheart, but I aim to find out. Why don't you set the table for supper while I try to calm Charity." He bolted the door as Star turned to her task. Then he led Charity into the bedroom and sat her down on the bed.

"All right, Charity, what's this all about? I know you're frightened of Indians, but from what Star tells me you had nothing to fear. The Indians were probably hungry and wanted food. Since the Clark expedition drove most Indians west from Virginia, we've had little to fear from them. Occasionally some of them make their way back during hard times, but they're not violent like they once were."

When Charity merely stared past him as if he didn't exist, Jed knew he had to do something to bring her back to reality. And it had to be something startling enough to shock her. He felt only a twinge of guilt as he sat down beside her, took her into his arms, and kissed her. With gentle expertise he coaxed her back to life with his mouth and tongue as he thrust past her lips to taste the sweetness he knew he'd find there.

Slowly, oh so slowly, Charity warmed to his touch, groaning deep inside her throat, overwhelmed by the taste and scent of him. Musky and male. Tender and rough. Never had she experienced anything quite like it in her life. She felt the torrid heat of his hands on her back as he pressed her against the hardness of his body. All her fears, her worries, faded away into nothing as she melted against him.

Shaking with need, Jed pressed her closer, closer still, wishing he could absorb her into his pores. When she made no protest, his hands traveled with slow deliberation to her breasts, caressing her nipples through the material of her bodice. Inspired by her acceptance, he kissed her wildly, her hair, her lips, her nose, anywhere his lips could reach.

Charity emerged as if from a dream, her body tingling, her senses careening wildly out of control. She felt Jed's hands scorching her flesh and his lips caressing her mouth and knew a fear not unlike that which she felt when she saw the Indians. But this was a different kind of fear, one that instinct told her could lead to pleasure. A pleasure she was not yet ready for.

"Jed, please." Her plea rolled off him like water off a duck's back. "Jed, I'm afraid." She had finally captured his attention.

His senses returned slowly. In an agony of need, he groaned and set her away from him. "Are you all right now? Do you want to tell me what happened here today?"

Feeling the need to lengthen the distance between them, he started to rise. Charity clutched him with frantic desperation. "They burst into the house without warning," she gasped breathlessly. "They talked among themselves and made motions I couldn't understand. I—I think they wanted food, but I was too frightened to react."

"I know Indians killed your parents, Charity, but that was a long time ago. Indians are no longer a threat to us."

"You wouldn't say that if you'd been in the root cellar listening to them kill your parents. They attacked at dusk one night when we least expected it. We lived near Jamestown at the time. My mother hid me in the root cellar while they fought for their lives. They saved my life but lost their own.

"The Indians set fire to the cabin and left. I crawled out of the root cellar in time to save myself and wandered around in shock until someone found me."

"Was that when the Kincaids took you in?"

"No, I lived with the preacher and his family a few months until he found a family willing to give me a home. The Kincaids had just arrived from England and were on their way to Williamsburg. The preacher convinced the Kincaids that I would be useful to them. I was nine years old."

"Useful," Jed spat. "Useful as a servant, you mean."

"They gave me a home," Charity reminded him.

"And you've been frightened of Indians ever since?"

Charity nodded bleakly. "I peeked through the cracks of the floor and watched them slaughter my family. I'll never forget their fierce joy when they—they took my parents' scalps." She shuddered uncontrollably. Jed wanted desperately to take her into his arms, but didn't trust his ability to do so without taking it further than Charity would want.

"Are you composed enough now to face Star? I brought you in the bedroom because I feared your hysteria would upset her. She probably has the table set by now and is wondering what's keeping us."

Charity gulped and nodded, realizing how foolish she must appear to Jed. "I'm sorry. It's just the shock of having my home invaded by savages. I'm fine now."

Jed stared at her, strangely pleased that she had referred to the farm as her home.

When he held his hand out to assist her from the bed, Charity suddenly recalled the Indians strange reaction when they saw Star.

"Wait, I forgot to tell you something. The Indians seemed surprised when they saw Star and began babbling language and gesturing excitedly. I don't know what it all meant, but they were frightened enough to turn tail and run."

Jed paled. "Are you certain it was Star they were looking at?"

"As certain as I could be under the circumstances. At first I thought they were merely surprised to see an Indian child, but it had to be more than that. Could Star's mother be from that tribe? Does Star look enough like her mother to be recognized as one of their own?"

"I can't say," Jed said tightly. Charity could tell he was worried, but his mouth was clamped so tightly she decided not to pursue the subject.

Star chattered happily during supper, their encounter with Indians already forgotten. But Charity could not forget so easily. Her eyes kept straying to the door, as if expecting it to burst open at any moment. She knew she wouldn't sleep a wink tonight.

After the meal she cleaned up while Jed put Star to bed. When he returned to the parlor, Charity lingered so long in the kitchen that Jed finally asked, "Aren't you tired tonight, Charity?"

Charity started violently. Her knees would have crumpled beneath her if Jed hadn't placed a supporting arm around her waist.

"You can't go on like this, Charity. You have nothing to fear from those Indians. Besides, 'tis unlikely they'll remain in the area long, they never do. Go to bed, I'll keep watch tonight."

Charity looked at the bedroom door, then at

Jed. "I'd feel safer if you slept in the bedroom tonight."

Her strained features gave hint of how difficult it was to ask that of him. "That's not a good idea, Charity. The room is hardly large enough for me to stretch out on the floor comfortably."

Swallowing her dignity, Charity said, "You could sleep on the bed." She feared Indians more than she feared Jed.

Jed's response was to close his eyes and groan. Just the thought of lying beside her was painful.

"I wouldn't bother you," she continued in a rush. "I take up very little room. And you could sleep on top of the covers."

Jed snorted in derision. As if he could actually sleep with her beside him, imagining what it would be like to lose himself in her sweet flesh. Charity must truly have been traumatized by their uninvited guests, he reflected, to suggest they share the same bed, even if he was on top of the covers. It was for that reason and that reason alone, Jed tried to tell himself, that he consented to Charity's request.

"Get into bed," he said gruffly, hoping to disguise the tremor in his voice. "I'll be in as soon as I bank the fire."

Charity hurried into the bedroom, grateful that Jed was allowing her time to undress and get beneath the covers before joining her. She knew she had been brazen to suggest such a thing, but she would definitely feel safer with Jed sleeping beside her. She undressed, washed quickly, and slid beneath the feather comforter seconds before Jed returned.

"Are you sure this is what you want, Charity?"

Charity swallowed and nodded. "I'd feel safer."

Jed limped into the room, sat down on the edge of the bed, and removed his boots. Then he lay down fully clothed on the bed, pulling a spare blanket Charity had placed at the foot of the bed over him. He stretched his right leg and groaned, plagued by a stabbing ache. The cold weather played havoc with his lame leg, and unconsciously he rubbed it to ease the pain.

If only he could relax, he thought irritably. His body was uncomfortably aware of Charity's small form lying but a hand span away. Suddenly he stiffened and jumped out of bed.

Startled, Charity rose up on her elbows. "What is it? Have the Indians returned?"

"No," Jed gasped, dancing around on his left leg. "Charley horse. The cold weather often affects my leg this way."

"Let me help." Scrambling from the bed, Charity gave him a gentle shove.

"What the hell!" He fell backward onto the bed. Immediately Charity was beside him, massaging and pummeling the corded tendons, trying to halt the painful spasms. She paid little heed to the withered flesh beneath her fingertips, concentrating instead on easing Jed's pain.

"Stop!" Jed gasped, embarrassed to have Charity witness his weakness. "I don't need your help."

"Jedidiah Wells! You're more of a child than Star." Her hands were magically soothing on his distressed flesh. "There now, doesn't that feel better?"

Jed groaned. His leg felt better, but another part of him ached most abominably.

Chapter Seven

Charity hunched over her work, counting stitches in the stockings she was knitting for Jed. She had decided to unravel a sweater of her own in order to make gifts for both Jed and Star. Star was to have a hat and mittens to go along with the birthday cake that Charity intended to bake for the little girl on Christmas Eve. When Star went to bed at night, Charity knitted on her gift, and when Jed was gone during the day, out came the stockings.

Feeling cooped up in the house, Star had gone outside to play, leaving Charity alone with her knitting and her thoughts. Despite her best efforts, her thoughts kept returning to that night Jed had allowed her to massage the knotted muscles of his crippled leg. He had allowed the intimacy until the pain eased; then he had rudely shoved her hands aside, declaring that he didn't need her ministrations. But she knew she had helped him despite his curt rejection. After that night he had returned to his bed beside the hearth.

Try though she might, Charity could not recall how his leg had felt beneath her hands. She had not dwelt on the withered flesh as she'd deftly kneaded the spasming muscles. All she remembered was the inherent strength beneath her fingertips. It mattered little that he was scarred in places that didn't count.

Suddenly the front door opened and Jed limped into the room, followed closely by Star. Not wanting Jed to see the stockings she was knitting for him, Charity thrust them behind her back, surprised to see him home so early in the day. He'd barely had time to finish the morning chores.

"I'm going to check on my traps and shoot a nice fat turkey for Christmas dinner," Jed informed her as he began gathering his equipment for an overnight stay in the woods. "The weather is cooperating, so I probably won't return until sometime tomorrow."

Charity paled. "Tomorrow? Star and I will be alone in the house tonight." Though no more Indians had appeared at her door, she was dismayed at the prospect of being left alone overnight. What if they returned while Jed was gone?

"You've nothing to worry about, Charity," Jed assured her. "Those Indians are probably long gone by now."

"We'll manage." Charity was glad he couldn't see her quivering insides. "Please be careful."

Jed regarded her intently. It seemed inconceivable that she cared enough about him to be concerned. Most women ran from him in terror. Of course, his surly manner and reclusive habits didn't endear him to women. But how could he bare his wounds to a woman during intimacy when he could hardly stand the sight of them himself? It truly surprised him that Charity seemed unperturbed by his injuries. She had touched his withered flesh without expressing revulsion. Just recalling her hands upon him made sweat pop out on his forehead. She was so damn beautiful and innocent, he felt like a depraved animal for wanting her so desperately.

"Trapping is a way of life for me. There is no danger involved when you know what you're doing."

"Nevertheless," Charity advised, "do be careful." She bit down hard on her lip, realizing how close she had come to cautioning him about his lame leg. He was such a proud man, the last thing in the world he'd want was her sympathy. She rose to walk with him to the door. Star skipped ahead of him.

Abruptly Jed stopped dead in his tracks, turning to face Charity. She bumped into him, coming up hard against him. He groaned softly, reaching out to steady her as she swayed on her feet. In a moment of intense yearning he pulled her close, the incredible softness of her body searing him from breast to thigh.

"I just wanted to say," he began hoarsely, staring down into the soft brown depths of her eyes, "that I should be home in time for supper tomorrow evening. I don't want to miss Star's birthday the next day."

Oddly reluctant to release her, Jed bent his head, tempted by her full red lips. His head slipped lower until their lips met. A jolt of raw heat ripped through him as he covered her mouth with his. He knew Charity felt it too by the way she shuddered and melted into his embrace. The heady scent of her skin glided across his senses, and his arms tightened, loath to let her go.

My God, he thought despairingly, how could this have happened? He was falling in love with his wife! He had known Charity so short a time, it hardly seemed possible that he could love her already. He had no business falling in love. Loving a decent woman was forbidden him, for his pride would never allow him to bare his body in the act of love to any but a whore. He was doomed to love Charity from afar, fighting the compulsive need to taste her sweet flesh.

Charity's heart nearly erupted from her breast, slamming the breath from her as Jed's kiss went on and on. Against her will her hands crept around his neck, tunneling through the hair at the back of his neck as she gave herself up to the pure magic of his mouth. How was it possible to enjoy something as shamefully delicious as a kiss? In all her years with the Kincaids she'd never witnessed the slightest hint of intimacy or closeness. She wanted the kiss to go on forever. She wanted more . . . much more . . .

but had no name to put to her need. And her limited experience told her Jed felt the same way.

Jed indeed felt the same way. But he was made of much sterner stuff than Charity. Stiffening his resolve, he broke off the kiss, carefully set Charity aside, and backed away.

"I'm sorry, Charity, I didn't mean for that to happen. You're too inexperienced to know what this sort of thing could lead to. I made you a promise when we married and I intend to keep it. I just hadn't counted on feeling this way about you. Don't worry, though, I won't ever place you in the position of running from me in disgust."

"No, I wouldn't . . . I don't . . ."

"You don't know," Jed said softly. Then he turned abruptly and limped out the door. Charity wanted to call him back, but the lump in her throat prevented her from doing so.

The afternoon dragged by as Charity worked diligently on Jed's stockings. A light snow was falling but it didn't look like anything to worry about. She tried to imagine Jed's surprise when she presented him with her gift on Christmas Day. He had such a low opinion of himself, she knew he expected nothing from her.

Living with Jed these past few weeks had shown Charity a different side of him, a side only Star had been aware of. He wasn't reclusive by choice, she realized. The townspeople had forced him to retreat from society to protect his Indian daughter from their cruelty.

Connie Mason

Charity now understood that Jed had retreated from society because he scorned pity. He deliberately discouraged friendships with his surly manner and dark moods. Her heart went out to him. Though she was inexperienced with the opposite sex, there was one thing of which she was absolutely certain. Her feelings for Jed had nothing to do with pity.

"Charity, I've finished the handkerchief for Papa, do you think he will like it?" Star held up the square of cloth for Charity's inspection.

Charity laid down her knitting needles to inspect Star's handiwork. The initial was crudely wrought on the square of linen and the stitches were uneven, but Charity knew Jed would appreciate his daughter's effort.

"It's wonderful, Star. Your father will love it."

Star beamed happily. "I'll hide it until Christmas. Only two more days till my birthday. I hope Papa gets here in time."

"He'll be back," Charity assured her. "We'll make something special for him for supper tomorrow night. Maybe the chickens will cooperate and lay a few eggs for your birthday cake."

Star brightened. "Maybe they already have. I'll go look in the chicken coop." She jumped from the bench, retrieved her coat from the hook beside the door, and removed the bar from the panel. Since the Indians had burst into the house, Charity had been most diligent about barring the door.

Charity smiled to herself as she gathered the ingredients to prepare a small lunch for herself and Star. She had never imagined she could be so happy living with a man. Or so accepting of an Indian child after her harrowing experience with Indians when she was a youngster. Suddenly her reverie was shattered by a piercing scream. Star!

Charity rushed to the door and flung it open, finding her way barred by an Indian whose fierce expression made her shrink back in terror. "What have you done to Star?" she cried, peering past the Indian for a glimpse of Star. Star screamed again and Charity spied her by the chicken coop, being carried off by a fierce-looking Indian.

"Oh, God, no!" Stark, black panic seized her when she saw Star struggle in her captor's arms, kicking and screaming at the top of her lungs. When Charity tried to follow, the Indian beside her shoved her backward into the house, slamming the door in her face and sprinting off after his companion.

Stunned, Charity stared at the closed door, listening to Star's screams growing weak in the distance. She tried to move but her legs were numb, refusing to obey her silent command. Fright was like a ravening beast within her. She knew she must do something, but what? She had no idea where to find Jed and there were no close neighbors whom she could turn to for help. She wrung her hands pitifully, struggling to overcome her fear. She could barely breathe, let alone think.

Indians had taken Star! The words reverberated in her brain.

She thought of Jed and how deeply he loved his daughter. She could well imagine his horror when she told him Star had been kidnapped by Indians. Would he blame her? Charity wondered. Did she blame herself for failing to protect Star? Marshaling her courage, Charity realized she must overcome her fear and use her wits if she hoped to rescue Star.

Cowering in the house was a coward's way and she was no coward, she told herself. For Jed's sake, Charity knew she had to follow the Indians and beg them to release Star. Since neither she nor Star had been harmed, she had to assume their motives weren't vicious. Perhaps they had recognized Star as one of their own and wanted her back. Whatever the reason, Charity knew she couldn't live with herself if she didn't attempt a rescue.

Gathering the tattered edges of her wits, Charity donned her warmest clothes and left the house before she lost her nerve. Walking into an Indian camp was going to be the most difficult thing she had ever done in her life.

There was a light dusting of snow covering the ground, so Charity had no difficulty following the trail left by the Indians. Twice she thought she had lost them in the woods, but her persistence paid off when she picked up the trail once again. It was nightfall when she stumbled into a camp of a dozen or so lodges hugging the riverbank. She was exhausted, hungry, and nearly petrified with fear. But when she thought of how frightened Star must be, she willed her feet to move.

The camp dogs caught her scent and set up a terrible ruckus. Frightened beyond reason, Charity came to an abrupt halt as the dogs snarled and nipped at her heels. Almost immediately people came running from their lodges to investigate. They stared at Charity curiously but did not touch or menace her in any way. They appeared to be waiting, and when Charity saw a tall, handsome Indian emerge from the lodge, she knew instinctively he was the man who held her life in his hands.

Then suddenly a tiny body bolted from one of the lodges. A small cry of gladness escaped Charity's throat as she fell to her knees and opened her arms. Star rushed into her embrace, hugging her tightly.

"Charity! I knew you'd come. What do the Indians want with me? I want my papa."

"Your papa will come, sweetheart," Charity said soothingly. She patted Star's dark head, trying not to convey her anxiety to the frightened child.

Charity cried out when Star was torn from her arms and carried back into the lodge. The child's heartrending screams gave Charity the courage to leap to her feet and give chase. To her chagrin, she was forcibly restrained. When she protested vigorously, the chief stepped forward, pointed to himself, then to Star, and said, "Father."

Charity went still. "Father? Are you saying you're Star's father?"

Once again the Indian pointed to himself and then to the lodge into which Star had been carried. "Father," he repeated, gesturing wildly. "My child."

Charity was struck nearly dumb. If this Indian was Star's father, who was Jed?

*   *   *

Jed limped into the yard late the next day, excruciatingly aware of his throbbing leg. He'd told Charity he'd be home for supper and he'd made it with time to spare. Tomorrow was Christmas Eve as well as Star's birthday, and he wanted to be with her to give her the gift he had purchased recently in town. After he rested his leg he planned to cut a Yule log to burn in the hearth. Luck had been with him and he'd shot a magnificent turkey for Christmas dinner. Later he'd gut and pluck the bird and ready it for the pan.

Jed smiled all the way to the house, thinking how wonderful it was to have Charity waiting for him. He'd never imagined that having a woman in the house could be so rewarding. If only he dared ask her to be a true wife to him, he thought wistfully. He was so irresistibly drawn to Charity that his entire life had been subtly altered by his strong feelings for her.

Moments before Jed lifted the doorlatch, he was assailed by an ominous foreboding, giving him a sinking feeling in the pit of his stomach. Something was wrong! The bitter taste of fear spurted into his mouth as he shoved the door open and stepped inside. The house was cold and silent as a tomb.

The fire had gone out. The ashes in the hearth were cold. An oppressive emptiness, more profound than any he'd ever felt, plunged him into the darkest hell.

"Charity!" The name echoed hollowly in the room. "Star!" Before the words left his mouth he knew there would be no answer. They were gone. Where?

He saw at a glance that their coats were missing, but a search of the bedroom and loft revealed that none of their belongings had been touched. The only thing he could be certain of was that their departure had been sudden and unexpected. A quick survey of the kitchen told Jed that Charity had begun preparations for a meal. Yet he knew that it hadn't been today's meal, for the ashes in the hearth were cold. That meant they had been gone since yesterday.

Jed rushed outside. The fading light revealed two sets of moccasin prints and a pair of smaller boot prints. But the tracks he was most interested in were those leading away from the house into the woods. Fortunately, no new snow had fallen and the tracks could easily be followed. At first he was puzzled by the impressions left in the snow, until he figured it out. Signs indicated that Indians had carried off Star, and Charity had followed some time later.

Jed was amazed that Charity had mustered the courage to follow Star. But the proof was indisputable. Ignoring the stabbing pain in his right leg, he hung the turkey in the smokehouse and followed the tracks leading from the house into the woods.

Chapter Eight

A woman entered the lodge where Charity was confined and set about lighting a fire. She spoke no English. She did her work efficiently, shaking her head when Charity inquired about Star. Since she had been taken to the lodge, Charity had neither seen nor heard anything of Star.

It was full dark now and Charity looked up, shuddering in revulsion as the chief entered through the open doorway of the log and bark structure, bending low to clear the entrance.

"Herowan say," he began, pointing to himself, "you go now, no come back."

"No! Not without Star," Charity replied defiantly. "Where is she? I want to see her."

"You go now," Herowan said, pointing at the door.

Charity pursed her lips belligerently. "No. I told you, not without Star."

The chief took a menacing step forward and Charity cringed, trying desperately to control her fear. Though she was quaking in her shoes, she was determined to remain until she could take Star with her, no matter what the Indians did to her. Deliberately she thrust from her mind the image of her parents as they'd fought for their lives. Lifting her chin at a stubborn angle, she knew she'd defy the devil himself if it helped bring Star back home safely.

Herowan spat out something in a language Charity didn't understand, then turned abruptly and left. Charity nearly collapsed with relief. A short time later she was surprised when the same Indian woman who had lit the fire in the hut brought her food. She eyed the mixture suspiciously, but it smelled so good she tasted it, finding it a simple concoction of vegetables and wild game. She scraped the bowl clean, then set it aside.

Though Charity tried to remain alert, she dozed fitfully during the long night, praying that Star was warm and safe.

Cursing the darkness that prevented him from following the tracks left by the Indians, Jed was forced to stop for the night. Curling up against a large rock, he munched on jerky and parched corn he had packed in his pockets before he had left to check on his traps and thought about Star and Charity.

He had a vague idea why the Indians had taken Star. The one thing he'd feared since he'd brought home the newborn babe had come to pass. Never in his wildest dreams had he imagined that the Algonquian tribe would return to the area. The Algonquian were not nomads. They were farmers who lived in villages and stayed in one place, grew crops, and built their lodges from logs, bark, and grass. He suspected the hard winter had something to do with their migration into the area again.

Even more astounding was the fact that Charity had followed the Indians to their village. He would have thought her terror of Indians would keep her from venturing after Star. Her courage amazed him, and his heart filled with an emotion so foreign it took him a while to identify it. He felt love for Star, but it was a father's love for his child, and he'd thought he loved Hilda Appleby at one time. But what he felt for Charity went beyond anything he'd ever felt before.

A man unaccustomed to prayer, Jed nevertheless believed in a higher being and silently sought His help. It was nearly Christmas, a time of miracles, and he prayed for the safety of his loved ones. Jed recalled how Star had come to him, which was a small miracle in itself, and how precious she was to him. Then he thought of his wife, startled at how important she had become to him in the short time he had known her. He wished desperately that one day she would love him as much as he loved her. He fell asleep with a prayer on his lips.

* * *

Charity awoke abruptly when a small body hurtled through the door and fell into her arms. Tears came into Charity's eyes as she hugged Star close, surprised to see that daylight had arrived. "Star! Thank God you're safe. I've been so worried."

"I'm not Herowan's daughter, I'm not!" she exclaimed, her eyes wild with fear. "I don't care what Pomeca says, I belong to Papa."

"Who is Pomeca?"

"She's Herowan's sister."

"How did you understand what Pomeca said?" Charity wondered curiously.

"Songbird taught me some Algonquian, but I don't think she belonged to this tribe."

Suddenly Herowan poked his head inside the lodge. He saw Star and smiled. Then he frowned, pointed to Charity, and said, "You go now."

Charity took Star's hand and led her from the lodge, hoping Herowan had had a change of heart and would allow her to take Star with her. But she was disabused of that idea when the child was torn from her grasp by the irate chief, who spouted words Charity did not understand.

But Star must have understood for she started sobbing as if her heart were breaking. "Herowan says I cannot go. He says I am the daughter of his dead wife, Timacan. He says . . ."

Her words faltered, then stopped altogether as a great commotion erupted on the perimeter of the village. Charity's gaze swung toward the noise, and her heart nearly stopped beating when she saw Jed pushing through the crowd of Indians who had come from their lodges to investigate. Jed spied Charity and Star, and his relief was so profound his lame leg twisted beneath him and he stumbled, having tested it severely trekking through the woods without respite. No one made an effort to stop him as he strode toward Charity, his gait uneven but purposeful.

When Star caught sight of her father, the little girl broke from Herowan's restraining grasp and flew at Jed. He caught her handily, swinging her into his arms and hugging her against him while his anxious eyes sought Charity, needing to know that she was unharmed. What he saw must have satisfied him for he turned abruptly to face the chief. Charity was surprised when he spoke to Herowan in the Algonquian tongue. But she should have known that if Songbird had taught Star the language she certainly would have taught Jed also.

They spoke at length, sometimes heatedly, often drawing angry howls from Herowan's people, who were listening intently. Suddenly the argument stopped abruptly and Herowan turned and walked away. The moment he left, Charity and Jed were surrounded by tribesmen brandishing spears, forcing them into the lodge where Charity had spent the night. Star was forcibly restrained from joining them.

"What are they going to do with us?" Charity cried once they were alone. "Why do they want Star? Oh, Jed, I'm so frightened."

Jed took Charity in his arms, crushing her against his heart, needing to know that she was unharmed. "They're not going to harm us," he consoled. "They only want what is theirs."

"You mean Star?"

He nodded gravely. "They can't have her," he said. "They lost the right to her on the day she was born."

Charity looked at him curiously, making no effort to leave the safety of his arms. The comfort of his strength—she never once considered him weak because of his disability—lent her courage. It felt so right to be in his arms like this; she never wanted to leave.

"I don't understand any of this," she said, bewildered. "I thought you were Star's father."

"Come here and sit down, Charity," Jed said, urging her to sit on the ground before the fire. He dropped down beside her, sliding an arm around her shoulders, pulling her close. "I'm not really Star's father. I found her in the woods where she was left to die when she was but hours old and I've always considered her mine."

"You found an Indian baby and raised her despite the fact you're not related?" She shook her head, finding it difficult to believe that anyone would do such a thing. Especially a man like Jed, whose fearsome wounds and resulting disability had turned him into a bitter recluse. "I still don't understand. I'd always heard Indians loved their children. Why was Star left in the woods to die?"

"I never knew for certain, I could only surmise. Herowan confirmed my suspicions when he told me why Star had been abandoned."

Charity stared at him, realizing that she had barely scratched the surface of this complex man. She thought he must have the purest heart of anyone she'd ever known, so different from the Kincaids, whose greedy and sometimes cruel natures resided behind a facade of religious zeal. She waited for him to continue, fearing he'd be reluctant to share his innermost thoughts with her. But she needn't have worried. Jed drew a deep breath and continued.

"I have to begin at the beginning for you to understand. I was wounded in the war by British cannon fire. When Sir Henry Clinton sent 3,500 men south to Savannah, I joined Howe's army to fight for American freedom. The British brought up their cannon and fired into the line of attack. Unfortunately, Savannah fell. During the battle I was severely wounded. The bones in my leg were smashed and couldn't be set properly. Most of my body is scarred by shrapnel.

"I wasn't expected to live," Jed continued, haunted by the memory of his harrowing experience. "And when my wounds finally healed, it was a long trek home. I arrived in Virginia on Christmas Eve, 1780."

"Star was born on Christmas Eve," Charity said, eager to hear the rest of the story.

"Aye. It wasn't as severe a winter as the one we're having this year," Jed reminisced. "I was within a few miles of home. I remember thinking about my mother and how surprised she'd be to see me. I was all she had, since my father had died the year before. And I thought of Hilda, wondering how she'd feel about marrying a cripple." His voice turned harsh with bitterness, recalling Hilda's revulsion the first time she saw him.

He shook his head to clear it and continued. "I heard a child cry. The cry was more animal than human, and I thought a kitten had gotten lost in the woods and was mewling for its mother. I don't know what made me interrupt my journey to investigate. Then I happened to glance up at the sky and saw a star. It was brighter than any star I'd ever seen. It seemed to be leading me, and I followed, propelled by an urge so compelling it was a driving force inside me. I'll never forget my astonishment when I saw Star's tiny face bathed in the bright light of the star that had led me to her."

"Just like the story of the Nativity!" Charity cried, entranced by the tale.

"Aye, it was my own Christmas star. She was strapped onto a cradleboard and left beneath a tree for wild animals to devour. I searched for her people, and though I saw signs indicating they had been passing through, they had already left the area. Continuing to search for her people was out of the question, for Star needed immediate attention. Had she remained outside an hour longer she would have been devoured by wild animals or died of exposure. Since I couldn't leave her, I brought her home."

"Did you not think of the furor you would create by raising an Indian child? People still think she is yours, that her mother was an Indian squaw with whom you had consorted."

Jed scowled furiously. "After Hilda rejected me, I cared not what the townspeople thought. My mother loved Star from the first. She raised Star the first two years of her life, until her death. Shortly afterward I found Songbird near death in the woods and took her in. She was the only mother Star knew until you arrived. I knew Star wouldn't be welcome in Williamsburg so I lived like a hermit, refusing all friendship for her sake."

"Until I came along and upset your life," Charity said lightly.

"You are the only good thing to happen to me since I found Star."

Shocked, Charity stared at him. "I am? Despite the fact that you were forced into marrying me?"

"Perhaps I was," Jed acknowledged, "but that changed quickly enough. I was too cowardly to admit that I was beginning to care for you. I have my pride, after all. I know how repulsive I am to women and don't delude myself into thinking you could care for me. I'm half a man, for God's sake! What woman would want me?"

"I want you, Jed," Charity said evenly. "But if there is some reason you can't be a—a . . ." she blushed furiously and looked up at him through lowered lashes "—husband to me, I'll understand."

"My God, is that what you think?" Shock colored his words. "The need to make love to you is like an ache inside me. Sometimes I think if I can't love you I'll die. And believe me, sweetheart—" he slanted her a crooked smile, "—I'm fully capable of being a proper husband to you."

"Why haven't you told me before how you feel?" Charity charged. "I thought you didn't want me, that you were grievously injured, or that you resented being forced into wedding me."

Jed smiled ruefully. "I have only my pride to blame. I thought all women were like Hilda. She was so repulsed by my limp she couldn't stand looking at me. She objected vigorously when she learned I'd brought home an infant for her to raise. She promptly married another man with a whole body and no children and moved to another city."

"I think you're perfect, Jed," Charity said, blushing. "You're strong and courageous and possess a heart as big as all outdoors. You may have fooled others with your churlish manner, but you don't fool me."

"You're much more courageous than I am," Jed told her. "Indians terrify you, yet you swallowed your fear and followed when they kidnapped Star. Few women would dare such a brave act."

"I couldn't live with myself if I stood by and did nothing. I know how deeply you love Star, and truth be told, I've come to love her myself. She's sweet and loving, and the color of her skin makes her unique. But I still don't understand how Herowan identified her as his daughter."

"Herowan told me Star had a twin sister, which I already suspected. Six years ago their small band was traveling through the area when his wife went into labor. As was the custom, she went into the woods to bear her child alone. She must have been horrified when twins were born, for they are considered bad medicine. When twin births occur, one of the babies is immediately killed."

"Oh, no!" Charity cried, aghast.

"Evidently Star's mother couldn't bring herself to kill one of her newborn daughters, so she left her to fate. Herowan never knew about his other daughter until just recently. He came back to look for her."

"Why didn't his wife tell him before? Where is Star's sister now?"

"They both died recently when a virulent fever decimated the tribe. His wife only told him about delivering twins on her deathbed. When two of his tribesmen saw Star that day they came begging for food, they realized that she looked like Herowan's dead daughter and rushed back to tell him. Herowan knew immediately that through some miracle his twin daughter had been spared, and he now wants Star to take the place of his dead child. He couldn't believe that she hadn't perished long ago."

"He can't have her," Charity said fiercely. "Star knows nothing of this kind of life and would be unhappy with her natural father. Is there nothing you can do?"

"I'll think of something," Jed said, not at all convinced he would succeed. His arm tightened around Charity, grateful to have someone with whom he could share his fears, his hopes, his dreams. Never in his wildest imagination had he thought he'd find a woman to love, a woman willing to accept his less than perfect body.

"Charity, when we get home I won't expect anything more from you than you're willing to give," he said earnestly. "You can't know or imagine the extent of my injuries. If you still want to be my wife in every way, I'll be the happiest man alive, but if you decide you cannot bear the sight of me, I'll understand."

"How you look has nothing to do with how I feel about you," Charity said shyly. "You're strong and handsome and kind, much kinder than the Kincaids. The day you found me in the snow was my lucky day."

Jed's eyes were glowing brightly when he lowered his head and kissed Charity. He kissed her with all the fervor he had denied himself these past weeks, groaning when her mouth opened beneath the pressure of his, allowing him to slide his tongue inside to taste her.

"Sweet, so sweet," he moaned hoarsely. "No man has ever wanted a woman as much as I want you."

Arching her back, Charity melted into his embrace, welcoming the heat of his hands as they learned the sweet contours of her body. Innocent passion coursed through her as she experienced things she'd never felt before, making her ache for more. If Herowan hadn't burst into the hut at that moment, she would have surrendered to Jed completely.

Herowan spoke to Jed, who shook his head in vigorous denial.

"What does he want?" Charity asked, frightened.

"He wants us to leave."

"Without Star?"

Jed turned to Herowan and spoke harshly. Now it was Herowan's turn to shake his head as he answered Jed's question.

"Herowan says we may stay for the feast to celebrate the return of his daughter; then we must leave . . . alone."

"Oh, no!"

"Don't worry, sweetheart, we won't leave without Star." His expression was so fiercely determined, Charity believed him.

Chapter Nine

Jed and Charity sat through endless hours of dancing and storytelling, which the Algonquian seemed to enjoy with great relish. A huge feast in Star's honor was prepared, and Jed choked down the food, trying to conceal his fear that they would be forced to leave without his daughter. At least Star had been allowed to join them, he consoled himself as he glanced down at her dark head. She sat between him and Charity, a confused look on her face. The poor child didn't know what to make of all this, and Jed hadn't had a moment alone with her to explain.

When yet another warrior stood up to relate a story of his bravery and prowess, Jed groaned inwardly. He had been searching his mind frantically for an answer to his dilemma and found himself butting against a stone wall at every turn.

427

Suddenly his attention sharpened as he realized it was Christmas Eve and he had a story to relate that was every bit as good as those he had just heard.

Fragile hope flared in his heart. Through Songbird he was aware of the Algonquian belief in things spiritual and sacred. Their lives were governed by mystical rites and taboos dictated by their gods. He hoped Herowan would be impressed enough by his story to change his mind about Star. The warrior had just finished his tale and was basking in the praise of his comrades when Jed leaped to his feet.

"I have a story to tell, Herowan, one I think your people will enjoy. Will you listen?"

Charity stared at Jed, wishing she could understand what he had just said to the chief.

"I asked permission to tell a story," Jed hissed when he saw her puzzled frown.

"A story? Of what good is a story when they are going to take Star from us?" Had Jed lost his mind? she wondered.

"Wait and see," he said in a hushed voice.

Herowan's eyes narrowed, considering Jed's request. He loved a good story as well as the next man, and in the end his curiosity won out. "Tell your story, white man."

"What did he say?" Charity asked.

"He gave me permission to tell my story. Pray, sweetheart," Jed urged, "pray like you've never prayed before."

Jed stood in the center of the circle, the leaping flames of the campfire warming his back. The

Algonquian gathered close, settling down to listen to Jed's tale.

"Long ago, at the beginning of time," Jed began slowly, "the Great Spirit above sent his son to earth in the form of a babe to redeem man's sins. He was born in a far-off country across the sea to a simple carpenter and his wife. Men came from all over the world to see this child, born during the holy season of Christmas. Among those who journeyed from afar to offer gifts to the Holy Child were Three Wise Men who had heard of the Savior's birth."

Totally absorbed, Herowan asked, "How did they know where to find this Holy Child?"

"They followed a star to the place of the child's birth. It led them to a humble stable, the only place available to the impoverished parents who had traveled far by order of their great chief," Jed explained. "They'd been turned away from the lodge because it was full and there was no room for them. They'd sought shelter in the stable, and there among the animals the woman gave birth to a boy child. The child was named Jesus.

"Guided by a brilliant star, the Three Wise Men found the babe and laid precious gifts at His feet." He smiled down at Star, who leaned against Charity, dozing, and his heart nearly burst with love for both of them. "Six years ago I saw a similar star shining in the sky."

"I do not understand," Herowan complained, disgruntled. "What does the star and the Holy Child have to do with my daughter?"

"I was returning from a great battle in which

I received grave wounds when I noticed a star shining brightly in the sky. It was very near the place where you are now camped. Winter was upon us, and it was the holy season of Christmas, when we celebrate the birth of the Holy Child. I heard the wail of a child and thought it was an animal. I was close to home and wanted to continue, but I couldn't. It was as if the star compelled me to follow. It was like a beacon, guiding me to my own little Star. I found a newborn babe abandoned by her parents a short time later, bathed in the brilliant light of the star. Had I not arrived when I did, it would have been too late. The star was a sign that led me to her."

"She is mine," Herowan said angrily. "She is of my blood."

"You were willing to let her die," Jed argued.

"It is our custom. Twins are bad medicine."

"Had your other daughter lived, you would not want her twin. I saved her life. I raised her. I love her. She belongs to me."

"What of the Holy Child?" a warrior called out as Jed and Herowan glared at one another. "Finish your story."

"Jesus was raised by His foster father," Jed continued. "You see, His real father was the Great Spirit above, who gave Him up in the form of man to be raised by His foster father. The whole of His life was spent in prayer, performing good deeds and teaching others to follow the word of His Father in heaven."

The Indians hung on to Jed's every word, transfixed by the story of the Holy Child and the star.

The analogy between the star that showed the Wise Men the way and the star that had guided Jed did not escape them. They stared at Star, clearly awed that she had lived despite the odds against her survival.

"Why do you tell us this story?" Herowan asked shrewdly.

"Can you not see the similarity? The Great Spirit placed the star in my path during the holy season of Christmas when His son was born. If I had not followed the star, your daughter would have died of exposure, or been devoured by wild animals. She was placed into my keeping for a purpose. I raised her with love, just as the Holy Child's foster father raised Him. If you take her from me now, both your God and mine will become angry and your people will suffer. Be grateful that your daughter lived and is being well cared for. For six years she has been mine. Are you going to risk God's wrath and take her from me?"

Awe-stricken, Herowan's people stared at Jed. The story had touched their hearts. Of course, they would uphold their chief's decision, but it was obvious their sympathy lay with Jed. The Algonquians believed in things mystical and possessed a spiritual nature. The story of the Christmas Star convinced them that Herowan's twin daughter had been spared for a purpose and given into another's keeping. They looked at their chief, waiting for his decision.

Charity stared at the Indians seated around the campfire, puzzled by the change in them. She had no idea what Jed had told them, but she knew it had affected them deeply. They seemed impressed by his words and enthralled by his story.

"What did you tell them, Jed?" Her voice shook with repressed emotion. Something momentous had just taken place and she had no idea what it was.

Her heart skipped a beat when Jed smiled down at her. "I told them the story of the Nativity and how the Christmas Star led the Wise Men to the Holy Child. I told them it was the same star that led me to Herowan's daughter, and that they must allow me to keep her or suffer God's wrath."

"What did Herowan say?" Charity asked, impressed by his cleverness.

"Nothing yet, but I think my story affected him deeply."

Her eyes filled with love as she regarded Jed. She knew no man as fine as he. If only she could help him in some way. Then she recalled that Herowan understood a smattering of English. Rising to her feet, she faced the chief and said, "I also love Star. I swear to raise her as my own daughter. Separating her from her foster father would be cruel and inhuman."

Herowan did not doubt the veracity of Charity's words. She had proven her love when she followed the child here and refused to leave when given the opportunity. He grunted and motioned Charity back to her place before the fire.

Jed grasped her hand, refusing to allow her to leave his side as he stood before Herowan, waiting for the chief to speak. Suddenly a woman cried out, pointing to the sky. All eyes turned upward. Jed gasped when he saw a single star high in the heavens, bathing them with a brilliance that dimmed all the million other stars twinkling beside it.

"Jed, look!" Charity cried, astonished. "It's almost as if—as if you had conjured up the star."

Charity wasn't the only one transfixed by the mystical phenomenon. Stunned, the Indians looked up at the sky, then stared at the man and woman before them as if they were prophets, or supernatural beings. A penetrating silence settled over the assemblage as the star hovered directly overhead, casting its light over the man and woman standing in the center of the circle. Suddenly little Star stirred and sat up, her eyes anxiously seeking Jed and Charity. When she saw them she smiled, picked herself up, and joined them.

Drenched in the light of the star, no one who saw them could doubt they belonged together. Least of all Herowan. His face was set in stone, his eyes bleak when at length he spoke.

"Your story touches my heart," he said slowly, placing a fist over the place where his heart beat within his chest. "Could the star that led the Wise Men to your Holy Child be the same one that guided you to my daughter? Could it be the same star that shines so brightly down on you now? If it is so, then I must assume the Gods favor your petition."

He gazed at Star, seeing in her his dead

daughter whom he had loved dearly. He saw how trustingly she regarded her foster father, how tightly she clung to his hand, how her eyes sought the woman who would be her mother, and he searched his heart for the right decision. He found it in the star that bathed the small family in celestial light.

"It grieves me to lose a child of my loins, but had she been devoured by wild animals I would never have known she existed. Twins are bad medicine, it is our custom to choose one and let the other die. Had I not lost Star's twin sister I would have been content, assuming the other was dead."

The breath slammed from Jed's chest. "Then you will allow me to keep Star?"

"My daughter was given to you by your Prophet. No mortal man has the right to take her from you. You may leave in peace."

So great was his relief, Jed's crippled leg nearly collapsed beneath him. "Jed, what is it?" Charity cried, alarmed. Had Herowan refused to give up Star?

"We can leave, sweetheart! Herowan has relented. Star is ours." He caught her around the waist and hugged her tightly. Then he picked up Star and swung her around.

Oblivious to the tense drama that had taken place, Star yawned hugely and said, "Let's go home, Papa. Today is my birthday and I didn't even get the cake Charity promised to bake for me. Or my presents. You did get me a present, didn't you, Papa?"

"We'll have a feast tomorrow," Charity laughed, "with a cake and anything else you'd like. And I wouldn't be surprised if there are gifts waiting for you at home."

Herowan's dark eyes were stark as he stared at Star. After a tense moment he rose abruptly to his feet and said, "When the sun rises tomorrow, two of my people will show you the way home." His shoulders were slumped ever so slightly as he walked away.

When they returned home on Christmas Day, Charity fixed a dinner fit for royalty. She cooked the turkey Jed had shot, prepared a variety of vegetables from the root cellar, and baked the cake Star wanted.

Star exclaimed wildly over the doll with a porcelain face which Jed had purchased for her in Williamsburg, and the hat, scarf, and gloves Charity had knitted from her unraveled sweater. Jed was rendered speechless when Charity gave him the stockings she had knit for him, and the rest of the day he wore a secretive smile.

Festive though the day was, Charity's nervousness increased as the day came to an end. No matter what Jed said, she wasn't going to let him sleep on the floor. She was his wife but she might as well be his sister, living the way she did. She wanted to be Jed's wife in every way, to experience the joys and trials of wedded bliss, to know what it felt like to be a woman. If she had to be bold, so be it. Jed had admitted he cared for her and wanted her. She had no idea what she had to do to convince him that nothing about him would shock or repulse her, but somehow she'd find a way.

Jed was even more nervous than Charity. He ached with the need to make love to Charity but feared her rejection. He couldn't bear it if she turned from him in disgust, and he wasn't certain he wanted to put her to the test. His emotions were too raw after years of virtual isolation from human compassion.

"Star is exhausted, Jed, why don't you put her to bed," Charity said, sending him a shy smile. Her voice shook from the combined forces of excitement and fear. No one had told her what to expect in the marriage bed. She just knew she wanted to be close to Jed, closer than she had ever been to any other human.

Jed started violently. He gave Charity a searing glance, sending heat coursing through her. Her eyelashes swept down to lie like butterflies against her cheeks. He decided to warn her one last time. "Charity, if you don't want—"

"No," Charity said, forestalling the rest of his sentence, "don't say it. I want to be your wife, Jed."

Jed groaned as if in pain, imagining her disgust when she finally saw the extent of his injuries. It would take a special woman to accept him as he was. He hoped Charity was that woman. "I want that more than anything," he said sincerely.

Alone in the bedroom, Charity stripped down to her shift, too shy to climb completely naked between the sheets. She hoped Jed would tell her what to do, for she had no idea what to expect. She closed her eyes and waited.

A short time later Jed entered the room and limped to the bed, gazing down at Charity with so much love and compassion that had she seen him she would have burst into tears. Disappointment jolted through him when she appeared to be sleeping. He started to turn away when she reached out and touched his arm.

"No, don't go."

"Are you sure?"

"I was never more sure of anything in my life."

With slow deliberation Jed removed his shirt; then he sat on the side of the bed and removed his shoes, stockings, and trousers. He stood up, his back to her, clad in his small clothes, aware of Charity's scrutiny as she made a slow perusal of his body. He knew that shrapnel scars peppered his back, and that his leg was grotesquely scarred and twisted, and he waited for Charity's reaction. When the silence grew oppressive, he slowly peeled away his remaining clothing. He wanted her to see all of him, to know the full extent of his disfigurement. Glancing over his shoulder, he wondered if she had been struck dumb by the gruesome sight and prayed she hadn't gone into shock.

Charity stared at Jed, transfixed by the powerful width of his back and shoulders, by the corded tendons rippling beneath his smooth flesh, by the narrow waist and slim hips. One leg was strong and muscular, the other she hardly noticed. If there were scars on his body, Charity scarcely saw them. What she did see was his handsome face, his strength of character, and the beauty of his soul. It was also the first time she had seen a naked male.

She stared at his body few moments, then reluctantly slid her eyes upward to his face. "I love you, Jed." Her voice shook as she pulled aside the blanket so he could slide into bed beside her. "You'll have to teach me what to do."

Jed wore a stunned expression. Having Star restored to him was a miracle, but the greatest miracle of all was finding Charity on that snowy night and hearing her say that she loved him. "I adore you, Charity Wells. I bless the day I found you."

He slid into bed beside her and took her into his arms. When his mouth found hers, she knew she had come home.

Outside, a bright star hovered overhead, drenching the lovers in the soft glow of fulfillment. It twinkled warmly when Jed gave Charity his Christmas gift, slipping onto her finger a wedding band he had purchased on one of his trips into town. For many days afterward, the Christmas Star rode low in the heavens, bestowing its blessings upon the Wells family.

The star provided Herowan's tribe with countless hours of entertainment as the story narrated to them by Jed was told and retold around the campfire. When they moved westward, the tale had been embellished until the Christmas Star had earned a place in the annals of the tribe's history.

MADELINE BAKER

The Queen of Indian Romance

Winner of the *Romantic Times*
Reviewers' Choice Award for Best Indian Series!

"Madeline Baker's Indian Romances should not be missed!"

—Romantic Times

The Spirit Path. Beautiful and infinitely desirable, the Spirit Woman beckons Shadow Hawk away from his tribe, drawing him to an unknown place, a distant time where passion and peril await. Against all odds, Hawk and the Spirit Woman will conquer time itself and share a destiny that will unite them body and soul.

_3402-6 $4.99 US/5.99 CAN

Midnight Fire. A half-breed who has no use for a frightened girl fleeing an unwanted wedding, Morgan thinks he wants only the money Carolyn Chandler offers him to guide her across the plains. But in the vast wilderness, Morgan makes her his woman and swears to do anything to keep Carolyn's love.

_3323-2 $4.99 US/$5.99 CAN

Comanche Flame. From the moment Dancer saves her life, Jessica is drawn to him by a fevered yearning. And when the passionate loner returns to his tribe, Jessica vows she and her once-in-a-lifetime love will be reunited in an untamed paradise of rapture and bliss.

_3242-2 $4.99 US/$5.99 CAN

RELUCTANT LOVERS
ELIZABETH CHADWICK

"Elizabeth Chadwick writes a powerful love story...splendid!"

—*Romantic Times*

Ever since her first appearance in Breckenridge, Colorado, Kathleen Fitzgerald has been besieged by proposals from the love-starved men of the remote mining town. But determined to avoid all matrimonial traps, the lovely young widow decides instead to act as matchmaker between her new admirers and the arrivals from her old hometown. Having sworn off love, Kat finds herself surrounded by romance, while the one man she truly desires leaves her body on fire, but refuses to ask for her hand. When even the girls in the local bawdy house begin to hear wedding bells, Kat knows the marriage madness has to end—but not before she herself gets her man!

_3540-5 $4.99 US/$5.99 CAN

NORAH HESS

Best Western Frontier Romance
Award-Winner—*Romantic Times*

DEVIL IN SPURS

In the rugged solitude of the Wyoming wilderness, the lovely Jonty Rand lived life as a boy to protect her innocence from the likes of Cord McBain. So when her grandmother's dying wish made Cord Jonty's guardian, she despaired of ever revealing her true identity. Determined to change her into a rawhide-tough wrangler, Cord assigned Jonty all the hardest tasks on the ranch, making her life a torment. Then one stormy night he discovered that Jonty would never be a man, only the wildest, most willing woman he'd ever taken in his arms.

_2934-0 $4.50

Winner of the *Romantic Times* Storyteller of the Year Award!

Storm Kennedy can't believe her bad luck! With six million acres of fertile territory open to settlers in the Oklahoma Territory, she loses her land claim to Grady Stryker, the virile Cheyenne half-breed she holds responsible for her young husband's death. And the only way to get it back is by agreeing to marry the arrogant Stryker and raise his motherless son. But while she accepts his proposal, Storm is determined to deny him access to her last asset—the lush body Grady thinks is his for the taking.

_3444-1 $4.99 US/$5.99 CAN

BRIMMING WITH PASSION...
BURSTING WITH EXCITEMENT...

UNFORGETTABLE HISTORICAL ROMANCES FROM *LEISURE BOOKS!*

The Magic by Robin Lee Hatcher. Destined for a loveless marriage to a virtual stranger, Cassandra Jamison finds herself instead swept aboard a notorious pirate ship and into its captain's arms. How can she hope to resist the most devastatingly seductive man she's ever encountered?
_3433-6 $4.99 US/$5.99 CAN

Ryan's Enchantress by Connie Harwell. When tomboy Susan Bradford meets her handsome new neighbor, she is shocked to realize that she longs for his tender caresses, longs to wipe the mocking grin off his face and show him how much of a woman she can be.
_3436-0 $4.99 US/$5.99 CAN

Fleeting Splendor by Julie Moffett. Trapped in a marriage of convenience with broodingly handsome Nathaniel Beauchamp, Alana MacKenzie makes the surprising discovery that love can sometimes blossom in the most unexpected places.
_3434-4 $4.50 US/$5.50 CAN

LEISURE BOOKS
ATTN: Order Department
276 5th Avenue, New York, NY 10001

Please add $1.50 for shipping and handling for the first book and $.35 for each book thereafter. PA., N.Y.S. and N.Y.C. residents, please add appropriate sales tax. No cash, stamps, or C.O.D.s. All orders shipped within 6 weeks via postal service book rate. Canadian orders require $2.00 extra postage and must be paid in U.S. dollars through a U.S. banking facility.

Name _____
Address _____
City _____ State _____ Zip _____
I have enclosed $_____ in payment for the checked book(s).
Payment <u>must</u> accompany all orders.☐ Please send a free catalog.